THE ILLUSTRATED HISTORY OF THE
SOVIET CINEMA

THE ILLUSTRATED HISTORY OF THE

SOVIET

CINEMA

Neya Zorkaya

HIPPOCRENE BOOKS
New York

Published by arrangement with
Novosti Press Agency Publishing House,
Moscow, U.S.S.R

Library of Congress Cataloging-in-Publication Data

Zorkaya, Neya Markovna.
    The illustrated history of the Soviet cinema / Neya Zorkaya.
    "Published by arrangement with Novosti Press Agency Publishing
House, Moscow, U.S.S.R."
    Bibliography
    Includes index.
    ISBN 0-87052-560-3
    1. Motion pictures—Soviet Union—History. I. Title. II. Title:
Soviet cinema.
PN1993.5.R9Z57   1989
791.43′0947—dc19
                          89-16594
                          CIP

Printed in the United States of America

Contents

Introduction

*T*his is not a textbook on the history of the Soviet cinema; nor is it a full account of its formative period and subsequent development. The story of the Soviet cinema (and of its predecessor, the cinema of prerevolutionary Russia) is a complicated one covering a vast amount of material. It has also proved to be an exciting one for art historians and critics, culturologists and sociologists, in fact, for all who are interested in the cultural trends of our times. No wonder, then, that it has long attracted the attention of researchers both in this country and abroad. Among the numerous Soviet publications on the subject are monographs by Nikolai Iezuitov, Nikolai Lebedev, Semyon Ginsburg, Rostislav Yurenev, Alexander Karaganov, Sergei Drobashenko, Yevgeny Gromov, Lyudmila Belovaya, Mark Zak, Yuri Khanyutin, Kora Tsereteli, the author of this book, and others, and a fundamental work, a four-volume *History of the Soviet Cinema, 1917–1964,* written by a team of specialists.

Among the works on the Soviet cinema by foreign authors, special mention should be made of those by the late Georges Sadoul (to whom all students of the cinema owe a debt of gratitude), in particular the posthumously published fourth volume of his titanic *Histoire générale du cinéma,* which gives a panorama of the Soviet cinema in the revolutionary twenties.★

★Georges Sadoul, *Histoire générale du cinéma,* IV (Paris: Editions Denoél, 1975). A Russian translations of this volume was put out by the Iskusstvo Publishers (Moscow) in 1982.

Jay Leyda, Jerzy Toeplitz, Jean Mitry, Ulrich Gregor, and Nina Hibbin are but a few of the leading world film critics who have written on the Soviet cinema. I should also mention the well-known French film critics Luda and Jean Schnitzer, authors of a two-volume *History of the Soviet Cinema* and several other books on the Soviet motion picture industry.

But here is a paradox: as more and more books are published on the subject, more questions arise, and there is a growing necessity of looking into problems that are still unexplored. It seems that the Soviet cinema remains largely a terra incognita: its major development trends are still insufficiently researched (maybe the time is not yet ripe for that!). What is more, there is no comprehensive account of its turbulent and dramatic history which began on the ruins of the cinema of prerevolutionary Russia and culminated in the Soviet motion picture industry as we know it today, which comprises film studios located in all the constitutent Soviet republics and in many major cities and which releases many hundreds of films a year.

The purpose of this book is a modest one: to conduct a brief survey of the history of the Soviet cinema from the vantage ground of the 1980s and the approaching world cinema centennial in 1995. I have tried to keep up with the tempestuous pace of development of the Soviet cinema over the decades, being aware that each decade is linked with all the others and represents at the same time something new, with a tone and hue all of its own, a "single musical impulse" (in the words of the Russian poet Alexander Blok) or the "color of the times."

We shall not be making new discoveries, but we shall consider the Soviet cinema from new angles. We shall come upon facts and details hitherto unknown. And what is most important, we shall put ourselves in a mood of retrospection as we go back in years and relive the times when the Soviet cinema emerged and developed. The "retro" style seems suitable not only for works of fiction but also for historical narratives.

The field of the film historian grows constantly. For with each passing year more and more material—what is topical and transient at a given moment—finds its way into the archives. Already at the beginning of this century people spoke of the unprecedented "acceleration of history." What about us?

Like the cinema of any other country, the Soviet cinema can be discussed from various points of view. In this book we shall consider it from the point of view of art. A film, regardless of its specific features, is primarily a work of art and as such should be judged by the same criteria as any other artistic phenomenon. And, of course, the sociological, historical, and cultural aspects of a film must also be taken into account, as is now generally recognized among film critics. In other words, a film is an interaction between the creative will of its maker and his epoch and milieu.

This brief survey of the Soviet cinema is accompanied by illustrations: photos with commentaries, which will be just as important as the main text itself, if not more so. I believe that in a book like this, pictures are more eloquent than words. Many of the photos selected for this book have not been previously published; others may have been forgotten or, on the contrary, are so well known that they have taken on a symbolic significance.

This book is intended primarily for readers in the United States. Therefore, whenever appropriate, I have emphasized the ties between the Soviet and US cinemas. Incidentally, this is a subject that has received relatively little attention among writers on films.

CHAPTER ONE

An Overture

The Birth of Russian Cinema

*H*ere they are, milling about in the street and laughing, jostling their way forward. A young woman tidying her coiffure furtively . . . a gentleman in a hat assuming a dignified air, his neighbor making a low bow to the camera. Even the fidgety boys have become quiet, waiting for the "birdie" to fly out. Hustle and bustle, and heads, heads everywhere. Peaked caps, hats, and colorful kerchiefs. Merry and inquisitive eyes, open faces, high cheekbones, snub noses—these are the Russians filmed by the first movie cameraman.

"Cinéma," "Kinemo," "Cinématographe-Lumière"—that's how movies were called in those days in Russia. They came to the country shortly after the first public showing of motion pictures in Paris on December 28, 1895, a date now considered the birthday of the cinema. The film attracted crowds, first in the Aquarium summer garden in St. Petersburg on May 4, 1896, and in Moscow's Hermitage pleasure garden on May 26, and then, all through the summer, at the National Exhibition in Nizhni Novgorod (now Gorky). It was a sensational success. Now a classic, it shows a train approaching the platform of a station, a child having his meal, workmen coming out of the factory gates after their shift, and a naughty youngster stepping on a hose, sending a jet of water onto the gardener.

The Russian viewers watched with alarm the iron monster of a steam locomotive moving upon them from the screen. "Look, the kid is like a real one!" someone cried with delight, and all laughed at the gardener being inundated with water.

In May 1896 Lumière cameramen arrived in Russia to do some filming. Among them was Francis Doublier, who had looked after the lights and the projector during the first film showing in the Grand Cafe of Paris on December 28, 1895.

It seems that Russia was an ideal locale for the newborn entertainment: it supplied both appreciative audiences and a wealth of material for newsreel and feature sequences. It attracted both enthusiasts equipped with a cinecamera and enterprising hucksters who smelled quick profit, and even downright shady characters. On several occasions government officials had to pay special attention to some overly audacious "newsreelers" loitering near army barracks or metallurgical plants in the Urals.

The vast expanses of Russia beckoned as a land of exotic sights and striking contrasts: ice hummocks illuminated by the northern lights in the Arctic, and the evergreen Crimea washed by the warm waters of the Black Sea in the south; the dense virgin forests near the western frontier, and the fantastic volcanoes on the Pacific Coast so much like those on Hokusai's engravings. Infinite possibilities for the cameramen! As to the people . . . "What a motley of dresses, tribes and tongues and faces!" wrote the great Russian poet Alexander Pushkin. The same idea was expressed by the official government newspaper *Sankt-Peterburgskiye Vedomosti (St. Petersburg Chronicle)* on May 21, 1896: "Of all the civilized lands, Russia alone, with its boundless expanses, has enough room for the nomad and the European alike, satisfying the tastes of both." Indeed, the expanses must have appeared boundless.

The first movie makers, both Russian and foreign, were eager to film local color—the sights, the customs, and traditions of the people—and they did it with enthusiasm. V. Sashin-Fyodorov, one of the pioneers of Russian "moving photography," a stage actor by profession and a photographer at heart, openly imitated Lumière and filmed a horse-drawn tram in Moscow, a fire brigade at Bogorodskoye, and . . . himself dressed as a gardener standing next to a flowerbed. A. Fedetsky, the owner of a large photo studio in Kharkov, filmed the entire procession of the transportation of a miracle-working icon from the Kuryazhsk Monastery on September 30, 1896. And he shot the most dramatic moments of Cossack trick-riding at the Orenburg Regiment. The cameramen of Lumière, Pathé, Gaumont, and other film companies traveled about Russia in search of "thrilling" scenes—fires, floods, train crashes, and the like. A series of films under the general title *Picturesque Russia,* from 60 to 165 meters each, were shown both in Russia and abroad and included *Blessing the Water from the Neva in St. Petersburg, A Naval Exercise on the Black Sea, Sketches of Life in the Caucasus, Fishing in Astrakhan,* and so on.

Of course, those early mini-reels were very superficial, and the selection of material was haphazard. There was no attempt at analysis, not even at a most primitive level. The camera fixed on the external side of a phenomenon, its surface. Yet this surface spoke volumes because of the exceptional ability of the screen to record events and its descriptive power. The filmmaker could capture life's fleeting moments, and humanity thereby acquired a new chronicler and observer.

Future historians will no doubt detect many signs of calamity, tragic ruptures, and turns of history in the silent reels made at the end of the nineteenth and the beginning of the twentieth century.

Russian documentaries hold a special place in the vast world cinema archives with their filmed records of the dramatic close of the nineteenth and the pompous (remember the 1900 World Fair in Paris!) opening of the twentieth century. The cameramen were neither politicians, social thinkers, nor forecasters. They simply filmed whatever was curious and exciting. But the camera registered real scenes: wretched strips of peasant land plots, primitive mattocks and wooden plows drawn by emaciated horses, and hamlets with straw-thatched huts (the straw wasn't lush and golden—it was caked and rotten). Here were the ragged villagers in the same footwear that had so much amazed Marquis de Custine, a European grandee traveling in Russia, some seventy years before. Yes, these were the Russian bast sandals which the peasants used to make during long wintry nights, in the dim light of a torch.

And then there was the famine in the Volga area, Russia's chronic plight; something that might seem inconceivable in a rich black-earth region near the great waterway. But the ruthless sequences show rickety children with swollen bellies and mournful eyes, young mothers (more skeletons than living creatures), and horse carts laden with dead bodies, as in the times of the medieval plagues.

Now, a different sequence: the tsar and the tsarina emerge from the Assumption Cathedral of the Moscow Kremlin at the head of a solemn procession. She is taller than her spouse, black haired, clad in a sumptuous white gown, with the plumes of her hat fluttering in the air. Next comes a servant, a robust man, carrying the invalid tsarevich in his arms, and then a long retinue of courtiers: the men a mass of shoulder straps, orders and medals, corpulent figures, gray beards, and moustaches, and the women with lace trains and necklaces studded with diamonds and pearls. It is as if the regalia, jewelry, plumes, and feathers are at this very moment moving past the crenellated walls of the Kremlin, in a display of wealth and arrogance. What we are witnessing are the festivities marking the tercentenary of the house of Romanov (the film was made in 1913). The coronation of the last Russian monarch, Nicholas II, was also filmed in Moscow, the old capital of Russia, in May 1896 (St. Petersburg was the official capital at the time). A team of filmmakers led by Francesque Doublier arrived from Paris, and the motion picture they produced is generally regarded as the world's first-ever newsreel.

The coronation ceremony was filmed in the Kremlin and on Red Square. Luckily for them the French filmmakers didn't go to Khodynskoye Pole in the city's outskirts, where popular festivities were traditionally held. Huge crowds of people flocked there on that day, attracted by the promise of a tsarist "treat" (a glass of wine, a loaf of bread, and half a pound of sweets) and entertainment. Two thousand died in the crush. The words "Khodynka" and "death in crowd" became synonymous. But the newly enthroned tsar did not cancel the ball planned for the evening of that horrible day. As Leo Tolstoi, the conscience of Russia, wrote in one of his letters:

> A coronation was arranged, terrible in its absurdity and insane waste of money: the dreadful misfortune of the deaths of thousands of people resulted from the authorities' impudence and contempt for the people, and the organizers regarded it as a small cloud over the festivities which should be not interrupted because of it. . . .[1]

So, that fatal May 1896 cast an ominous shadow on the first Russian motion pictures, their debuts and premieres. The fact that the beginning of the last tsar's reign coincided in time with the beginning of the Russian cinema was remarkable, though the real significance of this became clear only later. From 1896 on, the "tsarist chronicle"—royal receptions in the palace, audiences with foreign monarchs, troop reviews, and so on—was a regular feature that opened each film showing. Of course, no one had filmed the shooting of peaceful demonstrators near the Winter Palace on the "Bloody Sunday" of January 9, 1905. In general, at the time many filmed sequences never saw the light of day—a special Palace Department saw to that.

Incidentally, Nicholas II was fond of photography and liked to pose before cameras, even though he hated the cinema. Above all he feared the gathering of crowds at "electrotheaters," which he called "dangerous institutions." Several resolutions on the subject drafted by the monarch and preserved in the archives of the tsar and the Palace Department were made public after the Soviet government came to power. Beginning in 1908, the first year of independent Russian film production, Nicholas II did all he could to prevent the development of the Russian motion picture industry.

The tsar made his major "policy statement" on the subject in connection with plans to start a joint Russian-American film company. The episode has been described by I. Zilberstein, a veteran Soviet historian and archivist, who was the first to make public the tsar's resolutions:

> In the summner of 1913 Police Department officials inspected a letter sent by an American businessman from New York, A. V. Olster, to F. Rodichev, a member of the State Duma, in which Olster suggested that the Russian motion-picture industry should be improved and that the State Duma should take the matter in hand. Alarmed by the letter the Police Department sent a copy of it to Nicholas II together with a report on which the emperor penned the following comment:
>
> "I consider the cinema to be an empty, useless and even pernicious diversion. Only an abnormal person could place this tomfoolery on a level with art. It is all nonsense, and no importance should be attached to such trash."[2]

By 1913 quite a few Russian-made feature films had already been released, and Ivan Mozzhukhin had appeared in some of his star roles. In the United States cinematographers were striking out in new directions. The following year Charlie Chaplin was to make his debut on the screen. However, no cooperative undertaking of American and Russian film-makers was destined to materialize.

Trusted court movie cameramen (B. Matuszewski, K. von Hahn, A. Jagelski) filmed the private life of the royal family, their outings, picnics, and the like. The sequences showing a group of bathers in the palace swimming pool, with the emperor prancing about "in his birthday suit," as the saying goes, have been preserved to this day. The last film sequences of the royal family have to do with Nicholas II's abdication following the February Revolution of 1917. They show a special carriage moving on railroad tracks in a remote locality; the interior of the carriage with a lampshade, an icon of St. Nicholas the Miracle Worker in the corner, a large sheet of white paper with the monarch's signature; and the moment when Nicholas II, no longer an emperor, steps down from the carriage and, turning his back on us, walks toward a birch grove—now a common

Leo Nikolayevich and Sofia Andreyevna Tolstoi stroll in a 1908 still.

man in a gray military coat. Soft snowflakes whirl in the air and touch the ground.

So, the cinema willy-nilly became an annalist of the finale of a whole epoch.

The first Russian film producers and cameramen are usually dismissed as ignoramuses and profiteers. Well, the cinema didn't recruit its personnel from prestigious military colleges or schools for the sons of the nobility.

Take, for example, Alexander Drankov, the owner of a small photo studio in St. Petersburg. He borrowed a sum of money and went to London, where he acquired the latest equipment in photography and filmmaking and even got himself appointed the Russian correspondent for the London *Times*. In this capacity he gained access to the State Duma in Russia and became a regular phtotgrapher there and, later on, to the court. In 1907 he opened Russia's first cinematographic studio.

Rumor has it that after the October Revolution of 1917, Drankov turned up in Constantinople. Together with other Russian emigres, he organized an attraction known as "flea-hopping." Then he is said to have moved to America, where he resumed his old trade; he bought a movie van and hit the road, touring state after state. No more is known about him.

"A man of vast energy and enterprise, a gambler by nature,"[3] is how Semyon Ginsburg, the film critic, describes Drankov, whose activity was typical of the privately owned Russian cinema. But like many gamblers, Drankov was not without a certain charm and a business instinct. When he advertised "Filmed reels! Topical plots! Events inside Russia and in the outlying regions," he did not disappoint the audiences. His filmed reels showed episodes of fox hunting, the hunting of hares, bear hunting, or French wrestling, then much in vogue. Drankov went to the Khitrov Market in Moscow and pieced together a film which he called *The Have-Beens: Gorky-Type Characters*. It showed a doss house and its inhabitants, made famous by Maxim Gorky's play *The Lower Depths* and its stage production at the Moscow Art Theater. And there were filmed scenes of fires, cholera epidemics, and railroad crashes and a unique reel on Count Leo Tolstoi's eightieth birthday at his Yasnaya Polyana estate. Drankov also had the good fortune to film sequences with the Yasnaya Polyana hermit, as Tolstoi was called then, in 1910, shortly before the death of the great writer.

Hundreds of meters of film show Tolstoi during the last two years of his life: Leo Tolstoi with his family . . . on horseback . . . at a Moscow railroad terminal . . . visiting his daughter at an estate near Moscow (there is something "purifying" about these scenes) . . . then the last tragic days and the funeral . . . Russia's pilgrimage to the grave of her national genius. Such a chronicle, despite its naive and primitive techniques, was without peer in world cinematography of the day.

Drankov and his team also produced Russia's first feature film, *Stenka Razin* (known also as *Ponizovaya Volnitsa)*, which premiered on October 15, 1908. Stepan (Stenka) Razin, a popular Russian hero, was a Cossack from the Don who led a peasant uprising in 1670–1671. Till then the Russian cinema had virtually been in foreign, or rather French, hands: the Pathé Brothers flooded the Russian cinema market with their film productions and cine-equipment.

True, a year earlier, in 1907, Russian filmmakers had tried to shoot a screen version of Pushkin's tragedy, *Boris Godunov*. The very attempt was a bold one. But the filmmakers did not intend to probe the philosophical depths of the poetic drama; they just wanted to produce scenes of boyar (old Russian nobility) life. Even though the film was not completed, its significance in the history of the Russian cinema is undoubted.

Stenka Razin had better luck. This historical drama, 224 meters and 7.5 minutes long, was the work of scriptwriter Vasily Goncharov and director Romashkov. The actors were from a semiprofessional theatrical society. But the music (an overture) was written by Mikhail Ippolitov-Ivanov, a prominent composer.

It was an extremely primitive and clumsy production, crude "tableaux épinals,"[4] according to Luda and Jean Schnitzer, the French film critics. Indeed, it calls to mind cheap popular prints or woodcuts and their naive texts. The film consists of six scenes provided with long and semiliterate subtitles. The plot is based on the famous Russian song about the Cossack leader Stenka Razin. The stern ataman falls in love with a charming captive, a Persian princess. This causes discontent among his men ("he has changed us for a wench"). So they conspire against the princess and forge a letter for her intended bridegroom, Prince Hassan. In a fit of jealousy, the drunken ataman tosses the beauty overboard, into the "running Volga wave." Such is the plot.

The sequences were filmed in natural surroundings. The Volga and the rowboats, the island with a pine forest where the Cossacks pitch camp, the sunlit glade—all this is fascinating despite the clumsy direction and Drankov's lackluster camera work. In the last, tragic scene, the actors (poorly made up) rush in with cardboard daggers and goblets in their hands. They grimace and roll their eyes. The protagonists are just as bad: a bearded and stout ataman (played by Yevgeni Petrov-Krayevsky) and a plump princess in wide Persian trousers. There is no idea of action and movement, no awareness of the possibilities of the cinema.

But nevertheless it was a good lesson. First of all, it became clear that a histrionic style of acting was unsuited to the cinema. On the other hand, natural landscapes or sceneries—the wooden bow of a boat cutting across the Volga waves, the pinetops in the gentle breeze—filmed well. Second, *Stenka Razin* may be regarded as the first genuine national film. Of course, neither Goncharov nor Drankov pondered over the aesthetic questions involved; rather they were guided by intuition when they chose as the main character of the first Russian film a folk hero and a historical figure.

Despite the banality of staging and the primitive plot, the film, its title alone, conveys something of the spirit of freedom which the Razin movement symbolizes. The overture and the piano accompaniment have as their leitmotif the popular song "Down the Volga" (the tune was also played by the pianist in those places in the film for which no special music was written).

This firstborn of the Russian cinema was no more than a screen version of the folk pantomime *A Boat*. Film historians are quite right when they compare *Stenka Razin* to woodcuts or cheap popular prints, that is, the "pop culture" of the nineteenth century. As a matter of fact, the roots go deeper than that, as may be confirmed by students of Russian folklore. In this sense *Stenka Razin* is the point of encounter between Russian folklore and the mass culture of the twentieth century.

The success of the first feature film opened the floodgates: Russian cinematographers filmed scenes from theatrical performances and made films based on Russian classics and works by contemporary authors. Original scripts were commissioned. Leonid Andreyev, perhaps the most popular high-society writer in the years 1900–1910, summed up the trend:

> In the eight to ten years of its existence the cinema has gobbled up all the authors who wrote before it. It has bitten deep into all of literature—Dante, Shakespeare, Gogol, Dostoyevsky, even Anatoli Kamensky.★ No stove devours as much firewood as the cinema does—it grabs the stuff and gorges on it.[5]

★A pornographic writer.

The privately owned Russian cinema lived a short life, just a decade. Yet in this decade, between 1908 and 1918, more than 2,000 feature films were produced, along with a host of documentaries, newsreels, and educational films. Foreign companies, even the prolific Pathé and Gaumont, had found it had to compete with Russian motion picture companies on the local screens.

The winged horse Pegasus became the emblem and trademark of the A. A. Khanzhonkov studio. A Cossack officer of modest means, Alexander Khanzhonkov started on a shoestring—a mere four thousand roubles. In a few years he became Russia's foremost film entrepreneur and owner of the country's best film studio. Fitted out with the latest equipment, the film studio on Moscow's Zhitnaya Street had several departments, including one for science films and one for literature headed by Nikandr Turkin, a theater critic, playwright, and one of the first theoreticians of the cinema. Khanzhonkov organized a company of cinema actors, which was a major step toward professionalism in the cinema. He also launched *Pegasus,* the most informative and interesting publication among the prerevolutionary cinemagazines. This knowledgeable man of high principles rendered a great service to the Russian motion picture industry.

Within two years a million-rouble enterprise, the Joseph Yermoliev Film Studio, was set up in Moscow. Its emblem was an elephant. Paul Thiemann, formerly a Pathé representative, joined forces with F. Reinhardt, a tobacco merchant, and founded a large motion picture company with the emblem "Russian Golden Series." Films produced by this company were advertised as "delux" class. They might have not attracted many famous actors, but they were known for their sumptuous decor. Besides these major production and commercial centers of the newborn film industry, there were many smaller studios and motion picture companies. Competition between them was fierce.

Thus, the Russian cinema was born.

Film Library Gems

What kind of cinema was it? What was its artistic and social significance? What was its contribution to the art of the cinema, if any?

Cinema historians writing at different times give different answers to these questions.

The first Soviet film critics and authors of memoirs (Boris Likhachev,

Nikolai Iezuitov, Nikolai Lebedev, Semyon Ginsburg) were reserved, to say the least, in their assessment: the cinema of prerevolutionary Russia, in their opinion, was still in its infancy, a "diversion with only inchoate elements of art," . . . "triumphant middle-class mediocrity," . . . "purely commercial enterprise," . . . and so on and so forth.

The quality of the Russian cinema was indeed poor when compared with that of the literature, painting, music, and theater of the time. That was the "Silver Age" of Russian art and literature, the age of such prose writers as Leo Tolstoi, Anton Chekhov, Ivan Bunin, and Maxim Gorky, and of such poets as Alexander Blok, Andrei Bely, the "Akmeists" (Nikolai Gumilev, Anna Akhmatova), and young Vladimir Mayakovsky. It was the time of the Moscow Art Theater with its scenic reform, of Konstantin Stanislavsky's pioneering productions and the exciting experiments of Vsevolod Meyerhold in St. Petersburg, and of the sensational "Russian seasons" of the Dyagilev ballet in Paris. In painting there were several avant-garde groups including "The World of Art" and "The Knave of Diamonds." Against this background the film productions of the day—*Lunar Beauties, Aza the Gipsy, Magic Tango*—look insipid. In the 1910s the Russian cinema could not boast of a David Wark Griffith of its own. But it was to make up after October 1917. Its heyday was yet to come.

Some of the early film producers (Moisei Aleinikov, Vladimir Gardin, and Alexander Khanzhonkov) as well as film historians and critics of later years both in this country and abroad have a different view of the prerevolutionary cinema. They emphasize its democratic spirit, its popular appeal, and its educational and cultural orientation, and in particular its persistent efforts in making better known the works of Russian literary classics.

But, of course, turning to classics did not guarantee that the films based on them would be of a high quality. Even the best films merely borrowed the story line and the name of the main characters. The psychological and philosophical contents of a literary work, the "labyrinth of connections," which, according to Tolstoi, is the essence of a novel, were beyond the powers of the cinema then and indeed for a long time to come.

But it was in this field that the first, albeit modest, victories of the cinema as a form of art were scored. Thus, the screen version of Leo Tolstoi's *Anna Karenina* (1915) is not devoid of certain artistic merits.

The film was produced under the Russian Golden Series emblem by Vladimir Gardin, a novice in the trade. Gardin was to work for many years in the motion picture industry and, when he was already an old man, played the main role in the Soviet film *Counterplan,* one of the first sound films. Maria Germanova of the Moscow Art Theater, a pupil of Stanislavsky, appeared in the title role of Anna. The large fragments of the film that have been preserved attest to her subtle, in-depth interpretation of the role which was consonant with the image created by Tolstoi. Karenina's graceful carriage (this despite her being somewhat stout), black hair and light eyes, the unruly curls on the neck—Germanova had all that. Actresses who subsequently played Anna Karenina, including such stars as Greta Garbo, Vivien Leigh, and Tatyana Samoilova, have somehow failed to capture this inimitable plasticity of the original portrait.

The filmmakers were able to find a clue to the nightmarish dream haunting the heroine: the ogre of a muzhik (peasant), tampering with the iron and muttering some words in French. This image—the presentiment of retribution—was introduced with the aid of double exposure and combination sequences. There were two other outstanding performances in the film: those by Zoya Barantsevich, who appeared in the role of Kitty, and Vera Kholodnaya, a future "queen of the screen," who played the Italian wet nurse. Zoya Barantsevich was later to become a scriptwriter and the author of many decadent screenplays.

Also noteworthy are a film version of Dostoyevsky's *Crime and Punishment* (1915), made by V. Turzhansky, and *The Flowers Are Late* (1917), based on one of the early stories of Anton Chekhov, *Unnecessary Victory,* which was produced by B. Sushkevich. Both directors were from the famous First Studio of the Moscow Art Theater. The young actors were from the same theater; they combined sincerity of impersonation with masterly technique.

Finally, mention should be made of the best-known films produced by Yakov Protazanov: *The Queen of Spades,* based on a story of the same name by Alexander Pushkin, and *Father Sergius,* based on one of Leo Tolstoi's later stories.

These two films became famous thanks to Ivan Mozzhukhin, probably the leading screen actor of the time in Russia. After the October Revolution, Mozzhukhin emigrated to France where he mostly appeared in the roles of a satanic hero or a neurotic and, in a way, came to personify the "Russian style" for the European moviegoer. Unable to adapt to the talkies, he sank into obscurity and poverty.

Yakov Protazanov was the patriarch of the early Russian cinema and one of its leading lights. He was also a prominent figure in the postrevolu-

Still from The Queen of Spades *shows Ghermann-Ivan Mozzhukhin in 1916.*

tionary motion picture industry. He made numerous films which were most diverse. Having no predilection for any particular genre or subject, he abided by the Voltairian precept that "all styles are good except the tiresome sort." Protazanov has an impressive record: his films include comedies, the tragic *Nikolai Stavrogin* (after Dostoyevsky), domestic dramas, the mystical *Satan Triumphant,* and *Little Ellie* (after Maupassant's *La Petite Roque*), with Ivan Mozzhukhin in the main role of a sex maniac. He also produced *Drama by Telephone,* an extremely interesting adaptation of D. W. Griffith's *The Lonely Villa,* which was given a Russian setting.

The Queen of Spades (1915) and *Father Sergius* (1917) hold a worthy place in this motley crowd.

The first film has none of the refinement of style and subtle irony of the original. It is only a crude adaptation of the story by Pushkin. Nevertheless, it had a certain topical interest. In Mozzhukhin's interpretation the Pushkinian hero, a young officer, Ghermann, who dreams of entering fashionable society by discovering the old countess's secret about the three cards, is turned into a maniacal middle-class fortune hunter. Selfish, callous, and vulgar, with a demonical face and large glassy eyes staring out under dark brows, he is a doomed man. The final sequences show him sitting on an iron cot in a lunatic asylum, shuffling a pack of cards and each time turning up not the coveted ace but a queen of spades, a symbol of vengeance as well as retribution for the murdered countess.

This film is distinguished for an ingenious camera angle: Ghermann's tireless vigils beneath the windows of the countess's house were filmed from above, the way Liza, the countess's companion saw him. Deeply in love with him, the young lady used to sit in a chair at the window; she was all hope and expectation. Then we see Ghermann and his huge black shadow on the wall: the aquiline nose, unruly hair, the profile of a Napoleon. This was a novelty for the cinema of the 1910s, a bold experiment in developing the cinema language, its morphology and syntax. On the other hand, the faulty lighting robbed the sequences of the foreshortening effect and made the elaborate decor, executed by V. Ballusek, a noted artist of that time, appear flat and overburdened with detail. Thus, the film combined innovation and routine, brilliant ingenuity and dull commonplace work.

Protazanov began making *Father Sergius* after the February Revolution of 1917, which overthrew the Russian monarchy. The date is significant, for under tsarist censorship it was forbidden to impersonate a tsar (in this

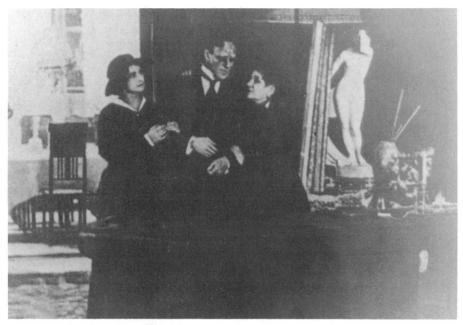

Space is broken in fragments with different perspectives in still from His Eyes *in Russian Gold Series of 1916.*

case Nicholas I) in a feature film or to deal with church affairs and monastic life. The hero of the film is Prince Kasatsky, an aristocrat who, disgusted with the hypocrisy and corruption of high society, takes monastic vows and becomes Father Sergius. The film is a serious attempt to translate Tolstoi's life of a saint (or rather "anti-life") into the language of cinema. It traces the life of the hero from his childhood years to his old age and shows his spiritual torment, his efforts in resisting temptations, especially that of deception, and his striving for true faith. Mozzhukhin, who played Father Sergius, gave on the whole an impressive performance, though it is somewhat marred by being bombastic and theatrical.

The best films made in those prerevolutionary years are based on literary works by Russian authors. An example is *Silent Witnesses* (1914), which, despite its modest aims, deserves consideration.

Silent Witnesses was produced by Yevgeni Bauer, with script by Alexander Voznessensky, a film enthusiast and author of many screenplays and literary essays. Yevgeni Bauer was probably the most remarkable filmmaker of prerevolutionary Russia, one might say a born cinematographer.

Silhouette photography and contre-jour *effects contrast black and white in* At Seven O'Clock, *1916.*

There is nothing unusual about the story itself: a young girl, a doorman's daughter, is seduced by a rich man. What makes the film unusual and interesting is the interpretation of the story, which in some ways anticipates the famous German film *Der letzte Mann (The Last Man)* made by Friedrich Wilhelm Murnau, with Emil Jannings in the main role. The outstanding thing about *Silent Witnesses* is not so much the acting (with A. Kheruvimov and D. Chitorina in the title roles) as Bauer's direction and the camera work of B. Zavelev, Bauer's close associate and one of the founders of the Soviet school of movie photography.

The film shows a cross section of a mansion with its drawing rooms and dining room, the master's study, the bedroom, the main staircase, the back entrance, the kitchen, and finally the doorman's lodge, where a liveried old man and his daughter Nastya, a housemaid, live. These are the two mute and humble witnesses of other people's lives, of their happiness. But they were lifted to the height of happiness themselves, only to be kicked aside the next moment: Nastya is seduced by the young master, who then leaves her without a thought. Meanwhile, life goes on in the big mansion: the cook prepares the meals, the young master returns at daybreak after a night's revelries, and the doorman announces visitors. The sorrow of the two "silent witnesses" is hidden deep inside them.

The film has no subtitles, which were an inevitable feature of earlier films. The narrative here is lucid and concise. Skillfully filmed and edited, the picture marked a big stride forward in the field of the cinema. It belongs to the tradition of the natural school of nineteenth century Russian literature, a tradition that goes back to Gogol's *St. Petersburg Stories* and Dostoyevsky's *Poor Folk* and to the populist literature.

Quite a different example are the animated cartoons of Wladyslaw Starewicz, a genre that he invented: three-dimensional cartoons with . . . insects as actors. Starewicz, a skillful cameraman and a magician of combination sequences, assigned the roles to bugs, grasshoppers, wasps, flies. These were handmade insects. Starewicz parodied melodramas and costumed plays based on historical themes and made use of stories from contemporary satirical magazines. Some of the titles of his productions are: *A War Between Capricorns and Stag Beetles, An Aviation Week of Insects,* and *The Cameraman's Revenge.* These witty cartoons followed the fabulist genre, above all the tradition of Ivan Krylov. Starewicz became famous thanks to his picture *The Grasshopper and the Ant,* based on Krylov's fable.

The influence of Leo Tolstoi's documentary work, *Sebastopol Sketches,* can be traced in Vasili Goncharov's film *The Defense of Sebastopol,* which was a landmark for the Russian cinema. The film was also influenced by the Russian school of battle-scene painting, in particular by Vasili Vereshchagin's sketches of the 1812 war against Napoleon and of the Turkestan War.

The Defense of Sebastopol was a full-length film—2,000 meters, 1 hour 40 minutes—something unheard of for 1911, the year when it was premiered. Just as surprising was the form. We may call it a "reconstruction of events," for the film had no plot as such and no clear-cut scenario either: the episodes of the Crimean War (1855–1856) alternated with documentary sequences from the battle scene. The portrait likenesses of the personages and real heroes of the war—Admiral Nakhimov, Admiral Kornilov, Pirogov (the field surgeon), the famous Koshka (the sailor), and Darya (the "sister of charity"), and many, many other real participants—are impressive indeed. The crowd scenes come off well: the evacuation of the city, a hospital receiving the wounded, a send-off of recruits, the siege of the Malakhov Kurgan. Two talented cameramen, A. Ryllo and Louis Forestier, presented the featured episodes in a manner of a war documentary. Louis Forestier came from France as a cameraman working for the firm Eclair, having made his debut in *Le Film d'Art* in Paris. He settled down in Russia and became a Russian citizen. Later he worked for the Soviet cinema for many years. His memoirs[6] have become one of the primary sources on the history of the prerevolutionary Russian cinema. In his memoirs he described the filming of *The Defense of Sebastopol,* made for the most part on the battle scene—at the Third and Fourth Bastions and at the Malakhov Kurgan. The first-ever field expedition of Russian filmmakers!

The present-day viewer will find many emotional and thrilling episodes in this film, not to speak of its historical and documentary value. As to the ending, it rather looks like a television program of our time. The film shows veterans of the Crimean War, those who had lived to see the year of 1911, against the backdrop of a war memorial. Former army soldiers, seamen, lieutenants, and captains appear as elderly men with many orders and medals on their chests. Former nurses are now grandmothers, many in widows' weeds. The cinema camera moves along their rows as if presenting them one by one to the audience.

Mention should also be made of the films produced by Vsevolod Meyerhold, the outstanding stage innovator and modernist: *The Picture of*

Dorian Gray (1915) and *The Strong Man*. Unfortunately, no copies of these reels have been preserved. Both productions represent a break with conventions and, showing excessive refinement, must have appeared "elitist" for the film audiences of the day. They were not popular.

Meyerhold (a superb drama actor and Stanislavsky's pupil, the first performer of Treplev's role in *The Seagull* by Anton Chekhov at the Moscow Art Theater) played the part of Lord Henry Wotton. According to critics and authors of memoirs, the film failed to convey the paradox of relationships among the heroes (Dorian Gray, Basil Hallward, and Lord Henry) that was so exquisitely treated by Oscar Wilde in his novel, a variation on *La Peau de Chagrin* by Honoré de Balzac ("the original is eternally youthful, it is the picture that withers and decays with age"). By transferring the Wilde prose to the silent screen, Meyerhold sacrificed the delicacy of its fabric. The best point of the film is in the decor: in the chiaroscuro (light and shade) effects, in the luxury of the setting and interiors, and in the interplay of carpets, porcelain, wood, and flowers—chrysanthemums in vases and orchids in buttonholes. Failing in the literary texture of the film, the producer gained in its pictorial imagery. Vladimir Yegorov, the designer, and Alexander Levitsky, the cameraman, the producer's coauthors, skilfully blended the elements of film art: the composition of a sequence and the rhythm of montage, the mise-en-scène and lighting. Discouraged by the cool reception of the public, Meyerhold turned his back on the movies and returned to the theater, to traverse a long and arduous path in the service to it. True, he reappeared once as an actor in the role of a tsarist dignitary in Yakov Protazanov's postrevolutionary film *The White Eagle,* a screen version of Leonid Andreyev's short story. However, *The Picture of Dorian Gray* can be qualified as the first experimental Russian film, a brainchild of the cinematographic avant-garde. Its vivid, pictorial style and chiaroscurist eloquence certainly influenced many prerevolutionary reels, at least those where the makers would search for *speaking pictures* and not just go ahead and "shoot off" in a pavilion or from life.

It is indicative that Fedor Chaliapin, the great Russian bass who captivated generations of music lovers all over the world, turned to the cinema as well. He successfully combined his prodigious voice with outstanding dramatic talent.

The mass, popular nature of cinema art appealed to him. Coming from common folk, Chaliapin thought of the many thousands of provincial

29

Newsreel of November 1918 shows empire facade of Bolshoi Theater at the time of the VI All-Russian Soviet Assembly.

Russian spectators who could thus gain access to art and see the stars of St. Petersburg and Moscow. Although the silent screen robbed him of the opportunity to use his unsurpassed voice Chaliapin took his chance, pinning all hope on his plastic gestures and facial expressions. Proceeding from one of his starring roles, that of Tsar Ivan Grozny (Ivan the Terrible) from the opera *Maid of Pskov,* Chaliapin offered a filmed version: the full-length picture *Ivan the Terrible* (1914). The production (carried out by V. Vegorov) was not very successful. Chaliapin carried over to the screen some of the theatrical, histrionic cliches—the emphasis on gestures and the tense facial features—in spite of his obvious attempts to overcome them. Nevertheless, the film was a landmark. The forceful Chaliapin conjured up the image of the tyrant tsar, an intriguing and horrid figure of Russian history, with all the dichotomy of his soul and with such intrinsic traits as power and guile, brutality and slyness, acumen and spiritual savagery. The actor impersonated all this with natural ease—quite an achievement for the silent movies! Since the film has come down to us, we may form a firsthand impression. For all its production drawbacks, the picture is second only to Sergei Eisenstein's *Ivan the Terrible,* produced as late as the 1940s, with the classical Nikolai Cherkasov in the main role, even though the cinema had turned on many occasions to the image of the first Russian tsar.

In general, prerevolutionary Russia's cinema is a treasuretrove of cultural values. It has succeeded both in documentaries and in feature reels in preserving for the future generations a broad panorama of Russian artistic life during its Silver Age, including the élan of Anna Pavlova's dancing and the dramatic style of Yevgeni Vakhtangov's acting. It has also poked fun at "trendy" vogues in the parody *Drama in the Futurists' Cabaret No. 13,* in which the artists Natalia Goncharova and Mikhail Larionov were engaged. It has filmed the *Cricket on the Hearth* staged at the Moscow Art Theater, one of the favorites among Moscow theatergoers, enlisting the best theater actors. Yet, here credit goes to the cinema as a medium and to the smart owners of film companies who were never tired of attracting celebrities for both prestige considerations and profit.

As for the purposeful quests, these—like in the cinematography of other countries—were of secondary importance, clashing as they did both with the commercial interests of the entrepreneurs and with the primitive tastes of the broad audiences—the country folks of yesterday, now factory hands, who had left their native parts to flee poverty. Uneducated masses, they would swarm to the "flics" to get a kick for their five- or ten-kopeck coins.

So the screen had to cater to their tastes by offering crude adventure stories with robbers—the Russian counterparts of Cartouche and Rinaldo Rinaldini, such as Vaska Churkin (advertised as a "Russian Fantomas"), Anton Krechet, or the pretty female thief from Odessa, Sonka the Golden Hand. Those were the carbon copies of popular "kopeck" literature (dime novels Russian style) that flooded the book market by the millions—Nat Pinkertons, Nick Carters, and their Russian cousins. All this notwithstanding, a stratification process set in, first among the cinema-goers, and then in the repertoire.

Cinematography grew into a multistoried structure with its aesthetic "top" of artistic experiments and conquests, the "basement" of cheap crude pictures, and the middle-level tiers of mass consumption in between, later known as "show business," or "pop culture."

Accordingly, different production levels applied for the makers and for those who gave them the money. And so, smallish and ingenuous nickelodeons, that is to say low-farce booths with highfalutin names, gave way to fashionable cinema theaters with large ornate halls and damask armchairs and just as extravagant "alien" names as "La Parisienne" on Nevsky Prospekt in St. Petersburg, "Le Moulin Rouge" (in St. Petersburg too), "Le Moderne" as far away as Ashkhabad on the outskirts of the Karakum Desert, and even "A. M. Don Othello" in Irkutsk, deep in the heartland of Siberia.

"The Silent Ornaments of Life"

Inside, in the mesmeric darkness of the hall, an endless cinema drama unfolded on the screen.

"Last night I was in the Kingdom of Shadows. If you only knew how strange it is to be there. It is a world without sound, without color. . . . It is not life but its shadow, it is not motion but its soundless spectre."[7] Such were the opening lines of the first cinema critique carried in the Russian press. The author was a young provincial journalist, the great proletarian writer of the future. He was Maxim Gorky, the founder of the method of socialist realism in Soviet literature. Gorky was spellbound by the enchanted world of Merlin and the phantasmagoria of the screen, by the magic of a bundle of rays projected onto the screen, by the electric aura about the heroes, their faces, and movements, and by the clicking race of sequences.

Russian cinema did not produce its own genre of film comedies or Westerns or no-prose varieties in the garb of detectives and thrillers. Even though the Russian audiences were mad about all kinds of tricks, gimmicks, and gags on the screen, Russian cinema in the 1910s offered mostly imported productions. The public was wild about comedians; it worshiped the Frenchman Max Linder, who, when he made an appearance in Russia in 1913, received a royal reception.

But homegrown talent enjoyed no popularity. Neither Anton Fertner, a Polish-born comedian, in his role "Antosha the Dandy," nor Arkadi Boitler ("Arkasha"), who followed in his footsteps, nor the fatty "Uncle Pood" (V. Avdeyev) achieved acclaim.

Apart from its indisputable contributions and innovative approaches in the realm of literary adaptations, Russian cinematography expressed itself, it seems, in a single original genre only. The ads called it a "psychological drama," or just a "cinema drama." Yet if we stick to more exact terminology, the word is "social melodrama." No new genre, of course: with its roots back in the eighteenth century, social melodrama became widespread in the theater and world literature of the nineteenth century. The cinematographers took a fancy to it. Why? Because as a conservative medium it could not catch up with volatile artistic ebbs and flows. In all events, social melodrama found favor in the cinema, with the blessing of Russian cinematography.

On the bosom of such psychological drama, the aesthetics of the Russian cinema, with the gaudy and ornate decor of its settings, was taking shape and substance. So was a company of cineactors and cineactresses. The first "stars" were already twinkling in the cinematographic firmament of Russia in 1914–1915.

"Added to the perennial topics of those days about the war, Rasputin, State Duma and theaters," recalled the veteran cinematographer Ivan Perestiani, "was a new one, the cinema. It had its prophets. . . . A queer cineterminology was coined: 'king of the screen,' 'stella of the canvas sky.' . . ."[8] All, or nearly all, "kings" and "queens" of the cinema rose to a fame they could never have dreamed of in the theater.

The screen metamorphosed the theatrical types and characters. Thus, the traditional "hero lover" changed into a "tail-coated fop," a man about town; he became a Bohemian, a "gilded-youth" type, a gentleman of the "upper crust," and a heartless enchanter. He seduced in seduction reels like *Withered Chrysanthemums, A Life for a Life,* and *Fata Morgana.* These roles were acted by Vitold Polonsky, Peter Chardynin, and Osip Runich, or by Vladimir Maximov, who impersonated a lyrical, romantic image of the same type.

Yet a pivot of the psychological drama was the heroine. Vera Coralli (the Bolshoi prima ballerina), Zoya Barantsevich, Natalia Kovanko, and other belles graced the screen. But one eclipsed them all—the glamorous Vera Kholodnaya, a household name in the Russia of those days and remembered even now. Although Vera Kholodnaya lived a short life in cinematography, just four years, and only a few of her films have come down to us, her fame has been passed down from generation to generation: Vera Kholodnaya, the legend of the screen, the beauty who knew no rivals, the star of stars.

Vera Kholodnaya, star of silent film, was the ideal of feminine beauty in pre-revolutionary years.

A young woman from an intellectual milieu, she came to the A. Khanzhonkov studio with no professional background and no stage experience but only with love for the cinema and the passionate desire to become a film actress. She had something else to offer though: large gray eyes, long eyelashes, and a petite foot.

Her debut in the *Song of Triumphant Love* made a hit. Vera's pictures adorned the covers of cinema magazines. Her fame grew rapidly. Kholodnaya left the Khanzhonkov studio and joined that of D. Kharitonov's. She was offered enormous fees for those times. Poets devoted their poems to her. Alexander Vertinsky, a popular singer, dedicated his poems and songs to her. Vera Kholodnaya's name on billboards guaranteed huge receipts.

Young girls saw in her their ideal of beauty, grace, and style, a fancy world poles apart from their bleak existences. Kholodnaya played sundry heroines: Maria Nikolayevna, the wife of a small government official; Nata Barteneva, a young poor girl brought up by a woman millionaire; Marianne, a girl earning her living by recitation; or Paula, a girl from the circus. At first, all of the heroines wear motley dresses: a modest white blouse and skirt, or the "Pieretta-style" garb; a girl student's hat; or a muslin gown of a young lady from a rich family. But this is before good luck lifts them up the social ladder. Then they don modish apparel, depending on the fashions of the day: décolleté evening dresses, fur-trimmed capes, elaborate afternoon gowns, necklaces, hats with ostrich plumes, Greek shawls, and so on.

The same perennial motif of the lustful, pernicious sway of wealth over a frail woman's soul, of the fatal leap "upstairs" to the resplendent world of luxury and graceful vice permeates the two-serial film *Silence, Melancholy, Silence! (Love's Dear Tale)*. The producer, Peter Chardynin, managed to engage the cream of the actors for the all-male cast playing opposite Vera Kholodnaya, who, as the heroine, had to relive her classical, stereotype role over again. A swan song of old Russian cinematography it was—the film appeared on the screen after the October Revolution of 1917.

These pictures are tainted with malignant vapors of mammon and "easy money": windfalls descending upon luckless minions of fortune; forged promissory notes, legacies, money marriages, and bankruptcies; feasts with dainty dishes and champagne. The films showed picnics, restaurants, furs, gorgeous interiors (salons, drawing rooms, boudoirs, private picture galleries, lavish decor, frescoes, embroidered screens), shooting boxes, extravagant villas, and automobiles, of course, with their bright headlights piercing the night darkness, that symbol of luxury, that novelty of the century. Never appearing were traces of the war bleeding Russia white beginning from 1914, even though the scene of most of the films was set in the present. Yet it is a fancy and rootless present that leaves no room for the war and no room for the imminent revolution either.

Old Russia's cinematography had closed its ears to the rumble of artillery cannonade and to the sullen murmur of the people. Instead, it sang praises to Russian capitalism, post factum, with a historic lag. It was on the screen that the viewers could read its last chapter, even when the days of the February Revolution had come and gone and October was but a few days away. In secluded mansions with their splendid halls with illuminated columns and potted tropical plants fateful destinies continued to be decided on the screen.

Yet quite a different film was on its way. The producer was Yevgeni Bauer, assisted by a group of artists, young Lev Kuleshov among them. They, together with cameramen Boris Zavelev and Alexander Levitsky, showed perfect mastery of the pictorial style, a hallmark of Russian modernity in the cinema.

On October 24, 1917, in the cinema theaters of Moscow, the center of Russian cinematography, a new film entitled *The Silent Ornaments of Life* was shown. It was a cinedrama about complicated relationships between a Prince Obolensky and two beauties, tender Claudia and willful Nelly. The very name of this film has become a byword. Next day, on October 25, the Socialist Revolution triumphed in Russia.

CHAPTER TWO

The Tempestuous Twenties

Is State-Run Cinema a Real Thing?

*A*ugust 27, 1919, the day Lenin signed the "Decree on the Transfer of the Photographic and Cinematographic Industry and Trade to the People's Commissariat of Education," is considered the birthday of the Soviet cinema. All privately owned motion picture enterprises—studios, movie theaters—were nationalized. The entire industry was drastically overhauled. With the passage of ownership into government hands, no longer was cinematography a commercial private enterprise; it was now the cinema of the socialist state, a medium of ideology, propaganda, enlightenment, and education.

October 1917–August 1919 was a transitional period in the Soviet cinema burdened with difficulties arising out of economic disarray, foreign military intervention, and civil war. Yet, despite all the obstacles, revolutionary programs were tenaciously pursued in the cinema industry.

37

A historian who decides to trace the progress of a particular society by analyzing the development of one of its specific spheres would find the Russian cinema to be excellent material, perhaps a better source for study than other forms of cultural media.

Like Janus, the two-faced Roman god of gates, cinema also faced in two directions at once, looking upon both art and commerce.

The privately owned Russian cinema took no note of the historic day— October 25 (November 7 by the Gregorian calendar), 1917. Engrossed in spinning black-and-white years of the "silent ornaments of life" and "fairy tales of romantic love," it failed to hear those eventful *Ten Days That Shook the World,* the written account of the enthusiastic and sagacious American John Reed, who probably saw more and better than many onlookers who had no idea of what was happening in the outskirts of Europe. The revolution in Russia, a backward country that had lived only fifty years without serfdom (abolished in 1861) and only eight months under a provisional government that had succeeded the paralyzed autocracy, seemed to be no more than another regular riot which the authorities and the gendarmes were sure to quell the way they had done before.

Although he had to bear the brunt of administrative and other types of duties as the head of a revolutionary government, Lenin showed much concern for the film industry. Besides the decree on its nationalization, Lenin left a number of remarkable documents and pronouncements in relation to cinema. His popular expression that "of all the arts the most important for us is the cinema,"[1] is the most well known in the Soviet Union. But I am afraid we are running ahead of our story. These words were uttered at a later date, when the Soviet government had become more stable and the time had come to build a new culture.

In fact, Lenin's interest in the cinema dates back to earlier times. One of his closest associates, Vladimir Bonch-Bruyevitch, recalls what Lenin told him in 1907:

> So long as it remains in the hands of vulgar profiteers, the cinema will do more evil than good. More often than not, it corrupts the people with abominable content. But . . . when the people take over the cinema and put it in the hands of true representatives of socialist culture, it will become a powerful media of enlightenment for the masses.[2]

These words vividly show Lenin's attitude towards culture and arts and underlie his plans for their development. Recall his article on "Party

Organization and Party Literature" (1905), a true manifesto concerning the inevitable choice of "party" literature over "bourgeois" literature. In the article he said that the idea of socialism and sympathy

> with the working people, and not greed and careerism, will bring ever new forces to its ranks. It will be a free literature, because it will serve, not some satiated heroine, not the bored "upper ten thousand" . . ., but the millions and tens of millions of working people—the flower of the country, its strength and its future.[3]

What a good example of enthusiastic and infectious optimism! Thinking back to those turbid times of 1905, when the tsarist regime went to any lengths to suppress revolutionary action of any kind, one can imagine the impact of these meaningful words, so consonant with aspirations of the progressive Russian intelligentsia. This is essential to keep in mind in order to fully understand the social processes preceding the October Socialist Revolution.

Returning to the cinema however, the following statements about the present and the future of Russian cinema show that Lenin's contemporaries held much the same views as he did himself.

"There sits an ugly Toad-the-Peddler in the bulrushes of cinematography," noted Leo Tolstoi.

"The cinema—purveyor of movement. The cinema—renewer of literature. . . . But the cinema is sick. Capitalism has covered its eyes with gold. Deft entrepreneurs lead it through the street by the hand," indignantly said Vladimir Mayakovsky.

"Before it serves science and helps people to improve, the cinema will help popularize debauchery," prophesied Maxim Gorky.

That's what the progressive-thinking public believed. And a closer look at the tenets behind Lenin's concept of art would show us that Russian cultural tradition is one of its main points of origin.

Spiritually, love for one's fellowman was always characteristic to the Russian democratic intelligentsia. Pain and a constant sense of duty toward the humiliated and oppressed, empathy with those deprived not just of life's cultural needs but even of the bare necessities, the ardent desire to "sow the seeds of the intelligent, good, and eternal" were felt by all. In contrast to Oswald Spengler, the author of the *Decline of the West,* Russian thinkers did not dread a cultural twilight of modern civilization. The specifically Russian "Kulturtraeger" trend accepted the cinema, that "offspring of industry and technology." All that was evil in the film industry came from the bourgeoisie. Revolution, the cherished dream of the progressive-minded intellectuals, was seen as a savior of the dying Russian society as a whole and of the Russian national screen.

On the historic night of October 25, immediately after the victory of the Socialist Revolution, Lenin raised the issue of mass education as a matter of high priority, recalled Anatoli Lunacharsky, the appointed People's Commissar for Education. The next day, commissars of the revolutionary government and the painter as well as art critic Alexander Benois (heading the "World of Art" Association) drew up a plan for "protecting artistic treasures" and inspected the famous collections of the Hermitage.[4]

On November 24, 1917, the People's Commissariat of Education passed a resolution to establish the State Publishing House. About its tasks the resolution said: "First of all, inexpensive, popular editions of the classics should be published and, where circumstances allow, distributed gratis, through libraries serving the working democracy."[5]

Apparently, cinema was among the primary concerns of the revolution. Thus, one of the first events offered by the Soviet cinema was the widely advertised Turgenev Scenario Competition held in August 1918 and specially timed to coincide with Ivan Turgenev's birth centennial.

It can be seen from the above that the long, substantial history that preceded the Lenin's Decree on the Nationalization of Russian Cinema had a distinct cultural educational orientation. Middle-class commercial potboilers—"whiny plots," ridiculous absurdities, depraved fancies—became the arch enemy. One looked forward to a new, socially conscious proletarian viewer who embodied Lenin's dream. The first "movie train" whistled across the country, resounding "The cinema lightens darkness, it enlightens the poor. . . ."

Lenin asserted that recording chronicles was a good way to start the new Soviet cinema. The new leadership, needing active support, demanded that its documentary material show urgency, persuasiveness, and a direct link to current events. As early as 1918, weekly newsreels started coming out.

"Black Evening . . . White Snow"

Events directly related to the proclamation of Soviet government were too dynamic to be recorded on film. It was somewhat later that *October*

Coup: A Second Revolution, a documentary pieced together from odd filmings, was released. The reel contained shots that are now considered classic: sentries at the entrance of the Smolny Institute, which was turned into the headquarters of the revolution; townsfolk near the Winter Palace after the arrest of the provisional government ministers; even the destruction wrought in Moscow by the clashes between the Red Guards and the counter-revolutionary cadets. These sequences did have a high documentary value, but they failed to show any *appreciation* of the fact that a totally new system and era had come into existence. The old system was as good as dead.

Of course, it would be wrong to say that the old Russian cinema ignored real developments altogether. For example, it responded to the February Revolution of 1917 and the downfall of the Romanov dynasty with the fast-released sensations of *People of Sin and Blood (Sinners from Tsarskoye Selo), Grishka Rasputin's Amorous Escapades,* and *The Disgrace of the Romanov House.* These pseudo-revolutionary films raked up the filth of Rasputin-type erotic mysteries with relish. With the censorship on depicting the tsarist family and court lifted, smart hucksters of every stripe competed with one another in depicting the horrors of the deposed regime. Sundry "fighters" and victims of tsarist tyranny were quickly "revolutionized" and released on the screen. But, alas, not one film reached a level above low-grade commercialization.

Meanwhile, private cinema firms continued to operate right up to the passage of the nationalization decree. As many as one hundred fifty pictures[6] were produced in 1918 alone; but while thematic diversity within the repertoire was maintained, very little innovation was shown, almost as if no revolution had occurred. Notable exceptions, however, were two Neptune Studio productions starring Vladimir Mayakovsky. The poet starred in *The Young Lady and the Hooligan,* which was based on an Edmondo de Amicis story but set in Russia. A similar "translocation" was done to Jack London's *Martin Eden* in the film *Creation Can't Be Bought.* Here the Mayakovsky hero was called "Ivan Nov," or "New Ivan." In both movies Mayakovsky infused hot temper and coarse virility into a plebian's passionate love for a young girl from the intelligentsia. He used no makeup, a bold departure from contemporary tradition. Just the image of the "hooligan," the law-breaking pariah endowed, nonetheless, with a tender heart and passionate soul, continued the nineteenth century romantic tradition of social outcasts as heroes. A new, more straightforward

The Young Lady and the Hooligan *was one of the first films released after October.*

manner of presentation was found, presaging a general change of style: the turn of the century "moderne" was giving way to constructivism, futurism, and other "leftist" artistic currents of the post–October years.

Definitely, the air was rife with the change of time. Although the *Dying Swan, Satan Triumphant* and *Last Tango* still flitting across the screen, the colors of time were changing quickly. Sharper features characteristic of the epoch and its art were starting to appear.

The prerevolutionary 1910s were robed in violets and dull greens. "The City," for example, the poet Alexander Blok's prophetic cycle, poignantly forewarns about "invisible changes and unprecedented revolts." These colors appear in the vignettes and exquisite watercolors of Konstantin Somov and Sergei Sudeikin. They can be seen in the tints of high society salon draperies and beaded, sequined evening dresses. They show up in the limp, flaccid lines of the "liberty style" and in the opaque transparency of Galle's vases. For the sombre tones of Persian lilac, then the most popular color, it is enough to recall "Ice Creams from Lilac" by poet Igor Severyanin, an aesthete and idol of the public.

Last Tango, from the privately owned Russian movie industry, was a typical example of escapism into an imaginary world of peace and quiet.

Black, white, and sanguine red are the tricolor tones in Alexander Blok's "The Twelve," a poem written in 1918 which later became an epigraph to those tragic times. Black was the color of the wintry night in Petrograd, white the color of the blizzard, and sanguine the color of the revolutionary flag carried by a Red Guard patrol across the deserted streets.

> Black evening
> White snow
> Wind, wind!
> Careful, man, or down you go.
> Wind . . . wind . . .
> Roaring the wide world over!

Curiously enough, the same symbolic revolutionary tricolor scheme would inspire the famous Sergei Eisenstein: in each copy of his black-and-white film, *The Battleship Potemkin,* he would have the flag, hoisted by the revolutionary crew over its ship, hand painted in scarlet red. The Eisenstein classic was to become the emblem of Soviet cinema avant-garde, just

Inhabitants of Odessa mourn at the casket of Vakulinchuk in still from The Battleship Potemkin.

as "The Twelve" by Alexander Blok symbolized poetry born of the revolution.

But there was a long way to go to get to *The Battleship Potemkin.* In the meantime, private Russian cinema was getting closer and closer to agony and to its final collapse.

In 1918 an exodus of cinema entrepreneurs from Moscow and Petrograd to the south began. As early as spring of 1917, Alexander Khanzhonkov chose the lush Crimean resort town of Yalta as the site for his "Hollywood." Near the fountains on French Boulevard in Odessa, A. Kharitonov put up a glass pavilion, with the hope of making his "Hollywood" near the Black Sea. Occupied by Entente and White Guard troops, Odessa and Yalta became the last footholds for the private Russian film industry; their ports were the last rickety bridges from which emigres going into self-exile could board their white steamships.

That exodus took with it a large number of cinematographers. Artists

In the finale, the revolutionary vessel Potemkin *passes the admiral's squadron.*

of the brush, sculptors, and stage actors had an easier time in finding their niche in the new Russia. They exhibited their works in town streets and squares, and they specially decorated them for the new national festivities in honor of the revolution. The most important day was changed from October 25 to November 7, as Russia had switched over to the European calendar. Eminent artists, including such celebrities as Isaac Brodsky and Natan Altman, were more than happy to paint portraits of Lenin in his study and behind the rostrum. Theater producers, inspired by the idea of resurrecting street shows, staged their experiments in front-line theaters.

However, cinema people depended a good deal more on their former entrepreneurs in matters that concerned film, cine-equipment, and money. Film entrepreneur Joseph Yermoliev started the "descension" of first- and second-magnitude stars upon the Franco-German horizon. These were the kings and queens of the screen: Ivan Mozzhukhin and his wife Natalia Lisenko, Vera Coralli, the beautiful Natasha Kovanko, Olga Gzovskaya,

Maria Germanova, Olga Baclanova, Mikhail Chekhov, Anna Sten, Vera Baranovskaya, and many others. Producers Protazanov, Volkov, Turzhansky, and Starewicz also left for the West. A glance into the *All Cinematography* handbook published in 1916 would show that over half the Russian filmmakers emigrated.

Those who left were in for different lots. Some, like Yakov Protazanov, for instance, having regained their senses fairly quickly, returned to Soviet cinema. Others, like Mikhail Chekhov, though homesick, stayed abroad and brought fame to Russian art there. The majority, though, vanished in the turbulent waves of European and American film industries. But even those who started off shining brightly in alien skies ended up in obscurity, as did Ivan Mozzhukhin, lonely and homesick. Acute and incurable nostalgia must be an intrinsic property of the Russian soul.

The Fates did not spare some of those who stayed at home either. In April 1919 the Spanish flu epidemic carried off Vera Kholodnaya in the prime of her beauty at the age of twenty-six. Thousands of people in

V.I. Lenin appears on the balcony of Mossovet in newsreel during meeting of January 19, 1919.

Odessa (where she had appeared in her last roles) bade farewell to their favorite idol of the screen. Clad in white and festooned with flowers, her embalmed body was buried in a glass coffin and placed in a chapel vault beside the remains of the illustrious Russian aviator Utochkin. Death also stole one of the most talented prerevolutionary producers, Yevgeni Bauer. Slipping and breaking his leg on a beach in Yalta, he wound up bedridden in a plaster cast and eventually died of pulmonary edema. Not long after him the handsome Vitold Polonsky also ended his earthly career.

New people appeared at the deserted film studios and ruined pavilions and took up the rusty, dust-covered cameras. The old social order was gone and replaced by a new one. The cinema of Russian capitalism was dying, but the cinema itself was immortal.

On December 19, 1922, the State Cinema and Photo Enterprise, Goskino (later reorganized into Sovkino Trust), was set up. Inevitably, a number of reorganizational periods followed (new enterprises came into being, the steppingstones to an integrated state-run motion picture industry). But the overall course of development was an undeviating one that would easily overcome any resistance. Restoration of war-ravaged studios began immediately after the end of the civil war of 1918–1920, for which essential film equipment was purchased from abroad. Progress was regularly discussed at Communist Party Congresses.

New filmmakers—producers, actors, and camera operators—were in the process of being made. On the battlefronts of the civil war, in major cities, universities, small Russian towns, even in Germany's prisoner-of-war camps, future leaders of the Soviet cinema were waiting for their chance to be called upon by the revolution.

Trailblazers' Laboratory

"THE KULESHOV EFFECT"

Some of the trailblazers, eager to plunge into the unknown, came from old private studios. Lev Kuleshov, mentioned earlier, was one of them. He may be called a godfather of the innovative, revolutionary film.

Kuleshov was born in 1899 into an impoverished family of the Russian gentry living in the old town of Tambov, south of Moscow. When he was only seventeen, he came to the cinema and worked under Yevgeni Bauer as a film designing assistant. In 1918 Kuleshov produced his first film, *Engineer Prite's Project,* at a private studio. He developed an ardent passion for constructivism and everything associated with machinery; in fact he later on distinguished himself as one of the first fans of auto racing.

While making films, a charming, good-looking Lev Kuleshov met a vividly striking Alexandra Khokhlova, a young actress of rare talent. The daughter of the famous Russian physician Sergei Botkin and grand-daughter of Pavel Tretyakov, the founder of the Tretyakov Art Gallery in Moscow, Khokhlova belonged to the Russian artistic elite. Their first encounter was a propitious one. Always together, they made a perfect match on and off the screen, the veritable Paul and Virginia of the cinema.

By nature an innovator, Kuleshov bravely rushed into the unknown. Leaving the paviliions of the Khanzhonkov Studio and the decor of Bauer films, he went off to join the Red Army units fighting at the fronts of the civil war. Later he prided himself on his achievements as a war correspondent and documentary producer during this "most significant period" of 1918–1920 until his dying day. At one time, he was even "in charge of the whole newsreel department," as he put it.

Already past his prime, Kuleshov wrote the following letter to the author of this book:

> I had to win cameramen and producers of documentary films over to the cinematograph based on montage, and most importantly, I carried out filming on assignments received from Vladimir Ilyich Lenin. Together with cameraman Edward Tissé, I shoot the Red Army's combat operations against Kolchak. I also filmed, on Lenin's instructions, *The Exhumation of the Remains of Sergei Radonezhsky* (which was erroneously ascribed to Dziga Vertov) and *The All-Russian Central Executive Committee Inspects the Province of Tver* (with Alexander Levitsky as cameraman); assisted by my pupils— M. Kudelko, A. Khokhlova and L. Obolensky—I shoot *The All-Russian Subbotnik★ of May 1, 1920*. In some of the sequences, I happened to be near Lenin, quite close to him. . . .[7]

Indeed, the first Soviet cinematographers were proud of their involvement in the revolutionary events of those years. They were happy to be the makers of unique historical documentaries showing Lenin.

However, it was not the documentary genre that brought the fame of a world cinema classic and trailblazer to the young and enthusiastic Kuleshov. His rival, Dziga Vertov, was to come into fame as the pre-

★Author's note: Subbotnik is voluntary unpaid work on Saturdays.

Dura Lex *is considered the masterpiece of Leo Kuleshov.*

eminent newsreel producer. Supposedly he made the documentary about the exhumation of the remains of St. Sergius of Radonezh. Kuleshov, however, claims authorship of the film, which showed the official opening ceremony of the shrine of St. Sergius, the founding father of the Trinity–St. Sergius Monastary (now the town of Zagorsk forty miles north of Moscow). Lev Kuleshov's pioneering discoveries—or as they are called in film literature, "The Kuleshov Effect"—lay elsewhere.

Kuleshov put his heart and soul into montage from the start. He just needed experimentation to confirm his conjecture, namely, that the combination of separate frames could impart a meaning not present in any one frame alone. His classic montage has been referred to many times in film literature: a close-up of the face of Ivan Mozzhukhin, acting out amorous passion in an old film, juxtaposed with a close-up of a bowl of soup. The message of the sequence came out to be pangs of hunger, not pangs of love. Edited with a scene showing a coffin with the body of a child, the same close-up of Mozzhukhin conveyed the father's inconsolable grief, and so on. Thus, a frame as such carries no independent meaning of its own: it is but a letter in the word, a brick in the edifice of a film. Montage is what makes a moving picture a work of art.

Not only that, Kuleshov found that by splicing still shots of the Gogol monument on Arbat Square in Moscow and of the Capitol building in Washington, D.C., he could show on the screen a setting that does not really exist. Filming the torso of one woman, the eyes of second, and the legs of a third, he could assemble an "unexisting" creature. So the conclusion was made, that with the aid of montage, one could create a new dimension of space and a new facet of nature. Herein lies the universality and omnipotence of montage. It is the absolute of the cinema, the secret of its success, even its alpha and omega.

Hot-tempered and prone to hyperbole (the sign of his times!), Kuleshov demanded that cinema function according to nearly all-encompassing and immutable laws. (Dziga Vertov independently came to the same conclusion somewhat later). However, the Kuleshov Effect was indeed a new phrase in the art of film. It fostered the conception of the cinema as an art of rhythm, movement, and ever-changing distance between the artist and the object, i.e. all that goes into the specifics of cinematography. At that time no filmmaker was so awake, in theory and practice, to the role of montage as Kuleshov was; he was its most zealous propagandist in the silent cinema.

In 1929 Kuleshov outlined his theories in the classic *The Art of the Cinema,* a book considered to be one of the keystones of cinematographic theory.

Kuleshov had another cinematographic passion which was destined to play a major role in his career. That was the "American bug" or "Americanschina," as one of his articles is entitled. The Russian-born Kuleshov started shooting pictures about . . . America and Americans.

In his famous picture *The Extraordinary Adventures of Mr. West in the Land of the Bolsheviks* (1924), one of the first "travelogues" to follow a foreigner's journeys around the Soviet Union, Kuleshov brought an American to the Soviet screen. This was one of the popular genres of the Soviet cinema in the 1920s and 1930s.

For Kuleshov the film was another witty and funny cinematographic combination. Washington, D.C., by the miracle of montage, was transplanted to the banks of the river Moskva. Playing up that kind of ironic incongruity gave him great pleasure. The hero of this film, Mr. West, was played by P. Podobeda, a spitting image of Harold Lloyd, which added spice to the amusement. Attired in a hat, which hovered over a shy, slightly silly smile, and a shaggy fur coat and holding an American flag in

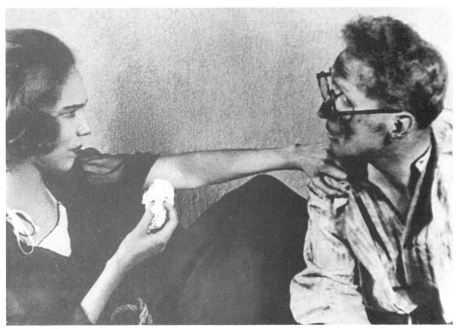

P. Podobeda plays Mr. West and A. Khokhlova plays the supposed Countess Saks in Mr. West in the Land of the Bolsheviks, *1924.*

his hand, his droll figure looked quite a sight beside agile waifs, the Cathedral of Christ the Savior, and the old Moscow tracks of the A tram. Or take the cowboy landing in Moscow—watching the brawny, dexterous Boris Barnet was almost as good as watching the real McCoy. What a store of merry, rib-tickling episodes he had up his sleeve!

Against a backdrop of Moscow's snow-ridden streets, Kremlin towers, and gold-topped cathedrals a fantastic chase scene unfolds, parodistically reminiscent of American comic films. Here one of the street teenage vagabonds hanging around the railway station promptly makes off with Mr. West's briefcase upon his arrival in Moscow. To save the dignity of his compatriot, Jeddy, the cowboy, rushes off in hot pursuit. With skill and dexterity he takes the heavy-set Moscow drozhki-driver prisoner and lassoes him to a tree. He then hops onto the cabby's seat and lashes the poor bay, throwing a scare into Muscovites.

In another episode Jeddy makes his way across a street on a stretched rope from six stories up, goes through the roof, and ends up in an

American mission office. These sequences are full of resiliency, movement, and slapstick humor. Here much credit should be given to Levitsky, the cameraman (who performed miracles in spite of the poor supply of film, electricity, equipment, and all), and, of course, to the masterly technique of Kuleshov montage.

Poor Mr. West ended up in a quite parodic situation when he fell into the hands of some Moscow thugs. The American simpleton proved to be an easy dupe; using a seductive vamp as bait, they finagled money out of the otherwise ideal husband and had him imprisoned—right out of a lampoon about the Bolshevik regime, which Mr. West had read so many of at home. But a "real Bolshevik" in a leather jacket showed up to arrest the dirty-doers and rescue the unfortunate traveler. The Bolshevik showed a delighted Mr. West the sights of Moscow and even took him to see a Red Square military parade. Here Kuleshov inserted newsreel sequences, which now make the movie a rare historical document.

Based on a script written by the poet Nikolai Aseyev, the plot naturally could not be taken very seriously. Yet the comic and grotesque were spliced with sketches of the Soviet Union as it was in 1924—real situations, real people, and real cityscapes. And most important the film brought a string of expressive physiognomies and original personages to life.

In the *Extraordinary Adventures of Mr. West in the Land of the Bolsheviks,* Kuleshov showed the fruit of a five-year program on developing a new type of film actor: a "model" endowed with natural beauty, good health, and the ability to show expediency and purpose on the screen without "acting" or "recreating," unaided by makeup, wigs, and props, of course.

In the history of international cinema, Kuleshov's studio has gone down as the first professional laboratory for actors of film. He recruited applicants who were rejected at the entrance exams in the State Film School (now the All-Union State Institute of Cinematography, VGIK), which was founded in 1919. The school was headed by Vladimir Gardin, who earlier directed the Russian Golden Series and produced such thrillers as *Keys to Happiness.* After the 1917 revolution he made agitprop (propaganda) reels, including *A Spectre Haunts Europe, Cross and Mauser, Sickle and Hammer.* Gardin and other venerable directors taught from the old school of film acting. But not the Kuleshov studio! From the very first it set its sights on "left" theatrical currents, the avant-garde art.

The inside of the studios might have been cold but the Kuleshovites kept warm with their ardent love of the cinema. When no film was available they shot "pictures without film"—small scenes divided into individual, long-range, medium-range, and close-up shots. These photographed still pictures have survived and are now in cinema archives. "A Venetian Stocking," "A Ring," "Gold," and other sketches are distinguished for their youthful grace and optimism. The first presentation brought together many cultural personalities from various countries. Impressed, they hailed the students with an enthusiastic burst of applause. "Moscow is blessed in its poverty!" wrote a correspondent for the *Berliner Tageblatt*. "There is no sign of a Potemkin-style or old London palaces here. Rather Moscow will bring high-quality cinematography to Europe with its film students."[8]

These students were great talents, indeed: Alexandra Khokhlova, the actress; Vsevolod Pudovkin, a big name in international filmmaking, coming into prominence just five years after the pictures without film; Boris Barnet, a film producer of the future; Leonid Obolensky, a sound expert in the early days of talking films.

Another full-length feature made by the "Kuleshov team," as his most active pupils were called, was *The Death Ray,* a fantastic suspense story about the struggle of workmen in a capitalist state to obtain an apparatus that could send super high energy rays. We must do justice to the imagination of scriptwriter Vsevolod Pudovkin: laser has confirmed the reality of the "death ray." The plot was too confused, and the director just failed to deliver. Yet the imagery was excellent: striking contrasts of crowd scenes and solo episodes alternated with fantastic industrial landscapes and the mysterious interiors of an inventor's cottage tucked away deep in the woods.

A 1926 Kuleshov production of *Dura Lex (By the Law),* a screen version of Jack London's *The Unexpected* written by Victor Shklovsky, was remarkable with its charm and cinematographic lucidity. Paradoxically enough, the Russian born and bred Kuleshov was most successful with an American theme. The scene of *Dura Lex* is set in Klondike, among golddiggers staying for the winter after a successful gold hunt. There were only five characters in that film—a woman (played by Khokhlova) and four men. The camera work of Konstantin Kuznetsov was mainly responsible for the film's success. He shot the film as if with the express purpose of showing the boundless potentialities of the camera: flowing movement, sun and water, patches of light, and *contre-jour* effects (i.e., the classic composition of three subjects: human silhouettes, the contour of a pine tree, and the close-up of a swinging noose). Stylistically, it was one of the first Soviet psychological screen dramas where the heroes, their interrelationships, and conflicts rising from human greed were all thoroughly developed.

Meanwhile, Kuleshov's fledglings grew their wings and left the nest, one after another. Vsevolod Pudovkin became a producer in his own right, as did Boris Barnet, a man of great talent and charisma who was destined to write his page in the history of Soviet cinema. Kuleshov's student, Alexandra Khokhlova, faithfully stayed with her teacher and followed him through thick and thin, although as early as the late 1920's, artistic and productional misfortunes began to assail Kuleshov. For example, his psychologically interesting film *Your Acquaintance (The Woman Journalist),* in the production of which the gifted photographer and designer Alexander Rodchenko took part, was not appreciated by the public and became the target of film critics' slings and arrows.

The Soviet film pioneer did have one major productional success; it was *The Great Consoler,* one of the first talking pictures. More details about it will be given in the next chapter.

Kuleshov proceeded with his teaching activities. For many years he and Khokhlova were in charge of the film studio at the VGIK and taught generations of film producers. A master, professor, and a doctor of art criticism, Kuleshov had become a classic in his lifetime. It was he who opened the first constituent congress of the USSR Union of Cinematographers in 1965. He gave interviews to foreign correspondents and took part in the Venice and Cannes Film Festivals. Kuleshov died in 1970. The cineastes of Paris invited him and Alexandra Khokhlova to a ten-day film festival organized in their honor and accorded them with an enthusiastic welcome. Kuleshov and Khokhlova described their emotional and vivid reminiscences in *50 Years in the Cinema.*[9]

Lev Kuleshov went down in the history of filmmaking as an experimenter and pioneer. He blazed the trail in three crucial areas: (1) the Kuleshov Effect—two consecutive frames combining to give a new meaning, a semantic "third"[10]; (2) the film model school—the theory and methodology of training an actor specifically for the art shown on the screen; (3) the theory that cinema is a graphic art and an art of light.

All these experiments, discoveries, and conclusions came to Lev Kuleshov at the most romantic and yet most trying period in the Soviet Union's history.

"KINO-PRAVDA" (FILM TRUTH) OF DZIGA VERTOV

. . . I am the eye of the cinema. I am a mechanical eye. I am a machine, and show the world as only I see it.

. . . I am continual motion. I come up close to objects, and I move away. I crawl under them, and I leap atop of them. I trot beside the muzzle of a running horse, and I cut full speed into a crowd. I run ahead of attacking soldiers. I fall over onto my back, and I rise up into the air along with the airplanes. Up and down I go, up and down. My road leads to a fresh perception of the world. I uncode an unknown world and do it in a way that is absolutely new.[11]

These resounding and challenging words come from the "Kinoki" manifesto. They are more than mere poetic metaphors. The group of young documentary filmmakers led by Dziga Vertov was unique in the fanatic faith they displayed toward their principles. They were a ubiquitous, incredibly audacious group of people. The famous film *The Man with a Movie Camera* shows objects from absolutely unexpected angles: a train, for example, rushes up over your head from below. These people dubbed themselves "Kinoki," from the Russian abbreviation for cinema (kino) and eye (oko). A bold and reckless lot, a Kinok could parachute down, pressing his camera tight against his chest, to film a plane in flight. He could scale the dome of a church or lie low on railroad ties under the wheels of a train speeding overhead. Dziga Vertov and his team of cameramen were everywhere. Day and night, urban commotion, and the placid tranquility of country life—all nooks and crannies, all spheres of social life caught their eyes.

Dziga Vertov was the pseudonym of Denis Kaufman (1896–1954). The name Vertov, coined from the Russian word "verchenye," or rotation, greatly reflected the spirit of the times. The three sons of a lawyer from the small town of Belostok—Denis, Mikhail, and Boris—were all destined to work in film, although they pursued different cinematic paths. Denis became the creator of the documentary genre, of "Kino-Pravda," or Film Truth, and became famous as Dziga Vertov. Mikhail, his brother's faithful helper, an active Kinok, and cameraman of infinite temerity, lived a long life as a veteran of the Central Studio of Documentary Films in Moscow. And Boris, a proficient cameraman, had the fortune of filming such Jean Vigo masterpieces as *L'Atalante* and *Zero de Conduite (Nought for Conduct)*. Then he worked in Hollywood with Orson Welles and other celebrities.

It is impossible not to take special note of the montage artist Elizaveta

A Knok above Moscow appears in still from The Man with a Movie Camera.

A Man with a Movie Camera *was famous for its collage stills.*

Svilova, Vertov's wife and loyal friend. She, too, was one of the Kinoki group; and, outliving her husband, she preserved his archives and creative legacy. She also made a notable contribution in having the Vertov materials published in the 1960s, thus bringing back from oblivion the name and glory of the "Cinema Eye" creator. The history of Soviet cinema knows several such illustrious women—wives to whom their husbands owe posthumous glory. Among them are Kuleshov's widow, Alexandra Khokhlova; Sergei Eisenstein's widow, Pera Atasheva; and Julia Solntseva, married to Alexander Dovzhenko. They weren't seeking pecuniary compensation; they just wanted respect and justice for their late spouses' memories.

Dziga Vertov began working in film in 1918. He drew inspiration from Lenin's idea that the film industry should be started with documentaries and newsreels. Dziga's first productions—*The Anniversary of the Revolution* (1918), the first issues of the film journals *Cinema Weekly* and *Film Truth,* and the full-length *History of the Civil War* (1922)—were professionally quite sophisticated.

Even at that early stage of his work, Dziga was nurturing bold ideas of a "world without acting," of a cinema free of fantasy, literature, plots, props, and actors—of everything that goes into the notion of fiction: *only* documents, *only* facts, *only* things as they are, *only* chronicles were important. Vertov outlined this program in his manifesto of 1922, which he called *We.*

> We consider the psychological Russo-German cinematic drama, encumbered with visions and childhood reminiscences ridiculous.
>
> To the American adventure films, with the showy dynamism and productions of Pinkerton escapades—thanks from the Kinoki for a rapid succession of pictures and close-ups. . . . It is a notch above the psychological drama, but ill-premised all the same. Stereotype. A copy of a copy.
>
> We declare the old motion pictures—romances, theatricals, etc.—leprous.[12]

Who were these "We"? Vertov had in mind the Kinoki, of course, as opposed to the old guard of cinematographists, whom he dismissed as a "bunch of junk dealers." But not only Kinoki alone would have subscribed to this manifesto.

"We came to the cinema like bedouins, or a bunch of gold-diggers. We came to a blank spot. A spot concealing infinite opportunities," said

Sergei Eisenstein, the most colorful "nomad" and most fortunate "gold prospector."

A "blank spot" . . . These words would have made the late Yevgeni Bauer turn in his grave. Ivan Mozzhukhin, working with La Société des Films Albatros in Paris would have shuddered. A "blank spot" . . . These words would have outraged all of the Mezhrabpom-Rus Film Studio (formerly Rus, and subsequently Mezhrabpom-Film), which successfully continued in the old tradition of the Russian psychological film drama and which was supported by Anatoli Lunacharsky, the People's Commissar for Education. He frowned upon the leftist, or proletarian culture, rages of the Russian intelligentsia. But revolutionary film innovators found the Rus traditionalism simply loathsome. Especially Dziga Vertov, who called himself an "extreme leftist," although he did not belong to the Left Front Association. Not only were old plots unsatisfactory, but the very notion of the plot itself; not only were actors with teary eyes like Mozzhukhin detestable, but the class of actors as a whole.

It would be superfluous to point out the obvious erroneousness of some of Vertov's prophecies and judgments; the development of cinema in the Soviet Union and other countries has done well enough despite sermons and anathemas by him and his Kinoki. But the cinema has never gone back on its actors, literary plots, or fiction in general. Dziga Vertov brought little harm to Charles Chaplin, Giulietta Masina, or Dustin Hoffman when he introduced such fundamental concepts as film truth (cinéma verité) into cinema terminology. Several issues of the aforementioned film journal, such as *Pioneer Film Truth* or *Lenin Film Truth,* came out on the first anniversary of Lenin's death in January 1925. Today these techniques of montage sequences have been incorporated into the curriculum of schools of cinematography all around the world.

And other Vertovian concepts, such as "life on the spur of the moment," "the cinematic eye," "man with a movie camera," and "a world without acting," have entered cinematography's basic vocabulary as well. Vertov had the temperament of a polemicist, but his mind worked like that of a scientist; this was reflected in the universality of his manifestoes. He was an innovator with a capital *I.* His films laid the foundation not only for the genre of Soviet documentaries but for all cinematography as well. Of course he did have a unique source of material which proved quite fruitful: an old Mother Russia boiling with turmoil, rising from slumber, the "Sixth of the World" that became the first socialist state in the history of humankind. But though there were others who made films about new Soviet life—the subject material was very popular—it is the Vertov's films that have gone down in world cinema history.

The Film Eye, Get a Move On, Soviet, A Sixth of the World, Number Eleven, The Man with a Movie Camera, Enthusiasm or Symphony of the Donbass*, *Three Songs About Lenin,* and *Lullaby*—all these documentaries haven't lost any of their verve, even today, despite their old-fashioned naivete, so characteristic of those times. Their fresh vigor and authenticity capture the soul. Dziga Vertov's cinematic eye knew how to take in and fixate. The films not only capture a "presence effect" of catching someone by surprise anywhere at all (whether in a big city, in a Young Pioneers' camp, in a small town, in a coal mining village, on an animal-breeding farm, or in a desert) but also show an originality in production style and technique. They contain enough cinematographic "firsts" to be shared among many more filmmakers and many more films.

In spite of, or perhaps even because of, its lack of long-standing experience, the cinema has always harbored a certain weakness for classical examples and various kinds of myths. Many such examples can be found in Dziga Vertov's films, two of the most popular ones being the following:

Trying to prove that cinema can "reverse the hands of time," Vertov used reverse filming and montage in his *The Eye of the Cinema* to show: (a) the carcass of a bull hanging in a slaughterhouse turning back into a live happy steer once again grazing in a meadow among his herd; (b) a similar return of loaves of bread back to the bakery, the mill, and on to the field as stalks of wheat. One scene among the many tricks, inventive camera angles, and miracles of montage in *The Man with a Movie Camera* always stands out: where the Theater Square is displaced along side of a "split-in-half" Bolshoi Theater, making it look as though the trams are about to collide head-on . . . an optical illusion only a professional can explain.

But these attractions were more than mere street shows: a certain richness of life was felt, a richness of its multifacetedness most of all, as well as a love of this life and the people in it.

Take *The Film Eye,* where Young Pioneers' panamas dot the fields like butterflies or white little birds . . . or people are stunned by the sight of an elephant treading along, being led across a bridge to a zoo. Gazing motionlessly out of their windows onto a Moscow street, people resemble

*A coal region.

Poster for The Film Eye *publicizes the film of Dziga Vertov.*

framed family portraits of the lower middle class more than live persons. And the faces: captured with love are the physiognomies of Young Pioneers, Uzbek women (in *Three Songs About Lenin*), coal miners (in *Enthusiasm or Symphony of the Donbass*), Muscovites ordinary, and people not so ordinary, like a Chinese juggler on a rug demonstrating his magic or patients of the Kanatchikov insane asylum—an institution known in every household as something horrific. A raw and rugged reality nonchalantly managed to seep into the sequences of Vertov's early films.

Vertov was passionately in love with the revolution. Soviets, working men, Young Pioneers, street processions, co-ops, communes, municipal canteens, anti-religious propaganda, flags, banners—all were dear to his heart and inspiring to his soul. He believed in a world revolution and in the imminent collapse of capitalism. He had an abiding faith in the International. Lenin epitomized his ideal of a leader. Sequences showing Lenin alive between 1917 and 1922, up to the appearance of *Lenin Film Truth* in January 1924 depicting scenes where Lenin is buried to the poetic *Three Songs About Lenin,* mark the milestones of the Vertov "Lenin Series." Dziga's documentaries evolved from *The Film Eye* to the talking montage documentaries of the 1930s. Eventually his range of interests came to extend past shots of life on the spur of the moment to employing a cinematic technique that was specific and unified.

Vertov had a whole set of devices to offer international cinema. No matter which new technique of the 1920s and 1930s you take, the presence of this "film eye" poet makes itself felt: How he thought, what he was looking for, how he arrived at what he thought were the best solutions to the most difficult cinematic problems.

Unlike many other major filmmakers of the Great Silent Era who joined in a boycott against talking pictures, Dziga Vertov welcomed the talkies and predicted a great future for them. In his sound films, *Three Songs About Lenin* and *Lullaby,* the producer continued experimenting in montage, achieving a unique poetical grace and beauty; for example, maternal hands gently rock a cradle back and forth to the accompaniment of a soothing lullaby, under clear sunny skies, with rustling trees and fluttering leaves.

As befits the image of a "cinema eye scout," Dziga Vertov, camera in hand, makes his way through to the events of the day that were blasting over the waves of Communist International (first Soviet radio station), making the headlines of *Pravda* and *Izvestia,* and glaring down from giant red posters: three beautiful heroines—air pilots Polina Osipenko, Valentina Grizodubova, and Marina Raskova—carried out a transcontinental flight to Vladivostok from Moscow. Lovely Marina, after an air crash, wanders alone for days in the dense taiga, feeding only on tree bark and berries . . . Dziga is always on the scene. Sergo Ordzhonikidze, a popular leader and a veteran of the Communist Party, suddenly tragically dies, and Vertov is instantly at work on a commemorative film release.

Many of Vertov's adversaries, some of them respected and experienced names in cinema, criticized in his full-length films what they called a predominance of technique over substance. In *A Sixth of the World,* "factual accuracy clearly suffers," they said. "Substance has lost its substantiality . . ., it has become transparent like a symbolist work of art."[13]

The criticism is not unjustified. However, it should not be directed against Dziga Vertov alone but against the entire documentary film genre that professes poeticism and artistry. This reproach certainly holds for Walter Ruttmann and his *Berlin—Symphony of a Big City,* for Alberto Cavalcanti and his *Rien que les heures (Spare Time),* for Lionel Rogosin, Alain Resnais, and all other filmmakers claiming a poetic entity. It must be realized that the portrayal of an historical fact on film and the fact itself are two different things. Sometimes Dziga Vertov experimented too much, although he was saved by ingenuity, a boundless, insatiable curiosity, and a remarkable talent for production. In the *Enthusiasm or Symphony of the Donbass,* Vertov produced the first-ever sound interview. He interviewed a young female worker at the Dnieper hydropower project. The girl's several-minute monologue, syncopated to the montage and narration rhythm and addressed directly to the viewer, had a literally dumbfounding effect. Today, the simultaneous close-up interview is one of the most widely used techniques in film and television.

Dziga Vertov, a generator of imaginative, artistic ideas fifty years ahead of their time, can easily be called the Edison of the documentary film genre.

However, by the late 1930s and especially during the Second World War, his fame greatly declined and he lost his vanguard position in the Soviet documentary film kingdom. From 1941 on he did no more than just edit montage sequences of other cameramen, although from 1944 to 1954 he directed *News of the Day,* a documentary put out by the Central Studio of Documentary Films. Dziga Vertov, or Denis Kaufman, died in 1954 at the age of fifty-eight.

Dziga Vertov will always be remembered for his pioneering discoveries and achievements of the tempestuous twenties and early thirties. Hallowed by the lights of the October Revolution, he will always be considered a classic in world film.

THE GREAT EISENSTEIN

In 1925 Sergei Eisenstein (1898–1948) made his first motion picture. A good deal has been said about him; perhaps even more than about any other cinematographer. He has been the subject of books, essays, and articles in dozens of languages.

Sergei Eisenstein, as he looked in 1925, the year he did The Battleship Potemkin.

The bulk of his written legacy—scripts, sketches, research work, drawings, lecture notes—remains in the Central State Literature and Art Archives of the USSR waiting for publication. Private collections also house a good deal of material.

Organized by film critic and expert Naum Kleiman, the Eisenstein Museum in Moscow is a virtual Mecca for film devotees. Every day the museum is visited by researchers, publishers, and exhibitors of the great filmmaker's work from all parts of the world.

The Battleship Potemkin (1925), the most famous Eisenstein film, holds a record number of prizes and awards and is listed at the top of many film polls and questionnaires. A collection of all that has been said about the film by some of the brightest minds and cultural figures of the twentieth century would make many pages of interesting reading, not to mention the letters, memoirs, and press reviews published in the *New York Herald Tribune* (John Grierson's appreciation of December 1926), *The Christian Science Monitor, Morning Telegraph,* and other world-reputed newspapers.

When plans for this book were being worked out, I unthinkingly promised to substitute my own personal analysis of the *Potemkin* with that of the "greats," from Bernard Shaw to Albert Einstein, to which a very nice editor from the American publishing house wrote a letter requesting that this not be done, since, in his words, "everyone is tired of panegyrics."

What could I do? I had to refrain from including quotations. True, they wouldn't have been panegyrics; I never had that in mind—just thoughts on the film by people lacking neither in intellect nor in perspicacity.[14] Of course, the important thing here is not the elaborate praise, which Einsenstein doesn't need anyway, but, if you will allow, the phenomena of Eisentein himself and of the *Battleship Potemkin.* Both warrant at least some recollection, especially now, sixty years since the release of the film and forty years since the death of the filmmaker.

Eisenstein's most intriguing quality was probably his ingenuity, but he was a man of many talents. He was extremely educated and possessed a unique memory and a sparkling, energetic mind. Legend has it that, when Eisenstein died, the young doctor who was assigned to do the postmortem did not know whom he was examining. He was struck by the dead man's brain and asked,

"Who was the man? What did he do for a living?"

"He was a film producer."

"How many films did he produce?"

"Eight."

"What a pity!" the doctor lamented. "A man with a brain like that could have discovered a new theory of relativity."

Throughout his life, no matter what he took up, no matter what topic for film or article, Eisenstein meticulously and quickly learned all he could about everything he needed to know. He is justifiably considered to be a pioneer in the field of semiotics. Experts say that his discoveries in the psychology of creativity and the mechanics of perception opened up new avenues for research. Pedagogy also relies on his findings made when he directed a film workshop at the Institute of Cinematography and in several experimental studios. Eisenstein's theoretical works, such as *The Montage of Film Attractions, Vertical Montage, Non-Indifferent Nature,* and many many more (in fact, everything he wrote), are a fountain of information. They are original, witty, and full of fresh perceptivity, although at times the accuracy of events is a bit lacking and one doesn't necessarily close the back cover convinced. It is commonly believed that giants like Eisenstein are born at times of great upheavals, when "things are out of joint." Undoubtedly, there is some truth in that, especially considering that Eisenstein himself attributed his own and other cinematographers' achievements to the time he happened to live in, that of the Great Revolution. He summed up the way he and his generation lived with the following words: "Art through Revolution; and Revolution through Art." True, Eisenstein's talent of artistic perceptivity was a gift granted by nature; but it was a destiny, the artist's destiny at a crossroads of history, that gave this talent body and soul.

A recent book on Eisenstein, *Eisenstein at Work* by Jay Leyda and Zina Voynow,[15] features a very handsome centerfold. On the left against a backdrop of abysmal night blackness, a delightful-looking smiling young boy in a starched white collar and a posh checkered bow is reclining on a richly ornamented carpet. Bangs of flaxen hair brush gently over his high forehead. Next to him is a pillow with a book resting upon it. ("A boy from Riga," "Good Little Boy!" as Eisenstein was wont to call himself.) And on the right, set in a small frame, is the "Pale Horse," as the magician of the early cinema, Georges Méliès, dubbed the white skeleton of a horse that was harnessed into the Chariot of Death in a scene from *Les quatre cent farces du Diable (The Merry Frolics of Satan).* This film flabbergasted the eight-year-old Eisenstein in Paris, being the first film he had ever seen.

Charles Chaplin and Sergei Eisenstein (right) clown in Hollywood in 1930.

His family was well-to-do. His father, Mikhail Osipovich, was a civil engineer, the Chief Architect of Riga, and councilor of state. He had built many houses; in fact in New Riga on Krisjana Barona Street most of the buildings were constructed according to his design. These structures are remarkable for their eclectic style, rich decor, and lavish ornamentation, teasing the senses of those who gazed upon them. Sergei's father was a vivid and gifted personality. His mother, Julia Ivanovna, nee Konetskaya, was heiress to one of the wealthiest steamship companies in St. Petersburg and had innumerable relatives among the devout, ultraconservative merchant class. But young Julia, however, showed an independence unlike others from her social background. Fond of traveling, she trekked as far as the pyramids of Egypt, an unusual thing for those times. She also visited Paris frequently, taking her young son with her.

Eisenstein spent his childhood in a "gold cage," which he hated from early on. He was a precocious child with an observant eye, an unusual aptitude for drawing, and a startling command of three foreign languages.

The impressions of 1905—the ruthless suppression of the first revolution in Russia, the savagery of pogroms, the violence—all left their mark on the young Sergei, instilling in him thoughts about violent death and the suffering born of violence that lingered in his imagination. Thus originated one of the most forceful, obsessive motifs that permeated his films: the blind force of inhumanity, the malicious and senseless victimization, and the inevitable ruin of the weak and helpless.

It explains why the nineteen-year-old Eisenstein, a young man with a shining future ahead of him as heir of a model entrepreneurship, didn't hesitate about his attitude to the October Revolution. The elder Eisenstein joined the counterrevolutionary White Guards; his son Sergei joined the Red Army.

While the level of artistic quality in *Battleship Potemkin* is quite advanced, its magic is not there. Nor is it in its harmonic coherence, even though its presence is unmistakable. It is also not in the cinematographic technique, though that too is unimpeachable. World cinema knows quite a few pictures, made both before and after *Potemkin,* that are just as artistically perfect and brilliant. Harmony can be found in many masterpieces of the Great Silent Era. The miracle of the film is in something else.

The Battleship Potemkin, as subsequent decades have shown, was a prophetic reel. Whereas *Intolerance* by David Wark Griffith, Eisenstein's favorite film, evolved the "formula of enmity" in a generally philosophi-

67

cal, global, humanistic sense, *The Battleship Potemkin* concretized it socially and "chronologically" for the twentieth century, a century of mass movements and reprisals. This is the film containing what has prophetically come to epitomize the grief and horror of mass extermination: the scene of the baby carriage with a crying infant rolling down the steps to the sea and to inevitable death; the scene on the Odessa stairway of a bloody massacre when Cossack troops pounced mercilessly upon crowds of civilians.

Eisenstein had traversed a short but rough terrain on his way to the *Battleship Potemkin*. That way must have been foreordained for him. Upon his return from the civil war front, Eisenstein began his directing career by putting on controversial stagings at the Proletkult★ Theater, the most outstanding of which was *"The Wise Man,"* a modernized, mischievous version of the comedy written by the nineteenth century Russian Alexander Ostrovsky. The story of the young careerist, Glumov, was remade into something suitable for a circus or music hall: the play characters walked along a tightrope and balanced themselves on a perch. The original personages were replaced with an entirely different cast of characters. There was Pavel Milyukov, leader of the Constitutional Democrats during the tsarist reign, foreign minister in the provisional government, and then prominent counterrevolutionary and emigre. There was a fascist and a go-getter profiteer of the NEP★ period as well. Kozintsev and Trauberg, the young avant-garde directors of the FEX Group in Leningrad, performed a similar operation on Nikolai Gogol's play *Marriage*.

In *The Wise Man* there was much more done to provide entertainment and a test of ability than to portray actual reality. It was a search for a revolutionary style of theater production, of making an "anti-performance," so to speak, a kind of negative resolution of the theme!

Eisenstein's transition from the Proletkult Theater to the Goskino Film Studio was no minor move, as the young film industry gained an artist of the same calibre as Charles Chaplin. It gained a director who discovered a whole galaxy of thinkers, poets, and scriptwriters who would mold

---

★Proletkult—proletarian culture.

★★NEP is the acronym for the "New Economic Policy" launched in 1921 with the aim of postwar economic recovery and rehabilitation in Soviet Russia. It permitted limited private enterprise. One of the side effects of this policy was the proliferation of small-time entrepreneurs and hucksters, known as "Nepmen."

present-day culture as had hitherto been able only by the best in the writing profession.

Three Eisenstein films about the Russian revolutions, *Strike, The Battleship Potemkin,* and *October,* are symbols for the artist's unison with his time. Rejecting the traditional "fabulist plot," Eisenstein found a new springboard, the clash between the "haves" and the "have-nots."

In *Strike,* the search for perfect cinematographic imagery was evident. Eisenstein experimented with images of corpulent, obese bodies, with swollen features and cigars dangling between the teeth, to portray the evil incarnate, the powers that be, the factory owners. In an attempt to convey the multiplicity of human grimaces and deformities without makeup and patches, Eisenstein directed his search toward finding anomalous, aberrant types. He summoned a host of grotesque images to the screen: frolicking lilliputians, seedy prostitutes, and hoodlums; a monkey sucking on a milk bottle—the effigy of a police detective nicknamed "Monkey"; and the snout of a bulldog—the look-alike of yet another detective, "Bulldog." A real gallery of rogues!

The proletarian toilers, on the other hand, were shown as a swelling torrent crashing through the floodgates and spilling out onto the screen after a poignant close-up over the body of a workman who has killed himself. A hand-written sign, "Tools Down!" is held up and a surge of factory workers rushes to the manager's office. A steam locomotive, swarming with cheerful, jubilant workers, turns and crawls onto the audience. In the twinkling of an eye, the desolate courtyard next to the office building is transformed into a town meeting square thronged by thousands. The streets of the workers' township become swirling rivulets—the human streams flow down toward backyards where a vast pool of water glistens in the sun. A cart carrying flunkeys who are frightened out of their wits jogs along in front of the crowd. This image becomes fundamental in a comic rerun reminiscent of a Shakespearian intermedia: a band of barefoot boys, joyfully waving their hands about, runs alongside a cart with a frightened goat trotting back and forth on his unsturdy little legs. The strike takes place amid white birch trees in sun-drenched glades. It seems as though the whole town, the entire earth has been taken over by the proletarian storm.

Eisenstein unites history and man in a new way; and his works, which are autobiographic, reflect this. An event in history is an event in one's personal life; thus the revolution can be considered a personal milestone.

October, 1927, was one of the first representations of the image of Lenin in an artistic film. Nikandrov, who played Lenin, had an amazing resemblance to him.

Cossacks disperse a workers' picnic in film Strike.

No distance is put between man and history in *The Battleship Potemkin;* history is palpable and ever present. The tragedy of history takes second place to historic justice. Once he joins the revolution, the lonely, helpless, fearful individual, unprotected against malice and doom (like the panic-stricken crowd on the Odessa stairway), is no longer just a tiny chip in a maelstrom. Man is simultaneously the object and subject of history, its maker and its material from which it is made.

Of course, only an abiding faith in the revolution gave the artist such a feeling of assuredness. Eisenstein's concept of history is totally opposite to the concept of his great contemporaries. Take Hemingway for instance, whose heroes are always in conflict with history, perhaps with the exception of *The Fifth Column.* Henry and Catherine Barkley in *A Farewell to Arms* end up on Lake Geneva in a boat fleeing from inexorable pursuit. Robert Jordan and his sweetheart Maria, dishonored by the fascists, in *For Whom the Bell Tolls,* seek shelter under the nocturnal starry skies of Spain.

Marfa Lapkina, a peasant, proved to be an artistically talented woman in her role as organizer of a cooperative in Old and New.

History is not that inexorable juggernaut in Eisenstein's films. Why? Because man is not alone; he is among the millions who constitute the makers of history. Therefore, Eisenstein, poet of the revolution, has the human masses as the main hero. Individuals appear later, when he specifically investigates the impact of the revolution on the individual; what it gave the individual, the member of society; how it changed him. But for now there remain only two actors: history in the making and the artist, its observer and participant.

Like many artists of the twentieth century, Eisenstein transcends the conventional boundaries between the epical and lyrical and between the individual and social emotionality. Thus, in *The Battleship Potemkin* all conflicts are strictly social ones. The *Potemkin* crew is devoid of individuality; their destiny is indissoluble from the tide of events. Events are the be-all and the end-all. For instance, the cruel treatment of a young sailor and the anguish of despair on his tender, beardless face are immaterial per se, as far as the sailor as an individual is concerned. They are significant only in the social context, portraying the unbearable yoke of suppression and the limits of human endurance. The bewailing over Vakulinchuk, one of the dead sailors, is the most eloquent display of impersonalized emotion: grief and sorrow are expressed with a particularly striking force, but they are directed not so much to Vakulinchuk as a person as to the nameless victim, the unknown seaman, who lies on a jetty with a candle clutched in his dead hand, bearing the inscription on his breast, "Killed for a spoonful of borscht."

The heat and passion of public sentiment are elevated and hallowed by modern art, the art of the revolution.

Along with Mayakovsky, Brecht, and Picasso, Eisenstein belonged to those masters who made history the mainspring of action and conflict, the main plot in their works. And even though his montage of short film sequences may be outdated, "man through history" is a principle that will always endure.

Eisenstein began work on a sequel to his revolutionary epic with his film *Old and New* (or *The General Line*) right after he finished *The Battleship Potemkin* in 1926; but he finished it only in 1929, first completing *October* (1927), which was dedicated to the tenth anniversary of the October Revolution.

In *October*, Eisenstein addressed the Russian peasantry. He wanted to find out what the Russian peasant had gained from the revolution. He was fond of comparing two scenes in particular: the *Potemkin* crew's tense, frightful expectation of a tsarist squadron and a group of peasant farmers' expectation of the jets of rich milk from a separator in *Old and New*. He wanted to infuse an element of passion into the work and the days of a farm cooperative.

One of the film's characters, Marfa Lapkina, a real peasant woman from the village of Krasnaya Pakhra near Moscow, rose to become a "giant and symbolic figure," as le Corbusier put it, personifying an entire stage in the development of the Soviet collective farm industry.

Vsevolod Pudovkin, film luminary, reached his high point in the late 20s.

PUDOVKIN AND HIS HEROES

Vsevolod Pudovkin (1893–1953) is yet another luminary in the world cinematographic galaxy. He reached his highest point of artistic maturity in the late 1920s with the classical revolutionary trilogy *Mother, The End of St. Petersburg,* and *The Heir to Genghiz Khan (Storm over Asia).* At that time he also wrote his first major work on the nascent aesthetics of the cinema.

Pudovkin is frequently compared to Eisenstein, a tradition that started as far back as the 1920s and that was continued by many later film critics both here and abroad. It is a natural comparison, considering that both directors personify unique quests and accomplishments in revolutionary art and express the spirit of times in a profound and original manner all their own.

One of the creators of "poetic" montage, Pudovkin freely combined his innovative techniques with literary and stage tradition, namely, that of the Gorky prose writings and of the psychological school of acting. Pudovkin was the first to succeed in this bold artistic synthesis, which was quite unusual for those times. He united seemingly incongruous principles. Herein lies his contribution to the movies.

Vsevolod Pudovkin's rough and tumble life was typical of that of many restless, intriguing personalities of his generation. The October Revolution was a benchmark in history that forced him to grow up fast. He felt a need to transmute his experiences into artistic imagery, and he chose what the creative youth of the time saw as a promised land for ardent pioneers—filmmaking.

Pudovkin was born in 1893 in the central Russian town of Penza but grew up in Moscow. At school he developed a strong interest in natural sciences. Then he entered the Department of Physics and Mathematics at Moscow University. Drafted shortly before graduation during the First World War, he was sent to the front, where was wounded and taken prisoner. Back in Moscow, Pudovkin was admitted into the State Film School and became an active member of the Kuleshov team.

But something in Pudovkin did not mix with the Kuleshov school methodology. The cinema was infinitely more to him than pure artistic experiment; it had intimate links with real life.

Joining the Mezhrabpom-Russ studio, Pudovkin made his debut with a short two-part comedy, *Chess Fever,* which combined documentary sequences of an international chess tournament in Moscow with amusing tricks, similar to those in Kuleshov's film *The Extraordinary Adventures of*

Nilovna, a common Russian woman, represented the downtrodden and humiliated in Mother.

Mr. West in the Land of the Bolsheviks. A documentary made in 1926, *Mechanics of the Brain,* was a significant milestone in technique: Pudovkin perfected his mastery of montage, rhythm, and composition in the complex field of Pavlovian reflexology (conditioned reflexes).

From this modest educational science film, Pudovkin made a giant leap forward with his masterpiece, *Mother.*

"This theme was borrowed from Maxim Gorky" was written in the credits. Nathan Zarkhi, premier Soviet screenwriter, introduced changes into the original text that eventually became accepted principles of film art.

In his novel *Mother,* Gorky examined the large-scale maturation process of the revolution through the life of Pelageya Nilovna Vlasova, a common Russian woman. But Pudovkin proceeded from the whole to its parts, expressing the general through the particular. Thus the attention given to the everyday, the ordinary, in people. Hence the emphasis on the oppressed and ignorant state of the "mother," traits that made her an unwitting tool in the arrest of her revolutionary son Pavel. Nilovna typified many people who were downtrodden and humiliated, and she showed the nature and the historic inevitability of the revolution—a concept underlying many Soviet films of the 1920s that treated the motif of the revolution as a mass movement.

The film broke ground hitherto untouched by the cinema born of the revolution. It was not unwarrantedly viewed as an antipode of *The Battleship Potemkin*. Indeed, the story of one human being was the focus of the film, the very same "plot intrigue" of the individual which Eisenstein, Vertov, and other young filmmakers so ardently spoke out against.

The main roles were played not by "type" or "model" actors but by professionals from the Moscow Art Theater, Stanislavsky's pupils Vera Baranovskaya and Nikolai Batalov.

The "poetic" montage principle prevailed in the film. Viktor Shklovsky has aptly defined the *Mother* as a "centaur" incorporating both "poetry" and "prose." However, the cinematographic and literary traditions were more genuinely synthesized in it than if they were the components of an eclectic blend.

Pudovkin's hand and that of his cameraman Anatoli Golovnya are felt right from the beginning scenes: clouds scudding across spring skies, a giant stationary policeman—shot from below to accentuate his awkward massiveness. Thus, the montage juxtaposition evokes the two contrasting images: that of springtide delivery and renewal, and that of obtuse, all-crushing power.

The poetic, consonant image of spring grows as the film progresses: the merry gurgling of the streams, children rejoicing in the sun, the trees in bloom, and, finally, the mighty freshet with drifting ice, symbolizing the demise of winter and the awakening of Nature—which the director, striving towards optimal effect, spliced with mass demonstration scenes. The next image is that of the leitmotif, the forces of oppression: the close-up of the policeman's ruthless boot, his ramrod-stiff figure; inmates circling in a prison yard, reminiscent of Van Gogh's famous canvas; a courtroom with its disgusting types; and a Cossack squadron dispersing a demonstration.

There is a third force at work, too: A human figure, the Mother, stands out against the backdrop of the workmen's township. The camera focuses on her. Then a new visual leitmotif appears—close-up portraits of Nilovna. The Mother's sad and tender eyes illuminate the film.

The finale is built on the montage sequences showing a fatal clash between revolutionaries and a punitive detachment—just as in the Odessa stairway scene in *The Battleship Potemkin*. But here the Nilovna close-ups under the banner are the pivotal point of the composition. The climactic moment is reached when the heroine realizes that she is inseparable from her social class and its great struggle. Thus, the image of the individual is conceived in the epic narration.

"Clear eyes that look straight into your heart, gleaming white teeth, and though plain but infinitely charming face of young workman with prominent cheek-bones and wide smile. . . . He is good in the same way the youth of the Revolution is good." That's how Soviet film director Mikhail Romm described the hero, Pavel, played by Nikolai Batalov. And he continued:

> Everything in this motion picture is wonderful—temperament, innovative montage techniques, bold angles, daring metaphors, the splendid, clever script and the genuine mastery of young Golovnya. Yet, the finest of all is the Pudovkin eye. Where did he find all those people? How was he able to convey several chapters of Gorky's novel without a single word—with one look, a single turn of the head? Where does he get this power to convey the truth?[16]

The fat colonel (an actual tsarist army officer) who arrives with a search warrant; the prison ward inmate with deadpan indifference on his face; the rowdies from armed antirevolutionary bands; the visitors of the inn; old Vlasov, a sullen, morose man broken by years of back-straining work; and Nilovna beside her husband's coffin—all these types Pudovkin resurrected from real life in Russia, the way it was portrayed in the Gorky novel.

The next Pudovkin and Zarkhi film, *The End of St. Petersburg* (1927), combined the "long shots" of the revolutionary era with the close-ups of one individual.

The image of Lad, an anonymous character, seems to be a choice made at random, as though the camera stopped at the first person who came into its field of vision. It could look into any of the peasant huts in a village or shabby tenement houses in St. Petersburg. Thus, the seemingly random selection of an individual concealed what was actually an intentional display of typicalness.

The film opens with rural scenery: a quiet river, a windmill, straw-thatched huts, and fields under low gray skies. "Folks from Pensa . . .

Novgorod . . . Tver," read the captions. In a poverty-stricken peasant family, a woman is suffering labor pains. Another mouth to feed is born into a hungry family. Then the older son, Lad, is shown striding down a dusty dirt road to town—just another proletarian on his way to the capital to earn his living. Lad's is a typical story, and the film seeks to recount the plight of typical country folks from the old Russian provinces of Penza, Novgorod, and Tver. Here there is no Ivan or Peter from a certain village in particular. Lad is just as ubiquitous as are the landscapes.

Ivan Chuvelev, a stage actor, was used here as a prototype to typify "one of the millions." Lad's tousled blond hair cut Cossack style, coarse features, eyes sullenly looking out from under his brows, ragged clothes, and awkward, work-weathered hands form a picture that speaks for itself. The close-ups bring to mind the vivid canvases of the Peredvizhnik school of realistic painters, the heroes of populist literature, and other various associations forming a collective image of the Russian peasant.

The End of St. Petersburg, an epic embodied in the life story of an anonymous hero, was as gently lyrical and as touchingly human as *Mother.* This was revealed in the portrayal of a workman's family living in a miserable hovel; a sleeping child whose placid dream is metaphorically contrasted with the sailboat gliding on the smooth Neva (the light-hearted scene with a sailboat was inserted into a scene that showed ordinary everyday life); and finally, the visage of a country granny who has brought Lad to town.

The battlefront and revolutionary scenes in the latter part of the film are no more than fragmentary illustrations overburdened with detail. Lad's appearance is scattered; it is only at the very end that the Pudovkin device of combining long-range and close-up shots stages a comeback.

"Pudovkin achieves an inspiring, potent blend of narration and poetry. The Pudovkin metaphors are intimately linked with life, both in style and in meaning,"[17] wrote Alexander Karaganov in his book on the director.

The third part of the Pudovkin trilogy, *The Heir to Genghis Khan* (1929), was known in other countries as *Storm over Asia.* Here the Pudovkin metaphor truly reveals itself in both style and meaning, culminating in a dramatic finale.

Unlike Lad, the hero of this film is not from a peasant family but is a poor Mongolian shepherd who is heir to the legendary conqueror. The plot is based on real life: counterrevolutionary invaders capture a Mongolian freedom-fighter and discover in his possession a document

Ivan Chuvelev typified "one of the millions" in his role in The End of St. Petersburg.

Valery Inkizhinov plays the prisoner Bayr, who has just been declared heir to the throne, in palace scene from The Heir to Genghis Khan.

testifying that he is a descendant of the great Genghis Khan. Out to use him as a cat's paw, they proclaim him a "prince." But he escapes and returns to the revolutionary detachment. For all the exotic flavor and complexity of the plot (written by Osip Brik), the central idea of the film remains that of the average person joining the cause of the revolution.

The filmmakers trekked all the way to Mongolia where they filmed some unique scenes, including a ceremony with masks and ritual dances performed during the holiday Tsama. The festivities were filmed in an area at Lake Gusin using a method later known as the "reconstruction of events": the local lamas performed a genuine ceremony for the Soviet filmmakers and permitted it to be included in the final scenes. The final product was a film of extraordinary documentary authenticity and cinematographic expression. It was a true discovery of the East only minus the pavilion exotica and oriental decor which tended to abound in every scene set in Asia in both Western and Soviet films. Even today none of the scenes in *The Heir to Genghis Khan* has lost any of its profundity, sincerity, or human poignancy.

Pudovkin's last silent film, *Life Is Beautiful,* was a failure. It was released in 1932 as *A Simple Case.* The transition from films of widely encompassing themes proved to be a new ground of unavoidably rugged terrain.

FACTORY OF THE ECCENTRIC ACTOR (FEX)

In Petrograd in 1922, two young provincials who had just arrived there would make a name for themselves with a different style of cinema.

One was seventeen-year-old Grigori Kozintsev, born in Kiev in 1905 into a family of intellectuals (his father was a prominent doctor, and his sister Lyuba, a painter, was later to marry the eminent Soviet prose-writer Ilya Ehrenburg). In Kiev, Kozintsev attended classes at the studio of Alexandra Exter, an artist of the avant-garde. He had contracted typhus on the train to Petrograd and arrived running a very high temperature. The other was Leonid Trauberg, a young journalist from Odessa born in 1901. They became friends.

Shortly after their arrival on the frozen streets of the former imperial capital of Russia, there began to appear bizarre announcements of "Marriage: The Electrification of Gogol." At about the same time a thin pamphlet entitled "Eccentricity" came off the press. And, lastly, a rather respectable announcement inviting the youth of the town to join the FEX (FEKS) Studio, or the Factory of the Eccentric Actor, to study any of a wide variety of things, from acrobatics and pantomime to the history of the Italian commedia dell'arte. The culprits behind these eccentric offerings were Kozintsev and Trauberg.

The literary department of the Sevzapkino Studio, currently known as Lenfilm, was directed at this time by Adrian Piotrovsky, a connoisseur and translator of Greek and Roman classics and a man of versatile interests. Cinema had gradually become one of his favorite interests, and the first thing the cinematographer had to do to start work was to gather some new blood. Piotrovsky invited Kozintsev, Trauberg, and the rest of the FEXes, including such talents as Sergei Gerasimov, Yelena Kuzmina, Oleg

In expressionistic effects typical of Kozintsev and Trauberg, an amusement park attraction, the devil's wheel, changes in the eyes of the heroes suddenly into a gigantic clock face.

Zhakov, Alexei Kapler, and Yanina Zheimo, who won renown as professional cinema actors and directors. The first film of the FEX team, the three-act comedy *Adventures of Oktyabrina* (1924), was a cross between politics and buffoonery. The main character—a clever decisive young girl, a Komsomol member, in the capacity of house manager—had to deal with a NEP tax-evading entrepreneur and his companion, a representative of world imperialism nicknamed Coolidge Curzonovich Poincaré. Coolidge was trying to recover tsarist debts that were annulled by the Soviet government. But Oktyabrina would always foil the insidious schemes of world capital. Various cinematographic effects were employed: adventures, fights, sudden plot twists, even an unsuccessful suicide attempt by one of the heroes to hang himself on a suspender (which broke in the process), followed by a caption urging viewers to buy suspenders only in government-run establishments, not from private sources!

This film brought back the flamboyant, impassioned revolutionary posters: the camera eye absorbed the vast city, an entire world which could be surveyed and filmed from all different vantage points—from the dome of St. Isaac's Cathedral and the steeple of the Peter and Paul Fortress or from a motorcycle racing at full speed. Ostensibly the Kinoki group was not alone in the field.

In its other film, *The Devil's Wheel* (1926, based on the Venyamin Kaverin story *The End of a Thieves' Den*), the FEX crew attempted to create the contemporary melodrama: it saw ardent passion in modern Soviet everyday life; it distinguished between its good and evil and between its light and shade. An amusement park is full of temptations: the eerie rotation of the ferris wheel, circus girls dressed in skirts that glitter, and the turbanned "Mr. Question Mark," an illusionist of mysterious magic, who lured a young sailor from the Cruiser "Aurora," the same one that became the symbol of the October Revolution. This is the scene of the confrontation between two opposites: the whistle-clean ranks of sailors from the "Aurora" standing at attention and the criminal element in a big city carrying out various contracts, even if it meant operating in gambling parlors or committing murder.

Like Eisenstein in *Strike*, Kozintsev and Trauberg searched out unseemly types in various hangouts of ill repute and came up with obese wenches, ugly dwarfs, déclassé elements, and other sundry types. Like Vertov, they sought to portray the "bottom of the city barrel" in its true colors and thus used real sets and props. To film the skeleton of a haunted house, for example, they used a genuine run-down old house and genuine characters. The burglar's jump from the sixth floor and the house collapsing were exceptionally convincing. The FEX crew filmed the physiognomies of the shadiest urban characters, the grimiest of the human flotsam washed in by the turbid waves of the NEP era: a pock-marked butcher in a velveteen waistcoat with a bracelet charm, the leader of the crooks' den ("Khaza"), who looked like an elephant, and Mr. Question Mark (played by Sergei Gerasimov, a young pupil of the FEX studio) who, off stage, turned out to be just a regular, ordinary creep. Cloaked in melodramatic robes were characters from real life. While at work on *Devil's Wheel*, Kozintsev and Trauberg met cameraman Andrei Moskvin, who together with designer E. Enei and a young Leningrad composer, Dmitri

Shostakovich, would soon enable Kozintsev and Trauberg to form a high-class team. The camera wizard Moskvin "betrayed" this group only once—when he was invited to shoot the interiors in Eisenstein's *Ivan the Terrible,* including the classic feast scene that was filmed in color. When Moskvin died, his pupil, I. Gritsyus, stepped into his mentor's shoes to shoot Kozinstev's *Hamlet* and *King Lear.*

Only two months separate *Devil's Wheel* and the next of the FEX reels, *The Overcoat* (May 1926).

The script, based on Nikolai Gogol's story, was written by Yuri Tynyanov, a young author invited as film consultant. The idea was not so much to give an account of the life of a petty government clerk robbed of his new and very expensive overcoat as to show the world under Tsar Nicholas I's reign through "FEX-colored glasses." The result was a cinematographic Gogolian-based fantasy.

The insignificant clerk, Akaki Akakiyevich Bashmachkin, is portrayed both as victim and product of his time and environment. He is surrounded by blackness and a strange gloominess, by cold, by the alienating huge masses of the imperial capital, St. Petersburg. Behind an iron railing a soldier is made to run through a gauntlet for some minor offence. A Black Maria takes political prisoners to jail. A captured deserter is led along the street. The heavy dome of St. Isaac's Cathedral hovers above. A giant sphinx on the embankment obstructs the way of a wretched-looking little man. A monotony of tables, candlesticks, and quills drearily decorates the office where the clerk has dozed off into a pile of quills in the middle of taking care of his paperwork.

The boundary between the real and the imaginary in the film is very thin. On the eve of his death, Akaki Akakiyevich is visited by host of visions and recollections of his wretched miserable life. This constituted one of the earliest cinematographic attempts at psychological analysis—to look into a person's internal world and convey his unspoken thoughts and dreams. In the filmmakers' opinion, that was objective reality. *The Overcoat* was the first film to depict the cold, oppressive alienation of imperial St. Petersburg—the authentically classic Russian image given to us by Alexander Pushkin in *The Bronze Horseman* and continued by Nikolai Gogol and Fedor Dostoyevsky.

The Overcoat made just as significant a contribution to the language of cinematography. Directors and cameramen learned the art of conveying time and mood with the aid of visual effects: interiors, cityscapes, people in glittering evening dress riding in coaches or strolling down Nevsky Prospekt; someone walking alone under the arcade of some official edifice; a female silhouette standing against the backdrop of a hotel window. Dream scenes were shot using a patterned silk fan and out-of-focus frames; an atmosphere of obscurity and constant motion was created that was both irreproachably tasteful and true to life. Camerawork is definitely one of the best achivements in the silent cinema.

After *Bratishka* (*Little Brother,* 1927; the reel has not survived), the FEXes turned to nineteenth-century Russia and the Decembrists, participants in the uprising of December 1825. The cinematographers had no doubts that the film would be both an artistic and box-office hit.

SVD (*The Club of the Big Deed,* 1927, screenplay by Yuri Tynyanov and Julian Oxman) was named for the monogram engraved on a ring which the cardshark military cadet Medox won in a game of cards and gave out as proof of his association with the Decembrists' secret society. Medox was hunting and blackmailing Soukhanov, a rebel and former friend; but a general's wife, a society belle, was in love with Soukhanov and tended to his bleeding wounds. Stylistically the film was a romantic melodrama in both its dramatic approach and its acting technique. The general's wife, gliding about in soft satins, luxuriant turbans, and sables, over velvety carpets, might have been a figure in a Tropinin or early Bryullov painting. The battle scenes on a snow-driven field with smoke rising from the redoubts and lines of soldiers disappearing into the distance were inspired by paintings of battles done during Pushkin's time. *SVD* romanticized the material world according to the general stylistic principles of melodrama. Hence the picturesque compositions of a sentry standing next to a black-and white-striped post in the desolate dreariness of wintry Russian night, the flickering light of a lantern at the entrance to a gambling den, the dark poplars against the snow, and the lonely trudging figure of a wounded soldier—all combined in the leitmotif of a blizzard. Hence the striving for unusual, impressive locales: a skating rink and an ice palace in the dead of night or a magnificent cathedral. Some scenes unravel in a van of roving comedians, others under the cupola of a circus tent, and yet others in a governor's theater box. Victor Shklovsky has described *SVD* as "the most elegant reel the Soviet Union has."

The following picture, *New Babylon,* dealt with the Paris Commune of 1871 and was envisioned as a revolutionary epic. The directors themselves co-authored the screen play, which took them to Leningrad and Paris for

Scene in a gambling house from the film SVD romanticizes the material world. Sergei Gerasimov played the cardshark Medox.

filming. The Paris locales turned out to be particularly fresh and picturesque—blocs ouvriers, Ménilmontant, the Latin Quarter, the Père Lachaise cemetery; views of Paris in the haze; the chimeras of Notre Dame; the old, dented stones of the Paris pavements; the faces of veteran Communards, milliners, laitières, merchants from the market stalls; not to mention the tantalizing displays of silk, lacework, and brocade in the store windows.

Near one of the shop windows of the oriental department of one of the luxury stores stood a swarthy complexioned shop assistant; he was a wily fellow who wore a monocle and held an exotic dragon. Standing under ferociously grinning masks and Chinese lanterns, he eagerly made contact with potential buyers as they passed by. Vsevolod Pudovkin appeared in this cameo role.

Dmitri Shostakovich wrote the symphonic score for the film, making wide use of Paris tunes popular during the Commune times and offering an original arrangement of "La Marseillaise," which became the musical theme of Versailles and the suppression of the Commune. Shostakovich imparted humorous overtones to the music of "La Belle Hélene" by Jacques Offenbach, which thus came to symbolize the decay of the French bourgeoisie. He also provided musical arrangements for the cafe, bal-mobile, and operetta scenes. Unexpectedly, the Kozintsev and Trauberg style in *New Babylon* exhibited a tinge of reflection.

In 1928 protracted debates on formalism in art flared up. Actually the controversy was about the various approaches in Soviet cinema. *New Babylon* poured fresh oil on the burning flames. Some critics spoke out in strident and threatening tones; others gave the "thumbs up." Extremity of judgment was typical of the 1920s, and movies made no exception.

Like all Soviet cinematographers, the FEXes were tackling new problems of that critical period. Intellectual though they were, the extravagance they displayed was endemic to the spirit of the 1920s.

Although they were enamored of the revolution and its innovative, but crude, popular art and although they were practically building from the boundless vigor of youth and the prospects of artistic freedom, the FEXes were, nonetheless, unwitting participants in the restructuring of an anarchic, post-October cinema.

From the classics and historical revolutionary costumed productions, Grigori Kozintsev and Leonid Trauberg switched to a new genre in filmmaking. They would spend the entire 1930s making films on the Bolshevik Party activist, Maxim.

ALEXANDER DOVZHENKO, POET OF THE UKRAINE

During the years following the October 1917 revolution, Ukrainian cinematography underwent a turbulent period of development much like the one in Moscow and Leningrad, as the same people were working in both places. Vladimir Gardin, Peter Chardynin, and others worked at Kiev and Odessa. A constellation of Ukrainian stage actors, including Ambrosi Buchma, graced the screen. The Ukrainian cinema was living in anticipation of a national poet, and this poet came in the person of Dovzhenko.

Alexander Dovzhenko, a classic in Soviet cinema, was a "romanticist of socialist realism" and the author of about a dozen motion pictures. (One of the Soviet Union's largest film studios, located in Kiev, is named for him.) He traversed a long road to the movies. At thirty-two he knocked at the door of the Odessa studio although he had never tried his hand in the cinema before and had been but a rare visitor to the movies.

Dovzhenko was born in 1894 into the family of an impoverished Cossack farmer who had many children to feed. By the summer 1926, when Alexander Dovzhenko found himself at the Odessa film studio entrance on a fancy boulevard lined with chestnut trees and lovely mansions, he had already seen much of life. He was a student at a teacher's institute and then went on to become a teacher. Entering the Economics Department of the Commercial College, he headed the student organization and led many meetings and demonstrations during the grim year of 1918. He attended classes at the Academy of Art, where he was in charge of the Fine Arts Department and a commissar of the Shevchenko Theater. He served with the diplomatic corps in Warsaw and Berlin; he drew cartoons and worked for a local newspaper.

Shortly after he joined the film studio, Dovzhenko's name appeared in comic-strip captions of the eccentric *Vasya the Reformer* and in another short-length comedy, *Love's Berry,* which was based on his own script. He hit the jackpot when he released his revolutionary adventure film *The Diplomatic Pouch,* which became a perennial of the silent screen.

Yet it was not those early attempts, although they did have their moments of talent, that brought fame to the Ukrainian master. The Alexander Dovzhenko, who was destined to go down in the history of cinema, was born in the film *Zvenigora* (1928).

Zvenigora is the name of the memorable Ukrainian steppes between Kiev and the Zaporozhye Sech (Cossack Host) on which the historic battles against the Tatar invaders and the Polish feudal lords took place. According to old Ukrainian legends, the fortune of the Ukraine, wrapped up in a mysterious treasure, lay in various scythian burial mounds scattered about Zvenigora. Dovzhenko approached this legend from a different angle: the dawn of happiness for the Ukrainian people came with the October Revolution.

Delineated in this film was the image of a hero who would keynote all of Dovzhenko's subsequent productions.

The hero Timosh was played by Semyon Svashenko, who fit Dovzhenko's ideal of a man of that time. He was clad not in a velvety fur coat and wide Cossack trousers but in a ragged soldier's greatcoat. He was a handsome young fellow from the thick of the masses, with resolute features and clever eyes, a man whom neither poverty nor misfortune could crush.

The image of Timosh appeared among fancy meadows and leafy groves, placid lakes, and rivers. A captivating view unfolded from the very first scenes of the film shot by Boris Zavelev, the same Boris Zavelev who was the cameraman to Yevgeni Bauer, the best Russian prerevolutionary producer. Feathergrass bowed to the wind and patches of sunlight played upon the water. Maidens relaxed on river banks, making wreaths and setting them afloat downstream. Antique boats glided onto dry land. Out from a double vision on the screen returns a tale of the distant past— the story of the enchanted treasure of Zvenigora. Knights in battle brandished their swords, steeds flying; and a Catholic monk in a black cassock, looking as horrid as Death, crawls out from under the ground.

The script (written by two Ukrainian authors, M. Johanson and Y. Tyutyunnik) was heavy and confused, a crude mixture of fact and fancy. However, Dovzhenko was able to achieve a unique harmony that compensated for some of its incongruities.

Three folk personages epitomized the conflicting forces at work in the Ukraine. The thousand-year-old Grandfather (the People) had two grandsons: Paul, a mean skinflint and dastard, and Timosh, a nice, brave youth. The same allegorical triangle symbolized the revolutionary struggle: Soviet government (Timosh) and bourgeois nationalism (Paul), fighting for the Ukrainian people.

The dismal end of the wretched Paul is in stark contrast to the hour of glory of Timosh. This Red Army revolutionary boards a magic train speeding into the future with his grandfather. For all the patchwork of motley episodes, Dovzhenko's expressive hand is clearly distinguishable.

A Red Army unit leaves a burning village. Cavalrymen—one of Dovzhenko's pet motifs—gallop ahead at full speed. Like the poet Shevchenko's Cossacks, Timosh, prancing away on a fiercy stallion, feels no sorrow as he says good-by to his native village. Standing in the road beyond the outskirts of the village, his weeping wife tugs at the reins of the quivering horse, trying to hold him back. "I can't stand it, Timoshko!" she cries. At first Timosh tries to push her away but then gives her a parting kiss and gallops off. In a sudden fit of grief, the sobbing women flings herself onto the dusty road—the camera is focused on her clenched fist. It is from such a blend of folklore romance and cinematographic expression that the Dovzhenko style sprang. "He is ours, the flesh and blood of the traditions of our Soviet works. A master begging no alms from the Westernists. . . . Pudovkin and I owe him a good hearty handshake," recalled Eisenstein about the Moscow preview of *Zvenigora*.[18]

In his next film, *Arsenal* (1929), Dovzhenko infused epic blood into real historical happenings and not into the allegory of the search for a buried treasure and a vague, thousand-year feud when "nation rose against nation, and kingdom against kingdom." Here he depicted the factual World War I and the grief of the people: soldiers returning from the battlefields, the rule of the Ukrainian nationalist Central Rada (Council), and a revolutionary uprising at the Kiev Arsenal armory. Here Timosh appears as a front-line soldier and workman, representing the Bolsheviks in the Rada, and making the social message in this film more visible than it was in *Zvenigora*.

And Dovzhenko's style lost none of its originality in the process. Cinema historians may well remember the scenes of abject poverty in *Arsenal:* a wizened peasant woman, whose sons were sent off to the war, scattering seeds in the field; a one-legged cripple with a St. George Cross on his breast in an empty peasant house; a one-armed cripple beating an innocent horse in a fit of blind fury. A recurring scene has a German soldier laughing himself into convulsions on "laughing" gas (audiences recognized Ambrosi Buchma in this unforgettable portrayal).

The somewhat heightened emotionality of *Arsenal* is not particular only to Dovzhenko; it stems more from the Ukrainian national character and artistic tradition. Russian art, though of the same Slavonic family, is more restrained and sparing in its emotionality and is even more austere. Contrariwise, the Ukrainian poetic manner appears perhaps overly temperamental, gravitating to hyperbole and the picturesque. The Russian and Ukrainian filmmakers have naturally inherited respective national traditions. This is clearly apparent if one compares the contemporary revolutionary epics *October* by Eisenstein and *The End of St. Petersburg* by Pudovkin with Dovzhenko's *Arsenal*.

Although the films of Eisenstein and Pudovkin sparkle with metaphoric imagery, the threshold from reality is not crossed even once. But that is not so in the Dovzhenko films, where the real and even the documentary rub elbows with bold flights of imagination. Suffice to recall the classic finale in *Arsenal* when Timosh becomes invulnerable to enemy bullets: there he stands, the Ukrainian proletarian, shirt torn, baring his broad shoulders and breast. He stands, safe and sound, because, as Dovzhenko asserts, the revolutionary working class of the Ukraine is immortal.

Dovzhenko insisted that he didn't have any particular metaphors or

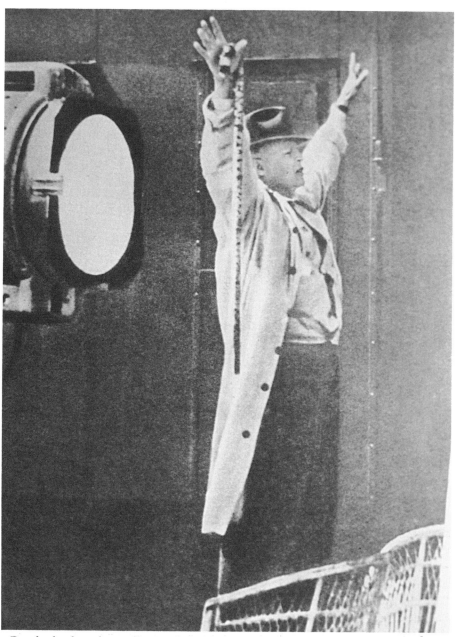
Dovzhenko, here during filming of Earth *in 1930, often crossed the threshold of reality.*

Semyon Svashenko plays the hero of Earth *as the tractor driver Vasily.*

symbols in mind; he just wanted to say one very simple thing: Revolution cannot be killed! Many, many years later, when things were quite different (in 1954), Dovzhenko mounted the rostrum at the Second All-Union Congress of Writers, where heated debates flared up about the crucial problems of the day, and talked at great length on outer space and the art that would soon have to depict life in a new, cosmic perspective. One by one the delegates exited the packed auditorium for a smoke, bewildered. But seven years later Yuri Gagarian was launched into space!

Dovzhenko remained faithful to his ideals until he died in 1956. His last screenplays, the *Poem of the Sea* (1958) and *The Flaming Years* (1960), were made into films posthumously, thanks to the efforts of his widow and assistant director, Julia Solntseva.

Dovzhenko drew a poeticized picture of the world of socialism, especially in his masterpiece, *Earth* (1930). In everyday language, this film is about the class struggle in the countryside during collectivization. The plot recounts the tragedy of Vasil, a collective farm tractor operator who is murdered by rich kulaks.

Yet Dovzhenko imparted a philosophical and symbolic significance that reflected not only the spirit of the times but his own individual spirit as well.

Life and death, the real and the illusory, the past and the future—all this was fused into one: Dovzhenko considered the distinction between "mine" and "yours" to be nonexistent. Hence, there was conflict neither between the private and the collective, nor between the ordinary and the festive. All living things on earth—people, plants, and animals—are of the same sinew. The terms "materialistic surrealism" and "dialectical surrealism" are found recurrently in foreign publications, but Dovzhenko is also called the Ukrainian heir to Homer and Hesiod and the Pindar of the October Revolution.

What Is He Like, The New Man?

The historic and revolutionary dramas and epics of Eisenstein, Pudovkin, and Dovzhenko shaped the edifice of the Soviet film art. Naturally, there have been subsequent changes and modifications based on historic developments, but the fundamentally innovative structure will always remain. In this lies the contribution of Soviet film to world cinema.

Social conflict and the victorious class struggle of the exploited over the exploiters were the prime forces of motivation.

In the twenties, the revolution had been won, the civil war was over, and the last rebellions of the White Guards, anarchists, and kulaks had been squelched. The country was throbbing with vitality in restructuring society's life. As far as the past was concerned, filmmakers more or less knew what was what. They could identify the enemy: the monarchists, capitalists, landlords, international capitalism, blood-sucking kulaks, and philistines. But that time was over; those enemies had been toppled and pilloried. What about now?

In those years socialism had yet to be built "from bricks left over by the old world," to use the then current phrase. Impatient artists, always prone

Earth *was about the class struggle in the countryside during collectivization.*

to daydreams and poetic fantasy, wanted to see the man of the future today.

What was he like? That was a simple question to answer if he was a Bolshevik who had worked underground before the revolution, or a progressive proletarian, or a naval leader (the Eisenstein-Pudovkin ideal again!). But what about the man of the future from the Young Communist League? What about family? Maybe the family was just a "vestige of capitalism." And love? What about love? Was that another remnant? What if a Young Communist fell in love with a married woman? What was the Komsomol cell to do about it? And the children and swaddling clothes. Wouldn't they drag the fighter of the future into the quagmire of the family treadmill?

As naive as those questions seem to us today, back then they didn't seem so, and with good reason. In a new world everything should be new,

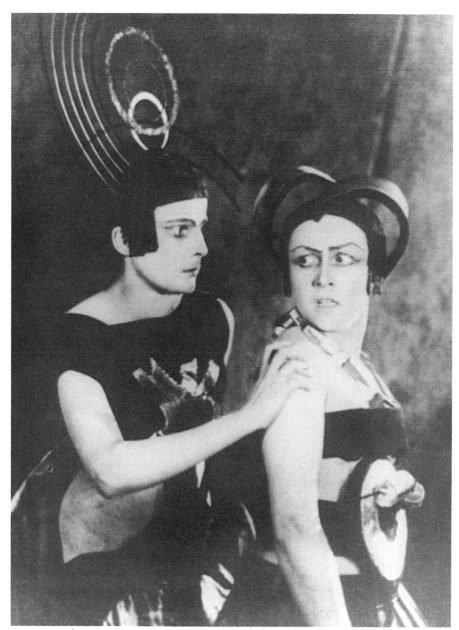

Julia Solntseva (left) plays the beautiful Martian in Aelita by Protazanov, with costumes designed by Alexandra Ekster.

including human relationships. Alexander Dovzhenko expressed this very idea in his poetic film *Earth*. The main character, Vasil, a tractor operator and a Young Communist, was engaged to the most beautiful girl in the whole collective farm village. Boys and girls would pair off and cling to each other in amorous languor. The rich, heavy branches of apple trees reached down to the ground (the apples and the giant sunflowers in *Earth* were the symbolic equivalents of Eisenstein's "milky rivers" in the *Old and New*).

All that naturally belongs to the realm of the poetic and fanciful. But what about reality, everyday life, and historical truth?

The film reserves of the Soviet silent movies offer a remarkable amount of information to the historian, sociologist, art critic, or the inquisitive person. That information draws a unique portrait of that time. Although decimated by the ravages of time and careless custody, the films still offer enormous material on a view of life in a country still out at the elbows, still shod in those bast-fiber sandals and worn-down boots of yesteryear; a country bursting at the seams to start work, to build, to storm the skies; a country full of mirth, energy, and hope! All this is fixed in the precious reels of the unforgettable twenties.

In *Aelita* (1924), produced by the "old man" Yakov Protazanov (considered "old" only because he was from prerevolutionary cinema; otherwise he was a mere forty), based on Alexei Tolstoi's novel, an engineer who works in the half-starving Moscow of those years designs a spacecraft and flies to . . . Mars. The scene shifts back and forth from Earth to Mars. There are two feminine characters—Natasha, the beautiful daughter of the Earth, and Aelita, the queen of Mars.

Films of everyday life in the 1920s are a source of diversion, variety, charm, and rib-tickling humor. Three filmmakers who are representative of that era are Friedrich Ermler, Abram Room, and Boris Barnet.

Originally from the small provincial town of Rezhitsa, Friedrich Ermler worked for a while as an apothecary's assistant. After the October Revolution, he served in the Cheka (the All-Russian Extraordinary Commission for Combatting Counter-revolution, Sabotage, and Speculation), after which he came to the Sevzapkino Studio in Leningrad. Despite a lack of years he had a keen eye and a good head on his shoulders.

His first major picture was *The House in the Snow-Drifts* (1923), a screen version of Yevgeni Zamyatin's story *The Cave*. This was a touching story about a strange musician, who felt unneeded and lonely in the new post-

October world. He had attempted to commit suicide and was on the verge of death when children of some poor people living in the basement saved him. The producer successfully captures details of the former Russian capital, Petrograd, snow-driven and plunged into darkness. It was the time of "tenant housing reductions," when workmen and their families who lived in basements and wooden barracks were moved into apartments occupied by families from the wealthy and middle classes. The current dwellers were forced to share their apartments with the newcomers.

Reduction—such was the name of the first "agitation" short. Tenant housing reduction became the subject of several other films (*The Golubin Mansion,* among others). *The House in the Snow-Drifts* was a film notable not so much for the thorough treatment of the topic of the day as for the wonderful actor who played the musician. That was Fedor Nikitin, a stage actor groomed at the Moscow Art Theater, ahead of whom lay a shining future in Soviet cinematography.

With his large radiant eyes and thin nervous Slavonic-looking face, Fedor Nikitin emotionally and physically resembled Fedor Dostoyevsky's Prince Myshkin *(The Idiot).* Quite an unsuitable character to be an ideal of those times, it might seem! But that was one of the zigzags, the marks of the early Soviet screen, that it was always in the process of "fermentation," in a state of contrast between light and shade. Nikitin gave just as shining a performance as a member of the intelligentsia: honest, gentle, yet strange, who lived "without fear and without reproach." He played this type of role three times: as Vadka Zavrazhin, a declassé hobo from Leningrad's "lower depths"; as Kirik Rudenko, a deaf-mute from the provinces; and as Filimonov, a former noncommissioned officer in World War I.

In *Katka's Reinette Apples* (1924) the beggar Vadka fusses over Katka, a charming fruit vendor, whose bandit lover, Semka Zhgut, has taken off, leaving her with an infant on her hands. In the *Parisian Cobbler* (1925) the same situation is set in a more social scene: the action unfolds at a paper mill in a small town. Katka (played by Veronica Buzhinskaya, who also starred in the first film) is a "shock-worker," and her lover is an active Komsomol member. Katka is expecting a child, but the Young Communist is afraid of "philistine degeneration" and tries to get the young woman to have an abortion. She refuses. Then the "evildoer" and his friends play a dirty trick on poor Katyusha. The tension is defused by the noble "Pari-

Fedor Nikitin (right) portrays deaf-mute Kirik Rudenko opposite Veronica Buzhinskaya as Katka in striped polo shirt and red scarf of the komsomols of the twenties, in Parisian Cobbler.

sian cobbler" (as emblazoned on the sign at the door of his pitiful shoemaker's shop); Kirik Rudenko shows up at a Komsomol meeting where the "case" of the girl, accused of "depravity," is being heard. In a splendid pantomime (the hero is deaf and dumb), Fedor Nikitin re-enacts the conspiracy by the dirty liars, and they are exposed in disgrace. Nikitin did just as well in the role of Filimonov, (*Fragment of an Empire,* 1929), a shell-shocked noncommissioned officer who suffers from amnesia. From the trenches of the war he is thrown right into the new, "red" Russia of 1929. The poor invalid has spent several years confined to some way station. In this film Ermler used what is called a "subjective camera" (a world of visions and flashbacks, temporal shifts) to achieve an exceptionally effective contrast between the horror of the war and the peace of socialist revival.

Two Moscow film masters, Abram Room and Boris Barnet, depicted their contemporaries with a probing perceptivity. Their keen, searching camera penetrated into the odd social mores during the NEP period.

Nikitin, after 40 years in films, takes the lead in the Nikolai Gubenko film Life, Tears, and Love.

In 1927, Room's famous controversial picture, *Third Meshchanskaya* (also known as *Bed and Sofa*), focused on the relationship among two workmen and a young woman who share a communal flat in Moscow. The situation develops into one of adultery, and the only thing that varies from time to time is the arrangement of the two beds and the sofa. It is the young woman that manages to break free and leave Third Meshchanskaya Street for good to make a fresh start in life. The theme of female emancipation was thus broached.

The light and witty comedies by Boris Barnet showed many colorful philistines of those unique times. The actress Anna Sten, a big-eyed, temperamental beauty, enlivened *The Girl with the Hat Box"* (1927) with her portrayal of Natasha, a milliner's girl, surrounded by a swarm of amusing admirers. In *The House on Trubnaya Square* (1928), Barnet gave a sectional view of an overcrowded apartment house in Moscow. The tenants, after much commotion, elect a young country girl, Parasha, as their deputy to the Soviet. A charming, talented actress, Vera Maretskaya, appeared in the role of the first Soviet "female cook who could head a government."

Later on, this prominent Russian actress would appear in many other roles personifying a Soviet woman from the working masses: in *Member of the Government, She Defends Her Country* (as the leader of an anti-fascist partisan detachment), and also in such postwar films as *Village Teacher* and *Mother,* directed by Mark Donskoi. This remarkable film producer, prominent in subsequent decades, was only starting to appear on the scene. Donskoi's first production, *In the Big City,* a film on young people, was shot at a small studio in Minsk. Situated close to the Soviet-Polish border, this city had been then the westernmost point of the Soviet Union's film industry. Now, although we have thus far been dealing with the motion picture industry of Moscow, Petrograd (Leningrad), and Kiev, the domain of the cinema during the latter half of the twenties actually encompassed a much larger territory.

The Map of the Soviet Cinema

The cinema industry of the Caucasian republics was making good progress. A new branch of the Georgian Goskinprom, AFKU, went into operation in Baku (Azerbaijan), where before the revolution several films had been made with money donated by local oil kings. In 1925 the motion picture industry made its debut in the Armenian capital of Yerevan. There, a series of national pictures was produced by Amo Bek–Nazarov (screen name Amo Bek). This talented man, who had played leading roles in prerevolutionary films, greatly contributed to the development of the early silent Georgian cinema as well. His films, *Namus (Honor), Has-Push, Zare,* and *Gikor* among others, exhibit not only his exhaustive knowledge of old customs and traditions but his intuitive sense of local color. They revive the image of Armenia's prerevolutionary past and medieval notions about family honor and power of money. These films reflected a predominant tendency in postrevolutionary cinema of the country to reassess the past sociologically and to understand the major changes taking place.

In the Caucasus, the first place in cinematography has always been held by the Georgian republic. Perched above the turbulent Kura River, in a garden not far from the famous Metskh Church, was the studio in Tiflis, where a number of cinematographic masterpieces have come out over the years. Naturally talented in the visual arts, Georgian filmmakers have been particularly successful in expressing themselves in the "seventh art." This was evident as early as 1923 when the Tiflis studio produced its first hit adventure, *Red Imps (The Young Red Devils)*, directed by Ivan Perestiani. In 1929, *Eliso* (a screen version of the story by the Georgian classic writer, Alexander Kazbegi) joined the hall of fame of Soviet film. Nikolai Shengelia, married to the late star of Georgian silent film, Nata Vachnadze, ★ produced *Eliso*, in addition to *Twenty-Six Commissars* (1933), filmed in Baku, in both of which he exploited various techniques of silent film, including shading, montage rhythm, and camera angling, to achieve a level of excellence in expressivity.

Mikhail Chiaureli, producer of such 1940s and 1950s films as *Great Dawn, The Vow,* and *The Fall of Berlin,* also made his debut in the twenties. His productions of the eccentric comedy *Khabarda* and the melodrama *Saba* distinguished him as a film director of originality and promise. Incidentally, in *Saba,* a small Caucasian inn featured unique frescoes painted by the great Georgian master of primitive art, Niko Pirosmanishvili. Unfortunately, the murals were later marred during repairs, but in the film they still retained their original beauty.

The twenties was also the decade in which the Georgian film comedy, which would win the hearts of viewers all around the world for years to come, made its debut. In the beginning the Georgian cinema produced splendid reels like *Samanishvili's Step-Mother* by Kote Mardzhanishvili, *Until We Meet Again Soon* by Georgy Makarov, and many others just as full of the southern sun and Georgian humor that bites like Kakhetian wine.

Others from torpid, sultry Central Asia also got involved in the "film-ification" process. The origins of the Uzbek national cinema date from the latter half of the 1920s. Those early reels treated predominantly social and moral issues. The arch enemy, besides prejudice, feudalism, and poverty among the peasants, is the exotic, so-called "oriental" film of the old school (harems, sultans, odalisques, eunuchs). In *The Moslem Woman* and *The Minaret of Death,* the theme of "the horrors of the past" (the Moslem

---

★This legendary and glamorous actress of the Georgian cinema was killed in an air crash. She left two sons, now well-known Georgian film directors, Georgi and Eldar Shengelia.

Turksib, a documentary of the Turkestan-Siberia railroad, shows the astonishment of desert inhabitants, including camels, to the "wonder of engineering."

law, vendettas, humiliation of the poor) takes on a Central Asian twist as the "emancipated woman of the East" becomes a key topic.

Victor Turin's documentary *Turksib* was remarkably original in both material and design. This Vostokkino release tells the story of the Turkestan-Siberia railroad project, showing the people's enthusiastic attitude toward work and the astonishment of age-old inhabitants of the desert, including Bactrian camels, at seeing the "wonder of engineering" speeding along the tracks in the sand.

Finally, moving even farther south, to the Soviet Union's southernmost border, we become acquainted with the youngest branch in the country's film industry—the Ashkhabad studio. A mystery to the people from the northern parts and located next to the Karakum Desert ("black sands"), Ashkhabad is the homeland of both the exquisite Turkmen carpets and horses. It was here that the young Moscow director, Yuli Raizman, shot his film *The Early Thirsts,* which was about the construction of a canal that cut its way across sands and age-old rocks, quenching the thirst of the parched soil. In those days everything old was shown with a "minus" sign (nomad tents and wagons, camels, rugs, yashmaks, piala bowls), while the new was always decorated with a "plus" (dynamite, construction projects, technology, meetings, slogans, flags). After many decades Khodzhikuli Narliev's film *Daughter-in-Law,* the pride of the Turkmen cinema of the 1970s, would show everything in a different perspective. But one had a long, long way to go to the seventies.

★ ★ ★

In 1923 the USSR State Planning Committee passed a resolution regarding the import of films. The purchase of many foreign films, primarily from the United States, was made. The floodgates to the American screen were opened with *The Virgin of Stamboul,* starring Priscilla Dean.

There are many reasons for this. As mentioned earlier, the Russian and American filmmakers did try to establish contact before the October Revolution, but any attempts were thwarted by the monarchy.

In October 1922 Lenin received Charles Recht in the Kremlin and discussed the progress of the cinema business in Russia with the American lawyer. Although French films were given the greatest preference during the 1910s, a trickle of American-made films did make their way through. The most noteworthy among these were films by D. W. Griffith. In 1916 a Russian entrepreneur purchased Griffith's *Intolerance* but did not succeed in having it released before the October events of 1917. The American masterpiece was first shown in 1918. In 1921 it was released for public viewing under the title *The Evil of the World* and became a smash hit. It suffices to recall what Eisenstein said in his article "Dickens, Griffith and We" or statements made by Vsevolod Pudovkin, Sergei Vasilyev, or Leonid Trauberg to get a sense of how the film was received by cinematographers. Griffith, along with the American producers Thomas Ince, Cecil B. DeMille, Charles Chaplin, King Vidor, and Josef von Sternberg, and such Hollywood stars as Buster Keaton, Fatty Arbuckle, Monty Banks, and Harold Lloyd were all familiar names to movie-goers in the Soviet Union.[19]

Edward Tisse, Douglas Fairbanks, and Sergei Eisenstein gather in the Sovkino film studio in Moscow in 1926.

In fact, American movies enjoyed a wide popularity in the Soviet Union. While on a round-the-world tour during the summer of 1926, Mary Pickford and Douglas Fairbanks visited Moscow, where they received a red carpet welcome. Documented evidence still remains: photographs, newsreels, and reminiscences, as well as two remarkable feature reels. These are *Mary Pickford's Kiss,* or *The Story of How Douglas Fairbanks and Igor Ilyinsky Quarreled over Mary Pickford* (directed by S. Komarov, 1927), and an animated cartoon-feature entitled *One of Many* (directed by N. Khodatayev, 1927). These comic reels featured documentary sequences of huge crowds gathered at the Brest (now Byelorussian) station in Moscow. As the train pulled in, the "golden pair" could be seen through the window: Mary looking charming as ever, and Doug flashing his gleaming smile. Later the guests paid a visit to the film studio where Mary contributed to the plot of the *Kiss* by planting a real kiss on the cheek of Igor Ilyinsky as he was playing the role of an usher in the up and coming Soviet *Harry Peel.* What priceless scenes! They are worthy of interest both as a page in the actual life of the "Great Silent" and as documentation

105

attesting to the rapport that existed between the two cinema powers all the way back in the 1920s.

In 1925 the Soviet Union started to export its films. The joint-stock company Amkino handled exports to the United States. Other countries could purchase Soviet films through Soviet trade offices.[20] The following is a list of several Soviet films that were exported: *The Station Master,* shown in 37 countries; *The Battleship Potemkin,* in 36 countries; *The Bear's Wedding,* in 35 countries; and *Wings of a Serf,* in 31 countries.

Despite the horrible fear of "red propaganda" and "communist infection,"* foreign trade businesses were eager consumers of films put out by the young Soviet film industry, for they were profitable.

Pleased over the strenghtening international ties and progress being made in the import-export business, the USSR's motion picture industry executives now sought to achieve predominance in the Soviet film market by the end of the 1920s, which it did succeed in doing.

Audiences came to love their young industry's productions and took an active interest in its problems. This led to the establishment of the Soviet Cinema Friends organization.

Soviet film advertisement was also coming along. Now in addition to the popular biweekly *Sovetski Ekran (Soviet Screen)* and other film periodicals and newspapers put out on a national scale, individual republics were starting to publish their own newspapers on the cinema as well.

The tempestuous, unforgettable, and fruitful twenties came to an end— a laboratory for original filmmaking, a labyrinth of creative search.

In one mere decade some fantastic changes had taken place. On the ruins of the old world, including the world of cinema, the Soviet "Great Silent" as it was reverentially called, grew up.

In the twenties a total of 1,172 feature films and cartoons were made in addition to a vast number of documentary, science, and educational films. The young masters of the Soviet revolutionary avant-garde—Sergei Eisenstein, Vsevolod Pudovkin, Lev Kuleshov, Alexander Dovzhenko, Grigori Kozintsev, and Leonid Trauberg—won worldwide fame. And the Soviet Union became one of the five occupants in the dominion of world cinema.

---

* We must not ignore the role of censorship, which was applied most strictly to films portraying actual revolutionary events.

CHAPTER THREE

The Thirties: Favorites of the Screen

The End of the "Great Silent"

*T*he close-up of a jangling alarm clock, the opening frame of the film *Alone* (1931), caused a furor in the cinema theaters. The people laughed and rejoiced. It was quite an event: the hitherto silent screen all of a sudden exploded with sound—and what a sound!—the clarion call of the workday world!

The alarm clock wakes up a chubby girl, the main character, who lives in a small room at the top of a tenement house. Humming a jolly ditty, she "pumps" her primus-stove (then a ubiquitous cooking apparatus) and makes scrambled eggs. A barrel organ is playing its plaintive tunes below, in the backyards. Cars honk, trams screech out in the street, feet stamp, news vendors shout.

The film *Counterplan* (a pledge of a work collective to meet the planned targets ahead of time) reproduces a real polyphony of sounds of a busy

Leningrad morning: the roll call of factory sirens, the clickety-clack of machinery, the splashes of water under motor launches on the Neva. Leningrad is at work. And the first hit song of the Soviet talkies, the light, boisterous "Song of the Counterplan" grew wings and left the screen, a catchy tune that was played over and over on the radio. It won a Grand Prix at a competition for the UN Anthem. A young talent wrote the music to the words of Boris Kornilov. He was Dmitri Shostakovich, who at that time was the composer of the opera *The Nose,* after the story by Nikolai Gogol, and of his First Symphony. He was to write yet another fourteen symphonies. Cinematography enjoyed the sheer novelty of word and sound. Like a deaf-and-dumb person who gained hearing all of a sudden, the cinema revelled in the concord of sounds. Noises and melodies, whisper and loud voice—everything seemed significant. A new world was discovered and it had to be explored. Recalling the predilection of the silent pictures for visual images—objects, lines, contours—it is no wonder that singers, musicians, and other "sources of sound" became heroes of the first talking films: Al Jolson in *The Jazz Singer* or the vociferous Lillian Harvey and Henri Garat in the French musicals.

At that critical time Soviet filmmakers were experiencing the same difficulties, joys, and doubts as their counterparts abroad, of course, notwithstanding the specific features in the development of post–October art—an art conscious of its socialist mission. Although the global process of the mastery of sound was universal, the Soviet cinema embarked upon a road of its own.

Numerous technical experiments paved the way for the talking era. In the middle twenties Professor P. Tager, working at Moscow University, set up a laboratory for research in sound-recording and sound-reproducing equipment. In Leningrad the laboratory under A. Shorin offered an original system for the sound movies. Even though the German sound system, Tri Ergon, was displayed back in 1927, preference was given to home-devised apparatus. Following the trial runs of the Tagephon and Shorinophon systems (one of the first showings was arranged at a congress of Russian physicists in 1928), the first sound films were shown to the broad public in 1929. Two cinema theaters, Khudozhestvenny in Moscow and Experimentalny in Leningrad, were eqipped for sound.

The early talking programs were in the form of filmed concerts featuring popular choirs and famous singers, symphony orchestras, jazz bands, folk instrument groups, and poetry recitals. The "talking stars" fad (tenors, saxophone players, tap-dancers) did not catch on for a variety of obvious reasons—the absence of a commercial interest ready to speculate on someone's reflected glory. The Soviet filmmakers would rather gear word and sound to cinematographic objectives of their own, to internal problems of the cinema—problems which, as it soon became obvious, were intimately associated with societal processes. In a nutshell: the sound, the sounding word, first and foremost would soon come to be subordinated to the propaganda objective of a new decade: that of shaping the image of a positive hero, a character for emulation and the prototype of a whole gallery of role models on the screen, drawn to infect the viewers with the urge "to model their life after," to quote Vladimir Mayakovsky's poetic line. Such a type emerged throughout the thirties.

The talkies were met not only with an enthusiastic welcome but also with some resistance on the part of the cinematographic elite. An aphorism was coined: "The talking cinema is just as useless as a singing book." There is nothing surprising about that if we recall that the fathers of the cinematography were dead set against the sound pictures. Charles Chaplin opened his mouth only in 1935: in the final sequences of *Modern Times* obstinate Charlie sang a ditty, but he preferred to use some gobbledygook (ostensibly of foreign origin) instead of plain words.

The accomplishments of the silent reels were too palpable to be abandoned for a "photographed theater." It was a pity to sacrifice the sophisticated montage code and the metaphoric mentality of the masters of the silent screen with their black-and-white phantasmagoria.

They feared most of all naturalism and flat imitation of life. This is why the triumvirate of film producers—Sergei Eisenstein, Vsevolod Pudovkin, and Grigori Alexandrov—came out with their *Sound Manifesto* (1928). This document advocated a "counterpoint of sound and image," a program relevant even today: the filmmakers opted for the sound as an independent artistic element within the integral montage structure of a film. In other words, they urged that the sound-word (naturalistic sound) illustrating, elucidating, or duplicating the frame be given up in favor of a poetically transmuted sound.[1]

What the masters of the "Great Silent" missed was this: the rich system of its expressive devices flourished in the absence of the audible, something that the cinematography industry had been longing for from its initial steps. Small wonder that recitation was one of the earliest forms of the "talking films" as far back as the turn of the century: an actor, standing behind the screen, supplied the action with sound and, as often as not, did a good job.

The din of a piano and even whole orchestras accompanied film shows in the twenties.[2] This way the screen sought to overcome its deafness. The same pattern would recur later, in the 1950s, for color. The screen would resist; it was none too eager to exchange its ascetic black-and-white dichromatism of *Otto e mezzo (8½)* or *Nine Days of One Year* for a rainbow feast of color. However, as early as the mid-thirties color reels were already being produced—the American best-seller film *Gone with the Wind,* which could well compete with its literary original, or the Soviet screen productions of Nikolai Gogol's *Sorochinsky Fair* and *A Night in May.*

Not only the Second World War but also misgivings on the part of filmmakers held back the development of the color film for as long as two decades. Such must be the law for any art; it applies even to the cinema with its dynamic, go-ahead idiom. In a way, art is a conservative medium that resists technical novelties for fear that the intruders might do no end of harm.

So, experiments, often mutually exclusive ones, were launched: from the search for abstract sound symbols to the natural sounds recorded on location. Thus, Mikhail Tsekhanovsky, a film director, came out with interesting experiments. In his short reel, *Pacific,* he sought for a correspondence between the visual and the audible. Taking Arthur Honegger's orchestral composition "Pacific 231," Tsekhanovsky joined sequences showing a steam locomotive and its parts with musical instruments shot from different angles and montaged accordingly.

A group of Moscow cartoonists known as "Ivvoston" (a pun on the names of the members, A. Ivanov, N. Voinov, and P. Sazonov) was engaged in interesting and bold experiments parallel, in a way, to the etudes and rhapsodies of Oskar Fischinger of Germany and Norman McLaren of Canada; they would put on the sound track geometrical designs and drawings that combined into consonances absolutely unknown to nature. Regrettably, these pioneering ventures drew no support. Incidentally, this is perhaps a typical trait of Russian inventiveness: a Russian finds it much easier to invent rather than patent his invention.

Experiments on "drawn" sound were the ultra-left for that day and age. Yet another trend was at work as well—the "sound unawares" that Dziga Vertov proclaimed in his *Enthusiasm (Symphony of the Don Basin).* This full-length documentary was released by November 7, 1930, the thirteenth anniversary of the October Revolution. In it Vertov played back a "live" recording of natural sounds—street and production noises, clanking, grating, whispering, and plain talking. Taking his camera and mike into the street during popular festivities or into factory shops and coal mines, he produced a "phonogram of reality." But Vertov went beyond the natural noises: he produced an effective counterpoint of word and image by superimposing a hit march song of the thirties, "Onward to Sunny Expanses," on sequences of popular processions with posters, banners, and masks.

Again, documentation, this untiring trailblazer, opened up new vistas for the feature film. The sound medium enabled the cinema, in pictures like *Counterplan* and *Road to Life,* to penetrate those spheres and problems that silent movies could only touch upon lightly.

In other words, sound helped the cinematographer in the realist portrayal and analysis of life. Sound was more humane, more democratic. Some films of the early thirties bear witness to this.

Take, for instance, *Road to Life,* shot at the Mezhrabpromfilm studio in 1931 by Nikolai Ekk (real name Ivakin). Long lines at box offices, a lively response in and outside cinema theaters, and debates and arguments all testified to its big success. But this popularity was quite different from that of the purely commercial, noisy *The Bear's Wedding* or some imported *Indian Tomb* of the previous decade. *Road to Life* raised questions of vital concern; it was a film from life, not from a dream factory. It dealt with "besprizorniki" (literally, homeless children), a word which, though not to be found in Vladimir Dal's classical dictionary of the Russian language, remained in Soviet vocabulary after the phenomenon of juvenile vagrancy had been eliminated.

One of the grave results of the First World War and the civil war, foreign military interventions, and migrations was the mass orphanhood of children who had lost their parents or were abandoned and lived on the streets. People of the older generation still remember the dirty ragamuffins of the 1920s warming themselves by the vats of molten asphalt used for covering stone-paved streets in big cities, nesting for the night in cellars and hovels, and subsisting on theft and cadging.

The viewers of *Road to Life* certainly remembered the shot showing a milling crowd at a railway station where the back of a lady's flowing karakul coat suddenly showed a vast white square where the fur had been cut out with a razor before everybody's eyes. Smudgy, dirty, raggedy

111

Nikolai Batalov has the image of a new hero as manager of a labor commune in Road to Life.

street urchins were not suitably made up extras but, alas, genuine types playing themselves. One of these performers was Ivan Kyrla, a teenager of unsavory appearance, with narrow, vicious little black eyes on a freckled mongoloid face. When the boys were handed back their disinfected clothes and were asked to dress, Kyrla chose such a hat and fashioned out such a get-up that Ekk decided to make the extra his main character. Thus was born the colorful figure of Mustafa Fert (Fop), a hardened thief who was reeducated and reformed in a labor colony and put on the right "road to life."

The film's concept and plot were prompted by the experiments of Anton Makarenko, the famous educator who had developed a system of "cure by work" of juvenile delinquents within the collectives of special corrective communes. One such establishment was shown in the film. The shooting was done in the real Bolshevo colony near Moscow, which certainly helped to make the film true to life and convincing, as did the participation of the actor Nikolai Batalov, who played the commune's headmaster, Sergeyev. This splendid performer, a disciple of Stanislavsky, made himself known in the cinema back in the 1920s (he played, in particular, Pavel in Vsevolod Pudovkin's *Mother*), but his principal roles were played in early sound films because he possessed, in addition to an expressive and characteristic appearance, a mastery of speech and a catching manner of speaking. Batalov was, in fact, the first impersonator of the new ideal of the social hero: a crystal-pure, utterly unselfish, clever, resourceful, and convinced zealot, unencumbered by dejection or anguish—a merry man of action. In *Road to Life* Batalov's broad smile flooded the screen. It was inconceivable even to think that in a few years that robust, broad-shouldered man who seemed splendidly healthy would die of tuberculosis in spite of treatment in sunny Italy and the best medicines of that time. Batalov had the gift of winning human hearts by instilling trust and faith in his truth, an essential gift for the hero in general and twice as valuable for the part of the Soviet hero leader he played.

Batalov's rival on the screen was Mikhail Zharov. He made his Zhigan, a leader of a gang of thieves, irresistable and fascinating in his own way; later on the actor would coin the cliche "mischievous villain" through his roles as the tsar's favorite and crony, Alexander Menshikov, in *Peter the First* and as Malyuta Skuratov, the blood-stained joker of the Russian sovereign, in Eisenstein's *Ivan the Terrible*.

The construction of the commune-town railroad, which Sergeyev succeeds in making an exciting game and achievement, on the one hand, and the alluring den of thieves with its wild revelry, vodka, girls, and the heart-rending songs of guitar-playing Zhigan, on the other—such are the clashing sides of the conflict. Zhigan wins in the *plot* and Sergeyev in *ideology*. The tragic finale shows the launching of the first train on the railroad tracks, which is to be driven by Mustafa. These are stirring and joyful minutes of expectation. But, as the train comes nearer, the faces of Sergeyev and of those waiting together with him reflect the impending disaster: the smiles die, the eyes darken. Moving into the picture is not the "locomotive of the commune," about which songs are being sung, but a funeral train; and the casket with the body of murdered Mustafa breaks the finishing tape. The words of the bewildered Sergeyev are sudden and very true: "Now how's that, Mustafa? Didn't you want to be an engineer?" The teacher seems to be scolding his pupil for another fault, with tears in his eyes. One can see how much Mustafa's uncomely face, now smoothened and ennobled, resembles Sergeyev's intelligent, winsome countenance. Mustafa died a *different* person, a son, not an orphan. His comrades also changed.

In August 1932 *Road to Life* and the silent films *Earth* (directed by Dovzhenko) and *And Quiet Flows the Don* (by O. Preobrazhenskaya and I. Pravov) were sent to Venice where, on Lido Island, the first international film festival in history was held, destined to become a highly prestigious competition. Twenty-nine films were shown, though there were no prizes as yet. Luda and Jean Schnitzer write in their *Histoire du cinema sovietique* that the management held a referendum among the viewers; the majority named Nikolai Ekk as the most talented director. This opinion is all the more significant since the other directors included Rene Clair, Alexander Dovzhenko, Frank Capra, Joris Ivens, Ernst Lubitsch, Alessandro Blasetti, King Vidor, and Rouben Mamoulian.[3]

Road to Life still often figures in Italian cinema literature. Thanks to its "engaged observation" method (shooting in the labor commune) and also to type orientation and naturalism, the film is considered one of the forerunners of Italian neorealism, a work of principled significance.

Dostoyevsky, the Soviet Approach; Classics on the Screen

The palette of Soviet cinema of that time was varied and rich. It transpired that sound cinema, far from retarding the search for new themes, genres, and images, actually stimulated it. But it also transpired that the very alternative silent or sound was of a purely intra-cinematographic significance. The really important processes in the development of socialist cinema art were the result not of aesthetic struggles as such but rather of broader and external factors of social awareness, the political slogans of the day, and the historical movement of society. This was particularly manifest during the 1930s, for Soviet history does not know a more turbulent decade.

The plans of collectivization of agriculture and of the national economy's industrialization were accomplished, which naturally resulted in numerous social, ideological, political, and cultural changes. The Seventeenth Congress of the All-Union Communist Party held in 1934 was pompously named the "Congress of Victors."

The authors of the collective academic work *History of Soviet Cinema* justly point out that the films of the 1930s

> certainly had truth that, if not always reflected the real processes of life itself, still reflected the mass notions about them. Art reflects life. But then mass notions, being one of life's inalienable components, can also feed art. In the early 1920s the broad masses of people lived in expectation of an imminent world revolution. History has shown those expectations were unrealistic at that time. Nevertheless art, spurred by dreams of an early revolutionary upheaval, reflected the mass, even though naive, conviction that the world revolution would take place very soon, maybe tomorrow.[4]

It should be added to these words that the screen of the 1930s not only reflected mass notions but also *formed* them in tune with Stalinist social mythology.

Indeed, events abroad, the international situation, and the relations of the world's first socialist state with capitalist countries greatly stirred Soviet filmmakers. Those were topical subjects, particularly at the beginning of the decade. Nearly one-third of the films released between 1932–1935 was devoted to the strike movement, the crisis, the international friendship of workers, and solidarity of all working people. Later on, the number of films in which the action took place abroad gradually decreased as the Second World War drew nearer.

Here are summaries of just a few productions of those years: *Tommy (Siberian Patrol),* directed by Yakov Protazanov (1941)—"About the awakening of the sense of internationalism in a British soldier"; *The Fugitive,* by V. Petrov (1932)—"An episode of the heroic struggle of German Communists"; *Together with Our Fathers,* by L. Frenkel (1932)—"About the participation of workers' children in the revolutionary struggle in the Western Ukraine"; *The Return of Nathan Becker,* by B. Shpis (1932)—"About the return of an emigre bricklayer to the Soviet Union"; *Heil Moskau,* by V. Shmidhof (1932)—"About fraternal solidarity of Soviet seamen and foreign workers on strike"; *Prosperity,* by Y. Zheliabuzhsky (1933)—"About American workers' fighting for their rights"; *The Sun Rises in the West,* by P. Pashkov (1933)—"About the growing political awareness of German workers"; *Torn Shoes,* by M. Barskaya (1933)—about the participation of workers' children in a capitalist country in the strike movement."[5] It should be noted that after 1933 the theme of international solidarity and workers' friendship gradually grew into an anti-fascist one, and later into the theme of defense, which dealt with the Soviet Union's preparation for a possible war.

The films of the "foreign cycle" were an approximation of the situations, settings, characters, and everything else. Nor could it be otherwise. Since joint productions and filming tours abroad were very rare, the filmmakers' knowledge of other countries and their customs was very limited. The portrayal of events was secondhand, borrowed as it were from books and films made in the West. The action took place particularly often in Germany or America, which was also by no means accidental.

The tragic events linked with Hitler's coming to power, the anti-fascist ardor, and, as we know now, a foreboding of the future drew the cinematographers' attention to Germany. Although most films showed that same unidentified Western capitalist country, not a real one, the screen still managed to some extent to preserve the truth of the time. It could be found in the *Deserter* by Vsevolod Pudovkin (1933), whose hero was Renn, a docker from Hamburg; in the *Revolt of the Fishermen,* made in 1934 by the well-known German theatrical director Erwin Piscator at the Mezhrabpomfilm studio with Russian actors; and somewhat later in the film version of the play *Professor Mamlock* written by Friedrich Wolf, who had emigrated to the USSR.

There was a different story with the United States, for it traditionally fascinated and attracted cinema workers in the Soviet Union from the 1920s, when most imported films came from America. The interest grew stronger in the 1930s thanks, in particular, to the numerous translations and publications of American authors, both classical and modern. At that time huge editions, typical of the USSR, were printed of the works of Theodore Dreiser, Upton Sinclair, Sinclair Lewis, Ernest Hemingway, Erskine Caldwell, and other prominent American prose writers; Eugene O'Neill was very popular on the stage (particularly successful was his *Desire Under the Elms,* which Alexander Tairov directed at Moscow's Chamber Theater); and cultural contacts broadened. At that time also, Eisenstein and his assistants Tisse and Alexandrov went on a tour of America (1930–1932). The trip disappointed him greatly because of the failure to carry out, through the fault of the company, the plans to shoot the films *Sutter's Gold, An American Tragedy,* and *The Black Consul;* the

A mask was one of the principal leitmotifs in Que Viva Mexico! *filmed by Eisenstein, Alexandrov and Tisse in 1931.*

footage for the film *Que Viva Mexico!* was to remain across the ocean. On the other hand, he carried away a wealth of indelible impressions after his acquaintance with a new continent, splendid artists, talented actors, and great film stars, some of whom became his good friends. America once again was featured in a film which its director Kuleshov entitled *Horizon* (1932) after the name of its main character, watchmaker Lev Horizon (played by the brilliant Batalov of *Road to Life* fame). It was Kuleshov's first sound picture. Life was hard on Lev in tsarist Russia, so he emigrated to America, which seemed the promised land to so many. During his eventful stay there he went through many hardships, met with poverty and humiliation, and returned to Russia, which was already Soviet, where he became an engine driver.

This story of a "returnee" or a settler in the USSR was told on the screen in many and various ways: from the horrors of the world, where grain is burned and milk is poured into rivers while children starve to death, from crisis, unemployment, exploitation, and the moral corruption of the top circles to the rising new world, to a new life under the red banner. This is how many film heroes came back home or acquired a new homeland, including those of American origin; these were first of all people who were called "spetsi" in the 1930s, that is, foreign specialists who worked in the Soviet Union under contract at the construction sites of factories, blast furnaces, or turbines during the first and second five-year plan periods, and cinema transformed reality into myths.

One such "spets," American engineer Clines, was played by Viktor Stanitsyn of the Moscow Art Theater in the film *Men and Jobs* (1932), directed by Alexander Macheret. The action developed at a major construction project. Clines, who led one of the teams, easily mastered the working methods and the equipment and left far behind the competing team headed by the Russian worker Zakharov, played by another splendid Soviet actor, the inimitable and attractive Nikolai Okhlopkov (he had already been seen in a comic sailor's role in the silent film *Death Bay* and would later play the worker Vasili in Mikhail Romm's films about Lenin and the redoubtable Russian warrior Buslai in Eisenstein's *Alexander Nevsky*). There is an ironic moment when the triumphant foreign engineer gaily laughs against the background of a flying streamer with the words: "Catch up with and overtake America!", a current slogan of the time. But this likeable character, superbly played by the subtly intellectual performer Stanitsyn (one of whose best stage roles was Dickens's Mr. Pickwick) celebrated too early. Zakharov and his team made an extra effort, displayed the proverbial "Russian sweep," and in the end overtook Clines' team.

Such an American, intelligent but simple minded, an excellent worker but a somewhat narrow and pragmatic person, who does not believe in the "Russian sweep" and is therefore good naturedly put to shame, was characteristic of the screen stage of the early 1930s. Even Nikolai Pogodin's popular plays, *The Rate of Advance* and *The Poem of the Axe,* invariably included such personages painted, it should be noted, convincingly and sympathetically. So it was in the cinema. Even if an American proved to be a saboteur (whose number grew in the films each year), as was the case, for instance, in the *Great Gamble* (1935) made by the Ukrainian director G. Tasin, the "bad" foreign engineer was always counterposed by a "good" one. Here, next to perfidious Chandler, stood the honest assistant Jansen, who gave all his knowledge and efforts to the

Soviet project. It was to be assumed that many of the guest specialists, including Jansen, would wish to remain for good in their new homeland; such were the happy endings of films. So there was nothing original about the return from across the ocean of the poor watchmaker Horizon, who became an engine driver in the end of Lev Kuleshov's picture. What was original was Kuleshov's second "American" sound film, *The Great Consoler* (1934), a free fantasy on the subjects of the literary works and biography of the American writer O. Henry, who was also very popular with Soviet readers.

A brilliant humorist whose witty stories were not free from secret sadness, the inventor of incredible plots, whose own fate was just another such plot with vertiginous turns, an author who often added gall and shadows to his gay portrayal of reality—such was to Kuleshov "the great consoler" William Porter, known in literature as O. Henry. He made his personal appearance (represented by old film actor Konstantin Khokhlov) in the film in striped prisoner's clothing (Porter is known to have spent several years in jail). Acting together with the writer were also the prototypes of his characters—burglar Jimmy Valentine, detective Ben Price, and others.

It is noteworthy that the filming team of *The Great Consoler,* acting in the spirit of the time, announced itself to be a "shock-worker team" and pledged to shoot the picture within two months, which drew favorable comment from the *Kino* newspaper of April 28, 1933. Thus O. Henry indirectly "participated" in socialist emulation drive.

The plot of the film *The Great Consoler,* which was written by journalist Alexander Kurs, was unusual for its time. It contraposed real life to a life transformed by art and back again to a life that was even more cruel compared to pretty imagery. This triad was fancifully and wittily executed by the three main characters: Porter (the artist), Valentine (literary hero), and young Dulcey (the reader), the last role being played by Alexandra Khokhlova with all her refined mastery.

Like a small diamond in a filigree setting, the miniature *Jimmy Valentine's Appeal,* made by Kuleshov in the "dime novel" style, sparkled with vignettes, little hearts, roses, and other furnishings of the mass editions of the late nineteenth century. Kuleshov's attachment to American province, to material which he who had never visited America "figured out" from the films of Mack Sennett and Chaplin, was manifested here in frank symbolism and amusing stylization. Things were much worse when it came to the portrayal of reality; this, regrettably, was pictured also symbolically, gaping with empty or rarefied frames, as was typical of Kuleshov's works which he made after his masterpiece *By the Law (Dura Lex)*. True, the director did not claim any "documentalism" in his depiction of nineteenth-century America. He rather provided an "outline" of reality wherein the little man, O. Henry's hero, languished and labored under the burden of poverty and injustice. Incidentally, later on, Soviet cinema and then also television would over and over again turn to O. Henry, to his paradoxical novels with unexpected endings as well as to his satire *Cabbages and Kings,* unfortunately without finding an adequate pictorial solution for his far from simple prose. When *The Great Consoler* was released in 1934, the film, despite its undeniable mastery and originality, was not a success either with the mass audience or with most professionals. "Ballet!" was the verdict of Kuleshov's younger colleagues, although Eisenstein and Pudovkin regarded the film as a "splendid thing." Those who turned to the theme of the West in those years would fulfil a "social order" much more precisely, which, as can be clearly seen now, was the opposition of "the way things are with them and with us." This aesthetics of the 1930s, born a decade earlier and reflected in propaganda art and the posters of the civil war, now having lost its original didactic directness, emerged as the content of art. The generation born after the revolution grew up with a sense of profound pride in their wonderful country. It didn't know much about other not so wonderful countries.

This view of the USSR as the center of attraction of the entire planet was largely strengthened by the visits of outstanding figures of world culture. Romain Rolland, Rabindranath Tagore, Henri Barbusse, Herbert Wells, Martin Andersen Nexo, André Malraux, and Lion Feuchtwanger came to the Soviet Union during the 1930s and on their return home wrote books about it. Also coming were professional reporters, such as the German Egon Erwin Kisch, who visited the USSR twice and left his testimony in books and document cycles, or the fearless traveler with a camera in her strong small hands, who was always drawn into the flaming center of the new and unexplored, the American Margaret Bourke-White, who visited the USSR in the 1920s and 1930s and who, in the early 1940s, was caught here by the first salvoes of the war. The fascination experienced by the Western cultural elite must have been truly great and irresistible if George Bernard Shaw himself, who visited Moscow in 1931, the skeptic and king of paradox that he was, excitedly wrote his guidebooks and manuals on socialism and communism, while Stalin's portrait hung over his bed. Poor Shaw . . .

> May we grow to a hundred
> Never reaching old age!
> . . . Hammer and verse shall glory sing
> To the land of youth!

The ringing verses of Vladimir Mayakovsky, the slogan "Life has become better, life has become jollier!", bracing march tunes, songs pouring out of loudspeakers on streets and squares—the whole tenor of life, toned up also by cinema art—were full of joy and vigor. They in turn inspired optimism in art, whose colors became brighter, more definite, and clearer as society advanced.

The year 1917 was certainly a historical landmark and the beginning of a new era. All of mankind's past was viewed with reference to the revolution, from the height of the October upheaval. It was like an overture before the real action which started in 1917, a prehistory as it were. In the light of the Soviet red dawns, the cinema reconstructed the "leaden iniquities of the past," as they said then, or the "vile Russian reality," as Vissarion Belinsky, the Russian revolutionary democrat and literary critic of the nineteenth century, put it. The striking contrast between the past and the present accounted for the sharp, exaggerated, grotesque forms of the new interpretation of the classical works of Russian literature; the old world, swept away by the revolution, loomed from the screen like an awesome ghost.

Sound cinema turned to the national classic treasures more willingly and frequently than silent cinema, which was impeded both by its muteness and the memory of prerevolutionary "flicks" that speculated on the names of great writers.

Vladimir Gardin of the academic school, a towering figure of the times of the Russian Golden Series and a film actor in Soviet time, played the miserable and cruel creature of Saltykov-Shchedrin, Iudushka Golovlev, in the film directed by Alexander Ivanovsky and based on the novel *The Golovlev Family*. Gardin masterly portrayed with passion and even relish the revolting miser and reprobate who was duly nicknamed Judas by his family and servants. The people near to Iudushka—the nieces ruined by him, the household staff, his concubine, his illegitimate son—were all depicted as victims of the "leaden iniquities" of the tsarist regime. In the end Iudushka, as a representative of the degenerating gentry, died leaving the historical stage to an even more fearful force—the bourgeoisie, the ignorant and uncultured merchants.

Vladimir Petrov filmed *The Storm* by Alexander Ostrovsky, a most popular play in Russian theatrical repertory, a story of a pure woman's soul suffering and perishing in a "kingdom of darkness." This definition by Nikolai Dobrolyubov, another Russian revolutionary critic, has become a set phrase denoting the ruthlessly ruled Russian family life, the stagnant and savage world of provincial merchantry. Katerina, a "ray of light in the kingdom of darkness," in the words of Dobrolyubov, was played in the film by Alla Tarasova, an actress of the Moscow Art Theater and a disciple of Vladimir Nemirovich-Danchenko. (Soon after, she played Anna Karenina on the stage of the Art Theater and impersonated on the screen Empress Catherine I, wife of Peter the Great.) Alla Tarasova as Katerina in *The Storm,* with her light brown hair, fine chiseled and gentle Slav profile, thin brows and clear light eyes, was an intimately lyrical image who evoked sympathy with and understanding of a suffering individual. And that is what the screen badly needed after a whole decade of concentration on social sentiment, passions, and actions of the revolutionary mass above all.

Now the cinema audience openly wept over the merchant's wife, Katerina Kabanova, who was unfaithful to her husband after falling in love with another man, for which she committed suicide. Still greater love by the viewers, which has lasted till our day, went to another of Ostrovsky's heroines, Larisa Ogudalova, a girl from a family of poor gentry, in the film *Bride Without Dowry* (1937), directed by the veteran of Russian cinema, Yakov Protazanov. The director boldly gave the role from the classic repertory (played in their time by the great tragic actresses of theater, Yermolova and Komissarzhevskaya) to the very young Nina Alisova, a charming black-eyed "gypsy." Touching, helpless, and doomed to perish in a world where everything is sold and bought, where all that she, a girl without a dowry, can do when her lover deceives her is to sell herself and become a kept woman, Larisa remains proud and pure even in humiliation and is incapable of such abasement.

An interesting attempt to screen Dostoyevsky's works was made at the same time by the directors Grigori Roshal and Vera Stroyeva in their film *Petersburg Nights* (1934), a cinema fantasy on the themes of the short novels *Netochka Nezvanova* and *White Nights.*

The relations between the cinema and Dostoyevsky had not been easy prior to that. His works were often filmed before the revolution (*Crime*

Heroine of Bride Without Dowry *by A.N. Ostrovsky, Nina Alisova, as Larisa Ogudalova, was the darling of the audiences of the thirties.*

and Punishment was made into a film several times), but the standard of the screen versions understandably could not compare with such theatrical productions as *The Brothers Karamazov* in the Art Theater. In the early post-October years Dostoyevsky was rejected by many as a preacher of humility, a "reactionary," and even a "religious obscurantist" (although serious and objective literary studies of his writings were published at the same time, for example, the *Poetics of Dostoyevsky* by M. Bakhtin, in 1929).

Just before *Petersburg Nights,* another film, in a way odious, was shot—*The House of Dead*. It was not an adaptation of Dostoyevsky's well-known *Notes from the Dead House* but a biographical film written by the prominent author and critic Viktor Shklovsky. The film showed, first, a young

Dostoyevsky, a member of a secret revolutionary circle, and then a used-up man broken down by years of hard labor in exile ingratiatingly conversing with the chief procurator of the Synod, the archreactionary Pobedonostsev. The picture *Petersburg Nights* was in a sense an attempt to exonerate the writer.

Its main character, serf musician Yegor Yefimov, a somber and lone genius who has lived a hard, tortuous life, rejecting, in particular, the revolutionary path, realizes that his existence was not meaningless after all when he hears rebellious weavers, now shackled and being sent to hard labor, sing one of his old and cherished songs. A tune composed by him, Yegorov, became a folk song!

Despite the extremely "bold" interpretation of Dostoyevsky's ideas (for nothing of the kind is to be found in his works), it was an attempt to overcome rigidly categorical evaluations, to make an allowance to the effect that an artist's creative work may prove more progressive than the man himself and reach beyond the author's political position. While handling the plot in a free and peremptory manner, transforming Yefimov, ruined by pride and drink and a half-talent eaten up by envy, into a potential revolutionary and transforming Dostoyevsky's "humiliated and insulted" ("poor people") into the victims of the "prison of nations" (the old tsarist Russia), the makers of *Petersburg Nights* nevertheless contrived to put across the peculiar atmosphere, landscape, and climate of the original short novels. Be that as it may, Dostoyevsky's "reprehensible" heritage was being reinstated for the new Soviet generations. Though the film did not outlive its time, it remained as its testimony.

No less eloquent, though testifying to its time in a different way (without the freshness of the *Petersburg Nights*), was another screen version of the classics, *Dubrovsky,* a film based on Pushkin's short novel and directed by Alexander Ivanovsky in 1936. The traditional theme of avenging the noble man who leads a "forest fraternity" to repay the enemy for his dishonor (like Robin Hood, Karl Moor, and other "robbers") was also interpreted here in terms of class struggle. The peasants from Dubrovsky's riotous band burned down landlords' estates the way it was done in 1917; they rebuked their chief for indecision and actually elected a new leader, the revolution-conscious blacksmith Arkhip. All this indicated that vulgar sociological approaches and the naive directness of the bunting-waving, sharply black-and-white, and rigorous twenties were not as easy to overcome.

A whole number of interesting, novel, and original films simply failed to arouse proper response or support at the time, remaining in the shadow, on the sidelines of the general process. For example, it would take thirty or more years for recognition and success to crown the works of Alexander Medvedkin, the creator of the unique film genre of satire in the form of cheap popular wood prints. His short silent satire-farces *Tit (Tale of a Big Spoon), About a White Bull Calf, A Little Log,* and others with their unusual expressive technique were so strikingly different from the general production that they were not understood, have not been preserved, and are now irreparably lost. Medvedkin's first full-length film, which he shot without sound in 1934—*Happiness (Snatchers)*—and which caused a sensation both in the Soviet Union and in Western Europe as a "revival" in the 1960s, was almost unnoticed when it was first released. It was a stylized Russian folk tale about a poor and lazy peasant by the name of Khmyr, who dreamed of becoming a tsar, eating his fill of pork fat and doing nothing (his idea of happiness), and his industrious wife Anna, who found real happiness on a collective farm after the revolution. The drawn scenery amusingly transplanted into cinema from popular Russian wood prints, the ingenious and always purposeful tricks, the hilariously funny scenes of the wanderings around Russia of a scraggy and vicious pilgrim nun, the talented sideshows of "dreams" and "royal repasts" of Khmyr—all this entirely grotesque world of the picture was crowned by the director's inventiveness which anticipated many postwar quests! Long before Bertold Brecht with his theory and practice of theatrical masks, Alexander Medvedkin let loose on the screen a whole platoon of tsar's soldiers with facemasks made from papier-maché; the soldiers sent to put down a peasant rebellion all had round, shining, and very stupid visages with gaping mouths frozen in an eternal "hurray!"

Also unique was the marionette film *A New Gulliver* directed by Alexander Ptushko (1935), a "modernization" of Jonathan Swift's *Gulliver's Travels* in which the classical traveler's role was given to young pioneer Petya and Lilliput turned out to be a militarized state.

A number of talented and merry comedies were produced in Georgia, famous for its humor. We may mention just one of the last Georgian silent films, *Until We Meet Again Soon,* directed by Georgi Makarov (1934), in which the serious theme of underground revolutionary struggle was played out with fiery, infectious optimism and with plenty of exciting adventures and comic situations.

Happiness, a satirical comedy of 1934 and Medvedkin's first full-length film, was a sensation as a revival in the 60s.

A curious phenomenon existed: fantasy and science-fiction films were almost totally absent from the repertory of the early 1930s, although the impressive success of the American-made *The Invisible Man* based on Herbert Well's novel, which was dubbed (for the first time in Soviet practice) and released in great numbers in 1934, was a clear indication of the spectators' interest in this genre. Only a few titles were to be seen on the bills after the silent *The Salamander* directed by Grigori Roshal and written by Anatoli Lunacharsky, the People's Commissar of Education (1929). Besides being a fantasy film, *The Salamander* set an example for subsequent cinema productions on the subject of internationalism, for it told the sad story of a Western scientist called Zanghe (played by the German actor Bernhard Goetzke) who conducted amazing experiments on salamanders in order to prove his materialistic ideas, for which he had to pay dearly. The makers of the film were interested not so much in the miraculous experiments on tailed amphibians as in the persecution of Zanghe, who was accused by capitalist obscurantists of corruption of minors and of falsifying scientific findings, which made the scientist escape to the Soviet Union where he acquired, as would soon become usual on the screen, his second homeland. So the real advent of science fiction to Soviet cinema was still in the future.

Yet the tradition of the early, if naive, Protazanov's *Aelita,* with its flight to Mars starting from Soviet Moscow, was continued. The film *Cosmic Voyage,* directed by V. Zhuravlev at the Mosfilm studio in 1935, was significant in that its heroes flew to the moon and even got to the mysterious unknown side of the earth satellite, where they walked about in lead shoes and space suits. But even more significant than that prevision (which was also naive in both scientific and artistic respects) was the fact that the film's consultant was Konstantin Tsiolkovsky, the forerunner of Soviet space exploration, who personally made thirty drawings of a space ship for the film!

The screen of the early 1930s showed, along with productions characteristic of the time and interesting for the historian, also films of major artistic value. Still impressive is the charming picture *Outskirts* made by Boris Barnet. This unpretentious, simple story about a quiet provincial town, a Russian backwoods village, affected from afar by the storms and explosions of the epoch—the world war, the revolution—was compared with Anton Chekhov's prose. Here triumphed Chekhov's principle whereby history was seen through the living flow of everyday events in the lives of most ordinary people with nothing heroic about them. The film presented a shoemaker and his two sons just recruited into the army, the owner of a shoemaking shop and his teenage daughter, an elderly German living in the town and young Germans, who are prisoners of the war that had just started, a student lodger, and so on.

Béla Bálazs, a prominent film critic and cinema theoretician, pointed out very precisely the peculiar features of the director's work in *Outskirts* in his review which he entitled "Greetings to Comrade Barnet." He wrote:

> You do not draw caricatures of serious things. You show them seriously because they are actually and really serious. But you do not sift or clean them of grotesque and comic details that may stick to the most serious

things. Shakespeare successfully mixed seriousness with humor. Yet the difference between the two concepts remained. They existed side by side. With you the same scene, the same images and gestures are simultaneously tragic and comic.[6]

Indeed, Barnet shows through sketches drawn with keen observation and humor, through the life of a town boulevard on whose benches human destinies are decided, love is declared, and farewells and separations take place, such serious things as War, Enlightenment, Death, Revolution. It was with a particularly gentle and kind smile that the story of the girl Manka, an "ugly duckling," played by Yelena Kuzmina, was told: the awakening of a woman, the first snubs from life, and the budding first love for another teenager who is already a war prisoner, a puny, tow-haired German boy, played by Hans Klering, a German actor living in the Soviet Union. (Many times later, during the war, he played Nazis—SS men, various storm troopers, and other Germans).

Finally the atmosphere of a cozy little provincial world was palpably real and drew the viewer into the *Outskirts*. It is getting dark on an evening street, lights go on first in one window and then another of a clapboard house (one is always curious to know, also in real life, what is there, in the window?), a love song is heard off the screen, a dog is barking sadly far away, boisterous laughter rings out in the darkness, then a titter . . . this soundtrack of life superimposed on the vibrant, airy picture was also caught by the director. However, the psychological elaboration of characters, close attention to a person's individuality, the "Chekhov principle" were all still in the distant future.

As regards its own time *Outskirts* was quite a rarity. Looking back today we realize that Barnet's film was much too "private," that it stood, in the idiom of that time, away from the "general line" of development of Soviet cinema. It was certainly realism, but for that time it was a little too refined, too highly polished as it were. Meanwhile the revolutionary theme awaited another interpretation.

"Quiet, Citizens. Chapai's Gonna Think!"

A stirring newsreel of the time shows a marching human column carrying the streamer: "We are going to see 'Chapayev'!"

The entire country had seen the film. Free tickets were distributed at

Chapayev provides a domestic portrait of the commander drinking tea in a film that everybody understood.

many factories and offices.

Everybody liked it. "Everybody understood it, from academician to collective farmer," as was then said by way of supreme praise. *Chapayev* conquered all contingents of cinema goers. Veterans of the civil war and the elite critics who had only recently sung praises to the "camera Muse" of cinema silence, and also Eisenstein and Dovzhenko, as well as towns-folk and peasants—all were carried away by *Chapayev.* Even youngsters watched it fifteen times in a row, hoping against hope that the glorious Red "Chapai," who is in the end drowned, hit by the Whites' bullets, would manage to reach the bank and wouldn't perish in the turbulent waters of the River Ural.

Frames from the film have become emblems and symbols of Soviet cinema: the orderly Petka crouching behind a machine gun and standing above him Chapayev with a Cossack fur hat rakishly crushed on his head, his hand thrown forward. On a hill in front of the future battlefield is a group of commanders with field glasses in their hands and Chapayev in the center on a white horse, his black felt cloak flowing down in rippling folds. Boiled potatoes representing troops are manipulated on a table by the impetuous Chapai giving an object lesson in tactics: "Where should the commander be?" Chapayev with a drawn saber leads a galloping cavalry squadron, his white horse floating above the ground, the black cloak billowing with the wind like a sail.

A person can hardly be found in the Soviet Union who has not seen this half-a-century-old picture or at least heard about it. Jocular and witty phrases and other quotes from the film have long become part of the vernacular. To this day children play "at Chapayev." Constantly growing are the extensive studies on the film and its two directors, the Brothers Vasilyev. In short, within the USSR, *Chapayev* is the No. 1 picture of the "golden stock" in terms of popularity. It is less known abroad than, for instance, *The Battleship Potemkin* and other classic silent films, which is understandable, for at the time *Chapayev* appeared sound (or rather language) was a barrier.

"Brothers Vasilyev" was the appellation chosen by the namesake filmmakers Georgi Vasilyev (1899–1946) and Sergei Valilyev (1900–1959). Contemporaries of the giants of Soviet silent cinema, representatives of the same creative generation born of the revolution, they attained fame by a longer and more tortuous road.

Both had handsome, soft, entirely Slavic features. Both were sons of professional men (Georgi's father was a lawyer and criminal investigator; Sergei's father was the keeper of military-historical archives). Both welcomed the revolution and served in the Red Army; both had worked at several occupations before choosing cinematography. Sergei studied at the Petrograd Institute of Film Art while Georgi attended the Young Masters art studio in Moscow and contributed to newspapers and magazines as a film critic. Later on they trained together, already as the Vasilyev Brothers, at Eisenstein's studio.

They met and became friends in Moscow, in a Sovkino laboratory where foreign films were recut and re-edited. The very possibility of such bold operations performed in the 1920s on films bought abroad, both by Soviet distributor agencies handling foreign pictures and by foreign distributors in regard to Soviet films, testified to the rudimentary or simply nonexistent copyright awareness in cinema,★ when a film was regarded

★This often remains the case to this day. Take, for instance, the arbitrary change of film titles by foreign distributors guided by commercial, psychological, and other considerations. Is it conceivable to alter, say, the title of a novel or a story translated into a foreign language without the author's knowledge?

not as a sovereign work of art but as an anonymous "commodity" or a "semi-finished product."[7]

But for all its barbarity, recutting was a good school. The Vasilyevs used to repeat later that they learned the craft on American films. And they learned it well! This was testified, among other things, by Sergei Vasilyev's book *Montage,* published in 1929.

The Vasilyevs decided to work together at the Leningrad Film Factory where they first made the documentary *Icebreaker Krasin* (a montage of newsreels about the rescue of the Nobile expedition, 1928). Then they shot two feature films, *Sleeping Beauty* (1930) and *A Personal Affair* (1932), which were very different. Each had merits of its own: the first was a silent montage film based on the contrast between the reality of the civil war and the staging of a classical ballet in a provincial theater, and the second was an "industrial film" about a factory foreman. It was then that these film directors, who had not yet found themselves, were offered the script of *Chapayev,* based upon a novel about the late Communist writer Dmitry Furmanov written by his widow. The script had long been on the studio's list and was marked "difficult." The Vasilyev Brothers accepted it immediately. They wrote in their director's application (a brief summary of the theme and plan of a future picture, which is an indispensable stage of Soviet film production): "This is a film about the Party's guiding role during the establishment of the Red Army."[8]

During 1919–1921 Furmanov was the political commissar of the famed Chapayev's division which fought against White troops on the Eastern front. He included his impressions, diary entries, and reminiscences in the novel *Chapayev* (1923), which was later proclaimed to be a gem of the literature of socialist realism. Although the material of the novel and of Anna Furmanova's scenario was considerably reworked in the script written by Sergei and Georgi Vasilyev and then further transformed in the cinematographic rendering, the basic plot remained unchanged. It revolves around the relations between the division commander and the political commissar (Furmanov) sent "from the center" to Chapayev's troops, who have still preserved the free-going guerrilla ways where the leader's word is indisputable and his figure almost deified. In one of the film's characteristic scenes, Chapayev's orderly, Petka (the irresistibly likeable snub-nosed lad, played by Leonid Kmit, promptly became the people's favorite), appears on the porch of a village house which is the divisional commander's headquarters, fires a resounding shot into the air,

131

pauses, and proclaims with pomp: "Quiet, citizens, Chapai's gonna think!" The noisy, vociferous crowd of soldiers subsides into awesome silence.

Confrontation, sizing up, sympathy, and finally genuine attachment—this how the film unfolds the changing attitude of Chapayev to the stranger, the "new boss" of his division. Furmanov for his part invariably faces the fearless Chapai, this natural genius of battle, with a keen, understanding smile and talks to him in a friendly, slightly ironic tone. The commissar, who is younger than the division commander, can talk to the latter as to a naughty child; he knows when to pull up Chapai, who is inclined to bluster, and when to play up to him. When he quoted the well-known phrase from Gogol: "To be sure, Alexander the Great of Macedonia is a hero, but why smash up the furniture?" to an infuriated Chapai, the later expressed utter perplexity. "Of Ma . . . Macedonia? Who's that? Why don't I know him?" It is quite clear why, since our "strategist," as he admits himself, "learned to read and write only two years ago."

Furmanov's paternalism, somewhat overstressed by the plot, is softened, if not removed altogether, by the performer, the good-natured, smiling Boris Blinov. He is a very sincere, honest, and quite young man. Spectators come to love him together with Chapayev. The actor, who, like Nikolai Batalov, was a natural image of the attractive Bolshevik, also died at a young age. Life went against the plot of the film, according to which the division commander perished but the commissar stayed alive. In fact, the performer of the main role, Boris Andreyevich Babochkin, had the good fortune to live a long and fruitful life as actor and theatrical director after *Chapayev*, although the laurels of Chapai alone would have lasted him for centuries. Babochkin died in 1975, and the civil funeral rites were performed at the Moscow Maly Theater, one of the oldest Russian theaters, where Boris Andreyevich worked for the last twenty years. At the feet of the casket stood one-role actor Leonid Kmit—orderly Petka—who had grown older but remained loyal to his Chapai.

There is no exaggeration in saying that Babochkin played Chapayev with exquisite excellence. The actor's inspired absorption in his character was combined with filigree nuances, plastic expressiveness, and a sharp outline of the figure, with the truth manifested by the slightest change of the eyes. The hero's portrait was undeniably live, unique, and individual, but it was also a certain type of his time. Chapayev, with his daring and

The Youth of Maxim, *starring Boris Chirkov, shared the first prize with* Chapayev *at the 1935 International Film Festival in Moscow.*

cunning, his boundless bravery and certain inner defenselessness, his intelligence, naivety, and openness, his sparkling talent seen in everything he did, was a true national hero, a purely Russian character. And, as is always the case with genuine art, it was an international figure, understandable to other peoples.

The film was successfully shown and awarded the Grand Prix at the 1937 Paris Exhibition and, somewhat earlier, the Silver Cup at the 1935

International Film Festival held in Moscow, where the first prize went *in corpore* to films contributed by the Lenfilm studio (*Chapayev, The Youth of Maxim,* and *Peasants*).

During the Moscow festival, a representative cinema competition, which regrettably remained the only one in prewar time, *Chapayev* was screened next to the American film *Viva Villa!* directed by Jack Conway and written by the famous playwright Ben Hecht. The performance of the main role by Wallace Beery had earlier won him a gold medal at the 1934 Venice Festival, while the jury in Moscow made special note of the exceptional artistic merits of the film and of the protagonist's perform-ance. Since then *Chapayev* and *Viva Villa!,* made in the same year, 1934, have often been compared.

There is certainly much in common, despite all the differences between these two figures of popular leaders, great commanders who came from the midst of the people, from peasant stock: Pancho Villa operated during the Mexican revolution of the 1910s while Vasily Ivanovich Chapayev was one of the celebrated heroes of the civil war of 1918–1920 in Russia.

The characters of these two men, raised aloft by the revolutionary wave, two counterparts from different hemispheres of the world, display a mixture of human traits which bring forth both admiration and a smile. Both, in Chapayev's words, "went through no 'cademies" but instead went through the cruel school of social injustice, which qualified them to take up arms and wield the avenging sword at the head of troops. Pancho Villa, as played by Wallace Beery, is a big, strong man whose eyes are not only fierce but also sad and gentle, a child at heart, a selfless and naive soul. The brilliant Hollywood comic actor projects with subtle sympa-thetic humor the attractive traits, the touching ruggedness of his fearsome Pancho, his unexpected reactions to the actions of people surrounding him just as Babochkin does in his portrayal of his impetuous, volatile, and quick-tempered Chapayev. Both the performance of the two actors and the directing of the two films convey an irrepressible nostalgia for the talented leaders slain by the treachery of the strong and resourceful en-emies, men whose images have so much in common with the brigand chieftains of days gone by, the legendary noble robbers such as Robin Hood or Rinaldo Rinaldini.

Babochkin wrote later about his hero:

> His death became inevitable not because his daring bordered on reck-
> lessness . . . but because a new epoch was moving in, and Chapayev as a

Still of partisan commander and his orderly in battle became an emblem of the film Chapayev.

historical type, as a representative of a definite type or species of a social formation which incorporated the spontaneous revolutionary force of the people, had to go.[9]

Also doomed was Pancho Villa, an early forerunner of future leaders who would in the second half of the century head the national-liberation movements of the "third world," having properly graduated from military academies and universities.

Chapayev's freedom fighters were opposed in the film by a formidable and well-organized force. Colonel Borozdin, who headed the White camp, had everything: ability, personnel, weapons, intelligence, culture, conviction, even compassion, to the extent acceptable to him, to "small people," say, to his own batman, a Cossack, until the latter rebels. The counterrevolutionary camp was shown in *Chapayev* in a true and impartial manner, which helped the filmmakers get rid of the caricature and the deliberate grotesque which were customary in depicting the enemy. One of the most striking scenes in *Chapayev*, its culmination and dramatic peak, is the famous "psychic attack" launched by elite officer units of the White army.

Three black columns are approaching from afar, across the sun-scorched steppe, to the dry roll of drums. The White guardsmen are marching with easy, firm cadence. When one falls, the black file closes in mechanically, remaining straight and fearless. The columns are approaching the thin skirmish line of Chapayev's poorly clad riflemen, who are supported by a single machine gun handled by a young girl, Anna, who is short of ammunition. The odds are uneven, and the columns are marching on inexorably like death. Leading the first file is an arrogant and smart first lieutenant with a swagger stick and a smoking cigarette in his mouth as an extra token of intimidation and "psychic" shock. Georgi Vasilyev took upon himself this unforgettable episodic role. He is marching into the attack and smoking in defiance of the "scum" in front.

The "psychic attack" is always compared in Soviet cinema literature to the scene of shooting on the Odessa stairs from *The Battleship Potemkin*. Both scenes are indeed a culmination, and both carry the charge of an ideological and artistic concept. They are also similar compositionally, showing as they do the inexorable advance of mechanical punitive forces on warm and palpitating life. But one can also clearly see the difference due to a decade's distance between the two films.

The Odessa stairs scene in Eisenstein's picture consists of two hundred sequences, so the camera's viewing angle changes two hundred times. The tragedy of the peaceful and guiltless crowd perishing from the salvoes of the tsar's soldiers and the mechanical tread of the bayoneted ranks are seen through the eyes of the camera, an eyewitness of the events. The witness's eye was able, despite the emotional absorption of an observer, to spot and follow the movement of a child's pram into the abyss of the sea. The pram with an infant bumping down the steps of the stairs is a "detail" expressing the entire cruelty and injustice of what is going on, the supreme degree of drama exploding with the salvoes of the battleship's guns at the headquarters of the punitive forces and the metaphoric jump of the stone lions. The entire poetics of montage cinematography was reflected in that scene.

The "psychic attack," which holds the same place in *Chapayev,* is built from only fifty sequences, but each has a much more profound content because of the greater duration of shots and the fact that taking part in the conflict are characters, heroes, living people whom the spectators know well and whose feelings are shared. Lying in extreme tension in the skirmish line in wait for the approaching black columns are the orderly Petka, Furmanov, the lovable Anna, with a young round face and a jet-black plait (played by Varvara Myasnikova), and other of Chapayev's fighters. The camera looks at the advancing enemy through *their* eyes.

The "deadly cigarette" of the officer with a swagger stick becomes the focusing "detail" of the whole scene. The White officers' steady marching to the drums' beat is headed toward our heroes and also at us, for the viewing point has changed and is now identical with the eyes of the Red Army fighter. This attitude of a participant, rather than onlooker, forms a new degree of involvement in the action.

The spectator, who is also a participant in the fight, watches with a quaking heart as the enemy comes close and launches a bayonet assault while the cigarette is smoking, but then Anna's machine gun begins to chatter and the black ranks are broken, confused, and retreat in disorder.

But this is not yet the end of the fight. The machine gun chokes, for the desperate Anna has run out of ammunition, and White cavalry is stampeding towards Chapayev's skirmish line. It is then that a cavalry squadron led by saber-wielding Chapayev himself triumphantly floats from behind a hill in a cloud of dust to the jubilant cheers on our side—sequences which are both vigorous and beautiful.

While the psychic attack was historically true and concrete, it had more general significance in the context of the time when the film was made and released. Of this Georges Sadoul wrote:

> The same mechanical, geometrically arranged march of war was lyrically depicted also in 1934 by Leni Reifenstahl in a fascist film about the big parade in Nuremberg. The treat of an "immense psychic attack" looms over Europe. The episode from "Chapayev" revealed the danger implied by the Nuremberg "parades," opposing conscious man to man-machine.[10]

The comprehensive and meaningful character of the psychic attack is undeniable. But *Chapayev* also brings home the idea which originally inspired Dmitry Furmanov's novel and then the film of Vasilyev Brothers, namely, of "the Party's guiding role in the period of the Red Army establishment," as was stated in the director's application. It found expression in the Chapayev-Furmanov confrontation, in other words, a clash between spontaneous revolutionary fervor and the purposeful, organizing, and guiding will of the Party. Viewed in retrospect, many films made during the 1930s after *Chapayev,* even if externally quite different from it, reveal its direct influence and are even similar to it in structure.

The film *We Are from Kronstadt* directed by Yefim Dzigan to the script of the playwright Vsevolod Vishnevsky (1936), moved the basic dramaturgical situation of *Chapayev* from the sun-parched plains south of the Urals to the Baltic shores, from the eastern to the northwestern fronts of the civil war. The time was October 1919, when Petrograd was being defended from the troops of White General Yudenich.

We Are from Kronstadt did not project such composite and sculptured characters as did *Chapayev.* Its images, though drawn with precision, remained personages of a multifigure composition meant to be seen and to affect the spectator as a whole. It was rather a collective image, "we," as was stated in the title. One was attracted by the very fabric and atmosphere of the film: the autumn wind whipping the leaden waters; the deserted streets of a seaside town; the farewell party to the strains of a tiny military band and the sad, awkward dancing; the pale, gaunt children playing with a machine gun in place of a hobby horse—all this was very expressive. The tragic pathos of the execution on the steep high seashore was severely restrained: a file of doomed men under northern pines, the endless sea beneath them, the long sorrowful twang of the guitar of a killed seaman, and sailors' caps dancing on the waves. The severe world of the film *We Are from Kronstadt* fascinated and convinced the audience without loud words and speeches, for the picture proved richer and stronger than words.

In this sense Dzigan's picture continued the plastic tradition of Soviet silent cinema of the 1920s but replenished it with the expressiveness of sound: the film has a broad gamut of "sounds of life" which implements the manifesto of Eisenstein, Pudovkin, and Alexandrov advocating the counterpoint of sound and image as opposed to a naturalistic and idly talkative screen.

Although Alexander Dovzhenko's film *Shchors* was originally conceived as a Ukrainian *Chapayev,* its director, a unique artist, certainly could neither repeat the Vasilyev Brothers' picture nor imitate them. *Shchors* is rather a literary metaphor, which seems quite in place, for the figure of Nikolai Shchors, a legendary hero of the civil war who died on the battlefield at the age of twenty-four, stands next to Chapayev in the pantheon of the revolution.

From the point of view of artistic method (or, more exactly, form), the two films had more differences than common features. *Shchors* is firmly linked with Dovzhenko's first pictures (*Zvenigora, Arsenal,* and *Earth*), for

Two seamen are threatened with bayonets of the executors in scene from We Are
from Kronstadt.

"crazy Sashko," as some called the director (Sashko is a Ukrainian dimin-
utive for Alexander), remained true to himself. Compositionally the film
was built like an epic poem. It traces the route of Shchors' cavalry division
across the Ukraine enveloped in the flames of war and bleeding under the
heel of the interventionists and Petlyurovites. With bold strokes
Dovshenko paints pictures unfolding before the Red Army fighters,
which are tragic and comic, moving and funny, highly dramatic and
sparklingly merry: a peasant wedding with the colors and beauty of
Ukrainian folk rituals; a farewell party in a village; the burial of a commander, when the stretcher, raised high by fighters' hands, slowly floats
above the steppe, with horsemen dashing past in the background.

Episodes are not tied together by the plot but are "stringed" on Shchors'
route, from battle to battle—Chernigov, Semipolki, Kiev, other liberated
towns, villages, and hamlets; winter roads and the sultry Ukrainian summer; a poetic scene of daydreaming at night.

But for all these purely Dovzhenko poetics, the common theme of the
revolutionary-historical films of the 1930s is present here, detemining the
"duet" of the film's main characters—Shchors and Batko (father in

139

Ukrainian) Bozhenko. A handsome young man with fair hair, light eyes, and high forehead, intelligent and self-possessed, Shchors was played by the Russian actor Yevgeni Samoilov; next to him was an old Cossack and veteran fighter, Batko Bozhenko, who was played by the Ukrainian actor Ivan Skuratov in a colorful manner reminiscent at time of Wallace Beery's Pancho Villa. There is a scene where the wise, cunning Batko unabashedly walks onto the stage of the Kiev Opera House pulling a machine gun on a leash and begins his address to the townsfolk who fill the multi-tiered auditorium: "Bourgeois citizens and characters . . . ."

This man, who had seen a great deal during his long life, reveres young Shchors, who is fit to be his son. The image of Shchors clad in a smart leather jacket with a tight belt, wearing a service cap, with field glasses on his chest, has nothing in common with the free and easy heroes of the civil war. Shchors combines in his person a political commissar and a commander of the regular Red Army. The nostalgia for a powerful Cossack chieftain after the fashion of Gogol's Taras Bulba is given to Batko Bozhenko. Although both Shchors and Batko fell on the battlefield at almost the same time in 1919, on the screen a funeral procession carries away the old warrior while the young Shchors and his cavalry forge ahead into the future. In other words, the balance of forces here is the same as in *Chapayev:* spontaneous popular revolutionary fervor gives way to the strict, military discipline of the regular army. In this sense the romantic, impetuous, galloping Shchors of Alexander Dovzhenko is indeed a "Ukrainian Chapayev."

It was certainly a matter not only of highlighting the past and its lessons but of orienting the audience to the current tasks as well. It will be remembered that the code of socialist realism (and the workers in the arts of the 1930s were particularly anxious to observe it) included "the ability to view the past from the height of the lofty objectives of the future." The propaganda aims of the films in question were to present a new type of army with a view to a possibly close war, to enhance the Communist's prestige, and to affirm the Party's leading role in all spheres of Soviet life.

Although the "theme of homeland's defense" (s it was called then) came to the fore of the film repertory only at the end of the decade, it had found expression earlier. Back in 1932 the same Ukrainfilm studio in Kiev which would soon begin to shoot *Shchors* made a film entitled *Possibly Tomorrow,* in which fascists unleashed war against the Soviet Union and enemy planes bombed a city. In the final sequence a worker was directly appealing from the screen to the spectators to be ready for war, which would begin "possibly tomorrow."

That was in 1932. In 1939 *Shchors* was released together with films like *Air Squadron No. 5 (The War Begins), The Fourth Periscope,* and *If There Should Be War Tomorrow.* The work on the "defensive theme" gathered momentum after armed conflicts began on the eastern borders of the Soviet Union—the events on the Chinese Eastern Railroad and the fighting at Lake Khasan and the River Khalkhin Gol.

A mere three years after *Shchors* appeared on the screen, in the harsh days of the retreat of the Red Army, Pravda published the play *The Front* by Alexander Kornelchuk (August 1942). It leveled scathing criticism at a certain front commander, Gorlov, a routineer and relic of the civil war. He and his antediluvian notions were to blame for Soviet defeats and calamities at the outset of the war, said the play. The filming of *The Front* fell to the lot of the Brothers Vasilyev. True, the situation changed while the shooting was in progress, and the film saw the light in late 1943, after the battle of Stalingrad and the turn in the entire course of the war.

It is noteworthy that Boris Babochkin played not Ivan Gorlov, an aged Chapai transplanted into modern war, but his opponent, the progressive General Ognev. Gorlov on his part acquired the traits of a commander resembling Bozhenko from *Shchors* without the charm of the man.

The play and film *The Front* summed up and put an end to the history of relations between a romantically inclined commander and a commissar who gradually assumed commander's functions and emerged as a military leader of a new type. However, dramatic action based on the contraposition of these two characters would not leave the screen or the stage. Further on we shall meet with different variants of this contrasting opposition.

Going back to the mid–1930s, when these conceptual values so important for Soviet cinema, their combinations and structures were only taking shape, we shall see that the theme of a Party member who takes the lead was elaborated in historical revolutionary films not only on the material of the civil war and army affairs. The film *Baltic Deputy* offered a "civilian" and somewhat complicated way of this theme's presentation. The film was made by two young Leningrad directors, Alexander Zarkhi and Iosif Kheifits, who were destined to live a long and creative life in Soviet cinema, though their tandem would fall apart, as was the case with many directors who began to work together (after the war Zarkhi worked in

Baltic Deputy *was a visual embodiment of the alliance between science and a revolutionary nation.*

Moscow while Kheifits remained loyal to Leningrad, where he met with his first success).

Baltic Deputy reconstructed, although very freely, facts from the biography of the prominent Russian scientist Kliment Timiryazev, who welcomed the October Revolution. The hero was named Professor Polezhayev, and his role was played by the young comic actor Nikolai Cherkasov. Cherkasov's particularly popular character was the eccentric scientist Jacques Paganel in the film *Captain Grant's Children,* based on Jules Verne novel, which was released a few months before *Baltic Deputy.* Paganel's merry song to a vibrant melody by Isaak Dunayevsky, with its rousing refrain, was sung with gusto by old and young alike:

> Captain brave, captain brave, give a smile, sir,
> For a smile is like the flag of a ship.
> Captain brave, captain brave, cheer up, sir,
> For the sea surrenders only to the quick!

The spectators were glad to recognize a familiar Paganel in the revolutionary professor. The combination of the performer's youth and his eccentric acting manner with the role of an elderly white-haired biologist, a honorary member of foreign academies, a scholarly recluse, was highly effective; and the emotional impact of the "young old man" with darting, inquisitive eyes was very strong.

Nikolai Cherkasov eventually became a prominent Soviet film actor, creating the classical images of Tsarevich Alexei in *Peter the First,* Alexander Nevsky and Ivan the Terrible in Eisenstein's spectacles, Don Quixote, and other characters. Zarkhi and Kheifits (together and separately) would establish themselves as masters of the psychological actor's film. They were particularly successful in portraying characters taken from life and spotlighted with love and sympathy.

In *Baltic Deputy* a Russian intellectual came face to face with the October proletarian revolution. The customary approach, dating from the 1920s, would be to show the confusion in the professor's mind caused by the alternative "to accept or not to accept." But in the late 1930s the question of one's attitude to the revolution was considered as settled; whoever "did not accept" had long emigrated to all parts of the world, while those who stayed faced quite different problems. Although the action took place right after the October events of 1917, when a major part of the captial's academics sabotaged the new government, groped in perplexity, or took a waiting stand, Professor Polezhayev entered the film with a ready and positive attitude toward the revolution. Moping and reflection were out of fashion; but the point was that the scientist was nominated a deputy of the Soviet of Workers', Peasants', and Soldiers' Deputies by the sailors of the revolutionary Baltic fleet.

The very title of *Baltic Deputy* was highly topical in 1937 when the film was released and when the first nationwide election to the Supreme Soviet of the USSR was under way. Preparations for it under the sign of the unity of the working class, collective-farm peasantry, and working intelligentsia had assumed the dimensions of an immense campaign. Not by accident were the characters' positions in the film quite definite in political terms. Fighting for the professor's soul were his two disciples. A vicious counterrevolutionary philistine, an academic with a pince-nez who was shocked by everything—rancid herring, food rations, the patrols on the street—stood against a Bolshevik scientist, Bocharov, who had just returned from Siberian exile and who ardently supported the professor's revolutionary sentiments. The dramatic development was built on the obstruction to the scientist on the part of the counterrevolutionary academics on the one hand and the very genuine "romance" between Polezhayev and the Baltic seamen on the other.

One curious feature, common for the majority of films of that time, was that characters who were conceived as the concealed prime movers, not the objects of the drama, projected less brilliantly from the screen despite all the efforts of the directors and the actors. They were also inevitably less popular with the people, who loved and admired Chapayev with his loyal Petka but not Furmanov, the eccentric professor but not the all-knowing revolutionary student Bocharov, or the guitar-playing sailor but not the too correct, although likable, commissar Martynov from *We Are from Kronstadt*.

There was a very real danger of establishing on the screen a patently dull figure with correct but uninspiring words, a function, not a living character. Such figures, wearing leather jackets and workers' shirts, with strong faces and steel-gray eyes—proper and ideal, traveling from film to film under different names—had also gone through the mill of Soviet cinema. The obvious and urgent task was to create a hero Communist who would be as loved as Chapai or merry snub-nosed Petka.

Bolsheviks: From Maxim to Lenin

Creating a hero Communist was best accomplished by Grigori Kozintsev and Leonid Trauberg in three pictures they shot to their own screenplays: *The Youth of Maxim* (1935), *The Return of Maxim* (1937), and *The Vyborg Side* (1939). Maxim, the hero of this trilogy, played by Boris Chirkov, took his place among the popular favorites of the screen of the 1930s, opening, along with Chapayev, a gallery of Soviet "superstars."

This gallery also included the film heroines played by Lyubov Orlova and Marina Ladynina, the doctor Zhenya working in the Arctic, or collective farmer Grunya, whom the actress Tamara Makarova endowed with her northern but warm beauty.

To this day older people remember and love, and younger generations recognize, on television or in revival movie houses the immortal and always young Maxim. Where the action of the third film took place, the former workers' suburb once known as the Vyborg Side, the attractive cinema house "Maxim" now stands on what has become one of Leningrad's thoroughfares, Smirnov Avenue.

144

Boris Chirkov, Communist hero in The Return of Maxim, *was a popular favorite.*

Cinema is well known for its special ability to fuse and identify the image and the actor. The image and its maker are often blended together not only for a naive or aesthetically unprepared spectator but even for a more advanced audience. An artisitc image born of fantasy is then perceived as a real person, and its maker (the actor) is attributed the qualities of the character and its fate. This is in fact the basis of such cinema phenomena as the star system, star myths, their cliches, and so on.

In the Soviet cinema of the 1930s this effect of fusion of the character and the performer was invariably in favor of the character. The spectators' hearts went out not to Babochkin or Chirkov but always to Chapayev and Maxim, the film heroes.

During the preparations for the first election of the Supreme Soviet of the USSR, the residents of a remote Siberian village nominated Maxim, the film hero, as their candidate. After long wanderings the paper with their meeting's resolution finally reached the Lenfilm studio.

Boris Chirkov had more than once disappointed the people who addressed him in the street as the real Maxim by admitting he belonged to the actors' guild. In his autobiographical book, *The Deep Screen,* Grigori Kozintsev described the preview of *The Youth of Maxim* in the Kremlin by Stalin (with the directors present):

> A voice rose several times during the preview. I tried hard to make out the words and grasp their meaning. This was not easy, for sharp, sometimes indignant comments were mixed with approving ones. But the anger and praise had no relation to the quality of the film. Gradually I came to realize that Stalin was watching the film not as a pictured story but as real events, as things being done before his eyes. . . .[11]

It all began with the script *Bolshevik,* on which the directors had worked at the request of the management of the Leningrad Film Factory since 1931, tirelessly redrafting the text in order to make the hero's image as typical as possible.

The authors' drafts show that they sought to avoid the cliche of that same "correct" but dull, "gray-eyed" Bolshevik "in a peasant shirt." One version of the script, published in excerpts in the *Soviet Cinema* magazine in 1933, described the worker hero as "a skinny fellow with intelligent eyes, a sharp nose, and an unruly shock of hair," a bookish character, a proletarian intellectual. He had no name as yet. It was planned to give the role to Erast Garin, an actor of an eccentric trend and a disciple of Vsevolod Meyerhold (he played Khlestakov in the latter's *Inspector General*).

The image was obviously far fetched. In search of truth the filmmakers went through mountains of archive documents, memoirs, letters, and photographs. Reminiscences of old Bolsheviks and their biographies which were then being published became their text books. Still more important were personal testimonies and the directors' own observations.

Nor would they wish to slip into the morass of everyday life, into naturalistic prose. They were helped by what seemed a sudden but happy idea that the Bolshevik should look like a merry and brave hero of Russian folklore—Ivanushka from folk fairy tales or maybe Petrushka the cheat and mischief-maker. One more exciting historical reference point was Charles de Coster's Thyl Ulenspiegel, the joyful drummer of the revolution who will be young forever and who will travel all over the world, fighting for happiness and truth.

Thus was taking shape the enticing genre of revolutionary legend, a parable of a Bolshevik, which was original and absolutely new to cinema. Later on it would give much trouble to the critics and film scholars, who would be hard put to say what exactly it was: an urban story ("There lived in Saint Petersburg, beyond the Narva Gate, three friends . . . ," said the film's titles, suggesting a narrative style), or a heroic comedy, or a film epic in many parts, or. . . .

But for all its free associations, the trilogy is strictly true to the history of the revolution. *The Youth of Maxim* begins during the orgy of reaction after the 1905 revolution, a period of arrests and exile when the Bolshevik Party went deep underground. *The Return of Maxim* took place in 1914, on the eve of the world war. The events of *The Vyborg Side* unfolded in the first postrevolutionary days of 1917. Through these three stages of Russian history, which were squeezed into a decade, Kozintsev and Trauberg followed their hero, first, as a careless young worker, then as a leading Bolshevik organizer, and finally as a commissar of the Soviet government.

The place of action was the capital of the Russian Empire. What was it like in the early twentieth century? It was not like Pushkin's St. Petersburg of elegant palaces and cast-iron monuments; nor like Gogol's, with the spectral and deceptive lustre of Nevsky Prospekt; nor like Dostoyevsky's, with its sickly air and huge dismal bulks of houses; nor even like the St. Petersburg of Alexander Blok, with its "nooks and crannies dark and somber." The film directors sought the image of capitalist St. Petersburg, which they identified with imitation diamonds in shop windows and advertisements proclaiming with boastful clamor the Ara Pills to be the best in the world. They also sought the image of the proletarian city on the banks of the Neva. Their picture of a St. Petersburg's suburb was a combination of a village with kilomter-long workers' barracks, smoking chimneys, and freight trains crawling along factory branch lines.

They saw in their imagination twilight skies smeared with soot, beer houses, swearing, distant locomotive whistles, and the warble and scream of harmonicas. Hundreds of harmonica-players were auditioned in the search for the suitable folk tunes. When one of them sang the now famous "The blue ball's a'whirling," the directors felt they had found their hero's image. Thus came into being Maxim—No. 1 fellow of the Narva Gate, a loyal comrade, witty and merry, a dashing suitor, and an admirer of the fabulous robber Anton Krechet, the fearless giant from the dime novels of the Kopeck publishing house.

As good luck would have it (Maxim was in general a lucky character), the right actor was found as a result of last-minute replacement. Boris Chirkov, a young actor of the Young Spectator's Theater, was at first offered another, smaller part, that of Dyoma, Maxim's comrade. The shooting promptly showed him to be the real Maxim. He was of medium height with plain features, somewhat high cheekbones, and a turned-up nose. In short, he had an unprepossessing, common appearance. But a smile lit up and transformed this face; his intelligent, cunning eyes began to sparkle with fervor and daring and to express enthusiasm and warmth. Maxim's outstanding personality and charm paradoxically arose through the concentration of the commonplace, the mean arithmetic.

From the unusual and eccentric to the common and simple, but seen with fresh eyes, to Maxim's final portrait—such was also the story of Kozintsev and Trauberg themselves, former FEXes, who evolved from the search for extravagant phenomena and monsters of their early youth to the poetic vision of everyday life. It may be noted that this evolution is typical of the genuine talent which only begins from "Left" extremism and then discards it as a temporary stage for the sake of simplicity and depth. The artificial goes while the vision grows sharper.

Turning back to the fifty-year-old reel and trying once again to solve the riddle of its success, we find the answer in three mainstays of the authors' style: humor, lyricism, and tempo. Funny scenes, witty rejoinders, comical quid pro quos—the authors fearlessly include all this into the most serious and seemingly dramatic episodes. The scene of Maxim's first interrogation in the prison invariably proceeded amid the boisterous laughter of the audience.

In *The Return of Maxim* the main sideshow, the key "feature" of the action, was a duel at billiards in a pub between Maxim and shop attendant Platon Dymba, "the king of St. Petersburg's billiards," a merchant's flunkey and informer. The performer of this part and Chirkov's worthy partner was Mikhail Zharov, who had played the thief Zhigan in *Road to Life*. The contest at billiards, which "the king" lost, forcing him to crawl under the table in token of shameful defeat, was only a means of finding out which of the city's factories had received a military contract, for Maxim, now a professional revolutionary, was doing secret work, fulfilling important Party assignments. Even in *The Vyborg Side,* where the background was much more menacing (a conspiracy of the Whites, anarchists, the ravaging of wine stores), the filmmakers included a tragicomical situation: Maxim was appointed the commissar of the State Bank in spite of the fact that he had never much to do with money, let alone financial operations.

Thus the Maxim trilogy brought the action to the moment when a Bolshevik political commissar appeared on the screen. The spectator was already familiar with the hero's history, simple as life itself; he knew Maxim's favorite song and his sweetheart, the winsome, round-faced, easy to amuse Natasha. Valentina Kibardina was truly convincing in this role of an intellectual woman from the masses, a Bolshevik "enlightener" who managed to give workers lessons of class struggle in an innocuous Sunday school. Natasha's dramatic line, like that of Maxim's, was gaily tied into adventurist knots. Just like Maxim, resembling his folk pro-totypes of the daring Petrushka and the clever Ivanushka, who played the fool but could always outsmart the jailer or policeman, so was Natasha, according to the plot, the queen of risk. She went about freely under the sleuths' very noses with forged documents in the name of the governess of a prince, drove around in posh droshkies, and in her flat, that nest of conspiracy, received with a steaming samovar the portly local police inspector, who was overwhelmed by the cozy respectability in the modest rooms of the new tenant. The audience was delighted, particularly since witnesses' accounts of Bolsheviks' secret operations, which spread by word of mouth after the revolution, were also full of particulars of trickery, cunning, and clever play, such as the type of underground print-ing press hidden before the search in a milk jug or the leaflets smuggled across the border in an infant's pram. Thus legend fused with true history, anecdote with truth, and fantasy with the chronicle of events, building up original and purely Russian poetics of the trilogy about Maxim.

One curious point: Maxim had no surname. This seemed to emphasize the symbolic and generalized nature of the image, yet people believed in him as in a living, real man. This was true not only of the naive provincial electors who wished to make Maxim their deputy but also of the socially aware spectators who proposed in their letters to the Lenfilm Studio to have Maxim's screen life continued in a serial of more and more parts ("Maxim the economic executive," "Maxim at Lake Khasan," "Maxim's children"). The spectators wanted their favorite to keep marching along in life together with them.

This merging of film heroes with their real prototypes in the minds of the spectators was facilitated by the fact that shown on the screen were impersonations of historically authentic persons hand in hand and on equal terms with imagined characters, the former being interpreted in a free manner reminiscent of legend. In *The Vyborg Side,* for example, Lenin, Stalin, and Sverdlov appeared next to the main characters.

Yakov Sverdlov, shot by Sergei Yutkevich in 1940, was a film about one of the founders of the Soviet state which also showed Lenin, Stalin, Dzerzhinsky, and Gorky. Incidentally, it happened to be the only film from a whole series of reels about prominent Bolsheviks planned for shooting in 1938–1939 (such biographical films were to made about Dzerzhinsky, Kirov, Babushkin, and others). Later on, Soviet cinema and television would turn to these personages more than once, but at that time top priority in depicting real historical figures certainly went to Lenin. The central works of cinematography during the 1930s were Mikhail Romm's *Lenin in October* (1937) and *Lenin in 1918* (1939), and *The Man With a Gun,* by Sergei Yutkevich (1938).

It will be remembered that about thirty newsreels were shot during Lenin's time. This film material, supported by numerous Lenin photographs, recorded speeches, and painted and drawn portraits taken from life by Nikolai Andreyev, Natan Altman, and Isaak Brodsky, was quite representative.

In the film epics of the 1920s, in Eisenstein's *October* and Barnet's *Moscow in October,* and in crowd scenes, Lenin was impersonated by Nikandrov, a worker who phenomenally resembled Lenin. Later on, when the part of Lenin, as written by Alexei Kapler in his scripts (*Lenin in October* and *Lenin in 1918,* the latter being done together with T. Zlatogorova) for Mikhail Romm's films and by Nikolai Pogodin for Sergei Yutkevich's picture, grew in volume and complexity, it required a masterful actor. Two prominent performers deemed it a great honor to be the first to create the image of Lenin. Boris Shchukin, a disciple of Yevgeni Vakhtangov and the leading actor of Moscow's Vakhtangov Theater, who had earlier played several parts in sound films, was given the role in Romm's pictures. Yutkevich chose Maxim Shtraukh, who had played in *The Wise Man* and *Strike* of young Eisenstein and who was now an experienced theater and cinema actor.

The first performers of Lenin's role shared different fates. After completing his work on *Lenin in 1918,* Shchukin died from heart disease half a year after the film's first run. Shtraukh continued to play Lenin for many years in films directed by Yutkevich (*Stories About Lenin,* 1958, and *Lenin in Poland,* 1965).

Boris Shchukin in the role of Lenin caused a sensation. Here in Lenin *in 1918, he is in the study of the Kremlin.*

The first appearance of the "living Lenin" on the screen caused a rousing sensation. Spectators applauded and jumped to their feet whenever Shchukin in Lenin's make-up entered the frame with the gait and manner of speech characteristic of the leader. Both Shchukin and Shtraukh also played Lenin on the stage, with equally great success, during the jubilee first nights to mark the twentieth anniversary of the October revolution.

In the subsequent fifty years, many actors tried their skill in recreating Lenin's image in Soviet cinema and theater, including such prominent masters as Amvrosi Buchma, Konstantin Skorobogatov, Innokenti Smoktunovsky, Mikhail Ulyanov, Alexander Kalyagin, and Yuri Kayurov. But despite the masterful performances of some of these actors and because of the repetitious manner of others, the image gradually lost the jubilant brilliance and the joy of discovery which struck the audience in 1937. Probably only Shtraukh has succeeded in preserving and deepening the then discovered traits of "thoughtful Lenin," an image which took many long years to take shape.

The very first appearance of Lenin in the film *The Man With a Gun* pushed to the foreground the theme of Lenin the thinker. The moments of meditation, inner concentration, and self-absorption were the best parts of the role; some shots were like an animated portrait by Brodsky showing Lenin at the writing desk in his study. No less important for the actor was the episode in which Lenin meets soldier Ivan Shadrin, "the man with a gun," in the crowded corridors of the Smolny Institute. This meeting of the leader with a private soldier, the way Shtraukh played it, was not just a "human" episode but an impetus for Lenin's deliberation on the destiny of the masses, on the future. That was the director's idea, anyway.

Shchukin's interpretation was different. Shchukin created (especially in *Lenin in October*) the leader's image in revolutionary action, an image of great temperament and optimism. The director and the actor defined the action, or the kernel of the role as a whole, as "Lenin's irresistible will for the earliest implementation of an uprising." This was important because the scenes preceding the uprising showed Lenin in hiding (the leader's loyal "guardian," worker Vasily, concealed him from the police and sleuths of the Provisional Government), that is, forced to remain passive and wait. Shchukin and Romm managed to fill each scene with extreme tension.

On the other hand, the actor emphasized the leader's modesty, simplicity, and sense of humor—the human traits described in the memoirs of Lenin's friends and comrades-in-arms. Lenin as presented by Shchukin laughed heartily and infectiously and had a quick reaction and impatient movements and gestures. That man of medium height, no longer young (Lenin was 47 in 1917), was a live wire, a ball of youthful fire. The hour of his supreme triumph, the revolution, was approaching! The jubilant final sequences of the film show Lenin in the historic minutes when the great social transformation had taken place and the leader was finally in the epicenter of the popular storm. Here the inherent theme of revolution as a triumph is organically completed in multifigured mass compositions.

The general tone of Mikhail Romm's *Lenin in 1918* was different. Its action unfolded not in Petrograd, the "cradle of the revolution," but in Moscow where the Soviet government moved at the "critical" period of the new state (as Lenin described the summer months of that year).

Hunger, foreign intervention, rebellions in the countryside, treachery, conspiracies, and betrayals even in the very center of the revolution were the background of this film.

It was in this atmosphere of action, culminating in the extensive and painful scene of the attempt on Lenin's life by the terrorist Fanny Kaplan, that the image created by Boris Shchukin projected vigorous optimism. Each appearance of Lenin on the screen eased the tension. It was the same intelligent and cheerful man as in the first film who was confident of victory and could laugh heartily and joke. Shchukin epitomized in Lenin's image a man of action, a hero who clearly saw his purpose in life and was free of doubt, vacillation, or idle reflection. This interpretation vividly reflected the ideals, moods, and attitudes of the Soviet man of the 1930s, which were to a great extent instilled and cultivated by the cinema.

The somber background of the picture was by no means accidental, for in real life black clouds began to shroud the horizon. The combination of radiant, jubilant high spirits and a mounting alarm, an acute foreboding of danger next to the ironclad confidence in national strength, were a duality concealing the riddle, still probably unsolved, of the Soviet prewar years.

"When the country commands . . ."

Soviet history knows no other time when reality and cinematic art corresponded to each other as they did during the late 1930s.

"Life has become better, life has become merrier!" "Any one of us becomes a hero when the country commands!" The tunes of the composer Isaak Dunayevsky, the voice of the variety star Leonid Utesov, the living ornaments "woven" by sportsmen on Red Square, the heavy rumble of tanks during May Day parades, and the very mounting popularity of cinema created an atmosphere of a continual holiday. The time played up every feature of a happy, peaceful life, moving aside the memory of the past hardships.

Cinema created the mass Soviet song. This is a thoroughly original phenomenon, quite unlike the song hit of the West or a tune from a musical film.

Composer Isaak Dunayevsky, the song king of the 1930s, stated: "I am a singer of the Soviet success,"[12] which was true. He was the originator of the march song, the leading form of the Soviet mass song. Dunayevsky also pointed out that cinema did a great service in popularizing it.

153

The march song differed from the military march and from ordinary marching songs. It was distinguished by an entirely new texture of melody, which had an always joyful major tone, fast tempo, and vigorous rhythm. Probably this combination of mass, suprapersonal sentiments with a concrete film hero accounted for the special attraction of the Soviet mass song of the 1930s.

The best example is "The Song of Motherland" written by Dunayevsky to the lyrics of Vasili Lebedev-Kumach for the film *Circus* directed by Grigori Alexandrov (the greatest favorite of the time and also the greatest box-office success in the history of Soviet cinema), one of the most popular Soviet songs of all times. Before the war the song opened the programs of All-Union Radio, and its first line has remained Moscow's call-sign to this day. During the war years "The Song of Motherland" preceded the announcement of orders of the Supreme Commander in Chief. But this anthemlike song had another more personal and intimate aspect as the love theme of the film's heroes, Marion Dixon and Petrovich. The dazzling American circus actress Marion, played by Lyubov Orlova, the darling of Soviet cinema audiences, learned the song, amusingly mispronouncing Russian words. The heroes, a handsome and happy couple, sang this song as they marched in the front rank of a festive demonstration on Red Square.

Songs which were born by cinema half a century ago are still being sung by Soviet people regardless of the changing tastes and fashions. They now form the basic stock of Soviet musical folklore.

In August 1935 Alexei Stakhanov, a faceman at the Tsentralnaya Irmino mine in Donbas, set a staggering record of coal cutting. This event had a tremendous public response and started a whole movement of shock workers, the "Stakhanovite movement." In September of the same year the shock workers of the Ukraine and the Russian Federation called on cinema workers "to make films about heroic people of socialism."

The stars of the screen placed themselves at the service of the new, unheard-of "stars" in the ranks of labor. The Stakanovites' portraits were on the front pages of newspapers, schoolchildren studied figures of their achievements, pretty young weavers Yevdokiya and Maria Vinogradov were photographed together with Konstantin Stanislavsky at Barvikha sanatorium near Moscow, and children admired the exploits of the Tajik girl, Mamyakat Nakhangova, who introduced a new method of picking cotton with both hands.

This festive atmosphere, the aura of glory around labor heroes, popularized by newsreels and full-length documentaries, made special demands on feature films about contemporaries. To be sure, filmmakers had already made pictures about contemporary life, about people engaged in production or working at factories, mines, and collective farms. But now the latest news interfered with film production itself. For instance, Stakhanov's record brought about a change in both the plot and conflicts of the film *The Miners,* which Sergei Yutkevich was shooting in 1937. The screenplay, written by Alexei Kapler and entitled "The Gardener," initially deal with the improvements in a miners' settlement in the course of struggle for a "green Donbas" but was changed to make innovating miner Matvei Bobylev its main character

Stakhanov's exploit was central in Boris Barnet's film *A Night in September* (1939). One of its main scenes showed the miners marching to a night shift with the light of their lamps making strikingly bizarre designs of coal and soot against the white of the screen. The conflict in the film was based on class struggle: mine superintendent Poplavsky and his henchmen tried hard to foil the record (first they supplied rotten props, then even put dynamite into coal seams). Of course, the enemies were exposed and the People's Commissar of Heavy Industry, Sergo Ordjonikidze, came to the mine in order to support the initative of Stepan Kulagin (the main character). Even subtle and lyrical directing by Boris Barnet could not save the primitive script. Very promptly, that time shaped another cliche (previously the enemy was a capitalist or his hireling, a White officer, or a camouflaged "has been").

A similar conflict developed in the film *A Great Life* (Part I, 1939), written by Pavel Nilin. The cast included both the initiator of a new method of coal cutting and jolly, easy-going fellow, at first a scandalmonger and trouble maker, then a record-breaking hero. This character, called Khariton Baun, was played by Boris Andreyev, a gifted actor who was destined to rise to great heights in the war and postwar film repertory as the personification of Soviet man, a representative of the victorious people in pictures like *The Vow* and *The Fall of Berlin* directed by Mikhail Chiaureli. The Stakhanovite innovators in *A Great Life* were opposed by camouflaged enemies: saboteurs contrive a cave-in in the mine but are caught red-handed. The same old pattern was repeated. Thus, the figure of the enemy, saboteur, or wrecker rises on the screen next to that of a Stakhanovite, the "superstar" of labor, the "hero of our time."

Vera Maretskaya played a woman who became a collective farm chairwoman in Member of the Government.

Soviet cinematologists, the authors of the academic *History of Soviet Cinema,* give this aesthetic explanation to the typical conflict in most of the films of the 1930s which portrayed reality:

Cinematography fulfilling a direct social assignment, which read life "from the newspaper sheet," still wet with printer's ink, tried to respond to all ideological and political events of the time. An article in yesterday's newspaper, a reader's letter or court's records became a sort of an application for a screenplay. But there were also inherently aesthetic factors at work. Romantically oriented cinematography sought its motives in the arsenal of romantic consciousness. It shunned characters in which good and bad were intricately intertwined. Like all romantic art, it tended to the polarization of good and evil. An enemy, saboteur, wrecker, that is, an active villain corresponded better to such an orientation than a simpleton, an overcautious or ignorant person or a harebrained planner.

Looking back today and reviewing the extensive and varied film library of the 1930s, one realizes still more clearly why the people of that time were so fond of, and so ardently welcomed, laughter and joke, joy and optimism on the screen: they wanted to believe that all enemies would be defeated and that any citizen of the country could become a hero. The fates of invented contemporaries as shown on the screen were called upon to prove that.

Member of the Government seems a somewhat uninspiring title for a very moving film about the destiny of Alexandra Sokolova, a poor, downtrodden, "beaten by husband" farmhand, who became a collective-farm chairwoman and was later elected Deputy of the Supreme Soviet of the USSR. Actress Vera Maretskaya, who played the role in the film directed by Zarkhi and Kheifits, related that she found the key to the image from a meeting with distinguished women collective farmers: the women, illiterate and ignorant only a short while ago, who had just received government awards, "wept as they told the story of their past life, wept with happiness, with the awareness of their great importance for the country." And how many more women wept in the audience, sympathizing with Alexandra, admiring her stamina, and hoping that they would share her happy lot!

The heroic youthful films of Sergei Gerasimov, his joyful *The Brave Seven* and *Komsomolsk,* were permeated with the romance of distant travel, of the conquest of the Arctic and taiga, of formidable ice hummocks and turbulent rivers. These fresh and vivid pictures combined the director's orientation to "everyday heroism" with entirely "non-everyday" surroundings, and a precise and *detailed* vision (also categorically demanded by the director) with the ardent elation of struggle against the elements. Indeed, the neorealistic presentation of a Komsomol Arctic camp and of the faces of the young winterers at the beginning of *The Brave Seven* (1936) traditionally develops in the course of the action into the heroic romance:

Joyful film The Brave Seven *romanticized travel and conquest of the Arctic.*

the curing of a sick Chukchi collective farmer by the pretty doctor, Zhenya; the disappearance of the expedition leader and the radioman, who were proved to have been stalled by a blizzard and frostbitten but who, nevertheless, discovered a metal deposit; their rescue by Chukchis; and the happy termination of the wintering in spring.

In *Komsomolsk* (1938), the keen and accurate picturing of the city of youth construction in the taiga was regrettably spoiled by the banal "wrecker-saboteur" intrigue.

In his third film about working people, *The Teacher* (1939), Gerasimov produced an early version of "village prose" where the sufficiently detailed depiction of everyday life was not yet linked with the actual conflicts of collective-farm life and the motives and denouements were simplified. This triptych of films on contemporary subjects made by Sergei Gerasimov and his group of talented actors (Tamara Makarova, Boris Chirkov, Pyotr Aleynikov) opened up a distinct trend in Soviet cinema, a line to be followed for a half a century by Gerasimov himself, who displayed enviable loyalty to the principles then discovered.

And yet musical comedy was the greatest favorite with Soviet moviegoers in the late 1930s.

The term is, in fact, too general to characterize precisely the unique type of film which has no analogy anywhere else in the world of cinema. It would seem very simple to turn to the samples of Hollywood production, but the very first comparison (say, with *The Love Parade* by Ernst Lubitsch or with any other film starring Jeanette MacDonald or Maurice Chevalier) would reveal a profound intrinsic difference.

The point is that the American (as well as French or Austrian) musical film was a localized genre—entertainment first and foremost.

Soviet musical comedy, for all its gaiety and lightness, went beyond the confines of the genre; it claimed more than was commanded by the hierarchy of screen forms aspiring to present the truth of life. Even if it laid no such claim consciously through its authors and performers, it was *perceived,* was desired to be perceived, as the real truth. So it was received (just as in the case of historical-revolutionary films) not only by the most unsophisticated and naive audiences but even by professional film critics.

Thus one shall not find in the vast literature on Grigori Alexandrov's musical comedies an analysis of their entirely specific, integral, and open symbolism. They were, on the contrary, regarded quite seriously as realistic. This was not a mistake but rather a case of visual aberration when the screen and reality interlinked and interpenetrated in the minds of the contemporaries. In the same way, Ivan Pyryev's rural comedies were discussed in literature as absolutely realistic, true-to-life films: *The Rich Bride* was "about the life and work of young collective farmers"; *Tractor Drivers,* "about the fine exploits of the collective-farm youth"; *Cossacks of the Kuban,* "about the life of Kuban collective farmers." All this was in total neglect of a genre which could be named, after the manner of "musical comedy" (which has taken its place on the list of classic cinema genres), "collective-farm" comedy. Yes, a collective-farm film, with its distinct, declarative, and insistently impressive features derived directly from popular wood prints and the motifs of Russian folklore, formed on the screen a cinematic structure that had an unfailing effect on the audience. It was another myth of collective-farm prosperity.

Both Grigori Alexandrov and Ivan Pyryev hailed from Proletkult theater. The former was a colleague of Sergei Eisenstein and the co-author of the scripts of *October* and *The General Line,* and he accompanied Eisenstein on his trip to America. The latter also took part in the famous

A scene of a women's kolkhoz from The Rich Bride *by Ivan Pyryev promotes the myth of collective-farm prosperity.*

stage production of *The Wise Man,* where he and Alexandrov performed incredible somersaults and walked the tight rope in clowns' costumes. Despite the apparent departure from the historical-revolutionary, profoundly dramatic films of their teacher, these directors implemented Eisenstein's dream of the mass impact of cinematic art and brought to fruition (though, naturally, transformed in their own way) his experiments in the "art of millions."

Alexandrov's very first independent production, *Jolly Fellows* (1934), clearly showed that the director offered, even if only by way of active search, his own vision, rules, and methods of the Soviet comedy genre. The first version of the screenplay *Jazz Comedy,* written by Soviet satirists Vladimir Mass and Nikolai Erdman (the author of the plays *The Mandate* and *A Suicide*), resembled the internationally approved story of "the way to glory" only in general: adapted to Soviet standards, the hero, a new "jazz idol," is Kostya the shepherd, and the heroine is Anyuta, the pretty domestic servant. However, the entire system of characters, tricks, and eccentric numbers was a version of Eisenstein's "sideshow montage." The heroes' opponents were stupid Nepmen, the wicked beauty Lena, her mother the profiteer, and their monster guests.

In Alexandrov's next comedies, *Volga-Volga* and *Bright Road,* the story of "elevation," the "road to glory," was further localized in the spirit of the time: the heroine of the former was a provincial letter carrier and the author of a song who won a fight with a bureaucrat in charge of amateur theatricals and who persuaded him to lead a group of gifted amateurs to Moscow where, it turned out, all the people were already singing her song! *Bright Road* directly moved the Cinderella story to a textile town near Moscow. Cinderella's new name was Tanya Morozova, a peasant and then a weaver handling two hundred forty looms at once. The prince and the glass slipper were supplanted by inspired work: thanks to her industry, Tanya was invited to the Kremlin to receive the highest Soviet award, the Order of Lenin. Then she studied to become an engineer and was elected Deputy to the Supreme Soviet.

The leading role in all these and subsequent films of Grigori Alexandrov was played by his wife and beloved actress Lyubov Orlova. An actress of the Nemirovich-Danchenko Musical Theater with a special musical and choreographic education, Orlova would have been an ideal operetta performer had it not been for cinema. She made her debut in the film *Petersburg Night* by Roshal and Stroyeva, where she was admired for her excellent appearance, her original face with high cheekbones, and great, bright, slanting eyes. Curiously enough this "Cinderella," the domestic servant and proletarian of the screen, hailed from one of the oldest and most distinguished Russian families, the Orlovs, who were distantly related to the Counts Tolstoi. A photograph of Leo Tolstoi taken in Yasnaya Polyana shows the author of *War and Peace* with a pretty little girl on his knee, the future star of the Soviet screen. Well educated, disciplined, and industrious, Lyubov Orlova worked in the theater till an advanced age and died in 1975. Admirers from all over the country keep coming to her grave at Novodevichye Cemetery in Moscow. Grigori Alexandrov outlived his Lyubov (love, in Russian) just long enough to make the feature-documentary film *Lyubov Orlova.*

Alexandrov had the rare gift of spotting what was new, beautiful, and yet unfamiliar in life and presenting it as typical and common. He was able

Heroine of Volga-Volga, *played by Lyubov Orlova, is a provincial letter carrier.*

to attribute permanency to a holiday and to make weekdays festively colorful. Film workers still remember that while making *Circus* the director managed to shoot one scene on the roof of the Moscow Hotel, which was still under construction. When the film was released, the spectators were amazed to see its characters sit in a cafe on the rooftop and stroll around the hotel.

After the war Alexandrov directed the film *Spring* (1947), which had a modernized "twins" plot. Orlova played both scientist Nikitina and actress Shatrova, who in turn played Nikitina, and the action was built on numerous amusing substitutions, as befitted a picture about twins. As was usual with Alexandrov the action unfolded in luxurious interiors of the style which was later labeled "embellishment." The film was severely though belatedly criticized: "Do Soviet scientists live in such sumptuous mansions and villas?" All reproaches were futile. In a world without war, where white sailing boats cruised along the River Moskva at night while lovers strolled hand-in-hand along the embankments, dressed in evening gowns and tailcoats, in that cine-world scientists do and must live in villas with rambling roses.

Ivan Pyryev's collective-farm films hyperbolized the features of prosperity and happiness of Soviet life. The director did not conceal this exaggerated symbolism in the spirit of popular wood prints, amateur painting, and other forms of folk art. So in his films a water melon weighs not less than twenty kilograms, wheat stalks bend under the burden of heavy ears, grain fields are without bounds, the sky is endlessly high, and the teeth of the smiling lads and girls are dazzlingly white. The plot was usually based on a triangle. In the *Rich Bride,* a girl was vied for by two aspirants—one an excellent, perfect fellow; and other a funny, stupid but persevering character. The heroine, called the "rich bride," was not a daughter of a wealthy kulak or of a landlord but was a foremost collective farmer herself, rich with her plentiful workdays and government awards. Pyryev gave this role to Marina Ladynina, who projected a lyrical-comical image, a mixture between the soubrette and character parts: a short of stature, vigorous, and funny tow-haired girl with saucer blue eyes and a turned-up nose. She was always surrounded by a bevy of pretty girls. The fellows also came in a crowd, which followed the collective farm's leading gallant, Klim Yarko, who just returned from the army service (played by actor Nikolai Kryuchkov). In *Swineherd and Shepherd,* which was released during the war but which totally retained the prewar spirit, Kryuchkov was relegated to the role of the laughable rival Kuzma, the leading gallant being a handsome dashing mountaineer from the Caucasus in a black felt cloak and a tall fur hat sitting astride a prancing horse, with snow-clad mountains in the background, obviously also originating from an imitation oleograph or a colorful homemade carpet.

The music of Isask Dunayevsky, which invariably accompanied Alex-

Lyubov Orlova (center), most famous Soviet star of the 30s, is American artist Marion Dickson in Circus.

androv's films, with Ivan Pyryev assumed the collective-farm tone in comic ditties and a broad folk sweep in marches and solemn songs, as also did the Pokrass brothers' music in *Tractor Drivers* and that of Tikhon Khrennikov in *Swineherd and Shepherd*. The uniform musical style was, to repeat Dunayevsky's apt expression, "the style of Soviet success."

The sphere of action of Soviet cinema grew immeasurably during the 1930s. The government constantly gave attention to various questions of cinematography, which continued, as in the 1920s, to be discussed by Party congresses and which were reflected in top-level resolutions. For instance, the resolution of the Seventeenth Party Congress on the new five-year plan provided for increasing the Soviet cinema network to 70,000 projectors in 1938. The number of sound projectors grew from 498 in 1934 to 15,202 in 1939, the year of the Eighteenth Communist Party Congress. It is important to note that the cinema acquired sound only on

Marina Ladynina dresses in bridal costume of girl-swineherd Glasha Novikova in Swineherd and Shepherd.

the threshold of the 1930s and that most old cinema houses still ran silent films. It should also be pointed out that film import dropped to a minimum during that decade. The days of the cinema dumping of the twenties were over. Only the best films were imported from the United States, France, and Britain, including the masterpieces of John Ford, Rene Clair, and Alexander Korda. Soviet cinema employed only its own production facilities and material. The "old timers" still like to recall this golden age of the Goskino at their meetings and conferences.

In the spring of 1941 a wave of ceremonial meetings and sumptuous festive banquets marked an event of great importance, the award in March of the Stalin prize to most of the leading Soviet filmmakers. Then life began to settle into its routine pace. Shooting teams were preparing for summer expeditions.

But on June 22, 1941, Nazi Germany attacked the Soviet Union.

CHAPTER FOUR

All for the Front! All for Victory!

At the Price of One's Life

*D*uring July and August 1941, Soviet cinematography went through rapid military mobilization.

"All for the front, all for victory!"—the slogan that welded together millions and became the law of every individual existence—was inscribed on the filmmakers' banner from the first days of the war, literally and without rhetoric.

The Unknown War was the title given in the United States to a documentary epic of twenty parts, which included hundreds and thousands of feet of film shot by Soviet frontline cameramen. This gigantic picture was made in the late 1970s by a large group of film workers at the Central Studio of Documentary Films headed by Roman Karmen. Off-stage and on-stage commentary is by Burt Lancaster, who visited the key memorial places in the Soviet Union. In the USSR the film epic is known as *The Great Patriotic*.

Among those working on the "Partisans" episode of The Great Patriotic *are Burt Lancaster (third from left), Roman Karmen (second from right), and producer Vasily Katanyan (second from left) in the Museum of the Soviet Army.*

The appellation "unknown war," addressed to the American youth, certainly conveys challenge, bitterness, and reproach, for one wants to believe that every school pupil of the second half of the twentieth century should have read or heard about the Second World War and the incredible sacrifices and hardships that fell to the lot of the Soviet people who made a decisive contribution to the defeat of fascism.

In the USSR the words "unknown war" sound ridiculous even today, some forty years after, to a person of any age. This war was too well known. It stood on the threshold of every home. It is hard to find a family who does not mourn its relatives and dear ones who were killed at the front or who died during the siege of Leningrad. Although the third postwar generation is rising now and everything that was destroyed by bombs and shells has long been rebuilt, the unseen wounds of that war will never be healed.

In 1986 a very unusual film was produced at the Central Studio of Documentary Films by Alexander Ivankin (scriptwriter Lev Roshal). Its title, *The Trumpet Solo,* repeated the name of the famous segment from the march from *Aida,* which also was used as a leitmotif in the picture. The film documents the story of Lev Fedotov, a twenty-year-old Red Army private, who was killed in action in 1943 during a battle fought near the city of Tula. Only two or three snapshops from his childhood and several relics are all that remained of him. The most interesting is that the boy's diary of 1941 where he, then a secondary school graduate, predicted with a striking precision the date of the beginning of the war against the Soviet Union, its course, including surrender of Kiev and Odessa, the failure of the Nazis' plans to encircle Moscow and to strangle Leningrad by siege, and the time of the storming of Berlin. There remained also a collection of minerals classified by the boy, a score of *Aida* (his favorite opera) put down by ear as he had no musical education, and various drawings and sketches. This young man was exceptionally gifted.

Lev Fedotov's mother, now 93, tells about her son from the screen. Hers was also a life full of events and adventures. She met her future husband in New York, where she had worked as a dressmaker after leaving prerevolutionary Russia to earn her living. Lev's father was then a political emigre, a Bolshevik in hiding. They returned home in October 1917, called by the revolution. Her husband died long ago and she has been mourning her son for more than forty years, but she is still living. And how many more such mothers, widows, and orphans watch every

May 9 with tears in their eyes as the fireworks mark the Victory Day? So, was it really the unknown war? Certainly not! It will always remain for the Soviets the "Great Patriotic," a sacred war of liberation.

Film workers fully shared the trials of the war with the people, above all with the fighting army. This was first of all true of frontline news cameramen. By early August 1941 eighty film directors and cameramen joined the army in the field, plunging into the thick of battle. *Next to the Soldier* is the title of the war memoirs of the well-known Soviet documentary cameraman Vladislav Mikosha, which would be appropriate as the heading for several other books about the war covered by news cameramen. This title is neither a metaphor nor exaggeration. Vladislav Mikosha, who carried his camera with him from the first to last day of the war, in 1941 filmed the defense of Sevastopol and the retreat across the Sivash, near the Crimean Isthumus, as well as Arkhangelsk in flames after Nazis air raids. In 1942 he took part in military convoys plying between America and Britain and shot the ruins of London bombed by the Luftwaffe. Then came the storming of Kerch, the liberation of the Crimea, the triumphal march from Bucharest to Sofia to Warsaw, the spring days of 1945 on the Oder River. These are only a few pages of the frontline biography of one documentalist. Altogether, two hundred fifty news cameramen marched next to the soldiers along the deadly roads of the war. This is not a very high figure for the four years of fighting on fronts of enormous lengths. "Six or eight million men are fighting there, on the immense Russian front. This is the greatest front of struggle ever seen by the world," Thomas Mann, who emigrated to America, wrote in 1942.

These people, armed only with a camera, shot more than three million meters of film. Every fifth cameramen fell on the battlefield.

. . . Maria Sukhova was hit with a fragment from a German mortar shell while she worked in a forest held by partisans. Before she died she managed to whisper where the material she had shot was concealed; she was a very young girl with joyful Russian face and smoothly combed light hair under a garrison cap.

. . . Semyon Stoyanovsky died in Vienna while shooting the forcing of the Danube-Tisza Canal. When he was hauled from under the debris, mortally wounded with an arm shot through, he was still clutching his camera and whispering: "Camera, save the camera . . . don't spoil the film."

. . . Vladimir Sushchinsky shot his many newsreels on the Volkhov

River, near Leningrad, in the Crimea, the Carpathians, Poland. He wrote home in July 1942: "I have found an upright piano and also a grand piano in abandoned houses not far away and sometimes I play Chopin's preludes and Strauss's waltzes there. The instruments are badly out of tune, but still one can play. . . ."

He was killed in the battle for Breslau. When his film was developed after his death it showed fighting ending in an explosion: the man had filmed his own death. The can with the film was sent to Moscow by Sushchinsky's friend, cameraman Nikolai Bykov, who apologized: "I couldn't film him on the battlefield, as I was wounded by the same shell."[1] Bykov was also killed a few days later.

In 1945 M. Slavinskaya made Suschinsky's material into a film *A Cameraman at the Front—Vladimir Sushchinsky.* The shots had been made in extremely difficult conditions with great professional skill. They also portrayed a person of great courage who continued to film till the last moment of his life. This is more than a film about Sushchinsky; it is a monument to all those who did not live to see the victory.

All film studios of the USSR and Moscow's Cinema house have memorial plaques on which the names of frontline cameramen who fell during the war are inscribed in letters of gold.

Cannons and Muses

"When cannons talk the muses are silent" is a well-known maxim.

However, everything was done from the very first days of the war not to let the muses fall silent. Teams of performers were formed to give concerts for the army men in the field. Seven hundred such companies were formed in Moscow alone when the frontline was an hour's drive from the capital.

A stage was improvised inside a cramped dugout, on the deck of a battle-ready ship, or on an airfield with its constantly roaring engines. In the latter case the audience settled on the wings of planes ready for action. During a concert some of the spectators flew away and others returned from combat.

During their trips from one unit to another, the performers were bombed by enemy aircraft, and concerts were often interrupted by the call to arms. "At times the enemy could also hear our concerts, so close to the forward edge of fighting we performed," recalled Leonid Utesov.[2]

171

But it was impossible, of course, to arrange concerts for the entire army or for all hospitals. It was then decided to make *Film Concert for the Front* to be shown to as many units as possible.

The best singers of the Bolshoi, variety masters, the famed performer of Russian folk songs, Lidia Ruslanova, and others took part in this cinematic performance. In between the numbers, a frontline projectionist, played by the popular comic actor Arkadi Raikin, drove from unit to unit with film cans, ran films, and urged the soldiers to strike the harder at the enemy. The numbers showed performance of the concert participants in frontline units.

On May days in present time, when victory is celebrated each year, the *Film Concert for the Front* and other wartime reels are rerun on television. They are a profoundly stirring testimony to the vitalizing power of art which gave joy and vigor to people who were probably only a few steps away from death. Here is an excerpt describing the *Film Concert:*

> . . . the Leningrad Front. The variety star Klavdia Shulzhenko is singing "The Blue Kerchief" with tears in her eyes. For many years afterwards Klavdia Ivanovna and other singers sang this simple and moving song which was then as popular as "Katyusha," the favorite of all continents. But the film caught the unique moments of singing before an amphitheater of soldiers to the accompaniment of artillery, under the mortally dangerous cover of a white summer night, from which German Messerschmitt fighters could strike at any moment.

These frames recording the combat life of one of the most peaceful professions, that of an artist, are also incorporated in the heroic chronicle of the Great Patriotic War.

This chronicle is priceless not only as a vivid and irrefutable collection of historical documents and a record of the bloody battles which brought nearer the collapse of fascism but also as a testimony to maturing people's spirit and to the growing self-awareness of the art of cinema itself.

The Main Thing Is the Document, the Truth

The first response of art to the events of June 1941 was to a great extent immature; it followed the prewar pattern. Although the sunny Sunday morning of June 22 drew a fateful line that divided the country's life into

Eisenstein's sketch for historical Ivan the Terrible, *dated March 12, 1942, is here published for the first time.*

two epochs, the Nazi aggression was absolutely unexpected by millions of peaceful people and the first onrush of Nazi armies was strikingly fast. Therefore, the real scale of the calamity that had struck Russia was still unclear to workers in the arts, and the ardent desire to help the people through artistic means was not yet reinforced by the knowledge of truth about the war.

In those days, Moscow and Leningrad, the country's main cinema centers, had not yet lived the life of frontier cities. Food was still unrationed, practice alarms were conducted, and residents stood watch at night in house entrances. But a month after the war started, on the night of July 21, the Nazi air force showered the capital with high-explosive bombs. The Vakhtangov Theater, one of the country's best, located on the ancient Moscow street of Arbat, was ruined by a direct hit. The three talented actors who were on duty that night were killed.

The quickest way of contributing to the nationwide struggle against the enemy was for cinema workers to make short films with topical plots. They began to shoot such pictures in the very first months of the war.

The scenery was poor, the properties were hastily handmade, the crowd scenes were very small, but the task was urgent and clear: to glorify the people's exploits at the front and to inflame wrath and hatred of the enemy. Political topicality and ideological thrust were primary requirements of any cinematic production.

Thus came into being the *Fighting Films Albums* which carried the motto: "The enemy will be defeated, victory will be ours!" They consisted of several short stories—a screen version of a combat episode reported by the Soviet Information Bureau or described by a writer, a documentary sketch, a satirical scene, or simply a concert item, such as the recital of a piece of prose or poetry on a war subject.

In the autumn of 1941 the Mosfilm and Lenfilm studios were evacuated to faraway Kazakhstan. Camera rooms were hastily fitted out at the local film studio which was under construction in Alma Ata, capital of Kazakhstan; the Central United Studio of Feature Films was launched within three months. Thus the city near the spurs of the Ala Tau Range became for several years the cinema center of the Soviet Union. Ukrainian filmmakers and the Kiev Film Studio settled in Ashkhabad, next to the Kara Kum Desert. Some cinema workers were evacuated from the European part of the country to Tashkent, capital of Uzbekistan. There they established a small Film Actor's Theater which served military hospitals. They gave four or five performances a day in different parts of the city. Patients were brought to the concert hall on their beds, in wheelchairs, and in chairs. Sometimes the actors performed in wards from which the wounded could not be moved.

The good initiative outlasted the war, and the Film Actor's Theater continues to function in Moscow to this day.

Fighting Film Albums continued to be made for some time, but the hastily made scripts of the short films shot so far away from the war theater were plainly naive. Scenery was set, for instance, in a camera room of the Alma Ata studio, five thousand kilometers away from the supposed place of action, an imaginary European country occupied by the Nazis.

Young underground fighters in oilskin raincoats ran along narrow streets between houses with tiled roofs; they were hidden from the pursuing German soldiers in attics by gaunt women with sad, sunken eyes, and in the end all vigorously rose against the invaders. Real calamities were supplanted by adventures with a happy outcome. In Nazi-occupied villages shown on the screen, peasants disarmed enemy soldiers while boys and girls easily fooled the stupid Nazis.

Sergei Eisenstein wrote later: "From the very first days of the war a flood of short films, more passionate than well planned, more catching than well thought out, flew against the enemy as tracer bullets against enemy bombers . . . ."[3]

The *Fighting Film Albums* in effect reflected the attitudes typical of the first war months, or, more exactly, of the whole prewar atmosphere of the late 1930s. They combined illusions concerning a speedy end of the war, high patriotism, the indomitable will to win, and a sincere and ardent desire to stand together with the fighters. But life destroyed the naive schemes. Newsreels showing real battlefields killed the symbolic plots. The production of *Fighting Film Albums* (a total of 12 were made) ended in the middle of 1942.

Artistic comprehension of the new material of life, which is always difficult, is particularly hard during the grim times of war.

A glaring gap formed between the tragic truth of the war with its heavy fighting, killed and wounded, burned villages and ruined towns and the artificiality of the screen.

At first, even screen reporters were overawed and perplexed by the ugliness of truth. Vladislav Mikosha, a man of great personal courage and will, recalled:

> The world seemed to be collapsing. It could not, absolutely could not exist after the nightmares it had gone through. Thus came the sense of void; this was during the first hours. Then came fury, strength and hatred; but that was later. At the moment there was mistrust in the reality of what happened. In fact, I did not shoot all this for a very long time. I could not shoot the monstrous and senseless death of a man, the amazing power of everything living, even if maimed, or half-dead. I could not shoot the sufferings of people with which the future peace was bought. Why? We were firmly convinced that we ought to film heroism, and heroism, as everybody believed, had nothing to do with suffering. It was much later that I have realized that heroism is the overcoming of fear, suffering, pain

In newsreel still of battle of Kursk, 1943, German's pose and destroyed weapon are symbolic.

and impotence, the overcoming of circumstances, the overcoming of oneself.[4]

The first reports and short documentary episodes shot for newsreels were followed by films covering whole military operations and battles. The film of *The Defeat of the German Armies Near Moscow* marked a turning point in Soviet military documentary filming. The Academy of Motion Picture Arts and Sciences of the United States judged that film as the best work of 1942.

It described the offensive operation of the Soviet troops near Moscow in December 1941 January 1942, which countered the Nazi plan of surround-rounding and capturing the Soviet capital. Hitler is known to have counted on outflanking the Soviet capital. Hitler is known to have counted on outflanking the Soviet front and emerging in the rear of the Soviet troops. The plan further provided for flooding Moscow and turning the beautiful ancient city, a center of Russian culture, into a lake.

On December 6 the Soviet troops launched a successful offensive. They inflicted the first defeat on the previously invincible German army. the "blitzkrieg" idea thus exploded. The film *The Defeat of the German Armies Near Moscow* helped the world to learn the truth about the great battle.

The first liberated towns and villages and defeated Nazi divisions seen on the screen gave people hope and courage. Highly impressive were the shots showing the traditional military parade held on Red Square on November 7, 1941. The parade was not canceled, although the enemy stood at the near approaches to Moscow, where all windows were blacked out and many streets were barricaded with antitank obstacles and de-fended with barrage balloons in the air and antiaircraft guns on housetops.

During the parade, columns of armed soldiers marched with steady cadence past the mausoleum of Lenin in Red Square and dissolved in a snowstorm on their way straight to the front. Foreign correspondents saw in this march the image of "mysterious Russia" with its indomitable spirit.

The value of the film was not only in the showing of the Soviet first major victory but also in the revelation for the first time to the whole world of the ugly visage of fascism. The camera showed charred bodies of war prisioners, tortured and dead partisans, burning houses, gallows in Volokolamsk, the gaping windows of the New Jerusalem church, the ravaged museum-house of Leo Tolstoi in Yasnaya Polyana, and the half-burned house of Tchaikovsky in Klin, where the room in which the composer used to work was turned by the Nazis into a workshop for repairing motorcycles.

The film was made by directors Leonid Varlamov and Ilya Kopalin out of material shot by more than fifteen frontline cameramen. They worked under falling shells in 30-degree-below-zero weather. Thick snow filled their felt boots, got under sheepskin coats, and blinded camera lenses. Hands and face froze, and so did the camera movement; before an operator could begin to shoot he had to warm up the camera on his chest under his sheepskin.

Leading directors of feature films—Alexander Dovzhenko, Sergei Yutkevich, Yuli Raizman—also worked on documentaries during the war. The *Fight for the Soviet Ukraine* and *France Liberated* were full-length documentaries remarkable not only for their highly effective material but also for the mastery of montage, the directors' temperaments, and the precision of the artistic concept. Each of these grand films, which were in effect combination feature-documentaries continuing Dziga Vertov's traditions, portrayed a specific historical stage of the war. The film *The Defeat of the German Armies Near Moscow* recorded the first major rebuff suffered by fascism in the war, while Yuli Raizman's *Berlin* showed its final collapse.

During this concluding operation of the Soviet troops, the director and the shooting team were at the front, advancing to the Reich's capital with the Fifth Strike Army of the First Byelorussian Front. Each evening the film workers toured the forward edge of the offensive. Photographs made by newspaper correspondents show Raizman and his colleagues amidst Berlin's burning suburbs and next to the Brandenburg Gate. On April 30, 1945, cameraman Ivan Panov, scrambling his way toward the Reichstag with his orderly carrying a submachine gun, managed to shoot from a window of a four-story house on the left bank of the Spree the last minutes of the former German parliament with its bullet-ridden walls, smoke billowing from inside, and the remains of its stone columns. When the troops stormed the building, cameraman Ivan Panov was ready with his camera and entered the building under a hail of bullets with the attackers. In a few moments the red banner of victory was hoisted over the dome of the Reichstag.

This immersion in the very midst of events resulted in striking veracity and charged the film sequences with special color and vigor. The film *Berlin,* with all its documentality, is impressive with its mounting dynam-

Berlin, May 1945, by Yuli Raizman, showed the collapse of fascism, here in a scene at the Reichstag.

ics. Though the storming of Berlin began in darkness, the cameramen managed to catch close-ups of soldiers silhouetted by the flare of the shooting guns. Thus the general view of the mammoth artillery preparation by 22,000 guns came to include shots of some particulars of the artillery strike and of its participants. By and by, the tone of the film grew lighter and then the frame was filled with sunshine.

But besides the priceless value of these shots for the film chronicle of the Second World War, the more important and profound aim of the reel was the impact of the comprehension of Nazism's collapse and of the inevitability of the Soviet victory.

The film *Berlin* could be subtitled "Victory Suite" in keeping with the emotional counterpoint underlying the montage.

There is no need to repeat in the narrator's text or to express in the subtitles the biblical words "All they that take the sword shall perish with the sword"; this is plainly implied by the shots of the picture, such as the view of the Unter den Linden, Berlin's main thoroughfare, which has lost not only its lindens but even its pavement, ripped up and ploughed by shells and tank tracks, and which is lined on both sides with six-story houses flaming like torches, which look very much like the torches the Führer was greeted with, only magnified a thousand times. Or take other shots which convey the disgrace of defeat without any commentary: Berlin residents lining up at a Soviet field kitchen, a long line of emaciated people who had scrambled out of cellars and bomb shelters with mess tins and pots in their hands. The Führer promised them the whole world, and what they now get is a ladleful of gruel from the victorious soldier. Or there is the Soviet traffic controller at the Brandenburg Gate, the smiling, beautiful, young Raechka, who was made famous by the film. She seems to be dancing merrily as she turns to point the way to vehicles and marchers with her little flags. She grants an interview as a real "star" and is fully entitled to it. And a vast Reichstag stone column, scratched by shell fragments, bears the inscription: "We defended Odessa and Stalingrad and have come to Berlin. . . ."

At the sun-flooded, windblown airfield, where representatives of the Supreme Command of the Allied Troops met on May 8, 1945, planes are landing one after another. In attendance are Air Chief Marshal of Great Britain Arthur William Tedder, Commander of the US Strategic Air Force General Carl Spaatz, Commander-in-Chief of the French Army General Jean de Lattre de Tassigny—how young, smart, and full of joy these fine men look! What inner light illuminates the stern face of the Marshal of the Soviet Union Georgi Zhukov! The motorcade drives through the fallen, ruined Berlin to the Karlshorst suburb.

These "official" shots recorded moments of world-historic significance. Within the allotted strict limits, the cameramen managed to convey the general view and atmosphere of the event, the finest, accurately noted individual and psychological details, and the emotionally charged attitudes and moves of the participants:

. . . the solemn and sad (for the sacrifices made for the victory by his country are innumerable) expression of Marshal Zhukov, who opened the signing ceremony of the German Act of Surrender;

. . . the black gloves on the hands of Field Marshal Keitel; only one glove was removed for a minute to sign the surrender; Berlin was burning; the corpse of Adolf Hitler was left to lie no one knows where; but not a single muscle twitched on the face, and the hands were in gloves;

. . . the hawklike hatred-exuding profile of Nazi Colonel-General Stumpf;

180

The signing of the act of unconditional surrender was filmed on May 8, 1945.

. . . the dignified faces of the top Allied military leaders, close-ups of the generals, as if framed by the state flags of the USSR, USA, Great Britain, and France, over the long victors' table.

But the Soviet people and their cinema art had to traverse a long and thorny path before they came to this day in May 1945.

Countless Sacrifices of the People

Soviet writer Leonid Leonov said: "It is hard to delete in the logical chain—war-sorrow-suffering-hatred-vengeance-victory—the big word which is suffering."[5]

Most of the films of the first war years were devoted to the suffering and hardship of people who remained in the enemy's rear or lived on Nazi-occupied territory.

Within six months, director Ivan Pyryev shot at the Alma Ata studio the first full-length feature, *Secretary of the District Committee,* about partisan struggle led by a prominent Party worker.

Most impressive in the picture are the opening scenes of the town's evacuation: crumbling buildings, the flares of nearby fighting, refugees carrying bundles on their shoulders or pushing handcarts with their belongings.

181

But the notions of the partisan struggle still lacked substance. The fancily woven plot included pursuits, disguises, a spy with whom the heroine suddenly and fatefully fell in love, and the miraculous escape of the hero—everything that was so well known from adventure reels.

Scriptwriter Alexei Kapler and film director Fridrikh Ermler, amazed by the searing truth of *The Defeat of the German Armies Near Moscow,* wrote a long article about it and proceeded to make their own film, *She Defends Her Country.* Documentary films served as a tuning fork which set the tone for feature production.

Kapler had spent several months in the enemy's rear and had firsthand knowledge of guerrilla fighting. He wrote his screenplay on the basis of his own war reports.

The film begins with a montage of shots describing the prewar happiness of the heroine, Praskovya Lukyanova, a highly respected collective farmer, tender mother, and loving wife.

The sudden war destroys everything at once: her husband dies from wounds, her village is seized by the enemy, and her little son is hurled by a Nazi under the tracks of a tank. Vegeance is all Praskovya can think of now. She slides silently like a black shadow between the trees of a forest where collective farmers hide. At her sight, people fall silent and children stop playing. When Germans are said to have appeared nearby and everybody is ready to run in panic, Praskovya bars their way with an axe in her hand and the frightening cry: "Where to? Stop!" Thus ordinary, peaceful people become avenging fighters.

The camera records the ruthless shooting of the wounded and the killing of children. For the first time the war showed its horrible, undiguised face.

This gave rise to reproaches for naturalism and cruelty; some continued to think that feature films should be confined to the old methods. But the director could not conduct the entire film in a documentary style. The sketches from life and of concrete observation sometimes yield their place to the scenes full of passion and fury. Thus, having run into the murderer of her child, Praskovya jumped into a German tank and pursued him at its controls until he was squashed into the ground by the tracks. The film also had its "mollifying" lines of action: a traditional pair of lovers dreaming of a happy life after the war, the final rescue of the heroine from execution, and the liberation of the village by the Soviet troops. All this showed that the war theme had not yet been properly mastered. On the other hand, there was artistic veracity in the film, which stemmed largely from the brilliant performance of Vera Maretskaya, who continued to elaborate the familiar character of the Russian woman. Praskovya Lukyanova was in fact the twin sister of Alexandra Sokolova from *Member of the Government,* acting in new, wartime conditions.

Her furious eyes at the moment when she stopped her fleeing fellow villagers brought to one's memory the anguish-distorted face of another, real woman who demanded that the corpses of the hanged not be removed from gallows in liberated Volokolamsk so that everyone could witness the Nazis' crimes. That was a scene from the documentary *The Defeat of the German Armies Near Moscow.* Thus fact and fiction met.

The siege of Leningrad—how is one to describe the days when a ten-year-old girl, Tanya Savicheva, wrote in her diary:

> I am afraid. Bombs are falling. . . .
> Zhenya died at 12 hours 30 minutes in the morning of December 28, 1941. . . .
> Grandmother died at 15 hours on January 25, 1942. . . .
> Lyoka died at 5 hours in the morning of March 17, 1942. . . .
> Mama died at 7 hours 30 minutes in the morning of May 13, 1942. . . .
> The Savichevs have died. Everyone has died. I remain alone. Tanya.[6]

One of the first reels about the besieged city, *Leningrad in Struggle,* matter-of-factly depicted the details of life during the siege.

Leningrad, one of the world's most beautiful cities (the "Venice of the North"), stands frozen in the icy mist. Encircled by the enemy, it is continually bombed and shelled. There is no light, water, or heat. Stalled streetcars and buses are buried in snow drifts. Wires torn by bombing are hanging from lamp poles. Rare pedestrians, staggering with hunger, are dragging themselves along snow-covered streets. A woman is pulling on a sledge the body of her dead child. A scientist, wrapped in several shawls, is reading in a frozen hall of the public library, nibbling absent mindedly at his miserly bread ration until it is finished. An old worker at his lathe is trying to warm his hands with his breath. All these are pictures of the unbelievably hard life of the besieged city.

The cameramen suffered the same hardships. Hungry and exhausted, they lugged heavy equipment on their shoulders, took shots under falling shells, and developed the film in the freezing studio. But they fulfilled their task by showing that Leningrad would not knuckle under.

There is in the film a sequence where architect Alexander Nikolsky describes his design of the future Victory Arch to greet the fighters and shows his sketches. All this happens in a freezing cold house to the accompaniment of the air-raid siren and bursting shells.

Dmitri Shostakovich, standing next to a grand piano in a dark and cold room, is writing something on notepaper— this is the Seventh ("Leningrad") symphony in the making.

Scriptwriter Vladimir Nedobrovo spent in Leningrad the first, most terrible, winter of the siege. Film director Viktor Eisymont, swollen from hunger, left the city only late in December 1941. Both shared the hardships of the siege with their families.

They made the film *Once There Was a Girl*.

Children and war are probably the most incompatible notions. The film begins with the words of a fairy tale: "Once there was. . . ."

Only this is a true story of the twentieth century. A seven-year-old girl builds a bomb shelter out of cardboard boxes for her doll, anxiously awaits her father's letters from the front, goes to fetch water with a big bucket from an ice hole in the Neva, knows only too well what a food ration is and how it is "cut," and explains to another little girl the meaning of the military terms "encirclement" and "ring." For all that, children remain children, and their games in blacked-out rooms or near a house with the glass in the windows replaced with plywood emphasize with great force the unnaturalness of such an existence.

A different angle was given to the theme of the people's suffering and resistance in the film *Invasion* produced by Abram Room after the play of the same name by Leonid Leonov. Its hero, Fyodor Talanov, was an unusual figure both for the Soviet screen and literature. He is a person with a bad reputation, for he has been released from prison. The causes of his conviction are not explained, and the spectator is free to make guesses. One thing is clear: his conviction was unjust.

Fyodor, played by the talented and intelligent actor Oleg Zhakov, is a tragic figure. He forgets insults and injustice and wishes to join in the common struggle against the enemy. But he is not trusted. The chairman of the town's executive committee refuses to enroll him in his guerrilla detachment. What is more, his own father tells him: "I want to know who enters my house." These words strike Fyodor like a slap; he shrinks back with hunched shoulders and slowly goes away from his own home. Constant mistrust holds Fyodor in perpetual tension; he cannot relax even for a minute, hence his rude, defiant tone and his mockingly twisted figure, while his eyes are filled with endless sorrow. Fyodor can break through the wall of alienation and mistrust only at the price of his life. He kills a German colonel and goes to the gallows instead of the guerrilla commander, who a short while earlier refused to support him.

Characteristic of Leonov's manner of writing are heavy psychological strain and a certain symbolism in a situation. This is also felt in *Invasion,* but the film director placed the action in a realistic setting which reflects the hero's state. For instance, in the scene of Fyodor's passage through the town at night, the deserted streets, the violent wind, and the blind windows of abandoned houses emphasize his being condemned to misunderstanding and his aloneness.

Invasion linked the Soviet screen of the war years with the psychological insight inherent in Russian literature. But at that time Fyodor Talanov remained a chance and lonely character on the screen; it would take fifteen long years before art would turn for the first time to similar human destinies.

The theme of the people's suffering was projected with particular forcefulness in the film *Rainbow* made by Mark Donskoi based on a short novel by Wanda Wasilewska. Her story combined war prose and its grim authenticity with traditional Ukrainian prose with its heightened emotionality, pathos, and epigraphs from nineteenth-century poetry, folklore, and songs. The writer's truly happy finding was the image of a rainbow in winter, a rare natural phenomenon which, according to popular belief, is a sign of hope and happiness. Such a rainbow hung over a Nazi-occupied village frozen in despair.

The tone of Mark Donskoi's film was unusual, as if subdued. However, the impression produced by *Rainbow* on foreign audiences was akin to a shock. As to Soviet people, they were immediately astounded by something else: the matter-of-factness of the abysmally monstrous hell that was a Ukrainian village under the Nazis.

There was no explosive temperament here nor mounting tragedy, as in war films like *She Defends Her Country* or *No. 217* by Mikhail Romm. There was no striking contrast between the light of a peaceful day and the nightmare of Nazism, as in many pictures describing the fateful day of June 22, 1941. On the contrary, everything was quiet here, in fact too quiet. The war had lasted so long that it had become an accepted thing.

The village is ice bound and almost buried under snow drifts. The

Natalia Uzhviy plays the role of woman-partisan Olena in Rainbow by Mark Donskoi.

houses are overgrown with icicles. Even during the 1980s, when cinema techniques have gone such a long way and when much of the naivety of Donskoi's film is quite obvious, it is still hard to believe that this world of ice and snow was created in a Central Asian desert, in the scorching heat of Ashkhabad, with the help of naphthalene and various properties. The profound compassion for the distant sisters and brothers and artistic skill and talent of the filmmakers defied the vast distance separating the country's deep rear from the occupied Western regions.

Occupation—on the edge of the village the bodies of Soviet soldiers and partisans swing from the gallows. Threatening inscriptions are written on squares of wood: the same fate awaits all partisans and the disobedient. In the *Rainbow* peasant woman Fedosya comes here to visit her dead son. Swinging in the Nazi noose is not a corpse, for the frost has sculpted the young man's face into the marble head of an antique statue. And this is everyday life.

Olena Kostyuk comes to the village from her partisan detachment in the forest. The reason is simple and prosaic: the woman is near her time and has come to deliver a baby. The classical features and the vast bright eyes of Natalia Uzhviy, a star of Ukrainian cinema, are filled with silent, bottomless anguish. Heart-rending sequences show the torture of this poor pregnant woman and then mother, whom the Nazi sadist intimidates by manhandling the newborn. The shots would have seemed too naturalistic were it not for the restrained, internally overflowing but externally reserved performance of the actress.

While the German guard drives the tortured Olena across the snow, small Mishka, a son of young Malyuchikha, crawls out to pass a hunk of bread to Olena. The modest part of Malyuchikha (in fact, *Rainbow* had neither "first" nor "second" roles, the real hero being the village as a whole, the suffering people fighting to the last) was played by a very attractive and natural actress, Lisyanskaya, who was noted as a character actress by critics of different countries.

The Nazi guard shoots the child. There is bitter tenderness in the silent funeral rite where the mother and her other little children stamp down the earth into which they buried Mishka.

But the life of the village is not confined to a mother's meetings with her dead son and the death of a child. Commandant Kurt Werner, played by the German anti-Nazi actor Hans Klering, is quite comfortable and happy in "this barbaric country." He has a warm house, a batmen, orderlies, and a mistress, a local woman by the name of Pusya (a contemptible name for a German shepherd dog). Nina Alisova played that young woman, a capricious little fool, with great psychological skill and subtle contempt. A revealing scene shows the meeting at an ice-clad well of two sisters: Pusya in her permanent curls and fine clothes and the partisan Olga, a beautiful girl with a pure Slav face. The scene is a duel between a proud defender of her country and the slut and traitress who is her own sister.

The film has no plot in the usual sense of the word, but it has a core, a feeling, and tension. The rainbow in winter skies promises hope, early joy; the finale, the capture of the village by Soviet troops, is sudden and poetic: skiers dressed in white camouflage suits "fly into" the village like seagulls, liberating it from the enemy.

"The simplicity and lack of complexity of the plot are almost disappointing," admitted the reviewer of a French newspaper. "We are still poisoned by films with complex plots, our vision cannot stand this dazzling, like a snow field, truth."[7]

Mark Donskoi said that his personal impression helped him a lot: he had seen the first villages liberated from the Germans near Moscow, talked with people who had lived in occupied areas, and stayed with them for a while.

A peasant woman who lived in a dugout told him:

You evidently don't know what fascists are like. I have lost many of my relatives, there is only my daughter left. I have no house; the mailman brings letters from my sons who are at the front to the burrow which I dug where my house used to stand. And I tell you—I'll live till the day when the fascist will be retreating, and not the way he came here, but when he'll be miserable, hungry, shivering with cold, afraid to meet people's eyes, looking around like wolf. . . ."[8]

The director and Wanda Wasilewska used these very words of a peasant woman in their film.

Here is what Donskoi said about the actors' feelings at shooting:

When actress Tyapkina, who played Fedosya, mourned over the body of her killed son she was both actress and mother, for Tyapkina had recently learned that her son was killed at the front. When Dunaisky, who played grandpa Okhapka, spoke at the trial of the village elder, a fascist, it was not an actor but citizen Dunaisky whose family had been carted off to Germany.[9]

Young Giuseppe de Santis, who soon became one of the leaders of Italian neorealism, wrote:

> I want to address all who will read these lines: Hasten to see "Rainbow"! This is the best of films that have appeared on our screens since Italy, having rid itself of the fascist dictatorship, began to get foreign cinema production. This is a genuinely poetic work, a rare masterprice.
>
> In order to find something similar in world cinema one must go back to such films as "The Battleship Potemkin," "Variété," "The Tragedy of a Mine" and "La Grande Illusion."[10]

The naked tragedy of life's material shaped the cinema style of those years. That was when Roberto Rossellini made his masterpiece *Roma, citta aperta*. He considered himself a disciple of Mark Donskoi and followed him in boldly broadening the bounds of the permissible in art for the sake of portraying the truth.

Rainbow amazed and astounded everybody. The US ambassador in Moscow requested the Soviet government's permission for a copy of the film to be sent to President Franklin Roosevelt. Soon after the copy was sent to the United States, Mark Donskoi received a telegram in which President Roosevelt informed him that the film *Rainbow* had been shown in the White House. The President also added that the film was understood without translation, although Professor Charles Bowlen was asked to interpret, and that it would be shown to the American people with fitting grandeur and with commentary by Reynolds and Thomas.

The Light and the Shadows

Wartime cinema knew no halftones. We and they, heroism and cowardice, loyalty and betrayal, were the alternatives that dominated every plot, from a short item in newsreels to a full-length feature. All accents were marked beforehand. The enemies were inhuman, everyone of them. A woman or girl who was unable to wait long enough for her husband or bridegroom and betrayed him was despised as a pariah. All psychological excuses were rejected; only the very fact of cowardice and betrayal was considered important.

Twenty years later artists will closely scrutinize the inner world of a young girl which is overturned and crushed by the war. But during the forties the vacillations and fears of Veronica, the heroine of the film *The Cranes Are Flying,* would seem trivial, negligible, and unworthy of attention!

The poet Konstantin Simonov then addressed a wrathful "Open Letter" to a woman from the town of Vichug who had written to her fighting husband that she had married another man. The "Letter" ended with the words: "Disrespectfully, we are fellow soldiers of the deceased."

As a matter of fact, this sharp distinction of heroes and actions did not appear in the 1940s. One way or another it was present in the artistic works of the preceding decades. The film heroes of the 1920s and 1930s lived under a constant strain, always ready to fight. The type of the enemy changed with time, but the heroes remained invariably prepared to rush into a decisive battle.

Films called for struggle. It turned out, however, that what the fighters needed, maybe more than slogans, were lyrical works and stories about earthly life, about tenderness, friendship, and love. What was required were tales not only about heroes but also about plain, ordinary people.

There was a film conceived still in peacetime, altogether prewar and deeply rooted in the 1930s, which was released when its heroes and their coevals were already fighting. The dear, bright, already so distant prewar world stirred the heart with sad nostalgia in *Mashenka* by Yuli Raizman, with a screenplay by Yevgeni Gabrilovich. This film and the documentary *Berlin* are the two wartime mainstays of one of the best Soviet filmmakers, Raizman, whose works will be analyzed later.

Mashenka presents a modest, ordinary, slim girl in a plain beret, the story of her first love, offence, and separation. Love is here, for the first time in Soviet cinema, not as a sideline of the plot, but as the core of the film's content. This love began with a chance acquaintance during a practice air raid (a sign of the time), then was broken off by an accidentally seen kiss during an evening party with another, the heroine's girl friend. Mashenka meets her love again in a canteen on the Finnish front, then somewhere on the winter roads of the brief war. The film ends with another separation, the parting at a front crossroads, after an open declaration of love. This story, unfolding in the midst of urban life, is full of concrete and accurate details and features of the time and place.

Mashenka's simple story acquired a character of a refined artistic testimony. The heroine, with her moral principles, personified the traits of the generation which was born after the revolution and which came of age in

Valentina Karavayeva, heroine of the movie Mashenka, *brings love to the core of a Soviet film.*

1941. Her character was a fusion of youthful and somewhat rectilinear rigor, unselfishness, open-heartedness, friendliness, and trustfulness with quiet firmness and certain immutable notions and ethical norms. Young men and women took the era's slogans and melted them into the pure gold of their souls. That was priceless human material.

When Gabrilovich and Raizman painted in their *Mashenka* a portrait of prewar youth from life, they did not yet know all of its destiny or the feats it was soon to perform. But as soon as the film was released, during the early months of the war, the generalized meaning of the simple story about Mashenka, a girl from the post office, became quite clear. It was the discovery of a portrait character.

But Soviet cinema did not follow the way of *Mashenka* in the first postwar years. It sought to show the gigantic panorama of the great battle; and the filmmakers had no time, with rare exceptions, for a thorough study of an individual destiny.

For example, Vsevolod Pudovkin, while working with Konstantin Simonov on the screenplay of *The Smolensk Road* (about Moscow in 1941) wrote:

> We attempted to understand and generalize events in the sequence in which they were understood and generalized by people who began to fight at the Western Front on June 22. We led our heroes through the disappointment of the first days, through mistakes, through minutes and days of bewilderment and sorrow—through everything that the private soldiers and commanders had to go through in the war's reality—gradually revealing the entire meaning and course of that war.[11]

But this plan was not effected. Films about the beginning of the war were made differently at its end. More and more often the truth of the war was filmed with prompously enthusiastic or gigantically multifigured battle panoramas and, most important, by episodes in headquarters, above all, the Supreme Command Headquarters, with generals in conference clad in full-dress uniforms sitting under the portrait of Generalissimo Stalin.

During those years ordinary people appeared on the screen for a short time in order to fulfil a very concrete function—perform their little exploit and thus help implement the plans of the big war. So it was, for instance, with the driver nicknamed Minutka in *The Great Turning Point,* who, inspite of his mortal wound, clenched the ends of a broken telephone wire between his teeth and thus restored communication at a crucial moment of the operation.

This film, made by Friedrich Ermler to the script by Boris Chirskov, peculiarly forestalled the trend of Soviet cinema in the late forties and fifties. It was focussed, not on an individual fate or the story of one exploit, but on the depiction of the battle of Stalingrad, which was so important for the course of the war. For the first time the spectator was able to see the offices of the top chiefs and follow the implementation of the operation's plan.

War memoirs were not yet written; various documents, which are now well known, were not yet published; military-historical studies were only being conceived. Everything was unknown and secret. Therefore, the very possibility of having a look at the "sanctum sanctorum" was at first fascinating. Moreover, the film *The Great Turning Point* began in the Kremlin: the principal hero, General Muravyev, was carefully closing behind him a heavy carved door, beyond which, in the office of the Supreme Commander in Chief, he had received an envelope with the plan for defeating the enemy troops.

In aesthetic terms it was the cinema of the wartime years that discovered new strata of life, considerably broadened the limits of the permissible and customary in art, and saw a new hero. What is more, as the future was to show, it is from wartime films, above all from documentary reels, that the seeds grew of the artistic novelty which would later on mark *The Cranes Are Flying, Ballad of a Soldier, Destiny of Man,* and many other films of the great postwar war cycle, up to the tragic *Come and See* made by Elem Klimov for the fortieth anniversary of the victory in the Patriotic War, which recreated the horrible fate of the Byelorussian village of Khatyn, whose residents were burned alive by the invaders.

Soon after, as well as decades later, film directors will return to the war theme over and over again. Soviet artists will turn to the "fatal forties" as the pure source of the people's heroism. The screen will reveal the names of unknown heroes, the unknown pages of war history, under the noble motto "No one is forgotten, nothing is forgotten," the words inscribed at the Piskarevskoye Cemetery in Leningrad where the martyrs of the siege are buried. War will also extend from the memory of concrete events to the moral sphere and will become a metaphoric symbol of the hardest trials which befall man and demand that he muster all his strength.

CHAPTER FIVE

Cinema During the Thaw

A Renewal

*T*he film decade of the fifties made a dreary start. Only eight feature pictures were made in 1951. The level of Soviet cinematographic output had never been so low, neither in 1919 nor in 1943, the years of fierce fighting in war. A limit had been reached. "To make few pictures proved in no way easier than to make many," wrote Mikhail Romm. "The idea of concentrating on a few selected works (which was supposed to result in uniformly excellent quality) proved utopian."[1]

One cannot but agree with him when studying the pitifully brief list of 1951 productions.

Belinsky by Grigori Kozintsev was a biographical film about a great Russian democratic critic of the nineteenth century whose life was one of hardship, poverty, and civic heroism. Reviewing *Belinsky* today, one can hardly believe that it was made by a professional, so poor it was. It is still harder to believe that the same professional would make his *Hamlet* thirteen years later.

The second film of the same genre, *Przhevalsky* by Sergei Yutkevich, was somewhat saved by the picturesque landscapes of deserts and mountains shot in expeditions along the routes of the indefatigable discoverer of last century, the film's hero. Przhevalsky himself together with Cossack Yegorov, a "representative of the people," remained standard, copy-book figures.

The third biographical film of 1951, *Taras Shevchenko,* by the Ukrainian director Igor Savchenko, preserved the same dignified and smooth pattern of the "life of a great man," which suddenly was exploded by sorrowful and expressively tragic episodes of the poet's exile to a Caspian fort. The performer of the main role, Sergei Bondarchuk, a young disciple of Gerasimov, who drew general attention with his fiery temperment, was the only ray of joy and hope of the cinematic year 1951.

There were also two films on contemporary subjects—one shot in Moscow (the unfunny comedy *Sports Honor*) and one in Tallinn (*Light in Koordi,* on collective farm life); one concert film; and, lastly, following the pompous *The Oath* and *The Fall of Berlin, The Unforgettable Year 1919* made by Mikhail Chiaureli after the play of the same name by Vsevolod Vishnevsky, the "swan song" of the film cycle soon to be called the "personality cult in art." Such was the cinematic output of that year.

However, it was in the same year, and more frequently afterwards, that the customary assertions that Soviet cinema was at its artistic best were replaced by the official admission of an unsatisfactory state of affairs. Articles in the central press began to talk about the need for artistic search, criticized the lack of conflict in films and plays, and pointed to the deterioration of mastery in cinema art.

Cinematography needed changes and so did Soviet art as a whole.

The unsatisfactory state of affairs in literature and art was pointed out in the resolutions of the Nineteenth CPSU Congress (1952). A decision was passed to increase film production. Film output grew to 20 pictures in 1953, 45 in 1954, and 66 in 1955, not counting so-called spectacle films (slightly altered filmed stage productions), which had heretofore accounted for the lion's share of the annual output. In 1952, for instance, there were ten spectacle films and two concert films, while almost all other new films were screen versions of plays or other literary works, bringing the total to twenty-three. While spectacle films played their enlightening role and preserved for new generations the art of the stage and of its masters, they gave nothing to cinematography, so that film workers joked sadly: "It only remains to invent the cinema, wait for the brothers Lumière." Those were the last years of Stalin's reign.

The film-production situation was particularly difficult in Union Republics, which were almost totally limited to documentary work and dubbing. This picture scarcity at republican film studios resulted in stagnation, the waste of time of creative workers, and the deterioration of their professional skills. This was also recognized and reflected in the special decision of the CPSU Central Committee "on measures to increase cinematographic production in Union Republics" (1952).

Although increased production as such did not ensure a flowering of cinema art, it was the first requirement for leading it out of the impasse.

Things began to move. The process of renewal was fast and impetuous, for everything was ready for it, everything awaited big changes.

The first of all it became possible to broaden the range of subjects. The very choice of themes revealed a new attitude to urgent problems which seemed to be commonly known. Cinema began to abandon the established stereotypes. Here again an awareness of wrong attitudes and practices preceded new positive decisions. In 1952 the national daily *Pravda* and some other newspapers criticized the state of affairs in drama and censured the one-sided approach to contemporary man and the schematic and colorless presentation of his character: "Machinery is represented, and modern demands and the fulfilment of production plans are discussed. But people in their everyday life, their culture, their inner world are not shown."[2]

This was regarded as the first and foremost evil. A campaign was started against the "production" (in a negative and ironic sense) novel and film. Works were ridiculed where the conflict was between two methods of cutting or smelting metal. "The washer has ousted the man," raged the critics.

Also criticized was the habitual dramatic situation in which the opposed forces consisted of a young innovator fighting for a new production method and his antagonist the conservative manager (or some other superior) opposing innovation in every way. Reality was much more complicated and could not be reduced to the mere production relations between people. The problem was not in the fact that cinema concentrated exclusively on depicting this area of life, which is indeed very important for contemporary man and which takes so much of his time and strength. The problem was that production on the screen or stage was artificial and

197

thought up, and the conflicts were "made to order" and avoided real issues. In real life both the advanced innovator and the conservative bureaucrat were quite different from those shown on the screen or stage.

The change in the very approach to the depiction of man in his work within the system of social relations was a difficult matter. Here creative workers faced the greatest obstacles and had literally to "retrain" their vision and their pen. Although the "conflictlessness theory" was denounced by the press and public, it would take a very long time to eradicate it in practice.

However, the directions of *Pravda* editorials, which drew attention to the "insufficient coverage" of the personal life, relations at home, and the inner world of people, were useful. Soviet film workers were glad to turn to a sphere which had long been kept off the screen or was strictly rationed: the private everyday life of people and its ethical and family aspects. It was above all in this sphere that a qualitative renovation of cinematic art manifested itself.

The year 1954 saw the release of Ivan Pyryev's film *Test of Fidelity,* which was described in summaries and reviews as a film "about love and duty." Here the inner life of the heroes was controlled by uncomplicated moral rules: it is bad for a man to abandon his family and wife, and the person thus acting deserves punishment (in all cases!). The new element for the screen characters was that their private life was regarded as a matter of primary importance.

In the film *The Return of Vasili Bortnikov,* the last work of Vsevolod Pudovkin, which was released only two years earlier, a tight knot of the personal drama of three people was, in the course of action, virtually replaced by the so-called "production" issue. Yet that was a film which had every reason to become a principled work, as was Galina Nikolayeva's novel *The Harvest,* which served as the basis for the film's script. Both the novel and the film opened with theme of "coming back," the return from war of a man who had won peace for his country and intended to lead a new and happy life.

This theme would be extensively elaborated in Soviet art, in particular in such films as *Two Fyodors, The Chairman,* and *There Came a Soldier from the Front.*

The first of these soldiers, Bortnikov, met with grief at home, for his wife, wearied of waiting for him, fell in love with another and was unfaithful to her husband. Although the heroine Avdotya was somewhat

The portrait of a new social hero, Mikhail Ulyanov in the role of Yegor Trubnikov, the man returning from war to lead a new and happy life, became a popular theme in Soviet art.

"extenuated" by the war and her husband's prolonged absence (it should be noted that the time of action of Yevgeni Gabrilovich's screenplay was shifted from 1945–1946 to 1951–1952, which served to "exonerate" the unfaithful wife), the filmmakers did not dare make "the triangle" the principle conflict. They chose to elaborate other problems which required separate solutions, such as the manner of running a collective farm, the

199

bitterness of a person who deems himself wronged by life. Most regrettably they confined themselves to narrow "production" questions which concerned tractors rather than people. Because of this, *The Return of Vasili Bortnikov* remained at a crossroads, a timid harbinger of the coming spring.

A comparison with *The Chairman* (1964), a picture of the new time, which is similar to *The Return of Vasili Bortnikov* in the main "come-back" aspect of the plot, shows the great distance separating them. This is also confirmed by the comparison of the two portraits: Vasili Bortnikov, played by Sergei Lukyanov, and collective-farm chairman Yegor Trubnikov, played by Mikhail Ulyanov. The main difference was in the fact that Ulyanov's image was analytical and searching, while that of Lukyanov, who was a vigorous and colorful actor, was rigid and set beforehand. Cinematography had to master the art of painting a realistic character, which it had lost during the years of "picture scarcity."

The historians of Soviet cinema recognized as a film of genuine renewal another picture, *A Big Family,* made in 1954 by Iosif Kheifits based on Vsevolod Kochetov's novel *The Zhurbins.* Viewed in retrospect the film seems little different in style from its predecessors, but it included a plot situation and characters quite unexpected and unusual. There was a young unmarried woman with a child, the first "single mother" on the screen, who was not a frivolous, easy-going creature but the serious and pure Katya. Played in a noble and dignified manner by Yelena Dobronravova, it was this woman of "dubious reputation" that the youngest son Alexei dared to bring as his wife into the exemplary family of the Zhurbins.

This particular character and the exceptionally charming face of the performer, the young and then unknown Alexei Batalov, gave the fascination of novelty to the film. The young worker was quick witted, cultured, and sincere in his attachment to the girl he loved; he defended his love with enviable resolution before the eloquent and impressive authority of the older Zhurbins.

His generation particularly remember the young fellow with a high forehead and inquisitive, thoughtful eyes. The herald of the new screen, Alexei Batalov, was also a scion of a famous dynasty, like the Zhurbins, only of an artistic one. He is the son of Vladimir Batalov, who once played the merry driver in *The House on Trubnaya Square* by Boris Barnet, and nephew of the unforgettable Nikolai Batalov, the hero of Pudovkin's *Mother* and Ekka's *Road to Life.* Alexei Batalov, who inherited the charm of his elder relatives, was the first to appeal from the screen to the lofty concepts of morality, humanity, and trust. The theme broached in *A Big Family* was developed in Kheifits's next picture, *The Rumyantsev Case,* where the leading role was specially intended for Batalov and was written accordingly by scriptwriter Yuri Gherman.

It was at first sight only a detective story about a long-haul driver who was imprisoned on false charges and a good investigator who brought to justice the real criminals. But the film also spoke of the need for kindness and trust in man and of the belief in the triumph of legality and showed a hatred of bureaucracy. That was truly a film of the period after the Twentieth CPSU Congress, which was held under the slogan of restoration of the Leninist norms in social life. Although the film retained the inevitable and too easily attained optimistic finale and the victory of social justice (a typical happy ending), vivid signs of Soviet everyday life were shown on the screen. The truth of life was already approaching the screen through the realistically pictured long highways and the bold portrayal of the crook, working as the garage chief, and of his crafty profiteering tricks and operations with stolen goods. The portrait of the so-called "man in the street," truck driver Sasha Rumyantsev, whose principle feature was "a sense of dignity," marked a resolute protest against seeing in a man a function, a mere particle of the whole, a "cog in the wheel."

Life's Lessons in a Film Studio

The old and the new were intricately linked in the films made in 1954–1958 by the masters of the older generation. These were the films of transitional period between Stalin's death and the 60s.

In Alexander Zarkhi's *Height,* the familiar production confrontation between the innovator and the conservative is purely formal. The main theme in the film is found in the relations between two workers—a young fellow and a girl—with emphasis on the seriousness of their feelings.

The Lesson of Life, made by Yuli Raizman to a screenplay by Yevgeni Gabrilovich and originally entitled "The Wife," reappraised and censured for the first time, through the character of Sergei Romashko, one of the general types of a modern executive, a "captain of industry." Romashko was played by Ivan Pereverzev, who usually performed the roles of responsible officials, popular "positive heroes." Here, the very choice of the actor also played a role. Romashko still wore the romantic halo of the leader of a big construction project; his strong figure was painted against an imposing industrial background, amid flares and flashes, smoke and noise, the clanging and grinding of an industrial symphony masterfully recorded by the screen and the sound track. Romashko was denounced through a newspaper article and dismissed from the high post, which, as was claimed in the article, ruined the man and led him to abuse his power. Despite his admiration of the vigor, temperament, and strong will of this type of an engineer-manager, Raizman detected and revealed his callousness, crudeness, egoism, conceit, and at times downright brutishness.

An attempt was also made to study characters. Thus, Natasha, the somewhat outwardly dull and dry wife of the executive (which was both truthful and bold on the part of the film director), was subtly, gradually, and unobtrusively revealed as a sincere and out-of-the-ordinary person.

The next film, *The Communist,* made in 1957 by Gabrilovich and Raizman (both were then past fifty), grew out of their old artistic cooperation, from the distant *The Last Night* and *Mashenka,* where they tested the impact on the screen of seemingly simple, everyday, ordinary events and characters.

The word "Communist" is written in red letters over a still showing people on the roof of a boxcar. Then the picture brightens, the people in the sequence start moving, the film begins. It is the year 1918. Trainloads of people are rolling and crowds are plodding along towards a distant village hidden among peat bogs where a power station is being built. The hero's figure is not to be found easily among the shoddily dressed people—men in shabby soldier's tunics and women with heads covered with calico kerchiefs. Vasili Gubanov is not storming the Winter Palace, nor is he delivering important messages to headquarters; he is simply handing out drying oil or lime, procuring nails and screws, and providing food for the hungry women and children.

The title of the film is expressive, and so is the hero's occupation and his very appearance: the iron-cast torso, the sculptured features, and the youthful, dazzling smile of Yevgeny Urbansky, a young talented actor, who was destined, like a meteor, to trace his flaming way through several films, win the hearts of many, and burn in a motor accident during a film shooting on location in a desert.

Vasili's character is manifested in his every action and word. He manages to suppress his anger at a cruel and unjust insult when a worker spits

Yevgeny Urbansky, heroic as Vasili Gubanov in The Communist, *experiences difficulty in love for someone else's wife, Anyuta.*

at him accusing him of theft, wipes his face, and returns to the raging line of people demanding various supplies, somewhat abashed but determined to stick to his post. A self-controlled man, he is choking with joy and flailing his hands like a child as he runs along austere Kremlin rooms after Lenin himself has helped him to procure the nails so necessry for his construction site. In his kindness and tact that prompt him to bring presents from Moscow to the owners of the house he stays at (tobacco for Fyodor and a plain white kerchief for Anyuta), in his attention to any person he meets, and in his acute sense of responsibility for his job, a generous and powerful character is revealed most vividly.

The hero is, typically, a rank-and-file Communist and, typically, Vasili's love life is painfully difficult. Instead of a possible class-conscious girl student in a red kerchief, he meets the unhappily married peasant woman Anyuta. Vasili's death is also typical for a man of principle. A "canonical" film would be crowned by a completed power station even if the hero would die. Here, in the final sequences, the village is devastated by a fire, the project is far from completed, and bread has still been obtained at the price of a human life. All this heightens the dramatic tension and adds to the stern truth of the film.

The Communist confirmed the guiding principles of Raizman's works: discovering the complex in the simple, the unusual in the ordinary, the heroic in the non-heroic. These make the entire style of the film natural, including the key scenes in which Vasili fells innumerable trees or (like his cinema ancestor Timosh in a Dovzhenko's film), having been three times shot, rises to meet more enemy bullets. Even these legendlike scenes strike one as palpably true.

The carefully selected qualities, actions, and emotions of characters that dominated the films in the recent past were gradually giving way in the cinema of the late 1950s to the demands for the fuller reflection of life, naturalness, and variety. Pomposity and embellishment were being ousted by simplicity. The "phenomenon of veracity," seemingly elementary for cinema, did not come easily, as the screen often retained the old chill, discomfort, and ill-fitting decor. The new way of seeing the material and the radical changes in style which followed were manifested much more vigorously in the works of a new generation of filmmakers who emerged as an active creative force in the middle of the decade.

Young Filmmakers of the 1950s

In 1953 an assignment for an independent film production was given to two young directors who were graduates of all the All-Union State Institute of Cinematography (VGIK), Vladimir Basov and Mikhail Korchagin (the former became a well-known director and actor; the latter died prematurely). Their picture, *The School of Courage* (1954), based on a short novel by Arkadi Gaidar, produced a distinctly fresh impression on the audience despite its shortcomings.

Young directors were singularly lucky during that period, for more and more productions were assigned to them. In 1954 Grigori Chukhrai, who had worked for several years as assistant director, was offered a chance to make his debut at the Mosfilm studio. Vladimir Vengerov and Mikhail Shveitser codirected a film for the youth, *The Dirk,* at the Lenfilm studio. At the Odessa studio an independent production was entrusted to Marlen

Khutsiev, a disciple of Igor Savchenko. Alexander Alov and Vladimir Naumov, also graduates of Savchenko's class, who completed the film *Taras Shevchenko* (on which they first worked as assistant directors) after their teacher's death, produced *Pavel Korchagin* in Kiev in 1957, an expressive and nervous film which caused tubulent discussion in the cinema world because of its unexpected interpretation of the anthological Soviet novel *How the Steel Was Tempered*. The filmmakers were accused of being "pessimistic" and of "exaggerating the gloomy side."

Who were these directors of the new generation? First of all they were frontline soldiers who returned to their alma maters in patched-up tunics with wound ribbons or sometimes in bandages or on crutches. They were also younger people, born in 1929 and 1930, who had not been called up and still went to school during the hungry war years.

The distinct generation gap at the studios and in film production was felt, fortunately, with the same acuteness at the VGIK classes, at its directors' department where the younger generation was taking over the torch from their predecessors.

Stanislav Rostotsky, the son of a Moscow professor, was fortunate to meet Eisenstein back in 1935 when the director inspired the boy with his knowledge of literature, of the laws of creative work. His road to VGIK was by no means accidental. He finished school in 1940, became a soldier in 1942, and was badly wounded in February 1944. Rostotsky graduated from VGIK in the same class with Grigori Kozintsev.

Eisenstein's disciples—Mikhail Shveitser and Boris Buneyev, those of Sergei Gerasimov—Sergei Bondarchuk and Tatyana Lioznova, those of Dovzhenko—Tenghiz Abuladze and Revaz Chkheidze, and then, a year later, the disciples of Mikhail Romm and of other masters entered studios and "captured" them.

A jolly epigraph to this total debut was the comic film *Carnival Night* by Eldar Ryazanov released on the eve of the new year 1957, complete with paper streamers, garlands and silver stars, songs and laughter, snow flakes and carefree merriment, but also with daring, youthful ardor and witticism.

There was indeed plenty of music and variety in this picture, whose uncomplicated plot consisted in the preparation of a New Year party at the House of Culture and the party itself—a well-known and tested framework for a musical revue. But a device was used here which exploded the old form or at least exposed its conventional and secondary role for the

Dancer Lyudmila Gurchenko in Carnival Night, 1956, *demonstrates her spontaneity and vivacity.*

given occasion. Appointed as the chief organizer of the festive concert of the young was Ogurtsov, a middle-aged, flabby bureaucrat in art, totally devoid of any sense of humor or elementary artistic taste. *Carnival Night* became a story of young enthusiasts in the House of Culture who fought to "push" their concert program through Ogurtsov's censorship and save brilliant numbers, and of their success in the end.

Starting with the portrayal of life in the collectivized village, cinema workers turned to "urban" and "workers" themes. These were the subjects of the first films made by director Marlen Khutsiev, a VGIK graduate and a prominent figure in the cinema of the fifties and sixties. Although, from the very beginning, veracity was to him not the end but a means, not the goal of creative work but only its condition, Khutsiyev was promptly dubbed a "painter of ordinary life" and an "imitator of Italian neorealism." This judgment was passed on the basis of his first films, *Spring on Zarechnaya Street,* which he made in 1956 with Felix Mironer, and *Two Fyodors* (1959), in which Vasili Shukshin made his debut in the main role of a soldier who has returned home from the front.

In the case of *Spring on Zarechnaya Street,* the lyrical story of furnaceman Sasha Savchenko and of his love for teacher Tanya Levchenko, the critics, who received the film with warm appreciation, concentrated their attention, however, on the faithful depiction of everyday life. The detailed, unvarnished, and frank truth of the surroundings—when the screen showed, probably for the first time in twenty years, the ordinary, over-crowded, cluttered-up houses of a workers' suburb, the dirty streets, the class of a workers' evening school filled to capacity, the dull evening parties and joyless drinking, the provincial luxury of the factory club—led the critics to the conclusion that the film director was a "painter of ordinary life." In fact, this was the story of the awakening in the rough furnaceman of a hankering for light and culture which were personified for him in Tanya, a somewhat dull and not very attractive teacher, of how self-confident Sasha Savchenko began to ponder for the first time over his life and then came to the conclusion that there was something wrong with the way he had lived. The coming of spring caused confusion in the heart of a man who was by nature gifted and serious but who had already acquired brutish habits. Savchenko had become used to bonuses and awards and to arrogant statements that he was "the master of life to whom the whole world belonged." Suddenly all this proletarian glory, his well-earned wages, output quotas fulfilled half a year ahead, his handsomely careless manner of a lady killer were all reduced to nought by a new teacher, a haughty college graduate with immaculate hands.

Today's viewer of *Spring on Zarechnaya Street* will probably be impressed most of all by the stormy and inspiring passion of Sasha Savchenko, played with such power and temperament by Nikolai Rybnikov. He reveals a love that makes one's bones crack, that drives a man from place to place so that he walks about entirely lost, with his face distorted by a strong emotion.

Though the tracing of the stylistics of Khutsiev's films to Italian neo-realism was erroneous, they did contain features of a peculiar neoromanticism, a purely Soviet cinematic style of the late fifties. This was an art that intended to reject the flowery phrase but not inspiring words; a sober art that wanted to speak the truth, firmly believing in social reason and justice; and an art of great expectations, both civic and lyrical.

This credo of civic lyricism, of particular concern for ordinary people, was expressed in the film *The House I Live In* produced by Lev Kulidjanov and Yakov Segel and based on the script by the young playwright Iosif Olshansky (it won the first prize at the All-Union Screenplay Contest in 1956). It was a story of a big apartment house built in the late constructionist style of the thirties at Rogozhskaya Gate (then a suburb of Moscow), into which the film's heroes moved shortly before the war.

The film showed the ordinary life of the house tenants: shared flats, simple family joys, people going away on business trips, children attending school, ficus plants on window sills, and cheap lace curtains on the windows. The interior shots in a real house were unlike the plush chambers that had earlier been claimed to be the norm in Soviet life. The principle of describing the most natural flow of life was also observed in the presentation of the dramas taking place—partings, offended or betrayed lovers, the first sorrows, and the first disappointments.

But this unobtrusive and simple life of a house at former Rogozhskaya, now Ilyich Gate, is imbued with lyricism and a slight nostalgia. The childhood of the generation to which Olshansky, Kulidjanov, and Segel belong, which fell on the 1930s, was reconstructed in the *The House I Live In* in a halo of gentle sadness over the irrevocable prewar time. It was in the popular tunes of those years ("Rio Ritas," "Trot Marches," and so on), played on phonographs and heard from many windows, in the newly tenanted flats and rooms furnished according to the standards of the time, and in girls' dresses of Georgette crepe with frills that the directors sought and found their film's poetry, which contrasted with the cruel war colors. From *The House I Live In,* a kindly, wistful mist of retro, of reminiscences about the thirties, floated to *Clear Skies, Destiny of a Man,* and many other films made later. The thirties were already viewed as history. Take, for instance, this scene: as dawn rises over the Moskva River a young fellow and a girl are walking up a slightly ascending new street past the construction sites with their cranes. The camera follows their figures slowly receding into the distance—a long way to go, a happy journey! But out of the distance the flaming numbers "1941" rise on the screen, for this is the morning of June 22. And the ordinary colors of the film, its unhurried and detailed narration, and its rhythms become more rigorous and austere in keeping with the life that has changed. The destinies, characters, and faces which are in no way distinctive, deliberately "homely" at the beginning of the film, are now viewed in a dramatic, poetic light. Thus the ordinary and inconspicuous reveal the heroic.

The film tells of losses and grief without excessive pathos and tears, the effect being all the stronger. A glance exchanged between a young woman awaiting in vain for a letter from her husband and the girl letter-carrier speaks better than words.

The war is shown in the film through the scenes of Moscow as a frontline city, with barrage balloons, rationed bread, faintings from hunger, and window panes pasted over with paper strips. Victory came to the screen also not as scenes of festive welcoming of the triumphant soldiers but with the famous shot where the victorious and deadly tired fighter fell asleep with his boots on on the counterpane of a bed lovingly prepared for him, while the rockets of a salute in his honor were bursting outside but could not awake him.

The common features of the late fifties were best manifested in films about the war. Not only a person's actions as such but also the inner world and emotional condition of that person, which prompt him to perform a military exploit, were studied thoroughly and carefully. The individual destinies and characters of the ordinary man, a soldier, or his relative who remained in the rear replaced the generalized, monumental, and suprapersonal representatives of soldiers, workers, and the heroes of the front and rear as shown in the pictures of Stalin's personality cult period, *The Oath, The Fall of Berlin, The Battle of Stalingrad.*

The camera lens ever more frequently caught what only a few years before had been excluded even from the background: boxcars with the wounded, flea markets near railroad stations, profiteers and self-seekers thriving in the rear, overcautious characters in military headquarters, the ruins of towns, children working at munitions plants, evacuated people reduced to abject poverty—a true picture of a nationwide calamity, including all, even shocking and painful, details.

A private human destiny came into the focus of attention. Such a destiny, a happy life interrupted and broken by the war, was raised to a universal human level regardless of whether the actual actions and deeds of the person were heroic or reprehensible.

It was only then, ten years later in fact, that the broken line of *Rainbow* was continued, reviving the truth of the war, full of suffering, which had once been brought to the screen by frontline newsreel cameramen and the makers of the wartime feature films. Soviet cinema acquired new sincerity in the return to the war days, to nostalgia and sorrow over the irrevocable past, in the hallowed memory of those gone forever. The best films of the late 1950s, as if completing and summing up the decade, were about war.

Three Films and Three Directors

THE CRANES ARE FLYING BY MIKHAIL KALATOZOV

The film produced an astounding impression on professional cinema workers during its first run at Moscow's Cinema House. Its success with spectators began with the long queues near cinema houses in Moscow and reached distant foreign lands. The film was crowned with the Golden Palm Branch, the Grand Prix of the 1958 Cannes Festival, and many other international awards, but this was somewhat later.

The unusual impression was above all due to the fact that the screen told, with feeling and pathos, the story not of a glorious exploit but of guilt and atonement. The central character of the film could under no circumstances until then be a "positive example," yet the authors refused to pass judgment on the girl Veronica, who, under tragic circumstances, betrayed the memory of her bridegroom killed at the front.

The technique was also new. The black-and-white picture fascinated one by the brilliant "perpetual motion" shots of the hand camera, the play of camera angles and of light and shade, and the effects of short-focus optics. The vibrant and inimitable human life returning to the screen seemed to employ and rediscover the entire wealth of the metaphor, composition, and rhythms of cinematic poetry.

The script was based on Viktor Rozov's play *Eternally Alive*. The result of the crossing of the modest manner of the dramatist with the poetical uplift of director Mikhail Kalatozov and the expressive, romantic style of cameraman Sergei Urusevsky produced a peculiar fusion of different individualities.

Kalatozov (1903–1973), Georgian by nationality, first an actor, and then

Tatyana Samoilova as Veronica and Alexei Batalov as Boris in The Cranes Are Flying *by Mikhail Kalatozov brought long lines to movie theaters.*

a cameraman, was a very interesting and notably figure in Soviet cinema. The experienced and skilful master, who began his career in Georgian cinematography with the celebrated silent documentary sketch *Salt for Svanetia (Djim Shvante)* in 1930, subsequently remained in the background for a long time. Being always strongly attrached to sweeping romanticism, he preferred a hero of great stature and daring, as could be seen in particular in his film *Valeri Chkalov* (1941), where he showed the trials rather than the triumphs of the great flier. But Kalatozov as a master manifested himself more in his sticking to a once chosen range of artistic means of expression than to a definite theme. It is not easy to find the common line of a cherished theme and beloved idea and characters in such dissimilar works as the symbolic political pamphlet *The Conspiracy of the*

213

Doomed (1950), for which he was awarded the Stalin Prize, or *The First Echelon* (1955), a somewhat overweight with detail and unwieldy film about the development of virgin lands in Kazakhstan (a political campaign launched in 1950s). But these entirely different works also showed the director's close attention to the sequence of pictorial themes, his plastic talent, and bold selection of expressive techniques.

It is noteworthy that Sergei Urusevsky's shooting technique in pictures he made together with Kalatozov has much in common not only with *Salt for Svanetia* but also with Kalatozov's earlier camera work in *Gypsy Blood,* which had already revealed the range of the favorite devices of his future directorship: the play of striking, unexpected camera angles and the effects of light and shadow and, particularly, of foliage shot by a fast-moving camera and merging into a solid strip.

It could be said that Kalatozov found his "second self" in Sergei Urusevsky. For Urusevsky, the meeting with Kalatozov was also of special significance. Sergei Urusevsky (1908–1974), a painter by education and a disciple of the patriarch of Soviet graphic art, Vladimir Favorsky, came to cinematography with a backlog of pictorial tradition and proved to be a natural cinematographer who attained brilliant results with his camera. He worked with Vsevolod Pudovkin in *The Return of Vasili Bortnikov,* with Mark Donskoi in *The Village Teacher,* and with Grigori Chukhari in *The Forty-First.* But the decisive event in his creative life was the shooting of *The First Echelon* with Kalatozov.

After *The Cranes Are Flying,* Kalatozov and Urusevsky made *The Unsent Letter* (1960), a poem about geologists who perish while looking for diamonds in the taiga. Fantastic, lunar-type landscapes, the sinister sun over the primordial planet, and the loneliness of a tiny handful of people were shot magnificently. Nature seemed unrelated to people, to the relations between the characters, who were played by such performers as Tatyana Samoilova, Yevgeni Urbansky, Innokenti Smoktunovsky, and Vasili Livanov. The film remained an "experiment for cinematographers," which was also true of Kalatozov and Urusevsky's next work, *I Am Cuba* (1965), made in cooperation with Enrico Pineda Barnet and Yevgeni Yevtushenko. Here also the form was predominant (mass compositions, light and shadow effects, and the unrestricted play of the hand camera). Contentwise the film was a typified portrayal of the "flaming continent," of revolution in general.

Kalatozov's last picture, *The Red Tent* (1970), an Italo-Soviet production about the tragic fate of the Nobile expedition in the Arctic, was shot by another cameraman, Levan Paatashvili. Meanwhile Urusevsky undertook the directing of two films: *The Ambler's Race* (1969), adapted from the short novel *Farewell, Gulsary* by the Kirghiz writer Chinghiz Aitmatov, and *Sing Your Song, Poet* (1971), a fantasy on the themes of Sergei Yesenin's verses.

The wide variety of the material and subjects in itself testified to the fact that both masters, Kalatozov and Urusevsky, shared this weakness: their art tended to be dominated by form without a profound *insight into human hearts*. That is why *The Cranes Are Flying* has remained in the history of cinema as an epoch-making and classical film in which the discovery of a new theme and the original form were wonderfully blended.

In the film the private story of a woman's ruined life was magnified and sculptured on the screen by sympathy and compassion. Poor little Veronica struck the spectator with the sad blackness of her eyes, her original and memorable face, and her unusual character. She was played by Tatyana Samoilova (who would later play Anna Karenina in the film version of Tolstoi's novel). The part of Boris, Veronica's bridegroom, was played by Alexei Batalov.

The introduction to the film, reviving the happy peacetime days, is filled with bright morning sunshine and joy.

The film's poetics first attains its finest level in the crucial scene of the send-off to the front. The scene opens with the panorama of a schoolyard where relatives and friends say good-bye to the mobilized men. The moving camera shows many different and characteristic faces, snatches of private dramas, fragments of a shared disaster, of common woe. Every face is accurately spotted, revived in its main characteristic without details. There is a tumult of voices expressing sorrow, anxiety, fatalistic unconcern, faith, tears, and songs. Gradually, piercing the general noise, a woman's voice is heard ceaselessly repeating: "Boris, Borya, Borya!" as the fate of the film heroes, a tragedy of that love, with its foreboding, distress, and pain, merges with the common fate of the people.

The bewildered and sad face of Boris clearly shows that he cannot find Veronica. One effect of the scene is that, by fusing the vast common woe that is war with a single farewell that failed to take place—a purely private biographical fact infinitesimally small in terms of history—art put an equal sign between the two. An individual fate is welded with the fate of the people just as the faultlessly accurate thread of the action of the central characters is woven into the fabric of the scene: the episode at the recruiting station is followed nonstop by the shots of Veronica running along the city's streets; she is stopped by a column of heavy tanks, darts to and fro in the crowd, near an iron fence behind which the soldiers are filing in; overlapping this is Boris' inner tension, his concentration on what is now to him the meaning of his whole life, and the repeated call which he seems to hear.

The mounting excitement and the rumble, like that of a tidal wave, reach a climax. Then the old and familiar music of the "Slav Woman's Farewell" march is heard, the memorable sounds of 1941, devoid of martial fervor or the cadenced tread of soldiers' boots and conveying only sadness, preparedness, and courage. By changing the rhythm, the march divides the scene like the "golden section." The recruits have started to march. Peace has ended, war has begun. The old and dear "here" is giving place to the unknown and fearsome "there." As the column quickens its step the crowd begins a new movement—a recoil, an ebb—and the last turn of Boris' head in the column and the packet of biscuits desperately hurled by Veronica, which the recruits tread upon without noticing, conclude the farewell symphony. Quiet descends sharply on the screen, which is disturbed only by the whirring of the dialing disk of the public telephone: months have passed but there are no letters from Boris.

Another scene from *The Cranes Are Flying,* which carried a heavy charge and a seed for many subsequent images, was the death of Boris, who was killed in a forest near Moscow. This is where the famous superspeed camera showed within a few seconds the last vision of a falling mortally wounded soldier. What fascinated the spectator here most was not the vision itself, which seemed slightly jarring compared to Batalov's austere performance—a black tuxedo and bow tie, paper streamers, and bridal veil, the trivial attributes of an imagined wedding of a later period—nor the sequences with circling birches, which caused a long succession of various fantasies. The main thing was the heart-rending image of war and its unnaturalness, conveyed by the entire atmosphere of the scene: the autumnal coppice where the fighting was going on, the sucking clay, the cold and damp desolation. One felt an overwhelming pity, no matter how beautifully the birches waltzed, for Boris, who was dying in the coppice and who would never kiss his Veronica. This scene and the film *The Cranes Are Flying* as a whole revealed for the first time with such a fiery pathos the monstrous injustice of war to what is most natural: love, youth, and life.

Ballad of a Soldier *was the story of a man forced by history to become a soldier.*

BALLAD OF A SOLDIER BY GRIGORI CHUKHRAI

The screenplay of *Ballad of a Soldier* written by Valentin Yezhov, a former frontline soldier, vividly revealed, through the death of one of the millions (an ordinary Soviet Army soldier who had not even reached Berlin), the immense tragedy of the loss of one life, an irretrievable human life. Soldier Alyosha Skvortsov "could have become a good father and a wonderful citizen. He could have become a worker, engineer or scientist. He could have grown wheat and adorned the earth with gardens. But all he managed in his short life was to become a soldier. . . ." These final words of the author's off-screen text are highly significant. *Ballad of a Soldier* is in fact a ballad not about a soldier but about a man forced by history to become a soldier.

217

Chukhrai made his debut in 1956 and shot three films in five years—*The Forty-First, Ballad of a Soldier,* and *Clear Skies.*

Today this distinguished director makes one film after another *(The Quagmire, Life Is Fine),* but his "stellar hour," the breakthrough to revelation, dates back to the late fifties.

He was born in 1921. In 1939, when Chukhrai was admitted to take entrance exams at the Institute of Cinematography, he was called up to the army. Red Army Private Chukhrai could not take part in military operations during the Soviet-Finish war of 1939–1940 because his feet were badly frostbitten at its very outset. He was still in active service when the Great Patriotic War broke out.

Chukhrai was wounded for the first time on the second day of the war. Then followed years filled with events and circumstances which could be called extraordinary had they not also filled the biographies of millions of Chukhrai's contemporaries. He was at first a signalman, then volunteered for the airborne troops, and was repeatedly dropped in the enemy rear, taking part in complex and difficult operations. Chukhrai was wounded on several occasions, once very seriously; he was in the hospital at the time of Victory Day. After returning to his studies at the Institute of Cinematography with a still unhealed leg and an arm shot in several places, he had to undergo prolonged treatment, came down with tuberculosis, and had to walk with crutches for a long time.

Chukhrai made his debut with *The Forty-First,* a screen version of a short novel by Boris Lavrenev about the civil war. The heroine, partisan sharpshooter Maryutka, fell in love with a wounded White officer; he was that "forty-first" enemy whom she could not kill. Because of some circumstances they had to spend several days alone on an uninhabited island in the Aral Sea.

As Chukhrai once noted, the question of whether the heroine "had the right" to fall in love with an enemy did not then arise. For him, Maryutka's drama was not an alternative of choice or a conflict of remorse. Here love itself, this great feeling, was balanced against class duty.

There was certainly no question for Chukhrai what would tip the scale, and there was only one answer for Maryutka—class duty. The rifle shot at the "forty-first" was the inevitable and only possible outcome of Maryutka's love, and its supreme justice was not doubted for a second by either the heroine or the filmmakers. And yet Chukhrai gave all his temperament and interest to Maryutka's love.

The poetry of the most ordinary things also captivates us in *Ballad of a Soldier*. In the headquarters dugout the youthful private Alyosha Skvortsov, the hero of a recently won fight, tells the general about the leaky roof of his house in faraway Sosnovka and readily swaps a decoration for a furlough in order to see his mother and mend the roof.

The war in the *Ballad* is seen from inside, through a soldier's eyes. That is why the inside of boxcars looks so natural, soldier's tunics are bleached with wear, the mess tin is black with soot, and the water drawn into it from a tap at a stop is bubbling and must be deliciously tasty. Familiar also are glittering, dented heavy cans with American Spam and black lettering on them.

Both Chukhrai and his hero Alyosha find their bearings easily in the wartime world, which has been on the move ever since everything left its proper place. But while the dividing line between the rear and the front is fluid, the border between good and bad is marked very distinctly. To Chukhrai the main thing is that war, which had turned upside down all the previous life, also clarified, confirmed, and revealed anew its hallowed principles and mainstays, its goodness, its light, and its shadows. That is why Chukhrai's sympathy and anger are always expressed straightforwardly.

Close to each other in one film frame are two faces—Alyosha's fine Slavic countenance and the low-browed, pimply face of the sentry Gavrilkin. The latter is prepared to let the soldier from the front into a boxcar he guards only for a bribe, in this case the Spam. The two faces stand for two different moral types, and Chukhrai, devoted as he is to the good and beautiful, does not wish to conceal the existence of Gavrilkin with his vicious dumbness and kulak's greed.

This unambiguous appraisal and contraposition is felt in everything. Chukhrai is not afraid to look too primitive in the way he presents simple truths; and he proves correct, for there is a special epic feeling in his *Ballad* akin to the pure simplicity of a folk fairy tale, a song, or an ancient parable with their crystallized wisdom and justice of generations.

Ballad of a Soldier appeared at the Cannes Festival in 1960, the same year that Federico Fellini released *La dolce vita;* Michelangelo Antonioni, *L'avventura;* and Ingmar Bergman, *The Virgin Spring*. The very situation of the last named picture, where heinous forest bandits raped and murdered a defenseless child who had merrily ridden to church on a beautiful horse, the very metaphor of the world's evil, presented as a medieval legend, was in striking contrast with Chukhrai's film. *Ballad of a Soldier* opposed its faith to "noncommunicability," the "rupture of links and contacts between people," and "alienation"—the predominant ideas of Western art which were first proclaimed so sweepingly and tragically at the Twelfth Cannes Festival. Complexity was countered by simple truths; total relativity by an unsophisticated but certain knowledge of what is good and what is bad; the depiction of man's tragic loneliness by kindness, love, and human links which are formed in a world torn asunder in the hell that is war.

It was at the festival that the *Ballad* began to win hearts. The secret of its fascination for the modern West was best expressed at a writers' round-table held in Rome in April 1962 by Pier Paulo Pasolini: "Chukhrai is like a classic who has lived up to our time. It is like the unexpected finding in a city block of grey and mediocre buildings of the miraculously preserved ruins of a vast and mighty ancient structure."

This seems to be a just comparison. It was Pasolini who called the trend of the Soviet art of the late 1950s, in particular Chukhrai's work, "neoromanticism." The term, which was much used in the Italian and French press, marked the artistic uplift of Soviet cinema of that period.

Quite a lot has now been written about this film. Each episode has been analyzed many times over. A whole cinematographic tree has grown out of it, including significant and beautiful pictures as well as more modest ones. There are also naive and primitive imitations. But the important thing is that none of these films has repeated the "classic formula of the masterpiece" or said *what* Chukhrai spoke about and *how* he spoke about it. One sign of a great film is probably the fact that it is inimitable.

Later on people expected another *Ballad* from Chukhrai. Each of his films was compared with this remarkable achievement. But we all still have a great deal to learn about the mysteries of the day and hour, of the moment of the birth of masterpieces. *Chapayev,* for instance, was one of the first pictures of the Vasilyev Brothers but by no means the last.

DESTINY OF A MAN *BY SERGEI BONDARCHUK*

Sergei Bondarchuk added another tragic testimony of a destiny crippled by the war to the wartime tragedy of a ruined love *(The Cranes Are Flying)* and to the tragedy of the loss of a single priceless life *(Ballad of a Soldier).*

Mikhail Sholokhov's short story about the war prisoner Andrei Sokolov was broadcast over radio on New Year's Eve of 1957 and was of

Sergei Bondarchuk portrays Andrei Sokolov in Destiny of a Man *based on a short story by Mikhail Sholokhov.*

great public import because, until that time, captivity by Nazis had remained a forbidden topic in art, and Soviet war prisoners were not shown on the screen.

Sergei Bondarchuk was already a renown actor who had played Taras Shevchenko in the film of the same name, the Bolshevik Valko in Gerasimov's *The Young Guard,* and Doctor Dymov in the screen version of Chekhov's *The Grasshopper* when he made his debut as a film director in *Destiny of a Man.* Speaking about the film, Bondarchuk said: "The war still lives like an unhealed wound in the soul. The memory of war has seared every one of us."

Born in 1920, he was called up from a theater school in Rostov-on-Don, served his time, was demobilized, and came to the VGIK acting department in his infantry trench coat.

He must have felt attracted to independent organization of action and composition, for directorship finally became Bundarchuk's main profession although he continued to work as an actor.

Sholokhov's short story narrated in the first person acquires an epic force. The first shots of the film show Andrei Sokolov's prewar life. The fresh scaffolding of a construction site, a girl in a white blouse with her hair cut short in the Komsomol fashion of the twenties, the joy of the first date, the merry ditties sung to a harmonica in the evening—once again the bright prewar world was revived on the screen. The overture is necessary to the director for the sharp contrast between happiness and endless sorrow, calm and despair.

Truly tragic is the fate of soldier Sokolov, who lived through all possible war misfortunes: captivity, the loss of dear ones, humiliation, wounds, and pain. This path of sorrow is shown as a road of courage, endless suffering, and strength of spirit. Only in some scenes does Bondarchuk view his hero from a distance, and then the image acquires the features of lofty monumentality. But such moments are brief. On the whole the role is played and directed with great sincerity and is imbued with powerful hatred and love.

The Russian national character in the new social conditions is what Bondarchuk seeks above all to embody in Andrei Sokolov, providing his own, very purposeful interpretation of this multifaceted and very complex concept. He saw the specific traits of the Russian character neither in the traditional humility of Platon Karatayev, so admired by Tolstoi; nor in the contrast between external defenselessness and the inner moral purity of Alyosha Karamazov; nor in meek submission, spiritual ravings, or heart-rending tragedies. Sholokhov's Andrei Sokolov preserves unbending staunchness despite the severest trials. A reserved and reticent and all the more powerful temperament, mute stubbornness in the devotion to one's ideals, condensed will and unvarying kindness, concealed under an unobtrusive appearance—such is the portrait of a Russian man painted in the film. Bondarchuk added severer and more somber features to the image of the original story.

Destiny of a Man is a film of sharp expressive techniques. The director purposefully continued and developed the traditions of war films. The visage of war and fascist slavery is fearsomely ugly: the lacerated earth with a quiet birch grove as a surviving islet of nature, the black smoke billowing from the crematorium chimney in a concentration camp, the savagely cruel selection of victims, and the people lining before the crematorium.

The sound track includes abrupt contrapuntal turns. The extermination camp episode, for instance, is accompanied by the notoriously banal tune "O donna Clara." Through the barking foreign speech and singing, Andrei Sokolov suddenly hears the distant, dear melody of a lively Russian ditty: the sound plays the role of the hero's internal monologue. The film *Destiny of a Man* affirmed an active and emotionally charged mode of expression which was gradually becoming the sign of a new stage in the development of the cinema style, a style typical of the screen of the 1960s.

Released in the last year of the decade, *The Cranes Are Flying, Ballad of a Soldier,* and *Destiny of a Man* formed a triptych summing up the changes that had taken place in Soviet cinema.

Once again, as during the *Rainbow* time, which honestly told the contemporaries about the endless sufferings of Soviet people, these films brought into the world the unhealed anguish of the losses, the unmitigated sorrow, and the clear, unambiguous message of hatred of war. They answered the bitter rhetorical question of the well-known Soviet song, "Say do the Russians want a war." One had only to see *Destiny of a Man* or think of Alyosha Skvortsov and his mother in *Ballad* to realize how many bright hopes and how many lovers meant to make each other happy were buried by war in Russian forests.

Like *The Cranes Are Flying* and *Ballad of a Soldier,* the film *Destiny of a Man* received international recognition. It was equally successful in the same 1959 at a non-competition show of the Venice Film Festival and as a competition entry at the First International Film Festival in Moscow, where it received the main prize.

★ ★ ★

The international prestige of Soviet cinema was rising. The second half of the 1950s marked the second discovery of Soviet cinema, the first dating back to the revolutionary advance of Soviet films during the 1920s. Now Soviet films were winning high prizes at Karlovy Vary, Cannes, Venice, San Francisco, San Sebastian, Locarno, and Oberhausen. Although Soviet productions had been awarded international prizes before, the very comparison of titles indicated a great difference. For instance,

Sadko, an exotic film for the Western eye, and *Ballad of a Soldier,* a manifesto of a new generation of directors, were obviously works of essentially different ranks.

It should also be remembered that a great number of new names came to the fore in the world cinema of the fifties, and a process began which was changing the very "scale of values" at international festivals.[3] Whereas festival winners in the forties were, as a rule, films of the traditionally Hollywood type (even Rossellini's *Roma, citta aperta* was not understood and received only a honorary diploma), the contest of the fifties was centered around problematic, novel, and experimental works.

The international revival of Soviet films in the fifties introduces the Western spectator to a multitude of Soviet productions not released abroad earlier for various reasons (including censorship). Thus, *The Last Night* by Raizman was "discovered" in Paris, while *Film Eye* and *The Man with a Movie Camera* by Dziga Vertov became revival sensations at Cannes and Karlovy Vary. *The Battleship Potemkin* was again given first place at the international competition for the best films of all times conducted during the 1958 World Fair in Brussels, while *Mother* and *Earth* were also named among the best films.

The International Film Festival in Moscow, established in 1959 under the motto "For Humanism in Cinema Art, for Peace and Friendship Among Nations," is open for the latest productions not only of the world's leading film industries, starting with the United States, but also of the young or newborn cinematography of countries which are only beginning film production. Despite the inevitable disadvantage of this principle (due to the varying standards of films presented for general competition), the Moscow festival is today most democratic and representative.

New trends also make themselves felt in cinema life inside the Soviet Union. New films are now being discussed with the broader participation of the public, while previously the fate of pictures was decided predominantly behind the closed doors of the artistic council of the Department for Cinematographic Affairs or, quite often, "from above," by the order of the top official. Studios acquired greater independence.

The Organizing Committee of the Union of Cinema Workers of the USSR was established in 1957 and existed until 1965, when the First Inaugural Congress of Cinematographers was convened.

The need for creative consolidation of cinema workers had long been urgent and the Union of Cinematographers formed such a consolidating center, its plenary meetings and conferences at once becoming an arena of principled and heated arguments on burning issues of cinema life.

CHAPTER SIX

The Unforgettable Sixties

The New Outlook

*T*he Soviet sixties really denote the period between the twentieth and twenty-second CPSU congresses, that is, from 1957 to 1967. The cultural developments that gained momentum then later slowed down or lost their initial impetus. That time span marked the beginning of a different period, with problems of its own. But the sixties were invigorating and progressive times, not idyllic, but at any rate hopeful.

Our concern is the cinema, but we should re-emphasize the free and creative atmosphere of those days, characterized by heated debates at artists' unions and by the blossoming of new literary and art periodicals. The most remarkable of these was *Yunost* (*Youth*), the monthly edited by a writer of the previous generation, Valentin Katayev. Existing periodicals were transformed. In the vanguard was *Novy Mir* (*New World*), edited since 1958 by the poet Alexander Tvardovsky. Its title symbolized the new outlook.

Those were years of a public infatuation with poetry. Established poets like Mikhail Svetlov, Konstantin Simonov, and Boris Slutsky, as well as young but already popular poets like Bella Akhmadullina, Andrei

Voznesensky, Yevgeni Yevtushenko, Bulat Okujava, and Robert Rozhdestvensky, recited their verses in Moscow's packed auditoriums, performing in front of immense audiences gathered in the Main Hall of the Polytechnical Museum, where Alexander Blok and Vladimir Mayakovsky once appeared.

The reform involved the theater as well; and two new companies, the Sovremennik (set up in 1957) and the Taganka Theater (1964), competed for public attention. The former followed Stanislavsky, the latter Meyerhold, In the same years, cultural ties were expanded with many other countries. The number of translated books noticeably increased, and foreign companies performed in the USSR, among them the Berliner Ensemble founded by Bertolt Brecht and Peter Brook's Shakespeare Company. Both stirred the public imagination.

The general atmosphere encouraged progress in the cinema, which often anticipated development elsewhere. Film was frequently the first to explore new fields and offer new expressive means. Of course, literature was still the cinema's principal resource, supplying scripts, plots, and heroes. But film could register more expressiveness, scale, and impact than writing.

In the sixties the term "thaw" was replaced by other definitions— "flood," "spring," "ice-breaking." They implied the growth of democracy. Cinema's prestige was enhanced by productions like *The Cranes Are Flying* or *Ballad of a Soldier,* but these did not become models for the Russian equivalent of the "nouvelle vogue," which swept the Soviet sixties in one tide after another.

The World of Seryozha, Volodya, and Ivan

What had seemed to be documentary truth a short while before began to appear superfluous and general, as recent achievements were rapidly reviewed. What appeared to be true to life only the day before seemed affected, dated, and sentimental. Cliches were repudiated: off-screen female choruses accompanying emotional episodes; people running to symphonic music; "emotional" landscapes used to create a mood; and monologues of the heroes and off-screen comments that were seldom justified. The settings of even the best films of the fifties began to look artificial and theatrical.

Nor was the new awareness of the world satisfactory; filmmakers needed subtler instruments of research and presentation. Arguments against the aesthetic dogmatism of the past gave way to a positive realism that encouraged creative thinking. Filmmakers no longer sought mere role-models but tried to analyze a character in all its manifestations against a realistic background. Thus began the exploration of a new stratum of reality.

The yearning for a fresh and unbiased focus produced a new type of hero, a child. *Seryozha,* the first production made by Georgi Daneliya and Igor Talankin, became a major event almost despite itself. In *Seryozha* the world was shown through the eyes of a child. Street life, human faces and characters, landscapes, rain and the sun are all shown at a fresh angle, a special meaning being attached to every detail. The child's eye registers everything that escapes stereotypes and banal associations of the adult's. The child-hero helped develop a new cinematic vision; the film rendered the world of a boy who had survivied a long, horrible war and had experienced grief. Film characters of the preceding decade—Alyosha Skvortsov, Veronica, or Andrei Sokolov—were hero-martyrs, no matter how ordinary they looked. But in the sixties they gave way to a little person; the full title of Vera Panova's story that served the basis for the screenplay was *Seryozha: A Few Days of a Very Little Boy's Life.*

Never before had Soviet movies been so full of children and teenagers. Children's cinema (*Happy Vacations, Lone White Sail*) thrived, as it still does, but in the sixties children were chosen as a means to resolve acute and complex problems.

There were children, teenagers, and a father coming home from the war in the productions released a little earlier, for instance, in *Two Fyodors* by Marlen Khutsiev, where two wartime orphans, a soldier and a little boy (both namesakes), met among the ruins. The bitter wartime experience of the younger Fyodor had made him more mature than his namesake who had fought at the front. If we now turn to *Introduction* (1963) made by Igor Talankin soon after *Seryozha* and also based on a story by Vera Panova, *Valya and Volodya,* we will be impressed with the role of Volodya. The situation is both funny and disconcerting: a fatherless teenager who had grown independent and aware of the shady side of life too early patronizes his mother, still lovely and vigorous and somewhat light-minded (Nina Urgant created the character of a woman whom we were more likely to sympathize with rather than resent, which was unusual at the time).

Yuli Raizman, who made *And If It's Love?* (1960), took another aspect of the teenage problem. He focused on an urban residential area with its standard blocks of flats, yards, schools, shops, and clubs (in the late 1950s the USSR built many five-story prefab houses, unattractive but providing families with separate apartments). This was full-fledged postwar life, and Raizman tested its moral foundations. He used a conventional love story: teenage boy meets girl and is separated as they grow aware of their mutual attraction. Love is trampled by people whose obscure prejudices are disguised by a new morality.

The young couple, in a film which anticipated *Love Story* are a modern Romeo and Juliet. Ksenia, performed by the young Zhanna Prohorenko (who had come into the limelight after playing the lead in *Ballad of a Soldier*), and Boris are facing the "yard" as a symbol of conventional mentality. Common gossip, swelling like a snowball, leads to tragedy; the girl attemps suicide, and the boy has to leave the place for good. The sweethearts are separated. It isn't even love, merely growing mutual attraction, or a hint at affection, that is nipped in the bud by the yard's morality. The Yard is personified in Ksenia's mother (performed by Fedosova, who had played several middle-aged heroines in the sixties), a woman in her late forties, honest and dignified in her own way. She reared her children alone, and widowhood hardened her and deprived her of hope.

Ksenia is unmistakably her mother's daughter. Raizman is aware of her somewhat hard mouth, alarming commonness, and heavy chin. Yet, her eyes are childish and teasing. She is, in fact, human material that can be shaped into anything. Raizman, a sensitive artist, traces acute social problems and warns us against philistinism.

Showing life through the eyes of a child was a postwar tendency in other countries as well, manifested in Western Europe in a number of Italian neorealistic and post-neorealistic productions, such as *The Children are Watching Us, Shoe Shine,* and *The Bicycle Thief* by Vittorio de Sica. And think of Luca, the youngest brother in Visconti's *Rocco and His Brothers,* who gave us hope for a better future. Another typical production was *The Red Balloon* by French director Albert Lamorise. Obviously these trends had something in common, even if they occurred in the cinema or society of different countries.

The children's theme in Soviet movies (whose postwar advance was delayed but spectacular) was expressed in different genres. Some pictures were lyrical, others dealt with school life, and still others with parental problems. Among the latter was *Answer the Doorbell* (1965) made by Alexander Mitta and based on the screenplay by Alexander Volodin, a film dramatist with a vivid individuality that could not be obscured by the director's. It is a story of a little girl learning about the complicated relationships between adults. Another movie worth mentioning is *We'll Get by Till Monday* (1968), which was produced by Stanislav Rostotsky and written by Georgi Polonsky. It gave rise to heated discussions among teachers and schoolchildren. The male lead, played by Vyacheslav Tikhonov, was a charismatic and unorthodox schoolteacher. The actor previously worked for Rostotsky in his "country" film *It Happened in Penkovo* and later in *White Bim the Black Ear;* he starred as Andrei Bollconsky in Sergei Bondarchuk's version of *War and Peace.* Tikhonov reached the climax of his movie career when he played a Soviet intelligence officer in the twelve-part TV serial "Seventeen Moments of Spring" by Tatyana Lioznova, based on Yulian Semyonov's script.

Returning to the school theme, we could recall other pictures made in different genres, for instance, Elem Klimov's satirical comedy *Welcome, Or No Admittance* (1964). Its contradictory title announced the film's main topic—people's stupidity, red tape, and hypocrisy. The screenplay was written by Semyon Lungin and Ilya Nusinov. The comedy is set in a children's summer camp where young Pioneer Kostya Inochkin rebels against the camp manager, a bureaucrat called Dynin.

The comic effect of the picture comes from turning a holiday camp for children into a scale model of adult bureaucracy. The stupid but zealous Dynin adorns the camp with slogans, posters, and regulations and places horrendous plaster statues along its pathways. The children, naughty and happy like any kids on vacation, are yearning for the sunny beach and clear water, but the manager torments them with formal speeches of the kind made at official meetings of the staff. The parents' visiting day is turned into a formal occasion, like a reception of, say, a VIP delegation.

Welcome, Or No Admittance! was Elem Klimov's diploma picture—he graduated from the Moscow Institute of Cinematography in 1964. Before joining the cinema institute he had graduated from an aviation institute and worked as engineer and then became a journalist in radio and TV. When still a student at the Institute of Cinematography, his unorthodox talent for comedy brought him to the fore. His next movie, *The Dentist's Adventures* (1965, from a screenplay by Alexander Volodin), was also a comedy. (Incidentally, the dramatist also wrote scripts for a number of films, such as *Five Evenings* by Nikita Mikhalkov or *The Autumn Marathon* by Georgi Daneliya). This was the comic story of a dentist who could extract teeth painlessly, without an anesthesia. Its aura of nostalgia and the grotesque led the "Dynins" to find the poetic fable dangerous and have it shelved (not uncommon among movie administrators). Thus Klimov's misfortunes befell him soon after his brilliant start. Only in 1971 could he release his next film, *Sport, Sport, Sport,* in which documentary sports reels alternate with feature sequences connecting the present with the past and combining mime and ballet. Among the cast are Valeri Brumel, a Soviet sportsman of international renown, and a very youthful Nikita Mikhalkov. In a sequence set in medieval Russia, a young and beautiful tsarina is enthroned, clad in sables and fabulous jewelry. That vignette was performed by the witty and exquisite Larissa Shepitiko, Klimov's wife, who was also a film director. A pupil of Alexander Dovzhenko, she had recently become famous for *Wings.*

This brilliant young couple, gifted and handsome, later endured terrible trials; the still young Larissa died in a car accident. Suffering and tragic loss would tranform Elem Klimov's artistic talent, hardening him and eventually breeding the mournful but elevated spirit of his *Farewell* or the intense, condensed grief and anger of his *Come and See.*

Ivan is the title of a wartime story which Vladimir Bogomolov published in the *Novy Mir;* the film, produced by the Mosfilm Studios, was called *Ivan's Childhood.* The picture, ruined by some wreck of a director, was completed in haste by a recent graduate from the Institute of Cinematography and previewed at a conference held at the Filmmakers' Union in March 1962. Said Mikhail Romm, the then ardent supporter of young talents: "Remember his name: Andrei Tarkovsky . . . ."[1]

Ivan's Childhood begins with a shot of a forest on a fine day in June. The camera pans vertically along a sandy river bank, thick with twisted tree roots. The needles of young pines glitter in the sunlight. A cuckoo warbles. A fair-haired boy in shorts stares at the beautiful world around, his eyes wide open. Suddenly the camera jerks away to show the same boy, now deeply tanned and dressed in a well-worn padded coat, against the background of smouldering Russian land, thick with smoke. The boy makes his way through the thickets and across the moorlands, climbing over driftwood. Blackened trunks stick out from putrid water under his feet, and an unutterably sad musical sound soars over this land maimed by war. This one sequence was enough to realize that an artist was being born.

Larissa Shepitko is the tsarina in Sport, Sport, Sport, *an Elem Klimov film in which documentary sports reels alternate with feature sequences to connect the past with the present.*

231

Tarkovsky was a graduate of Mikhail Romm's celebrated studio (1961), also attended by Vasily Shukshin, Andrei Mikhalkov-Konchalovsky, and Alexandez Mitta. Tarkovsky came to the limelight when he made his first student film, a screen version of an Ernest Hemingway story. His diploma picture, a short feature entitled *The Steamroller and the Violin,* was shown to the public at large. It was a story of a child, something along the lines of Lamorisse's *Red Balloon,* but based on a purely Soviet situation and full of a romantic Moscow summer. Its hero is a young boy, Sasha, a violin student of a music school. His friend is good-natured steamroller driver laying asphalt in Moscow streets. That exquisite and innocent film was as fascinating as the boy when he played his violin. His babylike face with ruddy cheeks is transformed as he demonstrates his skill to his friend. *The Steamroller and the Violin* was about an emerging talent and a true calling, a short prelude to the amazing movie career of Andrei Tarkovsky, one of the most original and profound screen artists of the second half of the century, a poet of cinematography.

Ivan's Childhood was a step forward from his student films. It was so unusual that it scared off people. No matter how familiar and complex a child-hero might be and how many little wartime orphans adopted by fighting soldiers might appear on the screen, the character of the little avenger, ten-year-old Ivan, who fought against the enemy in a partisan unit, was unprecedented in film. The boy with adult eyes, whose hatred and courage surprised hardened soldiers, was a symbol of war that maimed young souls by filling them with hatred and a yearning for revenge.

Tarkovsky's *Ivan's Childhood* was an artistic revelation even after such pictures as *Rainbow, The Cranes Are Flying, Ballad of a Soldier,* and other European war films.

Military strategy, heroic endeavour, moral testing, and the suffering of innocents were all presented in many films, but *Ivan's Childhood* showed war as a distortion of human nature and as madness. That aspect was topical in the early sixties, the period of the struggle for ending the cold war. This was the era of summits between Kennedy and Krushchev. Andrei Tarkovsky always resented political time-serving; but he had an acute sense of time, which prompted his new interpretation of a wartime story.

Many critics who reviewed the film after it won the Grand Prix at the 1962 Venice Film Festival mentioned this unexpected angle. Italian newspapers discussed the film, as later did the left-wing French press and many writers and journalists (Sartre remarked that Ivan was as mad as war itself).

Ivan's Childhood anticipates ideas, plots, and elements of Tarkovsky's later work. More than a fresh interpretation of the valid story of a little partisan (it was too personal to be only that), the author's poetic mind, experience, and suffering were suffused into *Ivan's Childhood."* This became clear in 1975, when Tarkovsky's new film, *The Mirror,* with its strong autobiographical motifs, was released.

Tarkovsky, born in 1932 and attending junior high school during the war, chose a countryhouse far away from the front line, where he actually spent his wartime childhood, as set for this film. A son of a poet Arseni Tarkovsky, he was a Muscovite from a cultured family. When the war broke out, the boy and his sister were evacuated to the country.

His troubles and sorrows differ from Ivan's. They share only the pain of war. The author emphasizes that the scars of childhood trauma persist. A story of a little Leningrad evacuee and blockade orphan shown in *The Mirror* is based on that bitter awareness.

Another episode in the film also focuses upon war, privation, and famine. Alyosha (the hero) and his mother try to sell a pair of turquoise earrings to a wealthy woman living in a faraway village. The family is poor because the father is fighting at the front and cannot support them. Overcoming her shame, the mother offers her modest jewelry to the wealthy stranger. When the two women retire to the adjoining room to make a deal, the boy has to wait for a long time, and this waiting is unbearable. It is, probably, at this moment that he first becomes aware of himself as a person. His alienated eye falls upon a reflection in an oval mirror, forcusing on a strange boy with tousled hair, looking like a hungry young wolf, his ragged clothes soaked with rain, and a pool of water around his bare feet.

Thus the child's awareness of the world and of himself, first shown through the eyes of little Seryozha, led filmmakers far from that original idea to produce a new philosophy.

Soviet Ethnic Cinema

Soviet ethnic cinema was revived also by the theme of childhood, which helped it break through to the international screen.

Tengiz Abuladze directed Avtandil Makharadze, star of Repentance.

In 1956 the Cannes jury and the press were alerted by a short feature titled *Magdan's Donkey,* produced by the Georgian Film Studios. Two names among the credits—Tengiz Abuladze and Revaz Chkheidze—were new to the public. Sergei Yutkevich, who was on the panel, said later the picture meant the discovery of the Georgian cinema. The audience in the Cinema Palace in Boulevard de la Croisette knew nothing about the Georgians, let alone about Georgian films. Who were these dark-haired heroes, the "Russians" who looked more like Italians. A simple narrative of Georgia before the revolution, whose heroes were a widow's three children and a sick donkey called Lurdzha, was an event because of its very ordinariness, its serenity.

The two young Georgian filmmakers, both Dovzhenko's pupils, later worked independently; but the picture marked the beginning of the brilliant career of one of the most unorthodox Soviet directors, Tengiz Abuladze, later the author of a trilogy completed by the famous *Repentance* (the first two parts being *Entreaty,* 1968, and *The Wishing Tree,* 1977). It also brought to the limelight Revaz Chkheidze, not only as a highly professional director, but also as the efficient manager of the film industry. Since 1973 he had been combining his duties as Georgian Film Studios' general manager with intense creative work. His *Your Son, Earth* was based on modern Georgian themes, and he is now directing a new multi-serial version of *Don Quixote,* launched in 1980 and produced jointly with Spain. The part of Don Quixote is played by the subtle Georgian actor Kakhi Kavsadze.

But that is to anticipate. After *Magdan's Donkey* neither Abuladze nor Chkheidze deviated from their theme. Chkheidze soon made *Our Courtyard* (starring a number of emerging actors, who would soon become the backbone of the Georgian cinema). Abuladze produced *Someone Else's Children,* based on a newspaper feature about complicated relationships between two children, their father, and a strange girl who became a mother to them. On the verge of sentimentality, the plot of *Someone Else's Children* remains touching and innocent. Its atmosphere of a big southern city, Tbilisi, is spiced with original observations, folk scenes, and comedy.

The next picture by Abuladze, on a similar topic, was *Myself, Grandmother, Iliko, and Illarion,* from a story by Nodar Dumbadze. The wartime childhood of a Georgian country boy is the story of a simple soul, pure as the snow of the Georgian mountains, who nonetheless affects all around him.

That was the first peak of the Georgian "new wave," marking the emergence of an original local school. Its reputation was soon consolidated by *A Soldier's Father* by Revaz Chkheidze and starring Sergo Zakariadze in his best role. Having absorbed the folk tradition of the Georgian cinema of the twenties, the Georgian Film Studios have enhanced their reputation by the work of Otar Ioseliani, Lana Gogoberidze, Georgi and Eldar Shengelaya, Merab Kokochashvili, Alexander Rekhviashvili, and others.

In the early sixties every Soviet republic produced a film "through the eyes of a child," including *Children of the Pamirs* made in Tajikistan, *The Man Who Followed the Sun* released in Moldavia, *You Are Not an Orphan*

Repentance *was the last film in the triology by Tengiz Abuladze, one of the most unorthodox Soviet directors.*

produced in Uzbekistan, and the Byelorussian *Star of the Belt Buckle.*

Children of the Pamirs, poetic and unusual, was made by Vladimir Motyl based on a poem by Mirsaid Mirshakar. It was shot where the actual events took place—a Pamir high-mountain village, among snowy peaks and rapid streams, against a landscape of striking beauty and amidst beautiful people (there is a legend that the Pamir people are descendants of Alexander the Great's armies who crossed the Pamirs on their way to India). Shukhrat Abbasov's *You Are Not an Orphan* narrated the story of an Uzbek couple who adopted fourteen wartime orphans, all from different national origins.

Living Heroes (1960), directed by the emerging filmmaker Vytautas Zalakevicius, was the first remarkable production made by a new Lithuanian movie school. It consists of four stories about children. The first is set in the period of the bourgeois republic, the following two episodes during the war. The final, modern, one shows Soviet Lithuania through the eyes of a child. The episode titled *The Last Shot* and made by Arunas Zebriunas and Jonas Gricius (later one of the best Soviet camera directors; he shot *Hamlet* and *King Lear* for Grigori Kozintsev) was remarkable for its original style, lyrical landscape, special atmosphere, and unusual composition.

The Lithuanian school became world famous after the release of *Nobody Wanted to Die* (1966), by Vytautas Zalakevicius, a story based on the situation in Lithuania in the immediate postwar years. The plot, which depicts "forest brothers" hiding in the woods and terrorizing the locals, was well acted by an unmistakably Lithuanian cast adhering to a strong local dramatic tradition: Donatas Banionis, Juosas Budraitis, Regimantas Adomaitis, Algimantas Masiulis, and other young performers with brilliant subsequent careers.

Through the Eyes of an Adolescent

A teenager's world is different from a child's: he or she discovers it anew, and in conflict. Cinema and fiction could not ignore this: the conflict between generations and the desire of postwar teenagers to see the world's faults with their own eyes. In the late fifties and early sixties, Soviet cinema, influenced by contemporary drama and prose, developed a "youth" trend. The new type of young man who makes a hard start in life first appeared in Viktor Rosov's plays, such as *Good Luck!* and *In Search of*

Sofiko Chiaureli took the role of a mad peasant woman in The Wishing Tree, *a 1977 Abuladze film.*

Happiness, and in Vasily Aksyonov's story, *A Starry Ticket.* The young man rejects an imposed morality or refuses to follow others blindly because he senses the hypocrisy, groundlessness, and unreality of moral declarations. He resents the discrepancy between words and deeds, theory and practice. Becoming aware that some of the ideals suggested to him are hypocritical, he stubbornly denies all other moral values. He wants to investigate and find out what is true and what is false. The subsequent

Mzia Makhviladze, as she appears in Repentance.

careers of those who introduced this character to Soviet literature and cinema of the sixties took different paths. Viktor Rozov led the socio-psychological trend in drama for quite a time; but by the late seventies he seemed somewhat out of date, even in such an acute social drama as *The Deaf Man's Nest,* which depicted a now obscure type of Stalinist. Vasily Aksyonov, whose start was so promising, defected to the West.

The best film of that cycle was Marlen Khutsiev's *I Am Twenty* (1965), from a screenplay he wrote together with Gennadi Shpalikov (one of the best young scriptwriters of the sixties).

Sergei, Kolka, and Slavka, the three heroes, are childhood friends (following a centuries-old Russian tradition of portraying three friends, each of them playing out his own part).

239

Sergo Zakariadze has his crowning role of Georgy Makharadzeshvili in A Soldier's Father, *1964.*

Sergei (Valentin Popov) is a young, recently demobilized serviceman. He is the commonplace member of the trio, and we see the world through his eyes. More important than his individuality is the type he represents. He is a model of an ordinary Soviet man who combines work with evening college studies and social duties. He is perfectly healthy and handsome enough—a modern young man. He begins to ponder the meaning of life, of himself and his peers, like so many young people do no matter in what era or country they live. The main theme of the film is the maturing of his civic outlook, the determining of the evolution of Sergei's character. Important as his life story and love for Anya, a girl of a different social status, might seem, his inner development is the key. His friends are portrayed more realistically because they are shown through his eyes.

Kolka, played by young actor Nikolai Gubenko (it was his debut as a film actor, and now he is a prominent stage and film director), is a modern version of old film characters—charismatic jokers and real intellectuals in a middle-class milieu. Kolka, a raffish, irresistible charmer, in fact signifies a farewell to the familiar stereotype. This young man reaches the same stage of self-awareness as Sergei, only under more dramatic circumstances. Emancipation and inclination to reflection are results of trauma: an attempt to recruit him, the most loyal of the three friends, as an informer. Kolka works at a computer center, and a confidential talk with his boss, accompanied by oscillograph readings, delivers a final blow to his light-heartedness.

The role of the third member of the trio, Slavka, marked another debut, that of Stanislav Lyubshin, an actor who proved invaluable for the cinema of the sixties. Each period has its own faces and characters, and Lyubshin's were typical of a young man of the time—tall, with sharp features, shy smile, and thoughtful eyes. Slavka, an excavator operator, is the first of the trio to get married at twenty and have a place of his own in a new apartment block. He is dissatisfied with his existence, often rebelling against the marital yoke and quickly succumbing to his wife. There are times when he becomes vague and sits still, deep in thought. But he never indulges in philosophizing—his interest is soccer and the strength of the competing teams. This is his only refuge where he feels himself an independent man.

Khutsiev's characters seek meaning in life, like all young people, but who can help them find it?

Sergei's father was a soldier killed in the Second World War. The camera shows a face with a tender, innocent smile wearing an army cap with its red star. This image tells the son how the father was killed in an attack one early morning. This is one of the most lyrical sequences of the film. The twenty-year-old man meets his dead father, also twenty, and their two profiles lean over a soldier's face.

Sergei's growing self-awareness and maturing outlook are thoroughly analyzed by Khutsiev. The choice of Sergei's age as twenty is apt both psychologically and historically. The film was to be released in 1961, so its characters were born in 1941, when the Great Patriotic War broke out. "I'm dead earnest about the Revolution and I like the Internationale. I'm

241

quite serious about the fact that very few of us have fathers and I respect potatoes which helped us survive in those hungry years. . . ." Sergei's words are an emphatically expressed credo that inspired the neoromantism of the sixties. The viewer could only guess what happened to the trio next, but they are significant in themselves because they are individuals with firm convictions who are seeking internal freedom, independence, and the truth. The latter quality is not a state of mind, the way it was in the movies characters of the fifties, but a principle.

I Am Twenty, a democratic picture made in the post-Stalinist period, contains many beginnings and endings of later developments. It is an artistic summing-up of many discoveries of the sixties, for instance, the eternal theme of a recently recovered revolutionary ideal, of the national heritage, and of historical continuity.

In Khutsiev's film this theme is illustrated with classical and clearly symbolic scenes: the revolutionary sentry and change of the guard of honor at Lenin's bier—the obelisks of the revolution, the sacred tombs of the fallen.

Only a deaf and blind person could suspect Khutsiev of an attempt to paint Soviet reality black. What he made was a one-hundred percent pro-Soviet film, "involved" in the ultimate meaning of this word (the author's involvement is sincere and voluntary), romantic, and ultamodern. But the editors of the film drove the director to despair by their numerous corrections and cuts. The original version of his film, symoblically titled "Zastava Ilyicha" (Lenin District),★ was altered almost beyond recognition, some of its sequences replaced by new ones, and the documentary scene, shot at a poetry recital at the Polytechnical Museum, shortened a great deal (now it is regarded as invaluable documentary material). The very title was changed, for Lenin's name was considered to be out of place in a film like that. Actually, the title carried a double message: Zastava Ilyicha was a working-class area of Moscow, and its name was to remind us of the great leader of the revolution. The film was released only in 1964.

Editorial control was a most regrettable development that overcast the artistic horizons of the sixties. It occurred several years after the monstrous session of the Moscow Writers' Organization (1958) which expelled Boris Pasternak from the USSR Writers' Union. The film was released at about

★It was only in 1987 that it was decided to restore the original title, "Zastava Ilyicha," and reconstruct the original.

the time Nikita Khrushchev paid his notorious visit to an avant-garde art exhibition in Moscow and violently objected to its contents. Reactionary tendencies, rigid administration, and the incompetence of some art managers still existed in the sixties, which prevents us from defining those years as a golden age of the Soviet movies. But has there ever been a golden age in the international cinema?

Also characteristic of the sixties was the failure to make an issue of the liberation of innocent people who had been purged during Stalin's rule and sentenced to long terms in Beria's camps. The cinema took a passive stand, whereas literature produced such works as *One Day in the Life of Ivan Denisovich* by Alexander Solzhenitsin, *Kolyma Stories* by Varlaam Shalamov, and *Bas-Relief on the Rock* by A. Aldan-Semyonov. Filmmakers remained passive not because they did not sympathize with the innocent victims of the purges or admire the people who stuck to their moral principles even behind bars but because they faced strong opposition in the film industry's planned economy. Even if such a film were released, it was not copied or reviewed.

This happened, for example, to a powerful and original, though somewhat inconsistent, picture directed by Grigori Chukhrai, *Clear Skies*. Its hero was a war pilot taken prisoner during the Second World War. It seemed to elaborate the theme of *Destiny of a Man* by Mikhail Sholokhov, but Chukhrai in addition subjected his hero to a most severe test: he made him an outlaw who probed into a typically Stalinist psychology that evolved from the motto "You can't avoid chips when felling a tree," invented to justify the deaths of innocent victims of "the great goal." The main character, pilot Astakhov, repeats this motto, meaning himself to be a "chip."

Chukhrai showed a conflict of two outlooks, two approaches to man who had come to the fore in the time of "rehabilitation," even if he did it too straightforwardly and rashly.

The conference seated under a huge sculpture of Stalin pronounced a final verdict of "guilty" without ever doubting their decision and condemned Astakhov in cold blood. Humanity is symbolized by a loving, loyal woman, Sashenka Lvova, who preserved her affection for, and confidence in, the man she loved through every trial and who believed in the final triumph of justice. The final moments of *Clear Skies* showed that her faith and hope were not futile: Astakhov comes from the building of some important government organization clasping his restored Golden

Nine Days of One Year *reflected the conflict of the old and the new.*

Star of Hero of the Soviet Union in his hand. It happens on a fine spring day, and the sun shines from clear skies. Though the final sequence was somewhat too obvious and straightforward, it paid tribute to a society that rehabilitated its citizens condemned so cruelly and unfairly.

The picture was well received and awarded the Golden Prize of the Second Moscow International Film Festival (1961), which it shared with the brilliant *Naked Island* by Japanese director Kaneto Shindo. The press reviews were also favorable. The critics wrote about a triumph of humanity and restored justice. Regrettably, the issue raised was not sustained in the cinema of the sixties, though it was further elaborated in literature.

A collision of invigorating trends with imposed moderation in reform led to stagnation. This opposition existed throughout the entire period. Nonetheless, the wholesome powers of the cinema, the emergence of new talents, and a series of "new waves" came to change film. Inspired by new hopes and encouraged by the growing scale of production, Soviet cinema was going through an optimistic phase.

Mikhail Romm's Second Peak

Twenty directors made their debuts in 1964 alone, and a number of movie patriarchs (directors in their sixties) "recovered their breath" and continued to work hard, Mikhail Romm among them.

After his first successful films on Lenin, Mikhail Romm (1901–1971) was the acknowledged leading Soviet film director. He worked continuously and managed to produce several pictures even in the lull, including two films on military history, *Admiral Ushakov* and *Attack from the Sea.* Later Romm said unequivocally that the period of stagnation had irreparably damaged "not only those who were not allowed to make films but also the few chosen who were."

In 1956 Romm made a picture based on French material and titled *Murder in Dante Street,* which dissatisfied and frustrated him because its action was so theatrical, its composition artificial, and its situation not true to life. After that Romm did not produce anything for six years. He chose not to, though his reputation still stood high. He became artistic director at a Mosfilm Studios sector, drawing together his gifted pupils and teaching a course on direction at the Moscow Institute of Cinematography. Together with Sergei Gerasimov's studio, which was set up in the immediate postwar years when Gerasimov was making his *Young Guard,* Romm's school was in the vanguard of progressive reform. Romm trained a whole group of young directors, among them Chukhrai, Tarkovsky, Shukshin, Daneliya, Konchalovsky, Shepitko, Mitta, and many others. All of them owed professional skills and background to him. They could always rely on him while making pictures of their own. But perhaps the main role he played was extending their artistic horizons and developing their individualities.

Radical social changes made Mikhail Romm review his own values. His susceptibility to new ideas and his ability to keep up with the times manifested themselves once more, though he was well advanced in years at the time. He made *Nine Days of One Year* in 1962.

The film highlights the changes in cinema in those years. The traditional Soviet film hero sacrificing himself for the sake of science is shown at the crisis of his life (which is typical of all Romm's characters). But his individuality is revealed not through trials inherent in such a hero or dramatic situations he is put in but by his ability to think independently, by his analytical mind.

The main character, Gussev, coexists with another, Kulikov, who seemingly plays no definite role or carries no special message. He simply holds forth about all kinds of things, abstract rather than topical. This character gave rise to heated debates among critics used to thinking in terms of old dogmas who could not decide whether he was positive or negative.

Shortly before *Nine Days of One Year* was released, such a type as Kulikov (played by Innokenti Smoktunovsky), a cynical intellectual, always immaculate, would have been shown as a prospering Moscow careerist and a heartless egotist. But this stereotype was falling out of fashion, for no one doubted the right of individuals like Kulikov to exist and voice their opinions in films. The next stage would be to show the characters' everyday lives, ordinary and uneventful, instead of putting them through trials.

The very composition of *Nine Days of One Year* reflected the conflict of old and new. The plot is still based on Gussev's "case history": we keep wondering whether he would be exposed to neutron radiation for the third, fatal time. It shows in the acting: Alexei Batalov, who plays Gussev, makes it clear that his hero is doomed, and we can even imagine a martyr's halo over his head. The sinister omens of the nuclear age—radiation sickness, neutrons, and strontium 90—made the public apprehensive.

At the same time, a scientist sacrificing his life for the development of science is not uncommon for Russian prose and drama: suffice it to recall Dr. Dymov, who saved a sick child dying of diphtheria at the cost of his own life (*The Grasshopper* by Anton Chekhov), or Turgenev's Bazarov, a man who denied emotion but attended to sick peasants out of compassion and contracted a fatal disease from them. In addition to the plot, other elements acquired a special meaning in the film.

The apparently quiet and peaceful scientific towns of physicists with their houses built deep among pine trees, with their research institutes and underground labyrinths of concrete passages, their walls lined with dark cables looking like veins, and lights flickering over the doors—all have a lyricism of their own.

During the war Romm made a film titled *Prisoner No. 217* (1944), a story of a Soviet girl taken away to Germany for slave labor; it was a passionate, wrathful, and impressive picture condemning Nazism. It took the director many years to be able to return to such a theme. His next wartime film was *Ordinary Fascism,* based on a script by Maya Turovskaya and Yuri Khanyutin, both critics of renown. The title carried the film's message; it was an attempt to show the everyday manifestations, the face, and the psychological roots of Nazism. Sequences of German films of the twenties and thirties were used to expose the petty bourgeois' worship of uniform, his confusion in the era of social instability, growing yearning for revenge, and inferiority complex. Those episodes alternated with German newsreels of the time, which depicted torch-lit processions, military parades, uniformed Nazis, rejoicing crowds, and books being burned in street fires.

Romm's *Ordinary Fascism,* released in 1965, was ranked among such outstanding postwar pictures as *Night and Fog* and *Guernica* by Alain Resnais, *Mein Kamp* by Erwin Leiser, or *Hitler connais pas* by Bertrand Blier. No matter how expressive the title of Romm's film might seem, it did not fully cover its content and structure. Made in the USSR in the sixties, the film carried a message more profound than just tracing the origin of "ordinary Nazism," the plasma feeding on the soil of middle-class convention and boorishness and breeding the poisonous tree of fascism. Romm's film showed where a total madness manifested in bonfires, processions, and parades could lead. Romm believed reason and critical attitudes to be a guarantee of individual and social salvation, emphasizing this by introducing two series of contrasting sequences: one—demented crowds in the squares of Nuremberg and Berlin depicted almost graphically, and the other—the same Germans coming to their senses at the end of the war, shortly before their country was defeated. Their faces regained their individual features and became humane, brutality drained from them. Romm believed in human intelligence. Such an attitude was typical of the day.

Hero of Our Times

Farm Manager (directed by Alexei Saltykov and based on a script by Yuri Nagibin) was released in 1964 and became popular thanks to its unorthodox hero. It was a story of a farm manager, Yegor Trubnikov, a disabled war veteran who returned to his native village.

All the men of Konkovo had fallen in the battlefields, and the women had to plough the land in harness. Yegor Trubnikov, who saw them ploughing, took it as his personal disgrace. From then on he saw the purpose of his life in saving their collective farm and changing the farmers' life for the better.

Actor Mikhail Ulyanov created a realistic and complex character. Obviously fond of his hero and sympathizing with him, he does not try to show him a better man than he is. A progressive Russian literary tradition, whose characters are three dimensional, triumphed in *Farm Manager*.

The wholesome peasant philosophy and attitudes which had gone through many trials in the century since the abolition of serfdom in 1861 have survived, and many writers and artists tried to probe them. In the Soviet period, when all peasants were united in collective farms, the traditional image of a good farmer was bound to change. *Farm Manager* depicts two different types of farmers, Yegor Trubnikov and his brother, Semyon, who is his exact opposite. Ivan Lapikov, who plays Semyon, shows him as a hard and cruel man. In fact, the first part of the film is titled "Brothers" to emphasize their polar differences. Incomparable as they are, both men are dignified, and they are indeed brothers. Semyon is an individual farmer with firm principles, and Yegor is an ideal collectivist. In one of the sequences the two brothers are engaged in a mortal fight, and this scene is also highly symbolical.

An explanation of a character like Trubnikov can be found in the history of a whole generation. When still a poor country lad, working as herdsboy, Yegor Trubnikov believed in the new life born of collectivization.

Trubnikov is unselfish, disinterested: he has no personal ambitions or yearning for power. Mikhail Ulyanov (who won the Lenin Prize for the part) made the public ponder over his hero's story and realize the existence of many complex problems. Ulyanov created a tragic, charismatic, although unpleasant, character, without attempting to disguise Trubnikov's self-destructive fanaticism or the intensity of his emotion bordering on insanity. Trubnikov is shown as a product of his times.

At the time when it was essential to put an end to arbitrariness, Trubnikov looked too negative. Mikhail Ulyanov played many other characters and leaders of various ranks bred by the Soviet system, but his Yegor Trubnikov was the model character by which he tested all others.

In the sixties filmmakers became increasingly conscious of such complex, contradictory characters. Film director Andrei Mikhalkov-Konchalovsky showed a man similar to Trubnikov, severe looking but kindhearted and vulnerable, a fanatic dedicated to his ideals, in his film *The First Teacher,* produced by the Kazakh Film Studios (1965). It was a screen version of Chinghiz Aitmatov's story of the same title. Incidentally, the Kirghiz ethnic cinema began to show an interest in Aitmatov's work early in his career. Nearly all his early books were filed in his own constituent republic. The young Mikhalkov-Konchalovsky's interpretation of the lyrical story *The First Teacher* is authentic, and the tragic balance in his portrayal of uncompromising revolutionary struggle is worth a special description.

That was the struggle between new revolutionary ideas and the parochial, dreamy old ways of a mountain village in 1924. A teacher, Dyuishen, a civil war participant, came to set up a school and guide the local children along the path of the socialist revolution. Paradoxical as it might seem, not only the rich, insatiable, and omnipotent *bai* (local landowner) but also the peasants (unwilling to part with traditional customs and prejudices) resent the newcomer. Bolot Beishenaliev, a gifted and original actor, plays on his character's complexity and heightened behavior. Teacher Dyuishen's devotion to revolutionary ideals is appealing, but we instinctively resent his fanaticism and lack of compassion. We see him both through the eyes of Altynai, a girl who loves him because he saved her from the hateful *bai* (Altynai's part was the debut of a gifted actress, Natalia Arinbasarova), and through those of the local elders, *aksakals* (the wise men), and other residents. The finale is tragically symbolical: Dyuishen, who had seen his school burnt down by the local *bai,* is driven to despair; he grabs an axe and starts hacking at the village's only tree, the sacred poplar. Dyuishen raised his hand not so much against the innocent tree but rather against local obscurantism. It does not occur to him that the poplar was rooted deep in his native soil, the land of his ancestors, and that it provided shade for travelers and was the pride of the sun-scorched desert. Dyuishen, hacking at the tree in despair, is oblivious.

The locals stand around, alienated and scared. This is the climax of the film.

Mikhalkov-Konchalovsky's film was up to the expectations of his teacher, Mikhail Romm, and his senior colleagues, who had taken notice of him when his diploma picture, *The Boy and the Pigeon* (1962), won the Grand Prix for best short at the Venice Film Festival. Later the young filmmaker wrote a script for *Andrei Rublev,* together with its director, Andrei Tarkovsky. From Kirghizia in the postrevolution years (depicted in *The First Teacher*), Mikhalkov-Konchalovsky turned to modern times and Central Russia. All these two films had in common was the fact that their action was set in the Soviet period. His second and most original film, released in 1967 and based on a screenplay by Yuri Klepikov, was originally titled "Asya the Lame," later "The Story of Asya Klyachina, Who Loved But Did Not Marry," and finally "Asya's Happiness."

The film, shot in the countryside, was performed by amateurs. Only three cast members, among them the gifted Iya Savvina (who had made her debut as Anna Sergeyevna in the screen version of Chekhov's story *The Lady with the Dog* shortly before), were professional actors. This screen improvisation was made up of three stories, or rather monologues, based on close-ups and performed by novices. The first story is told by the farm manager, a hunchback with clear, trusting eyes; the second by an incapacitated war veteran, the husband of a local beauty, tall and strong Maria; and the third is the heart-rending narrative of an old farmer who had spent eight years in a Siberian camp.

The three life stories are told in a reserved, simple manner, but this unpretentiousness reveals an inner purity and nobility among those who somehow remain humane in the most inhuman conditions.

Such is the world of the blue-eyed heroine, lame Asya, a farm cook. Pure in soul and selfless, Asya follows her principles, which often makes her behavior unpredictable and impractical. She turns down a town admirer who offers her, a cripple, his heart, hand in marriage, and a good apartment: she is in love with another, a reckless driver who becomes father of her child. Asya is proud; and no matter how submissive she might look, this hidden pride (typical of a Russian woman!) plus the emancipated outlook of a Soviet farmer (Asya can always rely on the community for support for her child and herself) make a poetic Russian character, beautifully portrayed by the actress.

Regrettably, the film industry administration did not understand the

The Lady with the Dog *was one of the best translations of Chekhov's prose to the screen. Directed by Joseph Heifetz, it was the debut of the gifted Iya Savvina as Anna Sergeyevna.*

picture and regarded it as slanderous. Nonsense, of course, for though the director did not look upon reality through rose-tinted glasses, he obviously respected the rural lifestyle, ways, and traditions. Mikhalkov-Konchalovsky was not strong enough to stand up against the bureaucrats and prevent heavy editing: he agreed to make cuts and the time-serving corrections and alterations that followed. The shortened version of the film (it ran for less than ninety minutes), symptomatically titled *Asya's Happiness,* greatly differed from the original. In some sequences rough cuts disrupted the continuity.

It was a serious failure, and the director plunged into erratic experimenting. After an attempt to screen Russian classics, he made the obscure *Lovers' Romance,* then the four-part *Siberiada,* an epic of Soviet oil industry, and eventually a number of Hollywood-type pictures.

More regrettable than his personal failure was the fact that it nipped in the bud the filming of "countryside prose" as in his *Story of Asya.* The social portrayal of rural life, so remarkable in the film, continued the line started by Vasily Shukshin in his books and movies and anticipated the works by such outstanding Russian writers as Fyodor Abramov, Vasily Belov, and Valentin Rasputin, who founded a new trend in the Soviet literature of the late sixties. Of course, the cinema continued to explore this avenue, but such masterpieces as Elem Klimov's *Farewell* (after Rasputin's book *Farewell to Matyora*) appeared much later.

Artists working in other genres continued to create portraits of their contemporaries and analyze their characters, but the lovely Asya Klyachina remained unknown to the public at large.

Women as Directors and Professionals

Wings made by Larissa Shepitko in 1966 portrays a female version of Yegor Trubnikov, the "determined" character of *The Farm Manager.*

Many think film direction is reserved for men. That was what the sixteen-year-old Larissa Shepitko of the Ukraine was told at a session of the enrollment board of the Institute of Cinematography when she applied for entrance. As she was extremely good looking, they advised her to try the acting department, but she was determined to become a director. Her determination was so surprising for a young girl of her age and appearance that the great Alexander Dovzhenko, who was recruiting students for his workshop that year, enrolled her without more ado.

Larissa was up to his expectations, though Dovzhenko died before she completed the course. She graduated from the famous studio led by Mikhail Romm.

It is still unusual for a film director to make unfeminine films in harsh conditions, which usually requires a strong man of uncommon talent and not a tall and slender woman with intelligent blue-green eyes. Yet, that was what Larissa Shepitko looked like and that's how we remember her. Her name suited her perfectly: "Larissa" is the Greek for seagull, and she was a proud seagull who died a tragic death at the very peak of her career.

Like a true person of the sixties (later on this phrase was used to refer to artists who were part of the wave of social progress), Shepitko started with the films dealing with social and ethical problems. Her diploma film, *Heat* (1963), was produced by the Kirghiz Film Studios and based on another story by Chinghiz Aitmatov. Shepitko shot in the same virgin steppe where Konchalovsky's film, *The First Teacher,* was made. She sought to portray a character who was a product of the previous period—a kind of socialist superman praised to the skies by many and proud of his high status. Abakir, performed with intensity by a Kazakh actor, Zhanturin, was far more sophisticated in the film than in Aitmatov's original story, where he was plain, tough, and uncouth. Larissa was interested in the social and psychological reasons for his gradually developing heartlessness, and she discovered them. What made Abakir so inhumane was unlimited praise that spoiled the immature person who secretly believed in a strong man's power over the weak and subordinate, whose part the director took. Abakir's assistant, Kemel, a recent school graduate, awkward, unskilled, and frail, (symbolizing the weak), finally won a moral victory over Abakir. This aspect of the plot, ignored by critics of *Heat* who were carried away by the exotic desert, would become a principal theme for Larissa Shepitko later in the sixties. It can be traced in such later productions as *You and I* and *The Ascent,* as well as in other progressive filmmakers' pictures.

Shepitko made her *Wings* from a screenplay by Valentin Yezhov and Natalia Ryazantseva (the former was the author of *Ballad of a Soldier;* the latter, a subtle and intelligent screenplay author with a psychological bias, belonged to the same generation as Larissa).

The heroine of the film is a former war pilot, Nadezhda Petrukhina, whose portrait is displayed at the local museum. Principal of a vocational school, she sticks to army regulations and wartime laws when managing a postwar school. Absolutely honest by nature, she is too straightforward, boorish, and formal to get along with other people, among them her adopted daughter, students, and other young people. We are sorry for the woman who had suffered so much, but her anachronistic personality is not appealing. She is the tragic product of a certain period of Russian history. Actress Maya Bulgakova plays her subtly and tactfully. Two periods are touched upon in the film, the sixties in which the action is set and flashbacks of the war years, which emphasize the idea that the popular notions of female heroism have grown obscure and obsolete. None of this is to deny the unblemished purity of the heroine's soul, concealed by external boorishness. The positive traits of her character are more important than the negative ones. In the finale, two contrasting sequences show first the principal being so rude to the student she has been persecuting throughout the film that the boy cannot bear it any longer. He shouts in her face, "I hate you!" and slams the door behind him. In the episode that follows, Nadezhda Petrukhina, aimlessly wandering about the town, suddenly finds herself at an army airfield where pilots are about to take off. The contrast acquires a lyrical and highly symbolical meaning. The former pilot comes up to an aircraft, unnoticed by its crew, pats it on the side, climbs up into its cabin, puts her hands firmly on the controls, and takes off. Whether or not she lands safely, she has won a victory over herself.

In the sixties many filmmakers grew interested in a character or, rather, characters who maintained the continuity of the generations. Sons photograph their fathers and scrutinize their snapshots, aware of the paternal naivete and lack of refinement, but with no lessening of filial love.

The Byelorussian Station (directed by Andrei Smirnov, 1971) is a declaration of the younger generation's love for their fathers. Its action is set in the sixties, and its heroes are four ex-servicemen and their frontline comrade, a field nurse, now a single mother raising the child of a fallen comrade. In this case, too, the sons realized that their fathers were better men than the postwar generation—selfish, pragmatic, and increasingly consumerist in its attitudes. Such was the mood of the sixties.

Film director Kira Muratova created a different type of woman in *Brief Encounters* (1968). Kira Muratova is an outstanding and unorthodox movie personality. Like Larissa Shepitko, Kira Muratova refutes the stereotype male director. She proves that a gifted and humane woman can direct without making specifically "female" films or losing her femininity, un-

Regimental veterans meet in Byelorussian Station, *directed by Andrei Smirnov in 1971.*

derstanding, sensitivity, observation, patience, or keen eye for detail.

Kira Muratova graduated from Sergei Gerasimov's workshop at the Institute of Cinematography and made her director's debut in 1965. Her first film, *Our Honest Bread,* was produced in the Ukraine. She made it jointly with her husband, Alexander Muratov. It was actually a Ukrainian version of *The Farm Manager,* where the part of the "strong man" was played by the excellent Ukrainian actor, Dmitri Milyutenko. The realistic picture of contemporary rural ways shown in the film and appealing to many people brought the two directors to the fore.

Later the couple divorced and began to work separately, Kira more successfully than Alexander. Her *Brief Encounters* is still as topical as in the sixties. The film was ahead of its time, raising painful problems previously ignored by the movies.

Kira Muratova produced a version of the eternal triangle. Two women are brought together by their love of one man, but they see him in different lights, from their different backgrounds. Valentina is an emancipated, intelligent, and educated town woman, whereas Nadya is a country girl, young and naive, who came to town to work as domestic help. They have in common only their love for the hero, Maxim, a geologist, who is married to Valentina and who appears only in the two women's reminiscences. The lead is played by Vladimir Vysotsky, the author, singer, and actor of the Moscow Taganka Theater, whose fame grew throughout his life and turned into worship after his untimely death. An outstanding personality, Vysotsky appeared in several mediocre films, but *Brief Encounters* is different, even if Maxim is not his best role. Kira Muratova herself played Valentina, and the part of Nadya was the film debut of a young drama actress, Nina Ruslanova, who became a film star in the eighties.

Both the romantic figure of geologist Maxim seen as if through binoculars and the naively cunning, though emotional and integrated Nadya, the two sides of the triangle, only highlight the third character, Valentina, an independent woman, as businesslike and active as a man. This new type of woman has many advantages compared to her less emancipated sisters: financial independence, freedom, intellect, experience, a busy life, and unselfishness. Valentina is a public figure (she works at a city council and is preoccupied with other people's affairs and problems). But she is lonely, childless, and burdened with her undirected intellect. Nadya's life, uneventful as it is, compares favorably to that of her mistress. Maxim is more at ease with her than with his intellectual wife; it was his casual affair with the provincial waitress that made her move to town and work her way into the home of her lover's wife. But the hero returns to Valentina, as convention requires.

The film's relationships are complicated and confused, and the women are especially vulnerable in them. Life is not unalloyed joy, as Kira Muratova wanted to say in her next film, *Long Farewells,* based on a screenplay by Natalia Ryazantseva. Completed right after *Brief Encounters,* this film was released only in 1987, as were many other productions shelved for years for various, usually ridiculous, considerations. Thus *Long Farewells* was shelved for being "pessimistic." That film was the first attempt to show a divorced couple, the father living far away from town, and their teenage son, intelligent and sensitive, torn between his parents. This is shown without moralizing or preaching. The plot is centered around the mother, brilliantly performed by Leningrad actress Zinaida Sharko.

Actress Inna Churikova is Yelizaveta Uvarova, a mayoress obsessed with building a garden-like city in I Wish to Speak, *1976 creation of Gleb Panfilov.*

Brief Encounters, whose heroine is a public figure, is associated with a later picture depicting another female version of a tough Soviet manager, *I Wish to Speak* by Gleb Panfilov. This starred Inna Churikova as the mayoress of a typical Russian city, Yelizaveta Uvarova.

Gleb Panfilov (born 1934) made his first film, *There Is No Crossing Under Fire,* in 1964. It is a screen version of a story by Yevgeni Gabrilovich. The action is set in the years of the civil war (1918–1920). Both the picture and its unusual heroine immediately attracted the public attention. The girl, Tania Tetkina, is a field nurse, a simple and kindly soul with a gift for painting. Her unusual appearance, uncommon talent, and striking personality soon brought Inna Churikova to the fore. Later on, Panfilov and Churikova (who are married) chose the stories of artistic, unusual, and even exceptional women capable of daring actions, even when their individuality was obscured by everyday routine. In *The Begin-*

ning (1970) Churikova played a gifted amateur actress offered the role of Joan of Arc in a feature film. Churikova has created a number of original, very Russian characters, among them the mayoress in *I Wish to Speak.* Yelizaveta Uvarova represents a younger generation of Soviet functionaries emerging in the postwar years. She is eager to improve her town's amenities, speed up housing construction, and develop culture and art. She receives foreign delegations and can speak fluent French. She is always elegant and self-possessed. She has a family and a loving, or, at least, obedient, husband. Yet, she is very similar to Yegor Trubnikov and Nadezhda Petrukhina in many respects. She speaks in a peremptory tone, is obsessed with the notion of building a gardenlike city behind the river, and remains indifferent to her own well-being even though the period of self-imposed asceticism is over and her family lives in a comfortable apartment. She is pure in heart, honest, and convinced in the righteousness of the cause. She has a hobby that also links her with previous generations: she likes shooting in a shooting gallery, like the sharpshooters of her childhood.

Her character reflects the complexity of the times. She is opaque, a mixture of features both positive and negative, which have evolved in the controversial history of Soviet society.

Like Yegor Trubnikov, the character of Yelizaveta Uvarova caused heated debates among the public and in the press. The critics arrived at contradictory conclusions concerning the author's motivation. Some insisted it was a satire, others believed it to be a eulogy, and still others regarded the film as critical and accusing. The question of whether Uvarova is a positive or negative character is still open.

Panfilov tried to be objective. The evolution of the main character, tragic at times, revealed a living human, basically wholesome. This was realism that had absorbed the classical Russian tradition—a realism to which others are now returning.

History: A Touchstone for the Past and Future

Many filmmakers of the sixties turned to history to review the past or to resolve existing social problems.

In 1965 a screenplay titled *Andrei Rublev* and written by Andrei Tarkovsky and Andrei Mikhalkov-Konchalovsky was published in the journal *Iskusstvo Kino* (Nos. 4 and 5). It was a poetic, imaginative play whose genre was hard to define. The action was set in early Russia, at the beginning of the fifteenth century, when the country was under the Tatar-Mongol yoke. Strictly speaking, it was not a screen biography of Andrei Rublev, an icon painter of genius and a pupil of St. Sergius of Radonezh, who founded the Trinity–St. Sergius Monastery (now Zagorsk). It is apocryphal more than realistic. Neither is it a chronicle in the conventional meaning of this word, for the events of Russian history and the imaginary events of the plot are not important in themselves—they are shown through the eyes of Andrei Rublev, their witness or participant. The camera is Rublev's eye.

The great painter is shown to be part of his people, and his life as a righteous deed embodied in his icons. The icons symbolized popular yearning for peace, harmony, and fraternity at a time of barbaric feuds, from which came Rublev's famous "Trinity," the climax of early Russian art. The film was black and white, but the final sequences of the film show this beautiful icon from various angles, to music in harmony with the colors—ochre red, sky blue, and emerald green. Before painting his "Trinity," Andrei Rublev had gone through many ordeals.

The film consists of several chapters (including "Buffoon," "Holiday," "Passions of St. Andrei"), where the hero's life, wanderings, and doubts are shown against the background of folk life with its passions and suffering, the invader's atrocities, the perfidy of princes, and, above all, the people's toil and creative pursuits. Stunning scenes including the burning of the city of Vladimir, the iconostasis of the local Cathedral of the Assumption perishing in the fires of raiding Tatars, and the Russian Calvary where the passions of Jesus Christ are depicted against the northern winter landscape, the heathen festivity in the country, and the blinding of a group of artists all culminate in the sequence titled "The Bell." As a French critic remarked, "The artist and creator is roused and inspired by the people's enthusiasm."[2]

The impact of the film on the cinema in general and on the historic genre in particular was enormous. What was especially striking were the author's rejection of costume-drama and his successful attempt to show the continuity of history.

Others followed suit; Igor Talankin's *Daytime Stars* was released in 1967. Here a whole historical period and the people's tragedy are shown within the life story of a poetess. Here digressions into the past mingled with

In the Leningrad zoo scene from Daytime Stars *Alla Demidova is expressive as the poetess Olga with her father, a typical Russian man of the intelligentsia played by Andrei Popov.*

dynamic emotions. The screening of an autobiographical story by Soviet poet Olga Bergholz (played by Alla Demidova) gave the filmmaker an opportunity to bring together the past and the present most naturally.

Olga Bergholz's reminiscences of the Leningrad blockade of 1941–1943 and her childhood in the twenties alternate with sequences showing contemporary, peaceful Leningrad and follow the heroine's associations and thoughts. The red poppies on a spring meadow of her childhood, near the white battlements of Uglich, suggest another association: the red blood of the dead Tsarevich Dimitri assassinated on the white steps in the same town four hundred years before. The suffering of the people is evoked by unexpected images: the appearance in the Liteiny Prospekt of contemporary Leningrad of a medieval bell—once "executed" in Uglich for calling the townspeople to take arms (the bell is a symbol of early Russia). According to a legend, the bell's tongue was torn out in punishment.

The original form and inner monologues of *Daytime Stars,* authentic as they are, remind us of Federico Fellini's *Otto e mezzo* and Ingmar Bergman's *Wild Strawberries.* The director's ideas, the expert camerawork of photography director Margarita Pilikhina who succeeds in expressing the ethos of the picture through the medium of color, Alla Demidova's expressive performance (she was an emerging actress of the Moscow Taganka Theater at the time), and the acting of such an experienced actor as Andrei Popov made the film a masterpiece. Direct or indirect intrusion of history into action set in the present, as in *Daytime Stars,* and the historical parallels drawn to emphasize current problems again suggest the continuity of time. Many films depicting modern Soviet reality possessed some truly authentic Russian features.

Artists usually turn to classical works and interpret them in modern terms when their contemporaries begin to pinpoint the problems of their time and when a multitude of new problems and attitudes starts cropping up. Suffice it to compare the movies of the thirties with films made today to realize what great progress the Soviet cinema had made since. Any interpretation of a classical film should be up to date, otherwise it would turn into a textbook. The interest of the directors of the sixties in classics and the topical issues they raised in their films remind us of the pictures made by their colleagues today.

In the sixties many classical books were filmed: *The Idiot* and the four-part serial *The Brothers Karamazov* by Dostoyevsky (directed by Ivan Pyryev); Leo Tolstoi's *Resurrection* filmed by Mikhail Shveitser and *Anna Karenina* by Alexander Zarkhi; and, of course, the Chekhovian *A Lady with a Dog* starring Iya Savvina and Alexei Batalov. The most impressive historical epic of that period was the four-part *War and Peace* by Sergei Bondarchuk, from Leo Tolstoi's novel.

Bondarchuk sought verisimilitude, from large-scale battle scenes to minute detail: a candlestick in the Rostovs' household, a globe of the world in old Prince Bolkonsky's study, or the design of stirrups.

Fifty-eight museums placed their collections at the director's disposal. Thousands of people sent their antiques. Camera director Anatoli Petritsky, artistic director Mikhail Bogdanov, and other team members worked only in genuine interiors and at the site of historic events depicted in the serial. The battles of Borodino, Austerlitz, and Schöngrabern needed special equipment to film.

261

The main idea of the film is expressed in the opening sentence: the "unity of will of righteous people enables them to defeat evil and injustice." The inevitable victory of peace over war was suggested in the symbolical prologue, where the black color of gaping earth is suffused with the green of hope.

Bondarchuk next made *Waterloo*. The director, who spent ten years making *War and Peace,* regarded the new serial, a joint Soviet-Italian production, as a sequel.

The new production, made in Dino de Laurentis's studio, starred Rod Steiger as Napoleon, Christopher Plummer as the Duke of Wellington, and Orson Welles as Louis XVIII. The screenplay was written by G. A. Craig and the score by Nino Rota. The photography was directed by Armando Nannuzzi, and the rest of the team was also international. Thirty thousand extras were recruited among the troops of the Carpathian Military Region (the Ukraine). The action was set on a plain between Uzhgorod and Mukachev, where wheat was grown on a huge field to simulate the landscape of Waterloo. The battle actually took place on June 18, 1815, when "the beautiful days of Alexander's reign" (as Pushkin put it) were already over and when the victory of the Russian people over Napoleon that made them aware of being a European nation was already won.

While the events of *War and Peace* are shown from the inside, through the eyes of a participant, the one hundred days of preparation and the battle of Waterloo itself are presented in a detached and objective manner. Bondarchuk's work is remarkable for its purely Russian penetration into another nation's character and mentality.

The press noted the documentary authenticity of the battle scenes. Reviewers were unanimous in applauding the film's professionalism. The names of the French painters David, Gericault, Delacroix, and Gros were mentioned in every review.

Bondarchuk balanced the ugly and the picturesque, the horrible and the majestic, the real and the imaginary. Such is the French assault, with the little drummers in the vanguard, the blue tunics of the infantry, and a long, dry sound of drumming. Such is the attack of the French cavalry: an elevated camera makes it possible to cover the entire battlefield and register an unprecedented battle scene—the thirteen regular squares of the British troops dressed in red disperse before our eyes, perishing and turning into the ashes and soil of Waterloo. Or take another sequence, a

The most impressive historical epic of the 60s was War and Peace, *by Sergei Bondar-chuk, based on Tolstoi's novel.*

peculiar and unexpected scene of the British cavalry's attack, where light-gray horses shown in slow motion seem to soar over the land.

The effect is stunning, not only because of the wide frame or presence of a temperamental director capable of transforming the reality of battle into pure movement, but because the impact of the battle, no matter how fantastic the spectacle on the screen might be, is moral rather than visual. The battle develops parallel to the psychological duel between Napoleon and Wellington. The result is stalemate: Waterloo proved that war is absurd.

Innokenti Smoktunovsky plays Hamlet in screen version by Grigori Kozintsev in 1964.

Shakespeare was also well represented on the screen in the sixties. Consider *Hamlet* by Grigori Kozintsev, with a score by Dmitri Shostakovich. It is remarkable that the actor chosen to play the Danish prince, Innokenti Smoktunovsky, had already created a range of contemporary characters distinguished by their inner independence.

This screen version of *Hamlet* is a tragedy of conscience. Elsinore court makes futile attempts to mold Hamlet according to its own image, to win him with flattery, suasion, lies, and threats. The sequence showing Hamlet in conversation with the two provocateurs, Rosencrantz and Guildenstern, and the flute monologue determine the tenor of the film (unlike the classical screen versions focused on another monologue, "To be, or not to be"). As far as Kozintsev and Smoktunovsky are concerned, Hamlet is by no means a great doubter, sad and lonely and torn between his own power and weakness. He is a philosopher who uses thought and contemplation as his only weapons.

The famous monologue, "To be or not to be," is not the climax of hesitation but an answer to the eternal question: "Whether 'tis nobler in the mind to suffer the slings and arrows of outrageous fortune, or to take arms against a sea of trouble and by opposing end them?"

Resistance and struggle are Hamlet's noble and tragic lot. Kozintsev focuses on the intensity of this struggle rather than on the intricacies of the plot. He is more concerned with the Danish prince's life and destiny. We are made aware of the existence of tyranny personified in a petty ruler, who is worshiped and idolized. Hamlet's future is intertwined with that of his country, and the appearance of Fortinbras and his soldiers is not a solution. Only the death of Hamlet resolves the tragedy: a true man who personifies the humanitarian instinct and is a staunch fighter for truth and justice.

Kozintsev's next production, *King Lear,* continues his Shakespeareana and his reflections on history and its tragedies. The director worked at it for many years and completed it shortly before his death (1973). Pondering over the film concept, he grew acutely aware of the historical events of his own time. He wrote in his director's diary:

> The year that I have been making "King Lear" wars broke out in different parts of the world; every day someone was killed; fires burnt in the world's capitals—whole residential areas went up in flames; ghettos were blasted with tear gas; young people rioted. . . . Martin Luther King, who hated violence, was assassinated. What kind of age is this?[3]

★ ★ ★

We have looked in retrospect on the Soviet cinema of the 1960s and pointed to the radical changes that occurred in this decade. It was a time of revival and reform.

By 1967 the number of feature full-length films alone reached one hundred forty. Animated cartoons—stagnating for decades—also revived. Suffice to mention such cheerful cartoons as *Bonifacius's Holidays* by Fyodor Khitruk or *We Want a Goal!* by Boris Dezhkin and a full-length puppet version of *Bathhouse* by Sergei Yutkevich, remarkable for its technique and imaginative interpretation. It was an original screen version of Mayakovsky's satirical play.

The number of film projector units increased, and the construction of movie theaters gained momentum. In 1967 their number totaled 152,802 (compare it with 26,200 in 1932 and 120,010 in 1955).

The majority of the pictures were produced by constituent republic studios (twenty feature, and nineteen documentary and popular science ones). Scattered all over the country, studios occupied exotic buildings or stood in picturesque places. Thus the Lithuanian Film Studios occupied a Gothic building situated in the pine wood, on the sand bank of the River Neris, whereas its Georgian counterpart, a luxurious modernist structure built over the River Kura at the turn of the century, rose at the foot of the great Caucasian mountains. We admire the contrasts of the Alma Ata and Yalta, Kishinev and Ashkhabad studios, which deny the notion that all the film studios of the world are alike and standard.

In the sixties all the ethnic studios were operating at full capacity—both the old ones built in the last century, like the Georgian or Ukrainian ones, and the emergent studios set up in the Soviet period, like the Kirghiz or Moldavian studios. On November 23, 1965, the First Constituent Congress of the USSR Union of Film Workers opened in the Great Kremlin Palace. Organized in 1957, the union of Soviet filmmakers finally acquired all the rights of a self-governed artistic body.

The rejoicing filmmakers, anticipating a positive future, could not know that the situation would change and that they would encounter the disappointments of a period of stagnation. Yet the power of art and its cultural mission enabled them to rise above the mundane and urge people to fight and hope for a better future.

CHAPTER SEVEN

Time's Captive

The Seventies

*I*n the words of Boris Pasternak in "Night" (1956), "Oh, Artist, you're Time's captive, imprisoned in Eternity!" In favorable circumstances artists seeking new horizons may break through obstacles and restrictions. New manifestos and schools of art emerge. Team efforts produce a "new wave," the motivating force of which is a group of associates united by a common credo. Postwar art experienced many such periods, for instance, Italian neorealism; the Polish school; the French, Spanish, West German, and Hungarian new waves; and the Soviet "tide" of the sixties.

The wave subsides; and its champions, tired of manifestos, lose interest in public debate. What seemed an iron-clad credo proves not to hold water, for the future of all modern waves is uncertain, as their motivating force is external, stemming from a favorable social atmosphere and polemics with their predecessors or representatives of other trends. It is a law that manifestos and polemics, understood as an aesthetic purpose, soon degenerate into empty verbiage.

When they are exhausted, other personalities and trends come to the fore. They are the real hard-working artists whose works profess truth, goodness, and beauty, who never play with terms like progress and regress or us and them. Gimmicky trends, creating a series of identical master-pieces, give way to authentic art. Those works and artists independent of temporal factors are natural products of their time. They adhere to more profound and stable values. The criteria of quality, talent, and standard in art become all important. All that is true of the developments that took place in the Soviet movies in the late sixties and early seventies.

In the 1950s the cinema developed in cycles (for instance, a cycle of "country" films, then of films shown "through the eyes of a child," or of pictures "on the younger generation"). Now individual films became the staple. Filmmakers began to see themselves as authors, even if working on a team basis for a specific industry, or as individuals, like a poet or painter.

In the seventies a number of films giving their authors an opportunity for unlimited self-expression and confession and for drawing profound conclusions were released for the first time. Some preferred to make films dealing with current issues. The old idea of a "commissioned" film was rejected, and art became very personal. The best pictures of the decade, including some dealing with "sideline" problems, shared this quality. Among them were a screen version of a classical novel by Ivan Goncharov, *Several Days in the Life of I. I. Oblomov,* directed by Nikita Mikhalkov, and *The Autumn Marathon,* a tragicomedy by Georgi Daneliya. *Red Berry* by Vasily Shukshin was personal in a further sense—Shukshin himself wrote the script, directed the production, and played the male lead.

Another feature of the seventies was the growing interest in problems of morality and ethics. Filmmakers sought an ideal and looked for selfless, disinterested, and nonpragmatic persons among their contemporaries, people with a sense of social duty essential in the turbulent times, outgo-ing and compassionate. Such directors were truthful and open in the depiction of human predicaments. The educational role of the cinema and the artists' active support for high ideals were as important as ever. But in the seventies educational purposes were achieved in a subtler way: the screen discarded a black-and-white approach and appealed to the au-dience's own judgment more often.

The horizons of the cinema expanded, and filmmakers began to realize what kind of events were worth of depicting on the screen and what kind of characters should be portrayed. It occurred to them that their contem-porary should not necessarily be placed in a situation in which he had to act—it was far more natural to see him involved in everyday events or,

Scene in the Baykalov house from Red Berry *by Vasily Shukshin shows Lydia Fedoseyeva-Shukshina in the role of Lyuba Baykalova.*

quite contrary, in extraordinary situations which, however, enabled the authors to reveal his or her moral potential, strong and weak points, or rich or poor inner world. Suffice it to recall *Red Berry* by Vasily Shukshin, *You and I* and *The Ascent* by Larissa Shepitko, *Afonya* and *Mimino* by Georgi Daneliya, whose heroes were ordinary, unremarkable people. The cinema gave a priority to everyday life and contemporary developments. New artistic ideas and forms paved the way for a new content.

The seventies brought the artist's personality to the fore and gave him or her more independence in the choice of the plot, approach to it, and expressive means.

Meanwhile, the process of creative liberation that lasted throughout the seventies and well into the eighties was hampered by a growing pressure on filmmakers exerted by the USSR State Committee of Cinematography (Goskino) and the growing intolerance of editors at different levels, from studios to nationwide film boards. Many new scripts were shelved, and films were banned. Regrettably, filmmakers became too familiar with the verb "to shelf."

A process of unofficial stratification took place: filmmakers grouped around two poles.

One group willingly abided by the law of the Goskino, made "commissioned" films their superiors were sure to like, and thus earned "most favored nation treatment" as far as film shooting, funds, interesting trips, bonuses, awards, and other privileges were concerned. Alas, not only hacks but also some of really gifted filmmakers who had begun successfully in the fifties and the sixties made their fatal choice. By doing so they gradually gave up their artistic positions.

However, neither official recognition nor laurels could ensure the progress of art. That's why I have no intention of dwelling on the officious first-night shows of many mediocre pictures that did not deserve their awards or nationwide "fame"; they were typical enough of the seventies. They owed their VIP treatment to benevolent movie administrators who authorized unlimited copying, posh premiers in all the major cities of the USSR, and high fees for the authors.

I will be concerned only with the opposite group—searching and genuine artists who never betrayed their ideals and principles and who created immortal masterpieces—those "Time's captives imprisoned in Eternity." Even in the seventies their names were known to many true viewers, and they shine especially brightly now when the fresh winds of change have swept away the restrictions and bans.

Andrei Tarkovsky's "Depicted Time"

Andrei Tarkovsky defined the cinema as "depicted time" or "time shaped into facts," and this aptly describes his own productions.

There were not many of them—less than a dozen for the fifty-four years of his life (1932–1986), but every film was an event. Each of them was a milestone in the evolution of his self-awareness, a new stage in his service to truth and beauty, a manifestation of his yearning for harmony and integrity in a time full of worries, discord, and enmity.

Tarkovsky had a high opinion of cinematography as an art; he understood its global impact. Tarkovsky often repeated that the cinema is as important for the modern time as drama used to be in antiquity and the novel in the nineteenth century. "As far as I'm concerned, cinema is a moral rather than professional category," said Tarkovsky on the threshold of the seventies. "It is essential for me to maintain my perception of art as something very serious, stretching beyond the framework of such concepts as, say, theme, genre, form, etc. The mission of art is not only to reflect reality but also to arm man and enable him to face life." And in his last interview given a month before he died he insisted that "every artist, while he lives on earth, is sure to find and leave behind a grain of truth

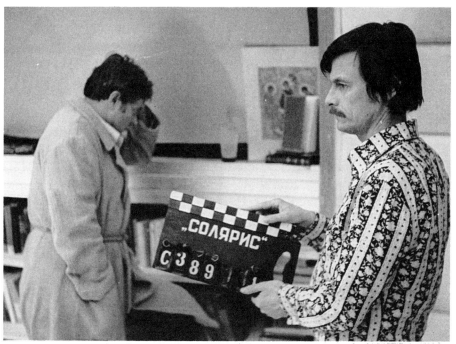

Solaris, *directed by Andrei Tarkovsky, was a philosophical film based on the novel by Stanislaw Lem.*

about the civilization and humanity, and his own vision of them." He remained loyal to his own principles to the end.

Andrei Tarkovsky, in his understanding of the role of art, adhered to a Russian cultural tradition and its basic principles. He inherited them both figuratively and literally. A son of the talented Russian poet, Arseni Tarkovsky, who was a younger contemporary of Anna Akhmatova and Boris Pasternak, a grandson of a nineteenth-century Russian revolutionary (Narodnik), and descendant of many teachers, doctors, and professors, that true elite of society, Andrei Tarkovsky absorbed his country's cultural tradition and applied it to the cinema. A pupil of Mikhail Romm and Alexander Dovzhenko (whom he always called the first among his favorite filmmakers), Andrei Tarkovsky developed into an outstanding movie personality.

His early films, *Ivan's Childhood* and *Andrei Rublev*, brought him international renown. He reached the climax of his career in the seventies. His

271

career made it obvious that an artist of his type was bound to encounter numerous problems. He was a true poet and prophet, and this is not an exaggeration.

> He looks upon that planet
> As if the starry sky
> Is an important object
> Of his midnight concern. . . .

These lines of Pasternak's apply to Andrei Tarkovsky, the author of philosophical films like *Solaris* (1972), adapted from the novel of the same title by Polish science fiction writer Stanislaw Lem, and *Stalker,* based on a script he wrote jointly with the two Soviet S-F authors, Arkadi and Boris Strugatsky. Actually, these films, though their action is set in an imaginary future—an orbiting space station in *Solaris* and near the Zone formed after a nuclear disaster in *Stalker*—also dealt with acute moral problems of his time.

Like *Andrei Rublev,* these two pictures are philosophical in delving into the meaning of human life. The intense, emphatic alternative of good and evil, faith and faithlessness, in man is invariably resolved in a humanitarian and optimistic way.

Tarkovsky interpreted the dilemma of man and his time as every person's responsibility for the rest of humanity and the future of the world, for one's nearest and dearest and one's own soul. The lyrical and the epic, the cosmos and the inner world are closely intertwined in all his films. Tarkovsky's film characters are overwhelming, highly individual, and charged with the author's own emotions.

The Mirror, one of the best films made by Tarkovsky, is made up of intimate reminiscences and real facts (for example, the prototype of one of the female characters, performed by actress Margarita Terekhova, is the director's mother, Maria Vishnyakova, a wonderful woman who was very beautiful in her youth). But even that story of two generations separated by war cannot be called a family chronicle because the author's childhood reminiscences are intertwined with reflections upon the destiny of his country, Europe, and the world at large (the crash of a stratospheric balloon, the civil war in Spain, the horrors of war and Nazism, and Maoist madness in China). The most important message of *The Mirror* is the role of art and the artist's vision of the world.

Tarkovsky's characters retire from the world of their own free will and take the oath of silence, the way Andrei Rublev did when he became aware of evil dominating Russia; or Kris Kelvin of *Solaris*, an astronaut who went to an orbiting station to shake the dust of earth off his feet; or the empty, instrumental, and antagonistic men who dared penetrate into the Zone seeking the enigmatic "machine of happiness" and the meaning of life. Another hero of Tarkovsky, Domenico, a madman and modern saint, decided to burn himself alive to warn humankind against the threat of self-destruction in *Nostalgia* (1983) and, eventually, so did writer Alexander in *The Sacrifice* (1986). The two last films, made in Western Europe, continued his Russian pictures and dwelt on the same problems in the same characteristic manner.

Naturally, the relationship between an artist on such a scale and Goskino (acting as his producer) was extremely complicated. Philip Yermash, who chaired the USSR State Committee of Cinematography in the seventies, was personally to blame for the fact that several ideas of Andrei Tarkovsky (in particular, his profound and original version of *The Idiot* by Dostoyevsky) were subject to long reviewing, were rejected, and virtually buried. The intervals between the films were too long, which had a negative effect on the impulsive, emotional, and reserved director. Not all of his colleagues chose to make an effort to support him in time of trouble. That was why Tarkovsky willingly accepted an Italian studio's offer to produce his film *Nostalgia* from the script he wrote in collaboration with writer and dramatist Tonino Guerra. It was, probably, in Italy that he became aware of the first symptoms of a fatal disease, lung cancer.

There is no denying that Tarkovsky, once he plunged into the Western film industry, could not feel contented or relaxed. Local producers were not exactly snatching the scripts of his unusual films from one another. No matter how cross Tarkovsky might be with some Goskino administrators, whom he considered his personal enemies, he repeated in many interviews published in the West that Goskino was the world's only producer who would permit him to shoot nearly an entire film anew because he was not satisfied with it, as happened with *Stalker*. Andrei Tarkovsky's unusual biography cannot be explained by purely political or publicity factors and neither can his tragically early death, which he predicted in his last two films.

On April 4, 1987, Andrei Tarkovsky would have been fifty-five. The Filmmakers' Club in Moscow held a memorial meeting preceded by a ten-day retrospective of his films. Audiences could see the artist's beautiful and enormous world, the "depicted time" of Andrei Tarkovsky.

The Mirror, *one of the best films by Tarkovsky, stars Margarita Terekhova in a role based on the character of the director's mother.*

Anatoli Solonitsyn (right) in episode from Andrei Rublev, *philosophical film of Andrei Tarkovsky.*

Vasily Shukshin's River of Life

Andrei Tarkovsky, a Muscovite with a sophisticated background, came to the Institute of Cinematography well prepared for its entrance exams, whereas Vasily Shukshin, who applied the same year, did not know much about film directing. No wonder: a native of the remote Siberian village of Srostki, he left home in the last year of the war so as not to starve to death. He had many occupations: a fitter, house painter, loader, sailor, radio operator, YCL functionary, and a school principal. It is amazing that he was enrolled and even more amazing that he became an outstanding director and actor.

Andrei Tarkovsky and Vasily Shukshin made friends in their student years and were always very fond of each other, no matter how their views differed. They presented two sides of the artistic Russian character, two

275

Andrei Tarkovsky (center) shoots Nostalgia, *with Oleg Yankovsky.*

poles of the national talent, one contributing sophisticated means of expression and the other a genuine folk spirit and close links with the people.

It was in 1964 that Shukshin made his debut as film director. His first film, *There Was a Lad,* was welcomed by a public fascinated by a new character—a driver named Pashka Kolokolnikov—and by rural Siberian landscapes and endless roads. The hero continued the pattern set by an earlier film character, Maxim, from the trilogy by Kozintsev and Trauberg—a cheerful, optimistic person who could not help regretting the world's imperfection. The director, a recent graduate of Mikhail Romm's workshop, had already performed a few successful parts in the movies.

Shukshin created an original world in his films. These stories had a limited set of characters, and their action was set in the same parts, on the banks of the River Katun in Siberia. The characters pass from one story to the next, thus creating a prose cycle.

Shukshin, who was very fond of his native land, immortalized it in his films and books. Indeed, he always preferred to write about his countrymen and he shot his films in Siberia.

Shukshin wrote the script for, directed, and performed the lead role of Ivan Rastorguyev, one of his favorite characters, in his next film, *Pots and Pans.* The plot is simple: Ivan and his wife set out to the south for a holiday and pass Moscow in transit.

Shukshin's acting in *Pots and Pans* is extremely funny, with an emphasis on details. Ivan Rastorguyev, an intelligent, cunning, and observant man, is at a loss in an unusual situation. Trying to conceal his bewilderment, that naive, kindly, curious, and touchy countryman is always on the alert. Though prepared to defend himself, he is unable to recognize danger in a busy city like Moscow.

If we were to choose the best films of the seventies out of a whole number of productions, good and bad, we would pick Tarkovsky's *Mirror* and *Red Berry* by Shukshin, the last picture he directed.

Red Berry appeals to the audience because it is so sincere, emotional, serious, and simple. Shukshin seems to be involved in a frank, bitter, and intimate dialogue with the viewer, hoping for the latter's understanding. His film is like a slice of rye bread, and not a gourmet's dessert, because content was more important to the author than form.

This is a story of a thief, Yegar Prokudin, formerly a country boy, who has served his sentence and has to make a choice. After many mistakes he

In Pots and Pans, *Vasily Shukshin has the role of kolkhoznik Ivan Rastorguyev.*

finally makes the right choice and is going to start his life afresh when the vengeful hand of his former accomplices strikes him dead.

Yegor Prokudin, brilliantly performed by Shukshin, is a controversial character, a man of contrasts who dropped out of his ancestors' world, his soul maimed by an unnatural way of life, but who has still retained his strong will power, bitter intelligence, sober self-esteem, and natural ability to do good. That screen portrait was a masterpiece of Shukshin's gallery of modern Russian characters.

We learn a great deal of Yegor Prokudin's life story, seeing how man is corrupted by a dishonest life and how hard it is for him to reform. We realize that such a man, even if he is following the right track, might fail to turn to good simply because he has no time. Such is the life story of a law breaker with several sentences, Yegor nicknamed "Woe."

We are also aware of another tragedy, that of man who ruined his life and failed to fulfill his destiny. Forgetting his nearest and dearest, defiling the sacred, and pursuing a dream which could never come true, he finds a poisoned feast. This psychic drama is the author's attempt to puzzle out the enigma of life and to express his yearning for his long-abandoned home. By that film Shukshin sought to stress the duty of the people to their homeland.

The drama would have been pointless if not for the hero's moment of enlightenment. Realizing his guilt he repents, seeking forgiveness in Lyuba Baikalova's love. The figure of a woman keeping the home fires burning is the most poetic image of the film. Yegor Prokudin is dead, but there will be other winters and springs, and the red snowball tree will blossom and bear red berries, and the home fires will be burning again.

Shukshin suddenly died on location in October 1974, and a green hill affectionately decorated with red snowball berries appeared at the Novodevichi Cemetery in Moscow, not far from the graves of Chekhov, Gogol, and Bulgakov.

Vasily Shukshin's grave is a sacred place for Soviet people, constantly visited by many. In 1980 another such grave appeared in Moscow, now at the Vagankovskoye Cemetry—that of Vladimir Vysotsky, an actor, poet, and author-singer. Neither of them will ever be neglected. As Pushkin put it, "The path to it will not o'ergrow beneath the people's tread."

A Farewell to Larissa

That was a time of sudden and irreplaceable losses for Soviet cinema. A year before Vysotsky died, filmmakers learned that at dawn on July 2, 1979, Larissa Shepitko who rode out to look for location for her new film, *Farewell to Matyora,* died in a car accident in the northeast of Russia. A charming, intelligent woman and mother of a six-year-old boy, she died in the prime of life.

The last years of Larissa's life could be referred to as the "ascent," the same as the title of her best film. The theme of moral choice that emerged in the cinema in the early seventies found its most dramatic expression in Larissa Shepitko's films, and its intensity grew with time.

The film *You and I* (1972), made from a script she wrote jointly with Gennadi Shpalikov, contrasts two doctors, both gifted surgeons, promising at the beginning but yielding to consumerism and pursuit of false values later in life. Thus the drama of sold talents repeated itself at a new stage of social development. "Comfort breeds traitors," wrote Russian philosopher Sergei Trubetskoy, who noticed the phenomenon at the turn of our consumerist century. Larissa shows the same phenomenon in *You and I*. The film portrays a medical researcher who is married to a soulless and petty woman and who leads a pitiful existence in the luxurious residence of a Soviet embassy in a quiet European country. But the time comes when this man feels he's had enough: he returns home, goes to Siberia, and resumes his surgical practice. The plot might look primitive in print, but it was certainly not so on the screen. The straightforward alternatives were given nuances by sincere and subtle direction.

Another film made by Larissa, *The Ascent* (1977), showed the director's concern for personal responsibility for one's actions and her uncompromising attitude toward behavior of a person in a borderline situation.

Sotnikov, a story by Vasil Bykov, served as the basis for the script. It was a wartime story describing an episode of the partisan resistance movement in Nazi-occupied Byelorussia. All the characters are scrutinized close-ups, and their conflict is glaringly accentuated. In the original story the writer explored the psychology of two partisans sent to get provisions for their unit. One died tragically, and the other became a traitor to save his life. Larissa Shepitko showed the last mission of Sotnikov and Rybak as a partisan Calvary and a moral ordeal.

The director managed to polarize the two characters to the extreme in a stark monochrome which condensed darkness against the background of sparkling snow. Sotnikov, a frail intellectual, bore his cross to the very end in a dignified way, despite horrible cold (the film was shot when the temperature dropped to minus 40 degrees). Walking in the deep snow, he did not utter a single complaint. The sophisticated, noble face of actor Boris Plotnikov, iconlike, contrasted with the mean countenance of Rybak (performed by Vladimir Gostyukhin) like light with darkness. That was, in fact, the contrast of the flesh and the spirit, of Jesus Christ and Judas Iscariot. The marble features of the hero hanged by the Nazis are beautiful. As for Rybak, who makes an attempt to hang himself in a dirty lavatory, like his predecessor, the unspeakable Judas, he cannot do even that, for his lot is to serve the Nazis and be tormented.

"The ashes of Claes beat against my heart," said Thiel Ulenspiegel, the noble-hearted hero of Charles de Coster's novel. The ashes of the innumerable victims of the war beat against Larissa's heart. It was her dream to shoot a film on the tragedy of the Byelorussian village of Khatyn, burnt to ashes together with its all population, women and children. She did not live to make it. Only many years later her husband, Elem Klimov, realized her idea in his apocalyptic film *Come and See*.

He also completed his wife's last picture, a screen version of a modern Soviet book. She undertook to dramatize Valentin Rasputin's *Farewell to Matyora*.

Her idea was to make a tragic film about a village deliberately flooded by an artificial sea, with its residents moved to townships against their will. The people had to part with their ancestral homes, the cemetery where their parents were buried, and every other thing sacred to them.

The noble, feminine heroine, village sorceress Darya, old in age and young in spirit, was performed by a talented Byelorussian actress, Stefania Stanyuta, who was chosen by Larissa. The first days of the shooting were happy and elevated.

The film completed by Elem Klimov and released in 1982 had a symbolic title, *Farewell*. A severe, dramatic, and classical picture, it betrays Klimov's mature style, realistic but phantasmagoric. Yet, no matter how unmistakable his manner might be, the picture was also a brainchild of Larissa, a ghost of her unforgettable character.

The "Fathers": Sergei Gerasimov, Yuli Raizman, and Iosif Kheifits

Death, cruel to the young, spared the patriarchs. Only Mikhail Romm, the leading director of the sixties, died, from a heart disease in 1971.

Fortunately, another patriarch, Sergei Gerasimov, lasted for many more years and achieved a great deal as an artist: he was professor, doctor of arts, writer, dramatist, permanent head of a studio at the Institute of Cinematography, Secretary of the USSR Union of Filmmakers, and an active film director, who never had intervals between his productions.

To demonstrate his creative longevity, it is enough to mention that he made a two-part film, *Leo Tolstoi,* based on his own script, when he was nearly eighty. He played the great writer, and his wife, actress Tamara Makarova, played the part of Tolstoi's wife, Sofia Andreyevna. The picture dwelt on the last period in the life of the Yasnaya Polyana recluse, as they used to call Count Tolstoi, Russia's pride and conscience. That was the period of intense spiritual quests and the rejection of temptations of high society life. His tragic departure from Yasnaya Polyana and his last stop at a little railway station in Astapovo, where he died, and the people's pilgrimage to the place where he was dying, along with his funeral, were all covered in the script.

The director scrupulously restored everything that was relevant to the action that Tolstoi's eye fell upon in his lifetime, from the terrace of Yasnaya Polyana to an old engine parked in Astapovo when Tolstoi was dying there. He never used copies—all those things were authentic. The film certainly required a tremendous effort on the director's part.

The list is long of Gerasimov's pupils who became Soviet actors and directors.

In private life Gerasimov remained cheerful, charismatic, and extremely agile till his last day. All the movie people knew about his hobby—cooking meat dumplings, Siberian style (Garasimov was born in Siberia), according to his own recipe—he could make five hundred of them at a time, which amazed people in many parts of the world, from New York to Novosibirsk.

The generation that came to the film studios after the October Revolution of 1917 in the unforgettable twenties all seemed to possess inexhaustible energy. Those "old-timers" gained in years but stayed young in spirit. Both those who died in the prime of their life, like Sergei Eisenstein and Georgi Vasiliev, but remained young in the memories of their colleagues and pupils and those who died in their eighties and made films till the very end were always in the vanguard of the cinema.

Yuli Raizman started his movie career as Yakov Protazanov's assistant director in 1923 and made the first film of his own in 1927. In 1982 he released *Private Life,* and two years later *Time of Desires.*

A director famed for his *Last Night, Mashenka, The Communist,* and *Your Contemporary* could certainly have rested on the laurels. Yet Raizman was involved in heated public debate even in his eighties. The main character in the film *Private Life,* a major functionary and administrator, had to retire when he came of pension age, but not only because of that. The man had become morally out of date, though quite fit physically, and the times required a more flexible style of management. That was the real drama.

Waving away all possible accusations of time-serving, Raizman enhanced that purely social issue, which seemed to have nothing to do with art, to the level of reflections upon the meaning of life and duty. The life of an administrator who had to vacate his beloved office grows meaningless. Overzealousness had alienated his family and the rest of the world. Raizman dwells on those serious and often insoluble problems without being didactic: he leaves them open to discussion after showing how acute they might be.

Raizman does not like public appearances and speeches; neither does he give interviews or write books. His life is dedicated to the movies and studio work. In private life he is a reserved, elegant, and smart "old Muscovite."

His Leningrad colleague, Iosif Kheifits, another movie veteran who used to work for the Lenfilm Studios even before the Second World War, is a living image of an old St. Petersburgian. He is also making films nonstop, without sparing himself. The maker of such classic pictures as *Baltic Deputy, The Big Family,* and *A Lady with a Dog* is still producing films up to the highest cinematographic standards, such as *Bad Good Man,* an original screen version of Chekhov's story *The Duel,* which starred Vladimir Vysotsky and Oleg Dahl; *Shurochka,* from Kuprin's *Duel;* as well as a number of pictures made from stories by Soviet authors, including *The Only One* (1975), *Married for the First Time* (1979), and *The Defendant* (1985). Kheifits's manner of direction, which is highly psychological and lyrical, has only grown more original and personal with time.

As to the "sons," they continue the cause of the "fathers," and not symbolically but in practice, attempting to enrich what they received as the heritage.

The "Sons": Muscovites and Leningraders

The Soviet audience warmly welcomed the debut of a young, smiling man in Georgi Daneliya's film *I Walk in Moscow* (1964)—he was regarded as a pleasant surprise. The part of Kolya was performed by Nikita Mikhalkov. His family name was known to everyone. His father, Sergei

Unfinished Piece for a Player Piano, *by Nikita Mikhalkov, was loosely based on Chekhovian times.*

Mikhalkov, was a renowned Soviet poet and dramatist; and his mother, Natalia Konchalovskaya, was a daughter of the famous twentieth-century Russian painter Pyotr Konchalovsky and a granddaughter of the celebrated artist Vasily Surikov. His brother, Andrei Mikhalkov-Konchalovsky, by that time had made *The First Teacher* and *The Story of Asya.*

"Indeed, why shouldn't the youngest of such a family try the movies?" some said in the early seventies, but they did not take his first pictures seriously. Yet they were watching the emergence of a gifted filmmaker.

Nikita Mikhalkov's movie career was rapid compared to other young directors. He released one film after another, working with a close team of associates and friends, among them the scriptwriter Alexander

Five Evenings by Nikita Mikhalkov was a reenactment of the 50s. Lyudmila Gurchenko plays Tamara opposite Stanislav Liubshin.

Adabashyan and cameraman Pavel Lebshev.

His first picture, *At Home Among Strangers, A Stranger at Home,* was a thriller shot in an expressive manner, fast moving and unexpected.

Another picture of his, *The Slave of Love,* was a retro-melodrama, a story of an actress who was associated with revolutionaries, and was based on a biography of a prerevolutionary movie star, Vera Kholodnaya (Yelena Solovei).

His next film was loosely based on Chekhov's early *Play Without a Title.* The most interesting sequences of Mikhalkov's *Unfinished Piece for a Player Piano* were the episodes where he showed an independent judgment in the use of Chekhovian ideas, where he altered the characters' stories, reviewed them, and made them think of the meaning of life.

Nikita Mikhalkov films Dark Eyes, *a joint Soviet-Italian production based on Chekhov.*

Several Days in the Life of I. I. Oblomov (an ironically modernized version of Goncharov's *Oblomov*) is a personal interpretation rather than a screen version of the book. The director deals entirely with the events in the life of the man whose name became a symbol of sluggishness during a period when his life could still give rise to a new Oblomov, one who had seen the light. The question was what kind of light?

Oblomov, a Russian gentleman, is compared to Stolz, of German extraction (they grew up side by side). Both are intelligent and talented, but Stolz is active, Oblomov passive. The film focused on Oblomov the person rather than on the social phenomenon he symbolized, leaving open the question of whether he should change at all without real purpose.

"Everyone's concerned with the meaning of life," the hero ponders. Perhaps passivity is better, more humane under the circumstances of old Russia's reality, rather than Stolz's activity.

Later Nikita Mikhalkov made several unexpected pictures. Parallel with *Oblomov* he shot *Five Evenings*—a picture both tender and hard, the story of a man and a woman who loved each other before the war, parted, and then reunited. Parting was presented as a poetic reminiscence, reunion more optimistically.

"*Family* is a noisy picture," the director warned at the premiere. Indeed, we hear all kinds of everyday noises: the rattling of a train, the revving of car engines, the cheers of the fans at the stadium, pop music roaring from stereo amplifiers. As a contrast to all this, a simple country woman comes to a town, to her daughter and granddaughter, eager to understand the alien world, to make things right, to help those close to her. Of course, her attempts to improve the world are futile. Upsetting routine relationships in a clumsy and tactless way, this kindly soul is out of place. The world around lives a life of its own, and she is not part of it.

The next film by Nikita Mikhalkov, *Without Witnesses* was the drama of a divorced couple. His latest production, adapted from several stories by Anton Chekhov, was entitled *Dark Eyes* (1987), and starred Marcello Mastroianni.

Director Vadim Abdrashitov and scriptwriter Alexander Mindadze began to work together in the late 1970s and early 1980s. Even before glasnost, they drew attention to negative developments in society, everyday confrontations, and the typical problems of the period, which they thoroughly analyzed.

In their debut *The Defence's Summing-up"* (1977), they showed a court case that resulted from an attempted murder of a young man by the girlfriend he insulted, who also attempted suicide. This was a study of serious psychological conflict. Another film of theirs, *The Fox Hunt* (1980), concerned the relationship between a boy detained by the police for picking a fight and his "victim." The hero, sentenced to penal servitude, is patronized by the man whom he abused and who undertakes to reform him. The case is regarded as charity, leading nowhere because it is forced on the recipient.

The two filmmakers probe further into contemporary reality in *The Train Has Stopped* (1982), where they show an "ordinary" railway accident with many people as the cause of it. The accident, obviously resulting

In the Vadim Abrashitov and Alexander Mindadze film Plumbum, *Anton Androsov is* Plumbum.

from sheer professional negligence, can also be presented as an act of heroism on the part of the locomotive driver who dies in an attempt to save the passengers. The film raises questions about the actual causes of the events. In their last two pictures, *The Planet Parade* (1984) and *Plumbum, or Dangerous Game* (1985), Abrashitov and Mindadze experiment with symbols, metaphors, and fables in order to drive the message home to the viewers by action rather than words.

Leningrad film director Alexei Gherman, a son of Yuri Gherman, the writer and dramatist, first drew public attention in the seventies by a screen version of *Lopatin's Notes*, a wartime story by Konstantin Simonov, entitled *Twenty Days Without War*. This film, though extremely realistic, was lyrical and poetic. Alexei Gherman, who belonged to the postwar generation, cherished the memories of those who participated in the war. It was a story of a frontliner, Lopatin, who spent twenty days far away from the trenches, in Tashkent, and fell in love with a woman he met on a train, whom he was to love till death. A simple love story suddenly develops into a story of the nation fighting a horrible war and revealing the best features of its national character. The picture of the poverty of the home-front workers, of teenagers working night shifts, of the people making a supreme effort to win was lyrical and realistic. The performances of the famous circus clown, Yuri Nikulin, who had also played many excellent film parts, and movie actress Lyudmila Gurchenko were superb. When we compare Yuri Nikulin's Lopatin, a soldier covered with dust, tired but handsome, as if transformed in the author's memory, with another character performed by the actor, a fantastic and slightly unreal figure of an old provincial collector and grandfather of a girl-heroine in *Weirdy,* we become aware of Alexei Gherman's specific manner of direction emphasized by a silvery black-and-white color range.

After a long interval the director released his new film *My Friend Ivan Lapshin* (1984), a screen fantasy from a work by his father. The critics have failed so far to define this unusual, though unspectacular, picture. What seems to be rough newsreels are combined with elaborately staged flashback sequences and the monochrome lighting of photographs typical of the thirties and printed by Soviet periodicals such as *Ogonyok*—snapshots with a dull bluish or greenish shade to them. But this was the technique used by Alexei Gherman to translate his father's prose into the film medium. His heroes were the people of the thirties, that enigmatic type who were idealists, loyal people who "had a worse life than we do but who were better than we are now," as the director said introducing his characters to the public. The truthful account and plain reconstruction of existence in communal flats in a provincial Russian town present the milieu of wholesome people like Ivan Lapshin, chief detective at the local homicide department. The director's partiality to the heroes of those days is felt very strongly.

Soviet Ethnic Cinema

The boom in cinema of Soviet constituent republics was continued into the seventies by a group of unorthodox artists.

289

Andrei Boltnev stars in fantasy My Friend Ivan Lapshin, *directed by Alexei Gherman.*

Among the first-class filmmakers operating in all parts of the USSR I would like to point out three—Otar Ioseliani of Georgia, Sergei Paradzhanov of Armenia, and Khojikuli Narliev of Turkmenia. They are no more talented than, say, Tolomush Okeyev of Kirghizia, Vytautas Zalakevicius of Lithuania, Emil Lateanu of Moldavia, or Ali Khamrayev of Uzbekistan; but all three of them belong to the Soviet school of cinematography. Their best films combine the individual and the ethnic, the national and the international.

Otar Ioseliani, who came to the fore with his first short documentaries, *Sakartvela* and *Cast Iron,* late in the sixties, was celebrated for his first feature, *Falling Leaves* (1967), based on a screenplay by Amiran Chichinadze. He is an artist with a well-developed sense of proportion. This quality was revealed in his best production, *There Lived a Thrush* (1971).

Ioseliani made few pictures in the four years between *Falling Leaves* and *There Lived a Thrush,* but he made them fast. Close to *Falling Leaves* in material, content, and style, the faces of the passers-by in *There Lived a Thrush* are shown from impressive angles amid the ironical spirit of the film, which is suffused with nostalgic and tender affection for Tbilisi, its old architecture, eccentricity, and songs.

The main character of *Falling Leaves* is an eccentric figure unlike the stereotype Georgian (a jovial man hanging about Rustaveli Avenue, toastmaster at fabulous feasts, or easy-going peddler). He finds himself within the framework of a conventional plot. Niko, shy, clumsy and awkward, does his best to have the standard colloid added to the wine casks at the vintners where he works after graduating. To do so, he has to defeat a crooked manager.

The plot is based on a standard "industrial drama," a typical confrontation of a bureaucrat and an innovator shown satirically. Ioseliani proved he can make good use of any material. He showed that the quality of a film depends entirely on its maker's talent. The idea that "industrial drama" is something artificial, unworthy of present day and too frequently expressed holds no water. The story of the young winemaker, Niko, revived a genre once discredited by mediocre pictures.

Ioseliani made *There Lived a Thrush* to explore unknown ground. It takes time and effort to probe its complex structure.

It begins with a story of a young man who cannot concentrate on his art Percussionist Giya Agladze, like Niko, belongs to the stratum of Tbilisi professionals. Ioseliani knows those people well and is fond of them. *Falling Leaves* has family breakfasts where a touching concern of the older generation for the younger is shown. This milieu is as patriarchal and traditional as it is open to everything new, and people like Niko with their firm moral principles are its natural products.

Niko was a clear-cut character, whereas the hero of *Thrush,* Giya, cannot pull himself together and act purposefully. That is why the big southern city, bubbling like champagne, with its easy ways and a kaleidoscope of faces and places drags him away from the most important thing in his life. The hero's dilemma results from his inability either to succumb to temptation or to write music. Swept away by the stream of life, his tragedy culminates in an arbitrary death as the result of a street accident.

The author makes no attempt to explain the drama. He leaves us to judge his hero in a finale set in a watchmaker's shop. The sound of ticking clocks, soft at the beginning and growing louder every minute, reaches its climax in the very last sequence, the longest in the film. The camera is focused on the rhythmic mechanism of a clock.

Ioseliani's literary mentors are hard to spot. His hero betrays his life, giving up his creative pursuits in a whirl of unreal, nonexistent, but allegedly important, events. Perhaps Ibsen dwelt on some aspects of this problem in *Wild Duck.* As to Federico Fellini and his *Otto e mezzo,* the hero's emptiness was attributed to his attempt to try on other people's lives amid an endless kaleidoscope of characters. Otar Ioseliani's tragedy shows that philosophic conflict, but in the shape of the witty and light-hearted story of an unfortunate musician constantly reprimanded for being late and unlucky. This philosophical picture was shot at the small Georgia Film Studios.

The fusion of philosophic fable and subjective narrative, using a documentary and realistic style, is typical of this director's work. In his *Pastoral,* in which a group of musicians go to a village on the Black Sea coast, in ancient Colchis, to have a rest and prepare a new concert program, Ioseliani compares rural and urban life—Georgian peasants involved in hard physical work and the intellectuals, the professional musicians: the former's apparent practicality and the latter's preoccupation with higher matters.

A "silvery thread" links up all the sequences of Ioseliani's apparently naive films. In his next picture, *Les Favoris de la Lune* (1984), shot in

France, the director shows the mutual bribing, cheating, stealing, and love affairs of a Paris residential area. The Laserlike beam of his camera penetrates the apartments of wealthy antique or arms dealers, a police superintendent, tradesmen, or thieves.

Some French critics described the film as "authentically French," of the kind that had not appeared in the home country of the cinema for a long time. Ioseliani could share a conviction common in his small but artistic nation: that it is "an island of Europe in Asia" and "a Transcaucasian France." Ioseliani was the third Soviet film director (after Andrei Tarkovsky filming in Italy and Andrei Mikhalkov-Konchalovsky working in the USA) who made a picture abroad. Before that only actors had taken part in foreign films, and directors participated solely in joint productions.

Armenian director Sergei Paradzhanov, also a Moscow Institute of Cinematography graduate, had made some unremarkable films before his sensational *Shadows of Our Forgotten Ancestors* (1965), based on stories by Ukrainian writer Mikhail Kotsyubinsky and produced by the Kiev Dovzhenko Film Studios (showed abroad under the title *Fiery Horses*). The film was a manifestation of Paradzhanov's many talents (he is a painter, sculptor, graphic artist, and art collector) combined with unorthodox, cinematographic techniques (unusual colors, images, and national Ukrainian music).

Shadows of Our Forgotton Ancestors is associated with the rich red of campfire flames, blood on the snow, scarlet wool woven into an ethnic carpet, and other echoes of West Ukrainian folk life, from ancient wedding chants to domestic utensils, each the work of a folk artist. This was the discovery of a country with a harsh terrain and a colorful lifestyle, customs, and legends. Paradzhanov's discovery of color and fabric made an impression not only in his country but in Paris haute couture, which borrowed and introduced West Ukrainian embroidery and other folk motifs.

The director's preoccupation with these elements partially obliterated the focus of the film, which later became Paradzhanov's theme in cinema: an individual's contribution to the national culture.

His interpretation of Kotsyubinsky's ideas in *Shadows of Our Forgotten Ancestors* was the first, though not wholly successful, attempt to embody his theme in a film. The love of a young Gutzul couple, Ivanka and Marichka, seemed to the director worthy of being immortalized for posterity. In his next film, *The Color of Pomegranates,* Paradzhanov made

A uniquely artistic rendition of the life of the great Armenian poet Sayat Nova is The Color of Pomegranates, *by Sergei Paradzhanov.*

the vaults of the temple shown in the final scene resonate with the voice of a poet of genius, the monk Sayat Nova. The love of an unknown peasant and the song of a great poet are both immortalized as contributions to culture.

We see an ancient book with an angular, geometrically perfect Armenian script, three pomegranates, a chiseled dagger, pomegranate juice split on the canvas, a bunch of grapes under the man's feet, three silvery trouts, a loaf of bread, and a rose turning into a rosehip. The open book is Sayat Nova's *Davtar,* and the off-screen voice recites in Armenian Ovanes Tumanian's verse dedicated to Sayat Nova.

The multiple images of *The Color of Pomegranates* are motifs of Sayat Nova's poetry. They symbolize Armenian culture and its landscape. They are metaphors of the poet's life: a closed poetic structure containing the poet's biography and his people's history and creative spirit.

The visual plane realized by Paradzhanov and others puts an end to the concept of the cinema as a junior brother of the fine arts.

Sergei Paradzhanov now works in his home city of Tbilisi, at the Georgian Film Studios. In 1984 he, together with Georgian director Dodo Abashidze, made *The Legend of the Suram Fortress,* a fantasy based on Georgian folklore and ancient history. While the dominant color in his picture on Sayat Nova was pomegranate red, *The Legend* is photographed mostly in niello silver. This is the color of the ancient chiseled work on Damascus steel daggers, of Georgian women's traditional costumes, or of Caucasian snow-capped peaks. Made after a long interval (for personal reasons), this film demonstrated the same subtle sense of color, line, and sequence composition. It is a hymn to love defeating death, to spiritual freedom triumphing over physical slavery, and to the hatred of tyranny.

The Legend of the Suram Fortress might not be historically accurate, and the director did not observe all the details of rites or customs; but the spirit of Georgian history, the beauty of monasteries, palaces, and churches are exquisitely depicted. *The Legend* is a purely Georgian picture in the same way as *"Shadows"* is Ukrainian and *"The Color"* Armenian, but all of them are undoubtedly by Paradzhanov.

Turkmenian filmmaker Khojikuli Narliev graduated from the camera direction department of the Moscow Institute of Cinematography in the early sixties.

His effort of making the screen image expressive and of bringing out every object caught by the camera's eye drew specialists' attention to his camerawork. His artistic quality became particularly clear in the first film directed by him, *Daughter-in-Law* (1972).

From the first sequence, the film is unique in every aspect—color, light, and movement. After an unexpected episode of a "tea ceremony" taking place amid vast expanses of sand there follows a series of subtle and elaborate scenes. There is nothing artificial; it is obvious that they spring from life. The outline of the yurta (tent) set up in the desert, a fantastic curve on a camel's neck and the animal's sad eye, the texture of astrakhan fur, and the wavy pattern of the sand dunes are Turkmenian.

In the seventies Oriental filmmakers, both emergent and experienced, undertook to translate ancient folk tradition on the screen, doing it naturally and inspiredly. Bypassing centuries of cultural development and styles and genres from the history of art, people developed a strong and objective interest in the cinema. That was the case with *Daughter-in-Law,* a very typical film in this respect.

In Daughter-in-Law *by Khodzhikuli Narliev, Maya Aymedova has the role of a Turkmenian woman awaiting the return of her husband from war.*

The heroine of the picture, Ogyulkeik, whose husband had gone to war, lives on two planes: the external one where she has to work hard looking after the sheep, fetching water, taking care of her parents-in-law, and doing many other household chores; and the internal one where she anticipates her reunion with her beloved husband.

This is the story of a Turkmenian woman who waited for her husband throughout the war. She waited even after the war—when her girlfriends' husbands began to come back, when her father-in-law waited no longer, and when others asked for her hand in marriage. The film is a poem to an enchanted soul of the desert and to eternal homecoming.

Valentina Alentova in the role of Katya Tikhomirova in Moscow Doesn't Believe in Tears, *by Vladimir Menshov in 1979, was a sensation.*

An Oscar for Katya

Moscow Doesn't Believe in Tears was an unexpected sensation. Its director, Vladimir Menshov, a former actor, made his debut in 1977 when he released *Practical Joke,* a school story appealing to the public and critics but not spectacular in any respect. His scriptwriter, Valentin Chernykh, a specialist in industrial drama, had published his story about three provincial girls who came to conquer Moscow in the late 1950s some time before. It was by no means a revelation and made little stir. The title,

297

Moscow Doesn't Believe in Tears, is a saying meaning "Don't you cry," or "Cheer up, everything's going be all right!"

Only a small number of copies was made, but people everywhere throughout the country lined up to see the film. In Moscow, where only two copies were available, half a million people saw the film within the first few weeks.

The success snowballed. When the film crew flew to Paris for the première, they were stunned by the commotion the picture caused in the French, capital. It was a success not only among Russians but in a country renowned for its sophistication. Menshov's colleagues were taken aback when the movie won an Oscar for best foreign production of 1981. They say that when someone phoned Vladimir Menshov at his hotel to break the news, he cursed and said that he did not fancy practical jokes that late at night.

Thus *Moscow Doesn't Believe in Tears* emerged as victorious as its heroine, Katya, a provincial girl who was seduced and abandoned by a Moscow Don Juan and who went on to create her own happiness. Katya did not weep in despair. She raised her daughter, worked and studied, and finally became manager at the factory where she had started as a rank worker. Later she met a worthy man and fell in love with him. Her lover, mechanic Gosha, was the aging but still charismatic actor Alexei Batalov. Vera Alentova, until then an obscure actress, played Katya, and a good comic actress, Irina Muravyova, played her light-hearted girlfriend, Lyudmila.

It was a truly realistic picture appealing to various types of viewers, including those who hoped to come across their own true love like Katya did on a suburban train. Some liked Menshov's flashbacks of Moscow in the fifties. Others were interested in a new stage of equality, when a woman had a higher social status than her man, just like Katya who was a factory manager whereas Gosha was a fitter, even if scientifically minded.

The film argued that a man's power is not in his social status or public rank; it is in the family, where he is the leader. When Katya realized that, she shut up like an ordinary housewife, and the audience greeted her with laughter and cheers (including the eighty million of Soviet viewers). Indeed Gosha could fix a fuse, if necessary, and make a salad or protect Katya's daughter from a rough suitor and his tough friends. This meant that the girl who had grown up with a dash for father's name on her birth certificate (the normal practice with illegitimate children at the time) did not feel fatherless any more. A song in the film is dedicated to Alexandra, the beautiful, free, and independent young Muscovite, the daughter of Katya.

The public, especially women, were pleased with Katya's revenge and complete triumph over her former seducer, Rudolph, a TV man. His luck ran out and he turned into a moth-eaten individual who assumed the trendy name of Rodion. Of course, the beautiful and well-groomed Katya who drives her own car and rules her factory wouldn't spite the poor wreck begging for her love and the affection of her daughter whom he had long abandoned. That pale copy of Pushkin's Eugene Onegin had to be satisfied with Katya's pity, just like his famous prototype was totally disheartened by Princess Tatyana's rebuff: "She left. Eugene stood robbed of motion, struck dumb as by a thunderbolt." In the final scene he sits on a park bench, watching Katya on her way to the man she loves.

No other Soviet films have ever raised such a number of social and psychological problems of women's life as *Moscow Doesn't Believe in Tears*. Suffice it to say that a positive and nice woman like Katya has an affair not only with the seductive Rudolph but later also with a married man. Her secret meetings with him take place in somebody else's flat, which is not fitting for a Soviet film heroine.

Actually, those who did not like the film (there were quite a few of them too) grumbled that it was sheer make believe, a Cinderella story. The first review of the picture published in the newspaper *Sovietskaya Rossia* was headlined "Variations on the Cinderella Theme." Those voices were drowned in a storm of cheers, however.

Indeed, the plot was more than familiar and stemmed from the fairy tale of an abandoned wife, neglected stepdaughter, pursued princess, or cheated maiden, whichever you prefer. Like any eternal story, it neverthe-less can always be updated and turned into art, as happened here.

The Crew by Alexander Mitta was released in 1980. Those who disliked the film compared it to a Western "disaster movie," which had never been produced in the USSR before. The second part of this long picture simulated an air accident and the crew's predicament. *The Crew* would not have been as successful if in the first part the director, an apt and cunning psychologist, did not make exhaustive use of family melodrama and other advantages of that popular genre. He first showed all the crew members at home and at work and only then sent them on a flight fraught with dramatic consequences.

Kristina Orbakaite, at 13, stars in Rolan Bykov's picture Weirdy.

But a well-made melodrama carries the same message and moral charge as the pictures addressed to a chosen and well-grounded audience.

Hi, Guys! was an example of such a melodrama, the exclamation mark in the title turning it into an appeal or reproach. The film focused on the same problem as *Moscow Doesn't Believe in Tears,* that of man's effemination. The hero of the picture unexpectedly becomes a father of three motherless children: his own daughter by a woman he had long parted with, now dead, and the woman's two children by other man. The film caused a tremendous response in the audience, especially in men, with letters arriving in dozens. It was astonishing since it's usually the women of all age groups who write letters to periodicals, film studios, and directors. What it meant was that *Hi, Guys!* had touched upon a painful and common enough social problem, that of fatherless children, single-parent families, and men's indifference to the children they have abandoned. The melodramatic motif is, apparently, an essential part of mass art.

Rolan Bykov's film *Weirdy* (1983), also makes us think of melodrama, that is, a sentimental story common enough in the last prerevolution decade. If it is a mere melodrama, one can't help wondering why millions of viewers who had watched it wept and argued about it so heatedly and

Natalia Andreichenko portrays Lyuba in Field Wife, *by Pyotr Todorovsky, 1984, about soldiers' wartime girlfriends.*

were so moved by its little heroine, a gifted, kind, and lovable schoolgirl, harassed by her wicked classmates. The picture mostly owed its success to the star, a talented and highly individual actress, Kristina Orbakaite, whom the public knew to be the daughter of the celebrated pop singer, Alla Pughacheva. Kristina was not the only attraction, though. The audiences were moved by the ethical problems raised in the picture and by its topicality: its appeal to one's good feelings achieved by showing scenes of children's cruelty that can either stay within the limits of practical jokes, not uncommon at this age, or turn into an evil doing. The picture warned the viewer by depicting the child's growing sense of despair. The final scene is cathartic as the culprits repent and weep.

In the eighties the concept of the author in cinema has extended. The filmmaker can express himself not only in a formal experiment, the way Alexei Gherman did, but also by seeking a new integral expression of his ideas on the screen. Today, bold camerawork typical of Sergei Urussevsky or the approach to direction favored by Mikhail Kalatozov in the past would look strange. The author's idea today can be revealed at its best by the choice of plot, sincerity of narrative, and a frank screen dialogue with the viewer, which is the shortest way to his heart.

All this refers to Pyotr Todorovsky's *Wartime Romance* (1984). A former frontliner, Todorovsky, who had been photography director in *The Spring in Zarechnaya Street* and other pictures, made his debut as film director twenty years ago. He produced *Loyalty* from a screenplay by Bulat Okujava—a simple story of a young soldier who went to war straight from school in 1941. Twenty years later we saw the same kind of youth in an ill-fitted army coat in the first sequences of Todorovsky's *Wartime Romance*. One might not have known that the filmmaker had waited for two decades to produce that film from his own script entitled *Field Wife*, a term used to denote the soldiers' wartime girlfriends who often shared their battle trials. One mightn't have known that the script was auto-biographical to a great extent, but one couldn't help feeling the author's deep personal involvement in the screen story. The audience wholeheartedly sympathized with the three-person drama set in the immediate postwar years, the late forties. One felt sorry for the youth in love with a beautiful blonde, his superior's girlfriend, and for the same woman years later, sick and hoarse, abandoned by her lover with a child to look after, and for another woman, innocently suffering, loving and not loved in return. The three stars engaged in the film, Nikolai Burlyaev, Natalia Andreichenko and Inna Churikova, subtly rendered all the psychological nuances of the eternal triangle.

Epilogue: The Beginning of Glasnost

*T*he films described above represented a variety of styles and artistic outlooks. One could also have mentioned quite a few pictures typical of the Soviet cinema of the early eighties and just as convincing. Yet the filmmakers grew increasingly dissatisfied with the situation in the industry and the falling number of moviegoers.

There was an obvious discrepancy between the cinema as an art and the cinema as an industry run by a supreme state body. The very name, Goskino, began to imply obstacles, barriers, and pressure.

A conflict arose between the immense creative potential of Soviet filmmakers and the obstacles to progress.

The conflict grew, and a single spark could have set the entire structure

The 15th International Film Festival opens in Moscow in July 1987.

ablaze. Then it happened. At this point our retrospective narrative turns into a newsreel.

The delegates and guests of the Fifth Congress of USSR Cinematographers are unlikely to ever forget the days of May 13–15, 1986. The Congress was held at the Great Kremlin Palace, where all important meetings of the professional artistic public usually take place.

We haven't described any Congresses held after the first constituent assembly that took place in 1965. No wonder: any constructive ideas or criticism were invariably drowned in the noise of formal speeches. During the eleven years since the first congress, the USSR Cinematographers' Union, which had started its activity with vigor and optimism, had eventually turned into a boring officious body utterly devoid of creative ideas.

The speakers who held the platform at the Fifth Congress subjected the Union to sharp criticism as soon as the opening speech and the report, smoothly running and full of praise, were over. The ancient Kremlin walls had probably never heard such ovation or indignation before. The lobby witnessed heated debates that overflowed from the auditorium.

It was, perhaps, for the first time that the filmmakers fully realized the meaning of glasnost.

A new board of the USSR Cinematographers' Union was elected freely and democratically. The new Secretariat—the supreme body of the Union—was now made up of genuinely talented and principled artists respected by everyone. Elem Klimov became First Secretary of the Union.

It marked the beginning of a new stage of Soviet filmmaking.

These changes would have been impossible but for the Twenty-seventh CPSU Congress.

Soon many excellent pictures shelved for years were released. They included: *Long Farewells* and *Brief Encounters* by Kira Muratova, *The Theme* by Gleb Panfilov, *Viktor Krokhin's Second Attempt* by Igor Sheshukov, and many others. There had been no reason for shelving them except bureaucratic caution. The fate of Alexei Gherman's *Trial on the Road* was typical. This unorthodox picture on the Great Patriotic War, remarkable for its direction and acting, was shelved for fifteen years!

Following the resolutions of the Fifth Cinematographers' Congress, a draft project of reform in the industry was worked out and discussed by professionals on a nationwide scale. In a nutshell, its idea is to make all film studios, their artistic councils, and staff absolutely independent.

The newly appointed Chairman of the Goskino, Alexander Kamshalov, emphasized in speeches and interviews that the introduction of the new "pattern," that is, of independence at all the levels of the film industry, is going to be extremely difficult, largely for economic reasons. No wonder: the Soviet film industry, like its counterparts in other countries, has not been profitable since 1986, which would make it hard for the film studios to attain real independence, financial included. Such an open acknowledgement of problems arising in the process of reform demonstrated the top executive's outlook and gave us hope. We have started to believe in a better future for the Soviet cinema.

Finally, the release of *Repentance* (made by Georgian director Tenghiz Abuladze in 1984) caused a stir not only in the movies but also in other spheres of the country's cultural, political, and civil life. The film is acutely topical today, at the time of reform, revival, and renovation because it returns to the abuses of the Stalin period and warns against the danger of forgetting the disastrous mistakes of the past. The picture had a two-month run in Moscow alone. The immense press coverage, a flow of letters from the moviegoers, heated debates, tears, blessings, and rejoicing

Tenghiz Abuladze and Milos Formann at the 15th Moscow Festival.

on the best part of the public and the stubborn opposition and ill-feeling of a minority adhering to the principle "Let the sleeping dogs lie" was typical of the first months of 1987, when *Repentance* was released in many regions of the USSR.

The picture, whose genre was defined as sad fantasy or tragic farce by the director himself, portrays two generations of a Georgian family and two eras, Varlam's and Abel's.

The beginning is weird: the dead body of a man called Varlam, once a top functionary, buried with all the tributes and homages, that same day has been dug out of the grave at night by a person unknown and "returned" to the family. The corpse reappears three times in the garden that belongs to Abel, the late man's son. This is an act of vengeance on the part of a woman called Ketevan, a daughter of painter who fell a victim of reprisals waged by the monstrous town mayor, Varlam. The court case of the heroine and her reminiscences are the apparent plot of the picture, but its action cannot be explained by the plot or sheer logic.

We are absolutely shattered by many sequences, such as a scene with the logs, where the women and children are looking for the names of their relations—political prisoners sentenced to penal servitude and felling trees in Siberia—on the butt ends of the logs, the "letters" from prisoners. Another distressing episode is the "inauguration speech" which the new mayor makes from the townhall balcony. The visit the dictator pays to the studio of the artist Sandro Barateli and the secret arrest of the latter that soon follows are equally chilling, as are the scenes of endless interrogations, confrontation of witnesses, physical torture, and executions.

Tenghiz Abuladze has a gift to show the inner moves of a human soul and to portray the daily cares and concerns of ordinary people, humble and humiliated, innocent and pursued, sympathetically and sadly. We feel that when following the story of the artist family, true intellectuals, the elite of the Georgian nation, cruelly persecuted and physically destroyed at the time of reprisals. Dictator Varlam, a totalitarian Oriental ruler and symbol of unlimited power, imposing in a sinister way, is dissected and exposed in the picture.

By showing Varlam's successors, his son Abel with his henchmen, their lifestyles and ways, the director portrays the era of stagnation, consumerism, and lack of spirituality and principle. The "romantic" villain, Varlam, is replaced by his son, Abel, a sluggish, cunning, and disguised scoundrel, who is no less dangerous. Yet, the time of judgment has come, and Varlam's grandson (Abel's son) Tornike, a pure and innocent soul, commits suicide because he cannot bear to know the entire truth about his grandfather and father. "Evil ruling the world will always lead it into a blind alley," said Abuladze commenting on the main idea of his film. "Social evil is so explosive that it eventually destroys itself."

Georgian actor Avtandil Makharadze performs the two leads, Varlam and Abel, brilliantly. The rest of the cast is just as splendid. The score, original scenery, and baroque sets have turned *Repentance* into a civic document and at the same time into a cinematographic event of highest artistry.

Tenghiz Abuladze's film appeals to such eternal categories and concepts as memory, evil, good, compassion, love, moral responsibility, life, and death.

The picture, philosophic and sophisticated as it is, can be regarded at different angles: it is complex and simple at the same time. The moral conclusions one can draw from it are clear and irrefutable. Soviet art needs films like that now that it is gradually giving up the Aesopian language inevitable in the previous era with its disguised ideas and forced formal experiments. *Repentance* has paved the way to free art capable of raising major social problems.

The secret of the Soviet cinema's viability is in its close ties with society. The screen depicts actual events typical of every particular stage of social development in the country. The cinema portrays, illuminates, and highlights the Soviet people's life. The role entrusted to the cinema by history places a tremendous responsibility on filmmakers, exposes them to the limelight, and does not let them rest on their laurels.

At the very beginning of the cinema in Russia the great Russian poet Alexander Blok wrote: "Eternal battle! Through blood and dust-clouds, peace is only a dream, alas!"

Every genuine filmmaker, from the eighty-five-year-old Yuli Raizman to an emergent professional who has just stepped across the threshold of a film studio, can put his name to these words.

Notes

Chapter 1

[1] *Tolstoi's Letters* (University of London: The Athlone Press, 1978), vol. 2, pp. 545–546.

[2] I. S. Zilberstein, "Nicholas II in the Cinema," *Sovetski Ekran (Soviet Screen)* (1927), No. 15, p. 10 (in Russian). Cited from: Jay Leyda, *"Kino": A History of the Russian and Soviet Film. A Study of the Development of Russian Cinema to the Present* Princeton: Princeton University Press, 1983), p. 69.

[3] Semyon S. Ginsburg, *Cinematography in Pre-Revolutionary Russia* (Moscow, 1963), p. 49 (in Russian).

[4] Luda et Jean Schnitzer, *Histoire du cinéma sovietique, 1919–1940* (Paris: Pygmalion, 1979–1980), p. 408.

[5] Leonid Andreyev, *Letters on the Theater* (Shipovnik, 1914), Book XXII, p. 242 (in Russian).

[6] Louis Forestier, *The Great Silent: Cameraman's Reminiscences* (Moscow, 1945), pp. 1–3 (in Russian).

[7] "Maxim Gorky on Art, Moscow, Leningrad" (1940) (in Russian). Cited from: Jay Leyda, *"Kino": A History of the Russian and Soviet Film,* p. 407.

[8] Ivan Perestiani, *75 Years in the Service of Art* (Moscow, 1962), p. 74 (in Russian).

Chapter 2

[1] *Of All the Arts the Most Important for Us Is the Cinema,* a collection of articles (Moscow: Iskusstvo Publishers, 1963), p. 124 (in Russian).

[2] *Ibid,* p. 93.

[3] V. I. Lenin, *Collected Works,* vol. 10, pp. 48–49.

[4] V. P. Lapshin, *The Artistic Life of Moscow and Petrograd in 1917* (Moscow: Sovetskii Khudozhnik, 1983((in Russian).

[5] *The Book About Books,* (1924), NN 5–6, pp. 75–76 (in Russian).

[6] *The History of the Soviet Cinema,* Vol. I, 1917–1931 (Moscow: Iskusstvo Publishers, 1969), p. 35ff. (in Russian).

[7] From the author's file, an unpublished "Open Letter to Comrades N. Zorkaya, Glushchenko and Teterin" of February 2, 1965. See also Y. Gromov, *L. V. Kuleshov* (Moscow: Iskusstvo Publishers, 1984), p. 184ff. (in Russian).

[8] *V. Shklovsky, S. Eisenstein, A. Khokhlova* (Moscow: Kinopechat, 1926), pp. 15–16 (in Russian).

[9] Lev Kuleshov and Alexandra Khokhlova, *50 Years in the Cinema* (Moscow: Iskusstvo Publishers, 1975) (in Russian).

[10] See the fundamental work by N. Kleiman, *Frame as a Cell of Montage.* "Voprosy Kinoiskusstva", 11, 1969, pp. 94–130 (in Russian).

[11] Dziga Vertov. *Articles, Diaries, Ideas* (Moscow: Iskusstvo Publishers, 1966), p. 55 (in Russian).

[12] *Ibid.,* p. 45.

[13] Victor Shklovsky, *Their Present* (Moscow, 1977).

[14] Those interested in the film may be referred to the book *The Battleship Potemkin,* in the series *Masterpieces of the Soviet Movies* (Moscow: Iskusstvo Publishers, 1969).

[15] Jay Leyda and Zina Voynow, *Eisenstein at Work,* Introduction by Ted Perry (New York: Pantheon Books, 1982).

[16] *The Art of Millions,* a collection of articles (Moscow: Iskusstvo Publishers, 1958), pp. 88–90 (in Russian).

[17] Alexander Karaganov, *Vsevolod Pudovkin* (Moscow: Iskusstvo Publishers, 1973), p. 112 (in Russian).

[18] Sergei Eisenstein, *Collected Works* (Moscow: Iskusstvo Publishers, 1964), vol. 5, p. 441.

[19] For a detailed list of American films shown in the Soviet Union in the 1920s, see *Kino i vremya* (bulletin), I (Moscow, 1960), compiled by E. Kartseva (in Russian).

[20] Film Directory, *Teakinopechat* (Moscow, 1929), p. 43 (in Russian).

Chapter 3

[1] The "document" was published in *Soviet Screen* (1928), No. 32.

[2] Such was, for instance, the orchestra which played from 1924 at the Moscow cinema hall "Ars" under the composer and conductor D. Blok. From the early thirties it functioned as a symphony orchestra of the film factory Mezhrabpom-film, scoring films (beginning with *Alone* by Kozintsev and Trauberg) with music by Shostakovich, Prokofiev, Dunayevsky, Kabalevsky, and other prominent composers. It has now become the State Symphony Orchestra of Cinematography of the USSR.

[3] Luda et Jean Schnitzer, *Histoire du cinéma sovietique,* p. 408.

[4] *History of Soviet Cinema, 1917–1987* (Moscow: Iskusstvo Publishers, 1973), vol. 2, pp. 177–178 (in Russian).

[5] Summaries from the catalogue *Soviet Feature Films, 2, Sound Films (1930–1957)* (Moscow: Iskusstvo Publishers, 1961) (in Russian).

[6] *Kino* newspaper, February 28, 1933.

[7] About re-editing of the 1920s in general and Georgi and Sergei Vasilyev in particular, see D. Pisarevsky, *The Brothers Vasilyev* (Moscow: Iskusstvo Publishers, 1981), pp. 40ff. (in Russian). This was also vividly described by Viktor Shklovsky in his book *Rewinder* (Moscow: Kinopechat Publishers, 1927). Shklovsky recalled, in particular, one of Georgi Vasilyev's tricks, which he called a "masterpiece": "He [G. Vasilyev] wanted the man /the actor/ to die, but he wouldn't. He chose a moment when his intended victim began to yawn, then multiplied the shot, thus stopping the action. The man froze with an open mouth, so it only remained to add the title: 'death from heart failure.' The device was so unexpected that nobody challenged it." Quoted from Shklovsky's book, *For Forty Years. Articles About Cinema* (Moscow, 1965,) p. 61 (in Russian).

[8] *Chapayev,* a collection (Moscow: Kinofotoizdat Publishers, 1936), p. 65 (in Russian).

[9] *"History of Soviet Cinema",* Vol. 2, *1931–1941,* p. 117 (in Russian).

[10] Georges Sadoul, *History of Cinema Art* (Moscow: Foreign Literature Publishing House, 1957), p. 303 (in Russian).

[11] Grigori M. Kozintsev, *Collection of Works,* vol. 1, pp. 343–344 (in Russian).

[12] Dunayevsky, *Articles, Reminiscences, Speeches* (Moscow 1952), p. 72 (in Russian).

Chapter 4

[1] V. V. Mikosha, *Next to the Soldier* (Moscow: Military Publishing House, 1983), p. 223 (in Russian).

[2] *Talent and Courage,* Book 1 (Moscow: Iskusstvo Publishers, 1967), p. 52 (in Russian).

[3] Y. Khanyutin, *Warning from the Past* (Moscow: Iskusstvo Publishers, 1968), p. 35 (in Russian).

[4] Vladislav Mikosha, *In Battle with a Camera* (Moscow: Molodaya gvardiya Publishers, 1964), p. 20 (in Russian).

[5] *Literature and Art,* June 5, 1943 (in Russian).

[6] B. Medvedev, *Witness for the Prosecution* (Moscow: Iskusstvo Publishers, 1966), p. 95 (in Russian).

[7] *Marseillaise,* October 20, 1945.

[8] Mark Donskoi, *A Collection* (Moscow: Iskusstvo Publishers, 1973), p. 23 (in Russian).

[9] *Ibid.*

[10] *La settimana,* April 12, 1945.

[11] Vsevolod Pudovkin, *Collected Works* (Moscow: Iskusstvo Publishers, 1974), vol. 1, p. 434 (in Russian).

Chapter 5

[1] Mikhail Romm, *Before the Broad Sweep of Art;* see *Works of Mikhail Romm,* 3 vols. (in Russian).

[2] "To overcome the backsliding of dramaturgy," *Pravda,* April 7, 1952.

[3] The catalogues of international film festivals confirm this. It is characteristic, in particular, that at the 1951 Karlovy Vary festival, the films *The Knight of the Gold Star* (Grand Prize) and *Donets Miners* were awarded prizes together with the Chinese film *The Steel Soldier* (Peace Prize), while the pictures *Maître après Dieu* by Louis Daquin and *Non c'è pace tra gli ulivi* by Giuseppe de Santis received no awards.

Chapter 6

[1] Mikhail Romm, *Dialogues on the Cinema* (Moscow: Iskusstvo Publishers, 1964), p. 304.

[2] *Cinema-70,* No. 144, p. 118.

[3] Grigori Kozintsev, *The Space of Tragedy* (Leningrad, 1973), p. 114.

Index

Actors

313

Directors/Producers

Films